ENDURANCE
The Complete Series

A. C. Spahn

Enduring Endurance was originally published in 2013.
"A Numbers Game" was originally published in *In Mount Diablo's Shadow Volume III*, 2013
Mightier than the Sword was originally published in 2013.
Under Cover was originally published in 2014.
Preferred Dead was originally published in 2015.
Wet Ducks was originally published in 2016.
This is the first printing of "Just Desserts."

Cover design by Jenny Zemanek at Seedlings Design Studio

ISBN: 9781791928179

For Justin

CONTENTS

Book One

Enduring *Endurance*

You were supposed to be excited when they promoted you to captain. It was supposed to be the best day of your life. You were supposed to celebrate with friends and consume an amount of alcohol that would get you kicked out of the service if Dispatch found out about it.

Thomas Withers did not have a party. No one came to see him off. Even his own former commanding officer barely wished him "good luck." In fact, since he'd first found out about the promotion, he'd done his best to avoid everyone he knew.

His footsteps echoed around the empty space dock concourse. Despite the fact that nobody was around, he kept his head down and tried not to think about where he was headed. He'd dreamed about this day—the day he took command of his first spaceship—from childhood. Now that he was here, he wished he'd stayed in bed.

It all came back to that moment three days ago,

when he received the ultimatum that landed him here and ruined the rest of his life.

* * *

"You screwed this up big time, Lieutenant!" Commissioner Wen's expression, like her crisp blue-and-black uniform, looked stoic as she paced in front of him, but Thomas couldn't miss the rage seething beneath her words. He stood stiffly at attention in her office at Dispatch headquarters, trying not to look as scared as he felt.

"Commissioner …" he started, but stopped when she held up a hand.

"Save it, Withers. I'm sure it seemed like a good idea at the time, but you made a bad call."

Thomas felt heat rise under his dark brown skin. "I saved that woman's life!"

"You ruined a five-year-long investigation!"

"But if I hadn't …"

"Spare me your damsel in distress story. I've heard it enough this week on the news." Wen brushed aside a strand of black hair that had escaped her bun and glowered at him. "Unfortunately, because the media has gotten so excited about your supposedly heroic rescue, we can't kick you out of the service without an onslaught of bad press. I came this close to doing it anyway, but we've decided on an alternative punishment."

Thomas felt a weight lift from his shoulders. He wasn't sure he could have lived with himself if he'd been fired, to say nothing of having to explain it to his family.

"Don't get too comfortable," Wen said. "You've lost Dispatch's trust, and that's not something we recover easily."

He nodded. "I know, Commissioner."

She crossed to the other side of her enormous desk and planted both her palms on it. "We're going to give you a choice. You can either stay at your current rank for the rest of your career and continue to serve as Captain Liu's first officer, or ..." She took a deep breath. "... we'll promote you."

Thomas's heart leapt instinctively at the word "promote," but his confusion stifled the reaction. "You don't trust me, so you're promoting me? I don't understand."

Wen's face twitched with annoyance. "Captain Jonah Davis has passed away. Old age. The *Endurance* is currently without a commanding officer. If you accept the promotion, that will be your new post."

Thomas's stomach sank into the floor. *No*, he thought, *not that ship*.

This was literally the worst news he could have received—worse than being dismissed from the corps. His parents might have gotten over that eventually, especially with the media on his side, but this ... there was no excuse for this.

The *Endurance* had a slew of nicknames among the United Earth Law Enforcement Corps: the "Misfit," the "Dead End," the "Quacker Barrel," and the "No-I-Quit-Instead" among them. It was the dumping ground for officers who had no business staying in the service, but who, for one reason or another, Dispatch couldn't actually kick out. To keep them out of the way, the *Endurance* spent all of its time patrolling the area of empty space around Neptune and running a handful of off-the-wall science experiments. It never did anything. It never saved anyone. It never stopped any crimes. The only time it had been in the news in the past decade was when one of its officers won the lottery and retired. Nobody, with the exception of Jonah Davis, ever wanted to command it.

That was the ship they were offering to him.

And he had to take it.

Ever since he was a boy, Thomas had dreamed of commanding his own ship—protecting civilians, fighting crime, and keeping space safe. He'd risen quickly through the ranks to lieutenant, and up until last week, he'd been the model officer.

Then that mess with the Uprising case went sideways, and his carefully constructed stack of cards came tumbling down.

This would be his only chance to make captain. If he refused it, his career would stall out. Of course, if he took it, his career was probably over anyway.

He swallowed and thought of the one thing that might possibly save his future. "If I accept the *Endurance* command, can I have a chance to prove myself?"

Wen watched him with a frown. "What do you have in mind?"

"I've heard the stories. I know the sort of nonsense that crew is known for. If I whip them into shape—if I prove that I can maintain Dispatch standards—will you let me transfer to a different ship?" Thomas held his breath.

The commissioner stared at him for a moment, then broke into a hearty laugh. "If you can ... if you can fix up *that* ship ... then by all means, Withers, you can transfer to any other ship in the fleet!"

Thomas wasn't sure if that was a real agreement or just outright mockery, but he would take what he could get. "Then I accept the promotion, Commissioner."

He hoped he hadn't just made the biggest mistake of

his life.

* * *

Thomas found his ship at the last airlock of the concourse. Though the outside was the same white metal as any other vessel, the rumors that circulated about the *Endurance's* interior (not to mention its crew) were enough to make even the most stoic captain cringe. He steeled himself. *Now or never, Thomas.* Taking a deep breath, he entered his authorization code into the airlock activation panel.

It beeped twice, and its indicator light flashed red. Entry denied.

So it began.

"Come on," Thomas muttered. He hadn't expected the problems to start until he was actually on board. He tried his code again, taking care to push each button correctly.

Beep beep!

"This is a joke," he decided. "This has to be a joke." He looked around to see if anyone noticed his embarrassment, but the area was deserted. Even if he wanted to ask for help, he couldn't.

He turned back to the panel and entered the code again, speaking over each number. "Work. You. Stupid. Piece. Of ..."

Beep!

The light flashed green, and the airlock slid open. Thomas blinked at the panel, then took in his first impression of the UELE *Endurance*.

The entry corridor looked surprisingly normal. The white metal walls, the plain brown carpet, and the overhead light panels all seemed perfectly functional, and perfectly standard among the United Earth Law Enforcement fleet. The corridor ran in both directions from the airlock, and the directional signs on the walls were both polished and mounted correctly.

A whiff of the ship's air flooded through Thomas's sinuses. There was something musty in the odor, but it smelled breathable, at least. He could hear a vacuum cleaner running somewhere down the corridor, evidently in need of a new sound damper. That would be easy to fix.

His first officer, Lieutenant Viktor Ivanokoff, was supposed to meet him at the airlock, but he hadn't yet arrived. Thomas took his first step onto the *Endurance*, keyed the airlock closed, and then stood in the middle of the hallway to wait.

And wait.

And wait.

The sound of the vacuum came closer, and Thomas concluded Ivanokoff had forgotten the time of the meeting. He wouldn't tolerate that sort of unprofessionalism in the future, but he could afford to give the man a warning.

He headed down the corridor to the right. The sound of the vacuum grew louder, and the musty smell stronger, until he rounded a turn and came into sight of Archibald Cleaver, the 104-year-old civilian who served as the *Endurance*'s janitor. The man had volunteered to work for the UELE fleet way back when civilians were still allowed to do that, and a small line in his contract said that he couldn't be laid off except for gross misconduct. Though he was well past retirement age, Cleaver was a very good janitor and simply refused to quit his job. So Dispatch had stuck him here, and over the years he'd become something of a running joke at headquarters.

Thomas passed him in the corridor and nodded to him. "Mr. Cleaver." The old man turned his half-bald grey head, nodded back, and continued pushing his vacuum down the hall. The smell faded as he walked away, and Thomas concluded the vacuum's filter needed to be replaced as well.

Right after he dealt with his wayward first officer.

He turned the last corner that would lead to the bridge and found the path blocked by the enormous form of a man, hands planted on his hips and a scowl on his pale face. The man's arms bulged with muscle under his black uniform shirt, and his thumbs were tucked into his belt next to a pair of customized handguns.

Ivanokoff looked like he routinely bench-pressed elephants, and Thomas had to fight his instinct to take a step back. Though he was just shy of six feet tall himself, he still had to look up to make eye contact.

The first officer, for his part, apparently didn't notice the overt hostility in his posture. "Captain Withers, I presume?" he intoned in a deep bass.

Habit took over while Thomas recovered his confidence. "At attention, Lieutenant!" he ordered. Ivanokoff's frown deepened, but he shifted into the proper stance. Thomas crossed his arms. "And you're correct—I'm Captain Thomas Withers. I had thought you would meet me at the airlock, but I assume something pressing came up?"

Ivanokoff shook his head. "I do not do airlocks."

Having no idea what that meant, Thomas settled for saying, "You do now." *That's right, Thomas. Show them who's in charge.* He nodded at the two pistols on the man's belt. "Those are hardly standard attire, Lieutenant. We're in green status, and at space dock. Why do you look like you're preparing for war?"

Ivanokoff seemed to have anticipated the question. "These are Dickens and Dante, sir. They never leave my sides."

Thomas blinked. "Dickens and Dante?"

"I like to read, sir." Ivanokoff shrugged. "Captain Davis understood."

"Well, I'm not Captain Davis," Thomas said. "As long as I'm in command of this ship, you will observe the rules for carrying weapons and leave them in your berth unless they're needed."

Ivanokoff cocked an eyebrow. "How do you know when they will be needed until it is too late?"

Thomas didn't have an answer for that. But he couldn't back down on the first order he'd given. That would set a bad precedent. So instead he doubled his resolve. "You heard me," he snapped. "I want those back where they belong as soon as I've inspected the bridge. Let's go." Thomas stepped past his first officer and continued down the hall. Ivanokoff hesitated for a moment, then followed. *Point, Captain Withers,* Thomas thought.

As they stepped through the hatch to the bridge, he felt a sense of relief. Though most of the stories about the *Endurance* were highly improbable (he hadn't *really* believed that the captain's chair was made of cardboard boxes and held together with packing tape), some of them had made him nervous.

Fortunately, the bridge looked adequately professional. In fact, the most unusual thing Thomas could see was his first officer standing next to him, fiddling with the handgrips of his guns. Even the other crew members seemed less odd than he'd been anticipating. The man at the defensives station was tapping his foot spasmodically, and the pale engineer standing over an open wall panel was sporting a unibrow, but they were all human, all standing appropriately at attention (more or less), and all seemed to have at least a general sense of what they were doing. This might not be so bad.

Then the engineer's wall panel exploded.

Somewhere amidst the smoke, the coughing personnel, and the apparently-too-sensitive fire alarms, Thomas heard Ivanokoff paging main engineering. The huge man found him in the chaos. "There are no flames; it is just an overloaded circuit," he informed him. "Chief Engineer Habassa will be here shortly to fix the problem and vent the smoke. In the meantime, I suggest we move everyone elsewhere."

"Obviously," Thomas tried to answer, but a lungful of smoke made the word come out in gasps.

They managed to get everyone out, though they almost missed the skinny man who had been at the helm. As they stood regaining their breaths in the corridor (though the old-vacuum smell lingered), a young woman with wavy black hair and deep copper skin came around the corner. She looked like a brand-new officer, and her black uniform shirt had only a single medical certification patch on its shoulder. Having only had time to familiarize himself with a few senior officers' profiles, most of which included outdated photos anyway, Thomas didn't recognize her.

"Well," she said with a nod, "what seems to have happened here?"

To Thomas's great surprise, Ivanokoff began to answer. The woman didn't look old enough to drink, much less to be in a high enough position that the first officer would bother to answer her queries. Or maybe Ivanokoff "didn't do" chain of command.

"And then the panel exploded," Ivanokoff finished.

"Hmm," the woman acknowledged. "Any injuries?"

Thomas hated rubberneckers, and this was starting to sound like the beginning of a gossip train. "Officer," he interrupted. "I'm Captain Thomas Withers, and I need you to move along. This isn't a show."

The woman, much to Thomas's confusion, did not redden with embarrassment and move away, nor did she seem the slightest bit perturbed. Instead she smiled at him and politely offered a handshake. "Pleasure to meet you, Captain. I'm Maureen, chief medical officer."

Thomas stared at her and, a little too stupefied to insist upon a proper greeting, mutely shook her hand. *You have got to be kidding me.* He cleared his throat and found his voice. "My apologies, Doctor. I didn't realize."

Again, to his great surprise, Maureen began to laugh, and chuckles arose from the rest of the group. "Sir," Maureen said through a smile, "I'm not a doctor."

Thomas was stumped. "I thought you said ..."

"I had some experience in caring for injuries, so after I finished at the academy, they assigned me here. They made me chief medic since we didn't have one yet."

Thomas could have slapped himself. He was a fool to think Dispatch would post an actual doctor to the *Endurance.* "Experience?"

A small man in his early thirties walked around the corner just in time to hear the captain's question. "Maureen was going to be a professional dancer. She's really good at treating injuries and being healthy."

Do people on this ship just chime in whenever they feel like it? Thomas wondered. "And you are?"

"Oh!" The man's face broke into an enormous smile. "Matthias Habassa. Chief engineer. Maureen's my sister." Indeed, he shared her skin tone, and though his hair was shorter, it sported the same natural waves. He seized Thomas's hand in an eager handshake.

"You're the chief engineer?"

"Yup!" Matthias continued to shake the captain's hand with more enthusiasm than he could stomach. "So glad to meet you, Captain. We heard about your big rescue on the news, and we're all really excited to have you. Dispatch sure sent us their best man! I just know you're going to love it here."

"I'm sure." Ignoring the reference to his supposed act of heroism and the unpleasant memories it surfaced, Thomas extracted his hand from the man's grasp and tried to regain his earlier tone of authority. "There's a situation that needs your attention, Lieutenant Habassa. One of the panels on the starboard bulkhead exploded, and ..."

"Again?" Matthias shook his head, though his grin did not fade in the slightest. "I just fixed it last week. No trouble, though. I don't mind fixing it again. If you love your ship, it'll love you back!" With that, he punched the panel to open the door to the bridge, releasing a huge cloud of smoke into the corridor that set everyone to coughing again. "Be right back!"

The engineer disappeared onto the bridge, the not-a-doctor began telling everyone to take deep breaths, the literary behemoth leaned against the wall, crossed his arms, and glared at everyone, and the old vacuum started up again somewhere down the corridor.

Oh yes. This was going to be *great*.

* * *

Once everything was finally repaired (Matthias assured him it would be at least a week before the panel blew up again), Thomas called a staff meeting for later that evening. He wanted everyone to hear the new standards he was instituting directly from him so that there could be no confusion about them. The meeting was set for 1900 hours in the rec room.

At 1917, Thomas decided he should have chosen to stay a lieutenant forever. Of the twenty-three people in the crew, only sixteen had arrived. Given that the ship was in space dock and didn't require a crew to man it, this was ridiculous.

Matthias and Maureen were present, the former swiveling his seat back and forth while the latter patiently sat with perfect posture. Archibald Cleaver had made his appearance at 1908, shambling in with vacuum in tow. The other crew members talked quietly in small groups, though Thomas could feel their gazes on him when they thought he wasn't paying attention. No doubt everyone was wondering about the temperament of their new commanding officer.

Viktor Ivanokoff was noticeably absent, as was the chief of the defensives department. Thomas was livid. Neither of his two most senior officers could be bothered to show up to his first staff meeting? It was unheard of.

"Ahem," Thomas cleared his throat, instantly silencing the room. At least they knew enough to let him talk. "It seems not all of the crew feels it is important to attend briefings. Has anyone seen Lieutenants Ivanokoff or Praphasat?"

"Excuse me," a soft voice said from behind him. Thomas nearly jumped out of his skin. He turned to see a woman looking up at him with dark brown eyes. Her heart-shaped face was a soft olive tone. Short black hair fell around her ears, and she looked to be somewhere in her mid-thirties. "Lieutenant Areva Praphasat, sir. I've been here since 1850 hours."

"Uh ..." Thomas was lost for words. He hadn't seen her enter the room, which he was certain had been empty when he arrived. Where could she have come from? "You were here when I came in?"

Areva nodded. "I like to stay out of sight, sir."

"Where were you?"

She pointed to a plant that sat in the corner. "May I go back?"

"Um ... yes, I suppose so."

The very millisecond Thomas released her, Areva darted back behind the plant and disappeared from view. Thomas had to admit, he was impressed with how well she managed to hide herself, though her choice of seating was pretty weird. He cleared his throat again. "In that case, has anyone seen Ivanokoff?"

Matthias raised his hand. "He doesn't do briefings," he answered loudly, without waiting to be asked to speak. He continued to swing his chair back and forth.

"He doesn't do briefings?" Thomas repeated. Matthias nodded, his ever-present grin still fixed in place. "And the other five missing crew members are ...?"

Eager to please, Matthias rattled them off. "Nina has the flu, Bernardo is on space dock visiting his mother, I think Paresh went with him, Rupin is always thirty minutes late for everything, and Grace is trying to fix a door that got stuck in the engineering section."

Thomas repressed a sigh. "Why doesn't she fix it after the briefing?"

"She's on the other side of it."

Of course she was. "Very well. I'll have a talk with each of them individually after the meeting." He straightened his posture. "I wanted to introduce myself to all of you ..."

"Excuse me?" The voice belonged to a white, middle-aged sergeant with short blond hair, a sharply pointed nose, and a three-stripe science patch on his shoulder. "What's the official position on how Captain Davis died?"

Before Thomas had a chance to answer, a female scientist answered. Her tightly curled hair was cut close to her head, and her warm brown face wore a no-nonsense expression. "Knock it off, Chris. You already know it was old age."

"So they want us to think," Chris said before fixing his attention back on Thomas. "What is United Earth saying?"

Thomas was about to reclaim the situation when the other scientist answered again. "Old age is what United Earth is saying. I'm telling you, there's nothing going on."

"I just want the details from someone with official authority," Chris said. "There's no way to tell who's a part of it, so we have to get every side of the story, Joyce."

Thomas's curiosity got the better of him. The more he knew about this, the faster he could return to the topic at hand. "A part of what?"

Groans from around the room informed him that he shouldn't have asked this particular question. Chris stared at him, as if studying his reactions. "A part of the extraterrestrial conspiracy to conquer Earth. Or the government conspiracy to cover up the time traveling accident of 2087. Or the conspiracy between the education system and the big grocery store chains to ..."

"I think he gets the idea," Joyce interrupted, rolling her eyes. "I'm sorry, Captain. My husband thinks Captain Davis was killed for knowing too much about aliens. Or the government. Or grocery stores. Or all of them."

"He was the highest-ranking officer to read all of my

research," Chris insisted. "It's not a coincidence that he died."

"He was 102 years old," Maureen said. "People die at that age."

Near the wall, Archibald Cleaver harrumphed.

"Present company excluded," she added with a polite nod.

Chris shook his head. "I'm not convinced."

"All right," Thomas said loudly, "that's enough. I'm not interested in conspiracy theories or questionable research ..."

"*Questionable* research?" Chris demanded, rising from his seat. "Do you have any idea who ..."

"Quiet!" Thomas's tenuous hold on patience vanished. This was ridiculous. It was time to make an example. "Mr. Fish," he said sternly, remembering Chris's last name from a list he'd read, "you are going to walk out of this room and go directly to your berth, and you are going to stay there until I have the time to have a one-on-one chat with you about proper respect. I will not have this kind of behavior on my ship! Is that clear?"

Chris's mouth hung open in surprise. "B ... but ..."

"And you're suspended from working on any side research for the rest of the week."

"But I have a grant from the ..."

"I don't care who's backing you! You work for the UELE. Your primary job is to keep this ship running, use it to catch criminals, and come up with better ways of doing those two things. Any other projects you might have the time and authorization to perform are a secondary concern. They've clearly become a distraction, and that is *not* going to be tolerated. Is that understood?"

Chris swallowed and nodded. Thomas continued to glare at him until he slowly rose from his chair and backed out of the room. He tripped over the hatch as he stepped into the corridor, and his footsteps broke into a run as soon as he moved out of sight.

Thomas turned his attention back to the rest of the crew, all of whom were now staring at him as if he'd just shot a puppy. He could tell he'd scared them, but maybe that was needed to get things in order here. He had a lot of work to do. Hopefully he'd just taken a step in the right direction.

* * *

No one dared speak to Thomas after the staff meeting unless they absolutely had to, with the exception of Matthias Habassa, who seemed to possess the unsinkable cheerfulness of a rubber ducky. Thomas overheard some hushed conversations that ceased as soon as he passed by and caught furtive glances between crew members whenever he entered a room. Each time, he nodded to himself with approval. His bad-captain technique had worked. Everyone was comporting themselves with the proper level of UELE discipline. If he could keep it up long enough, Dispatch was sure to take notice and forgive him for his past mistakes.

In the last round of communications before they left space dock to return to the Endurance's usual patrol, Thomas received a message from a Loretta Bailey. He didn't recognize the name, but the subject line was too familiar: "Thank you."

He'd received a fair amount of fan mail since the rescue, admiring his heroism, thanking him for protecting the community ... congratulating him on his promotion. "I'm so glad you received a proper reward for your bravery!" "You inspire us to do the right thing!" "The

UELE must be so glad to have officers like you!"

Right.

He'd finally asked Dispatch to stop forwarding them, so why had they sent this one? He considered simply deleting it, but if they'd bothered sending it, it must have some significance. He clicked it open.

Dear Thomas Withers,

I know this is a little weird, but I felt like I needed to write to you. I'm the woman you saved from that gunman at the lunar plaza. I can't imagine how hard it was to make the decision to shoot him …

He shut the computer before he could read any more. He didn't need reminders that he'd made a bad call.

Especially from her.

They took the ship out into space two days after he arrived, returning to the *Endurance*'s usual patrol around Neptune. Empty space, empty time to kill, and nothing to do but maintain vigilance and let the scientists run their little projects. It felt like exile.

Probably because it was.

After four full days of sitting in his office reading spy novels, wandering onto the bridge once an hour to see if anything had happened (it hadn't), and generally feeling useless, Thomas decided he might as well start tidying up the little points of order that were slipping in the ship's daily routine. The musty smell of the carpet had grown annoying, so he chose to first tackle the old vacuum cleaner.

He found Archibald Cleaver on the lowest of the ship's three decks, dutifully running his vacuum back and forth across the carpet at the end of a corridor. "Mr.

Cleaver," Thomas greeted him loudly so as to be heard over the machine.

Archibald turned around. "Hello," he said with a nod. He carefully turned off the vacuum. "Are you lost?"

"No. I'm here to talk with you."

Archibald did not look at all pleased with this news, but he remained silent.

"I wanted to discuss your vacuum. It's very old."

A nostalgic smile came over Archibald's face. "Yes," he agreed, "yes, she is. I've had her as long as I've been on this ship. She breaks down every so often, but Matthias always gets her running again. She does her job, that she does."

"I'm sure." Thomas suddenly realized this might not go as well as he thought. "I know this vacuum has worked well for you for a long time. However, I think it might be time for a new one."

Archibald's milky eyes grew very wide. "What?"

"As I said, this one is very old, and ..."

"You want to take her away from me?" The old man's voice now had a note of panic. "Why?"

"Wouldn't you enjoy using a new machine that works faster? I know there's been one in storage for years."

"Hah! Got no personality, those new devices. This vacuum and I know each other. We're comfortable together. No, thank you, I'll stick with what I'm used to."

Thomas knew that, having initiated the conversation, he couldn't back down. It would lead to all manner of discipline problems with the rest of the crew. "I'm afraid I have to insist," he said, moving to place a hand on the vacuum handle.

Archibald positioned himself in front of it.

Thomas raised his eyebrows. "Mr. Cleaver, are you

defying my order?"

"Well," Archibald drew out the word, "I hope you won't make it an order. But if you do, then yep, I suppose I'm defying it. If my vacuum goes, I go."

Thomas actually congratulated himself on that. Dispatch had been trying to get rid of Cleaver for literal decades; if he could get the man to quit, he'd be doing them a huge favor. "I'm sorry if that's your decision, but this really is long overdue." He held his breath and waited for the old man to pronounce his resignation.

Instead, tears started to form in Archibald's eyes. "You ... you think you can just come in here and change everything? You come and make one of your elders cry and leave his home of the past forty-seven years? Shame on you, young man! Show some respect."

People began leaning out of the doors further down the corridor. When the crewmembers saw what was happening, they began whispering to one another. Thomas distinctly heard the phrase "thirty on Arch."

Perfect. Gambling. Yet another problem he had to deal with.

Archibald was continuing to talk. "I worked this ship before you were even born! How dare you tell me to change my ways!" Murmurs of agreement arose from down the hall.

Thomas realized he'd played this horribly wrong. Instead of quitting in frustration, Archibald was turning the entire ship against him.

Before he could think of something to say, his first officer walked around the corner. "Is there a problem here?" Ivanokoff asked.

Thomas was about to tell him to leave when Archibald answered. "Ivanokoff, you know how important my vacuum is to me. Why, he's already made you give up Dickens and Dante. Next thing you know, he'll be telling Matthias he can't carry any tools with him!"

"He has a point," Ivanokoff told Thomas. "Dickens and Dante were not harming anything."

Thomas didn't think that was the janitor's point at all, but Matthias poked his head out of one of the doors before he could say so. "I'm not allowed to carry tools anymore?" the engineer asked.

"Of course you are," Thomas said hurriedly before he could be interrupted again. "This is only about the vacuum."

Matthias emerged fully from his room. "Oh, is it broken again? Let me see it, Arch, I'll fix it."

Archibald remained firmly planted between his vacuum and the rest of the group. "I'm not letting anybody near her until you apologize," he told Thomas.

"They're just weapons for self-defense," Ivanokoff muttered to himself.

"It's not broken?" Matthias asked, tilting his head to one side.

"No, she's fine," Archibald said.

Maureen came around the corner. "I heard yelling. What's going on? You'll wake up Nina, and it's hard for her to sleep when she's sick."

"Maureen, doesn't my vacuum do a good job cleaning your office?" Archibald asked.

"She still has that flu?" Matthias asked sympathetically.

"And weapons with artful names, too," Ivanokoff grumbled.

"No, now she has bronchitis," Maureen answered Matthias. "And Archibald, you've always done a wonderful job cleaning the office. Why?

20

"That's enough!" Thomas finally shouted, hoping to employ the same strategy that worked in the conference. Everyone jumped. "All of you, return to your duties."

"There's no need to yell about it." Maureen placed her hands on her hips and stuck out her lower lip. "I was just answering their questions."

Thomas softened. Yes, he was the "bad captain," but he also wanted to place blame responsibly. "I wasn't yelling at you ..."

"You've seemed very stressed since you stepped on board, and now you're showing signs of pent-up aggression. I think you could use some relaxation exercises. Just look at the way you're carrying your shoulders. I want to see you in my office first thing in the morning to go over deep breathing and other stress relief techniques."

Thomas decided to give up on the vacuum and try again when the entire senior staff wasn't watching. "That won't be necessary."

He moved to walk past the group, but Maureen stepped into his path. "Sir, I insist. And if you don't follow my advice, I'm legally required to file a report with Dispatch."

Thomas barely bit back a swear. She was right, of course. While the captain could refuse non-emergency medical advice, the review process helped ensure no one abused that privilege. A report filed during his first week of command was not going to improve his opportunities for transferring. "Very well, then."

Maureen smiled, then turned and waved graceful hands at the rest of the people standing in their doorways. "It's all right; everyone can relax. Take deep breaths and let them out slowly."

Next to Thomas, Matthias obeyed her. Loudly.

Maybe he should have stuck with the spy novels.

* * *

At 0600, Thomas obediently arrived at Maureen's office and rapped his knuckles on the metal hatch. A moment later, Maureen opened it. "Come in, Captain."

He stepped inside and Maureen shut the door behind him. The office was slightly larger than an average two-person cabin, though it sported the same brown carpet and white walls that adorned the rest of the ship. Two plain metal folding chairs sat in the middle of the room, and a cushioned table stood against the opposite wall, probably to serve as a medical exam bed. There was a desk near the hatch, topped by an enormous first aid kit, and a box of stretching aids and weights in the corner. A sign next to the hatch read: "Remember to turn off the gravity when you leave." That was it.

"This is the medical bay?" Thomas asked.

Maureen nodded. "I assume you were expecting something more elaborate, but since I'm not a doctor, I don't use any medical equipment. Dispatch took out some outdated things a couple years ago and never replaced them." She moved behind one of the chairs. "Please, sit down."

Resigned, Thomas did so, and Maureen arranged herself in the opposite seat. "Can you describe how you've been feeling?" she asked.

"A bit stressed, but that's typical for command officers." Thomas fully intended to give answers that were honest enough, but would get him out of the office as soon as possible.

"What do you think is causing those feelings?"

He thought that was a stupid question, but he bit his

tongue and answered politely. "Changing ships is always stressful, particularly when things are run so ..." Insanely. Crazily. Uncontrollably. Like-nobody-had-exercised-discipline-in-five-decades-ly. "... uniquely."

Maureen smiled. "All right, Captain. I'd like you to close your eyes." He obeyed. "Take a deep breath, and imagine you're collecting all of your feelings of anxiety in your lungs. Then breathe out and exhale the negative tension into the air."

Sure. Rolling his eyes underneath his closed eyelids, Thomas inhaled and exhaled, though he ignored the visualization part.

"And again," Maureen prompted.

He obeyed.

"And again."

Thomas was about to ask how many times he needed to do this when the ship suddenly lurched forward and threw him from his seat. He found himself lying on the ground, staring up at the ceiling.

"Captain!" In an instant, Maureen was helping him up, apparently having maintained her balance through whatever had just happened.

As soon as he regained his feet, Thomas tapped his personal intercom interface, a coin-sized device attached around his ear. "Page the bridge."

"Paging bridge," the computerized voice repeated.

At least something on the ship could follow orders perfectly.

More seconds than were strictly professional passed before the young man in charge of the night shift finally responded. "Uh, uh, Sergeant Ramirez here, Captain," his voice came through Thomas's interface.

"I just felt a sudden change in velocity. What happened?"

"Um, we aren't sure, sir. We lost helm control to the reactor room for a second, but we have it back now. I'm sorry it disturbed you, and we'll look into it right away, so please don't be mad, because it really wasn't anything we did, and ..."

"Calm down. Try to determine what happened. I'll be there shortly after I check on the reactor." Thomas tapped the interface again to close the connection and turned to Maureen. "I'm afraid I'll have to cut this session short."

She smiled at him and finished righting the furniture. "I understand. Just try to take deep breaths throughout the day. It should help you with your stress."

"Yes. Thank you." Thomas had no intention of following that advice. He turned to go.

"Oh, and sir?

He stopped and looked back at her.

She smiled apologetically. "Whatever caused that instability a moment ago, I'm sure it's nothing serious. My brother likes to experiment with new ways to improve the ship's systems, and sometimes when he makes changes to the propulsion system, it ..."

"Thank you for apprising me. I'll keep that in mind."

Considering Maureen's words, and how he should react if they turned out to be accurate, he headed to the reactor room.

* * *

The *Endurance* wasn't a big ship, so Thomas arrived in under two minutes. He found that he had intruded upon an impromptu party. The five engineers in the room each held a glass of champagne, and one of them—the man with the unibrow—was in the middle of some sort of toast. The group was facing away from the door, toward the Adkinsium reactor. The reactor itself looked a little different than normal, but Thomas didn't have time to reflect on that. Officer Unibrow was concluding his speech.

"… for inventing the most amazing breakthrough in propulsion technology, to Lieutenant Matthias Habassa!" The others applauded. "Thanks to him, the *Endurance* is now the first ship ever to leave our solar system."

"WHAT?"

Glasses broke and champagne spilled on the metal deck as the five whirled to face their captain. "What did you do?" Thomas demanded. Before anyone could reply, he whacked his intercom interface. "Page the bridge."

"Paging bridge," replied the interface, far too calm.

A moment later, Ramirez answered. "Uh, here, Captain. I'm so sorry, but we're still trying to …"

"Where are we, Ramirez?"

"Uh, sir?"

"Our location. Get a report from the helm. Where are we?"

Some muffled conversation carried through the channel, which quickly grew in intensity. Then Ramirez came back. "Oh my gosh, Captain, I swear it's not my fault!"

"What happened?"

"The solar system's gone, sir! All the planets, and the sun, and … I swear I didn't mean to blow it up!"

"You didn't blow it up, Ramirez." Thomas pinched the bridge of his nose. "Look at the stars, then use the navigation equipment to calculate our position."

"Um, okay." Ramirez didn't cover the microphone on his interface, so his next words nearly blew out Thomas's eardrums. "CHECK THE STARS, YOU

GUYS!"

Thomas forced himself not to raise his voice, but the sweat of anger began to form around his temples. "Where. Are. We?"

"Just a second." Thomas could hear someone reporting to Ramirez in the background. The sergeant swallowed audibly. "It seems we've, er, left the solar system, sir. We've traveled over twenty lightyears from Earth. But really, it wasn't anything we did! The view through the ports suddenly got weird, and Nina threw up, and now we're ..."

Thomas cut the channel and whirled on the engineers, all of whom were now staring at him with wide eyes. Twenty lightyears. At the ship's top speed, it would take them over 400 years to get back to their own solar system. As if the Adkinsium reactor would even last that long. He took a deep breath, gritting his teeth. "What did you do?"

Matthias raised his hand. "If I can, Captain? It was my idea. And I really didn't think you'd mind."

"You didn't think I'd mind that you took the ship out of our solar system without asking for my permission?" The beads of sweat began to run down around Thomas's ears.

Matthias shrugged. "To be honest, sir, I didn't think you'd notice, either."

Thomas lost it. "How could I not notice that you took us out of the solar system? How did you even DO that?"

Oblivious to the fury facing him, Matthias brightened as he launched into an explanation. "Well, sir, of course you know that faster-than-light travel is impossible, at least with our current technology. The power requirements would be ridiculous, and there's no way human beings could survive accelerating that fast, so instead of trying to break the light barrier, I went around it. It was an idea I had in grad school, but it wasn't until Captain Davis gave me permission that I started really pursuing it."

Oh no. Oh no, no, no. "You had permission?"

"Yup. I can show you the research order if you want. He got it signed by the R&D people at Dispatch and everything."

"Permission or not, you've effectively stranded us in the middle of nowhere with no way back!" Thomas couldn't believe he was going to starve to death on his first command—on the freaking *Endurance,* no less—because his chief engineer couldn't be bothered to have a little foresight.

However, that impression seemed to be wrong. Matthias looked appalled. "Captain, I would never do that! We were only in 4D for about ten seconds, so we should have well over 60 percent of our power left. And the prototype D Drive has at least another jump left in her."

"The what?"

"The D Drive." Matthias pointed at a large box attached to the top right corner of the reactor. It had most definitely not been there a few days ago. "It took me about ten years to get it working right. Had to renew the research permit a couple times, and it was pretty hard to get the testing phase approved, but Captain Davis was really nice about it. Basically, it projects an approximate four-dimensional axis onto the ship. That lets navigation calculate trajectories in 4D, so we can travel through it."

Thomas had earned his one-stripe engineering patch—a requirement for command—but the theoretical physics classes had been a while ago. Unfortunately, he needed to understand what had been screwed up so that he could fix it. He swallowed his impulse to start yelling again and instead managed, "Clarify on that."

"Okay." Matthias ducked behind a work station and came up with a piece of paper and an orange marking pen. Why he stored art supplies in the reactor room, Thomas had no idea. The engineer held the sheet up. "So, this paper has two dimensions. The X and the Y—length and width."

That much, Thomas remembered, but he managed to keep his cool. *Breathe, Thomas. Deep breaths.* He ignored the fact that he was following Maureen's stupid advice.

Next, Matthias bent the paper in half and held the two ends about two centimeters apart. "Now it has a third dimension—the Z axis, or height."

"Yes. I know that." *Deep, deep breaths.*

Matthias unfolded the paper again and drew two dots on it with the pen, one on either end, and labeled them "A" and "B." He held it up. "If you want to go from A to B in two dimensions, you have to go across the entire paper, about ten centimeters." He then folded the paper again, holding the ends with points A and B close together. "But if you add a third dimension, you can cut across it and shorten the distance by a whole lot." To illustrate his point, he drew a line through the air with his finger from A to B, which was about three centimeters.

Feeling a lot like a schoolchild, Thomas ground his teeth. *Keep breathing.*

The engineer put the paper down and beckoned around them. "Now, imagine that you can add another physical dimension—a fourth one. You could fold three-dimensional space and travel across the fourth dimension, shortening the distance you have to travel. That's what the D Drive lets us do. It doesn't make us go faster, it just lets us take shortcuts."

Thomas tried to picture four-dimensional space and found that he couldn't. Matthias watched him. "You're probably trying to picture four-dimensional space. It's not really possible, since we're three-dimensional beings, but the math works, and that's all that really matters. Want to see my calculations?"

"No. That's enough." Thomas's mind was reeling, but he had at least a basic understanding of what his chief engineer had said. And it obviously worked, so there wasn't much point in debating the validity of the idea. "You are going to turn us around and take us straight back to Earth immediately. As soon as we arrive, you are all confined to your berths, and will wait there while I look into disciplinary action."

"But Captain, since we have the research order, I don't think Dispatch will let you punish us. I guess we probably should have informed you, but I figured you had a list of all the current projects on the ship."

Yes, Thomas did have that, but the list had been awfully long. Of the project abstracts he'd read, he'd only understood a few, and he had given up after about an hour of trying to puzzle out the actual concepts.

Unfortunately, the research order meant that he probably couldn't have the engineers discharged from the corps, but he hoped to at least get an official reprimand in their files. "My orders stand. Get us back to Earth, now."

Matthias shrugged and turned to the D Drive. "Aye-aye, Captain."

"What a party pooper," someone whispered.

Thomas didn't have the patience to deal with that. He tapped his intercom interface. "Page the bridge."

A moment later, Ramirez once again stuttered into the conversation. "Uh, hi, sir. We're still trying to fix the problem, but …"

"The problem is under control, Sergeant. Set navigation back toward Earth."

"Um, yes, sir. Do you mind if I ask what happened?"

"Yes."

"Oh. Sorry."

Thomas reminded himself that this wasn't Ramirez's fault. "Just set the course."

"Yes, sir. Over and out."

As the channel went dead, Thomas glared at Matthias. "Progress?"

"Almost there, Cap. It's a prototype, so we have to be careful with it."

Thomas glanced at his chronometer. It wasn't even 0700 yet. He closed his eyes and took another deep breath. *Keep calm,* he reminded himself. This would all be over soon.

Matthias cleared his throat. "Hey, Captain? We have a slight setback."

Or not.

* * *

Thomas surveyed the faces staring at him from around the table in the conference room. Ivanokoff had begrudgingly attended the meeting, though he'd been three minutes late. Areva had again startled Thomas by appearing behind him, and when he'd ordered her to sit on a chair like a normal person, she slid most of the way under the table. Matthias was there, still smiling, which made Thomas want to punch him, and Maureen sat poised, legs crossed, hands folded on the table. Chris Fish, who represented the scientists as well the scanners team, stared at Thomas with narrowed eyes, probably trying to decide whether or not to categorize this meeting as part of a conspiracy theory. Thomas ignored pleasantries, as he wasn't feeling particularly pleasant, and laid out the problem at hand.

"Due to negligence and insubordination on the part of the engineering team during a risky experiment, we are now more than twenty lightyears from Earth. While it allegedly should have been a simple matter to return, the device that brought us here is in need of a replacement capacitor, which we don't have."

"Fortunately, I can build one," Matthias said. "We have all the materials, except that I ran out of chrioladium wire, so we need a little more of that."

"Which is why I've called this meeting," Thomas said. "We used scanners to determine that there's a solar system within a day's journey at our top regular speed."

"We were aiming for it. It's Struve twenty …" Matthias began.

"Lieutenant, that's enough."

"Sorry, sir." Though Matthias shut his mouth, he bounced excitedly in his seat, something he'd been doing since Thomas had first decided to investigate the alien system.

"As I was saying, scanners showed several gravitational sources—planets—orbiting the system's sun. Hopefully one of them has a deposit of chrioladium near the surface, and we'll be able to retrieve it, fix the D Drive, and return home."

"Question," Ivanokoff stated. "Who is to retrieve the materials?"

"That's part of why we're here. You're all department heads, so I need your input. We could use someone with geology experience to help find the compound in the first place. Then we'll need someone with a perfect spacewalk record to retrieve it."

Matthias's hand shot up. "I have a perfect spacewalk record!"

Maureen gently pulled her brother's hand down. "Matthias, you've done one."

"But it was perfect."

"I think the captain wants someone with more experience."

"Yes," Thomas agreed. "At least six."

"Areva has a perfect record with ten spacewalks," said Ivanokoff.

Thomas glanced at the chief of defensives, who was slouched so low that her face barely peeked over the table. "You do?"

Areva hesitated and nodded. "I like it out there. I volunteer when someone needs research done outside."

She wouldn't have been Thomas's first choice, but she certainly wasn't the worst. "Good. Then you can handle the retrieval part of the mission. Do any of the scientists have a background in geology?" He knew from the crew manifest that none of his team actually specialized in rocks, but he hoped someone might have taken a few courses or done some side research in the past.

Nobody raised their hands. Thomas frowned. "No one?" Certainly, they could use scanners to look for the materials, but without knowing where to look, a grid-by-grid search of even a single planet would take days. His frown deepened. "All right, then we'll need to deploy the backup scanners in order to ..."

"Ooh!" Matthias shouted. "I know! Ask Arch!"

Thomas stared at him. "Archibald Cleaver? The janitor?"

"Cleanliness enforcement specialist," Ivanokoff

corrected. "And I agree. Mr. Cleaver would be a valuable asset in this matter."

"He's very smart," Chris said. "Even without a degree. Maybe too smart."

"He knows everything," Maureen said. Even Areva popped her head up above the table to nod.

Having asked for their opinions, Thomas really couldn't argue, so he reluctantly called Archibald to the meeting room. The janitor shuffled in ten minutes later, beloved vacuum in tow. Thomas noted that Archibald kept himself in front of it, lest Thomas try and take it away again.

However, there were more important matters at hand. "Thank you for joining us, Mr. Cleaver," he said.

"So Mattie got us lost, did he?" Archibald asked.

"We're not lost," Matthias said. "We know exactly where we are. We're 25.428 ..."

"Lieutenant."

"Yes, Captain?"

"Stop."

"Sorry, Captain."

Thomas faced Archibald. "Yes, we're no longer in our own solar system. We can get back, but we need to find a nearby source of chrioladium. I was hoping something in your experience might help us locate it."

"Heck, lots of stuff on the ship contains chrioladium. Just use that."

Matthias shook his head. "Sorry, Arch. We need a lot more than that." Seeing Thomas's look, he shrugged. "It's a big capacitor."

"Of course it is," said Thomas. "Mr. Cleaver, do you know of any way to narrow down possible deposits on the planets?"

Archibald scratched his head. "Seems like I recall a

few pointers. What kinds of planets are we looking at?"

Chris pushed his computer pad toward the janitor. "We made a digital chart of each one's gravity field, estimated size, and projected orbit."

Archibald studied the data for a moment before speaking. "I'm thinking this one's your best shot." He pointed to the third largest of the seven planets in the system. "The gas giant's no good; if it did have the stuff, we can't get it, and we wouldn't get out of the gravity afterwards neither. These three," he gestured to the two smallest and the second-largest, "ain't dense enough to have the metals. That one's moving too fast for a safe landing. And that one," he pointed to the last eliminated choice, "is ugly."

Thomas paused. "It's … ugly?"

"Yeah. I don't like it."

He pulled the chart over. "There's no image here. It's just a list of numbers."

"I know. But I think it's ugly."

"You can't see it."

"I've just got a feeling."

"Arch's feelings have an 86.151 percent accuracy rate," Chris said. "I've tracked it."

"It is better than random guessing," Ivanokoff agreed.

Thomas held up a hand. "All right. We'll search the planet he suggested. I'll have the helm set our course for it once we enter the system."

* * *

The next twenty-two hours passed uneventfully, with one exception. When it drew near the time when the *Endurance* would enter the system, Thomas made his way to the bridge. Ivanokoff was waiting for him outside. "Sir, I would like to speak to you."

Thomas almost denied him out of spite, but he knew that if he disregarded his first officer without a good reason, it would probably get reported to Dispatch. "In my office."

The two made their way through the bridge to the little room. There was enough space for a desk, one chair on either side of it, and not much else, but Thomas had spent a large amount of time in the office anyway. His stack of novels sat beside the desk and his computer lay closed on top of it, but he hadn't decorated.

Thomas shut the metal hatch, more or less soundproofing the room, and turned to Ivanokoff. "Go ahead."

"May I speak my mind?"

Oh, great. "You may."

"You are a bad captain."

Thomas's insides lurched at the bluntness. "Excuse me?"

"You divided the crew by blaming the engineers in front of the staff."

"Our current situation is their fault, and it's time people on this ship learned to accept responsibility."

"Matthias is perfectly able to accept responsibility. He does not do any work unless he is proud of it. But the words you chose were meant to shame him and his team before the others. That will not do. A captain's job is to unite his crew. Under Captain Davis, the crew performed well and felt comfortable in their duties. Now they are quiet and rigid, the way you want, but only because they are afraid."

"*You* seem unafraid of speaking your mind."

Ivanokoff stared down his nose at Thomas. "I am

bigger than you."

That was true enough, but the phrasing made Thomas's blood boil. "Was that a threat?"

"No. It is an explanation. I am bigger than most things. The rest of the crew, they are not so big. You easily intimidate them. That is no way to maintain order."

"That's enough." Thomas drew himself to his full height. He still had to look up to make eye contact with his first officer. "I gave you permission to speak, but you are way out of line to question my entire system of command." Ivanokoff opened his mouth to retort, but Thomas didn't let him. "I've heard you, and now you're through. I will run this ship the way I see fit, not the way that makes everybody feel happy. You're dismissed."

"Captain, clearly you do not ..."

"I said you're dismissed!" Thomas moved to the other side of his desk, putting the barrier of officiality between them. "And the next time I have to give you an order twice, Lieutenant, I'll take you off active duty until you can learn to follow the chain of command."

Ivanokoff frowned and looked for the briefest of moments like he might argue, or possibly assault Thomas, but instead he turned, opened the hatch and ducked through. He slammed it shut on his way out.

Thomas stood in silence, staring down at his bare desk. This wasn't what he signed up for. All he'd wanted, for his entire life, was to protect people and train other officers to do the same. He couldn't do that while patrolling the emptiest space in the solar system, and he certainly couldn't do it if he died out here in the middle of nowhere.

He groaned and sank into his chair, feeling the old cushion sag a little. Up until two weeks ago, everything in his life had gone according to plan. Now it was all chaos.

His thoughts went back to that letter from Loretta Bailey, sitting unread in his computer. *You saved her,* he thought.

Yes, and look where it got you. You thought with your heart. Now think with your head, or you'll be stuck with these people forever. Or worse, you'll all die out here and no one will know what happened to you.

Hey, intruded his sense of optimism. The voice sounded annoyingly like Matthias. *If you get this ship back home, you'll have saved its entire crew!*

He groaned again and dropped his head against the desk. Dispatch might not consider that to be a good thing.

One way or another, he needed to keep going. With a supreme force of will, Thomas pushed himself back to his feet. The *Endurance* would reach the solar system in under an hour, and he wanted to be on the bridge to make sure they navigated safely to the planet. He could deal with the consequences of all of this later.

How he wished he'd just stayed a lieutenant.

* * *

Thomas couldn't shake his feeling of tension as he sat in the command seat, watching the little sphere grow larger on the scanners display. He couldn't yet see the planet out the windows, as the pilot was using the gas giant's gravity well to slingshot *Endurance* toward their destination. More people than were on duty filled the bridge, and their quiet conversations created a low murmur, but Thomas didn't care to listen.

He was about to send one of his crew out on a spacewalk on an alien planet hundreds of years' travel from Earth. Though the situation gave him a knot the size of Canada in his stomach, he knew on some level that if they made it back home, this would go down in the history books. He wasn't sure how he felt about that, and he wondered how many other "pioneers" of history had no idea what they were doing at the time.

"We're a third of the way through the arc now," the pilot announced. "The planet should come into view in a few seconds."

Everyone on the bridge leaned forward. Though the crew knew the size and approximate makeup of the planet through their scanners, they didn't know what sort of terrain they would face, if it would be possible to land, what sort of atmosphere—if any—it had, or any other details that could make the difference between success and failure. Their first glimpse of the world would reveal a lot of important information, including whether or not they had a chance of getting home.

Gasps arose as the planet came into view, and Thomas bolted up from his chair. "Are ... are those cities?"

They were facing the night side of the planet, and all across its surface they could see clusters of lights, dense enough to be visible even from space.

"It certainly appears that way," said Ivanokoff.

"No way ..." whispered Matthias. "What are the odds of that?"

"Of finding an inhabited planet by accident?" asked Chris Fish, also in a whisper. "About three point two eight ..."

Thomas held up a hand to silence them. He cleared his throat. "We don't know it's inhabited."

"Oh, come on!" said Chris, breaking the reverent mood. "What else could it be?"

"Sergeant, for the last time, you will address me with respect," said Thomas. "And it could be some kind of natural phenomenon. Or a mirage. Or ..."

"Or people," finished Ivanokoff. "Though we do not yet know whether or not they are hostile." His hands wandered to where he normally kept his pistols, and when he didn't find them, he tucked his thumbs in his belt instead.

"Or whether we can even breathe the atmosphere down there," Thomas countered. "There are a lot of things that could go wrong. Helm, take us into the upper atmosphere slowly. Sergeant Fish, tell whoever's running that chemistry set on the middle deck that I want to know the contents of the planet's air. Lieutenant Praphasat ..."

Areva appeared at his elbow, waiting for instructions. He was too distracted to be startled, still looking at the inviting lights below. "I think it's safe to say you should suit up."

* * *

Two hours later, the scientists had confirmed that the atmosphere was, indeed, breathable, and that the ship could safely fly in it. The bridge crew had used the time to take some high-resolution images of the clusters of lights on the night side of the planet, and had determined that they were, in fact, artificially-constructed buildings. Cities.

Thomas didn't know what to make of it.

On the one hand, discovering alien life was an enormous step forward in humanity's understanding of the universe.

On the other hand, this wasn't his job. He wasn't trained in diplomacy, he didn't know the first thing about studying new cultures, and he had no desire whatsoever to make mankind's first impression on another intelligent, city-building species.

Unfortunately, he couldn't send a message to Earth and ask for help, as it would take twenty-five years for them to receive it and twenty-five more to send a reply, if it even made it at all. He had to make this decision himself, and he was the only one who could do so.

"To land or not to land?" Ivanokoff muttered behind his command chair. "That is the question."

Thomas didn't answer. He stared out the window at the clusters of lights, wondering who or what they would find down there. He swallowed and hoped no one noticed. "We don't have a choice. If we're going to get home, we have to find that chrioladium. We're landing. Helm, put us down in the largest city on the daylight side. Try to find a building that looks important so we can talk to whoever's in charge."

Matthias whooped, and Chris pumped his fist in the air in an expression of victory. The pilot began guiding the ship down toward the planet's surface.

Areva stood near the hatch to the hallway, outfitted in her spacesuit except for the helmet. "Am I still going alone, sir?"

Thomas shook his head and stood up. "No. This was supposed to just be a resource-gathering mission, but now it's something bigger. I'm coming with you."

Chris, who had been listening intently, hurried over. "Can I come?"

"No."

"But I'm the leading expert on xenobiology ..."

"No, you're not," his wife called from the scanners station across the room. "That's not even a real field yet."

"It's about to be. I can't do any research if I don't get to see them."

"I only need one other person on the team," Thomas said. "Whoever we meet down there, they aren't going to speak English, or any other language of Earth, for that matter. So we'll need someone to help us figure out what they're saying."

"How do you know that they speak at all?" Ivanokoff asked.

"I don't. But I'm hoping they do, because otherwise we'll have a hard time explaining what we want." He looked around the room. "Does anybody on the ship have training in linguistics?"

"I have a little," Ivanokoff said.

"We can't have all three command officers off the ship at once."

"You do not have to come."

Thomas bristled. "Yes, I do. It's my ship, so Dispatch will consider it my responsibility." He felt a stone settle in his stomach as he realized he'd just referred possessively to the *Endurance*. "Besides, I want someone with more than a little training."

Chris raised his hand. "I've studied linguistics. And xenolinguistics."

"No, you haven't," Joyce said. She glanced at Thomas. "The xenolinguistics, I mean. He's telling the truth about the regular kind."

"Fine, then," Thomas said, "you can come." Chris started to pump his fist again, but Thomas continued, "*If* you can help us communicate. I don't want you trying to study them or anything."

"I won't."

"Good."

"But can I ..."

"No."

Chris frowned at him. "You don't even know what I was going to ask."

"The answer is still no."

"Sir," said Ivanokoff, "I recommend bringing a weapon with you."

Thomas shook his head. "No. I don't want to accidentally provoke them."

"But these are aliens, sir."

"All the more reason not to look like we're invading their planet. No handguns." An image of the aliens in a recent science fiction film—ten-foot-tall semi-robotic creatures that exhaled poison and bled liquid nitrogen—flashed through Thomas's mind, and he amended his orders. "But have someone standing by at defensives in case we need support from the ship's guns."

That seemed to placate the first officer, who inclined his head.

"Let's head for the airlock." Thomas glanced out the viewport, where the planet was rapidly growing larger. "This is going to be an interesting day."

* * *

As the exit ramp descended from the bottom of the *Endurance*, Thomas's stomach flip-flopped. He grimaced and berated himself for feeling nervous. Sure, it was a diplomatic mission. Sure, he wasn't exactly trained for this. But he was a captain in the United Earth Law Enforcement Corps, and he'd seen his share of action. "Butterflies" were for the newbies. He was going to step into this with confidence, with all the self-assurance he should have after his many years in the service.

Then the bottom of the ramp hit the dirt of an alien world, and Thomas thought he might throw up.

He, Areva, and Chris stomped down the ramp. Though far more flexible and less bulky than the equipment astronauts wore back in the 21st century, their spacesuits were still designed to ward off both extreme heat and cold, not to mention the vacuum of space. It made their footfalls heavy.

They'd landed in the middle of an enormous courtyard, surrounded on all sides by silver, reflective buildings at least five stories tall. The ground was made of flat, grey stones, arranged in a symmetrical grid, with small patches of flowering plants lining the walkways to each building and a design that looked like a seal or a crest laid into the middle of the courtyard where the four walkways met.

Two aliens waited at the bottom of the ramp.

As he descended to meet them, Thomas took in humanity's first look at extraterrestrials. They were both tall, about six-and-a-half feet, and slender. Their skin looked like a coat of matte grey paint covering their bodies, except where it darkened to black around their eyes. Their ears rose from the sides of their heads a good two feet into the air—creepy, spindly tendrils that swayed with the wind like antennae. They had noses and mouths, and were wearing clothes, which Thomas found reassuring—silky-looking garments that clung flat to their bodies. One wore a red thing similar to a dress, while the other had on a blue pantsuit-like outfit that had probably been tailored to fit him. The one in the blue was bigger than the one in the red, suggesting they might be different genders.

Oh, and they had a third arm sticking out of their chests.

Thomas tried not to stare at the creepy protruding joints as he reached the bottom of the ramp, and instead raised his hand in greeting. "Hello," he said. The sound came out of his suit's speaker sounding raspy, and he cleared his throat before continuing. "We're from a planet called Earth. Can you understand me?"

The pair blinked at him, and then Red Dress turned to Blue Suit and made a high-pitched, oscillating noise. Blue Suit waved his antennae, then pulled a small cube of about six inches on each side out of his pocket and pushed a few buttons on it.

Thomas looked at Chris. "Any guesses what that means?"

Chris shrugged. "Nope."

"What do you mean, nope?"

"What, you actually think I can translate this? Automatically, without any prior knowledge of the species?"

"Well, no, but I thought since you were trained in linguistics that ..."

"That's not how it works." Chris waved a hand dismissively. "If you gave me a couple of years to live with them nonstop, I might be able to put together a working grammar and syntax, assuming their language even uses things like that, but even then it would take a lot longer to gather enough of a vocabulary to start translating conversations on the fly."

Thomas frowned. "Why didn't you say so before we left the ship?"

"You didn't ask. And I wanted to come on the mission."

The two aliens watched the conversation, antennae-ears twitching whenever Thomas's voice rose. Thomas tried waving to them again, but they simply continued to watch. "We'll talk about this later. Right now, do you have any ideas for how to tell them what we want?"

"You could try acting it out. Like charades."

"I would like to see anyone act out 'chrioladium.'"

"Don't get touchy about it."

Thomas glared at Chris, and the scientist raised his hands. "Sorry. What if we just show them a sample of it? I can get one from Matthias."

"And then what?"

"I don't know. Improvise."

The alien in the red dress stepped forward onto the landing ramp. She hesitated a moment, then raised her left hand to mirror Thomas's greeting.

"Yes," Thomas said, raising his hand again. "Hello."

Red Dress tilted her head to one side, then raised her middle hand in the same gesture. It had a thumb on either side, and seemed able to pivot in any direction. Gross.

"Um, yes," Thomas said again, avoiding looking at the hand. "Hello."

This could be good, he thought. *Maybe this is progress.*

Red Dress watched him, then raised her right arm so that all three hands imitated the greeting. Then she started clapping both outer hands against the hand in the middle.

Or maybe not.

Thomas let his arm fall. "Okay. Let's get the sample."

* * *

The aliens let them retreat back into their ship's containment airlock without further interaction. Once safely secluded, Thomas activated his suit's intercom interface. "Page the reactor room."

"Reactor room, Matthias here."

"Lieutenant, I need a sample of chrioladium."

"Yes, sir! I'll suit up and bring it out right away."

"No, you're staying here. Just get it ready."

"Aw ..."

Just as he was about to head back out, his interface

beeped. "Bridge paging you," the computer announced.

"Answer."

Ivanokoff's voice came through in a booming bass. "We are having a problem with the computer, sir."

Of course they were. "What about it?"

"It seems that someone has accessed our internal database."

"That's hardly unusual, Lieutenant. There are over a dozen consoles with full access to ..."

"From outside the ship."

"... the complete database, and ..." It took a moment for the words to reach Thomas's brain. "From *outside* the ship?"

"Da. I thought perhaps it would be an appropriate time to arm the crew with ..."

"No, don't do that!" Thomas said with more than a little alarm. "The last thing we need is to start a war with these people. Maybe they're just ..."

"Invading our system, sir?"

"Trying to learn more about us, Lieutenant."

Ivanokoff grumbled. "Very well. I will wait." He cut the line.

Thomas rushed back to the exit ramp. Areva and Chris looked at him with concern. "Is something wrong?" Areva asked.

"Maybe. Maybe not. We're going back out."

* * *

The second time they descended the ramp, the two aliens were standing in the same place, except Blue Suit now had the six-inch cube held in two hands in front of him. Red Dress once again lifted her right hand in mimicry of Thomas's greeting.

"Um, hi," Thomas said. "Look, I know you don't understand me ..."

"But of course we do," said Red Dress.

Thomas blinked. Areva squeaked. Chris gasped, then said, "I understand them now!"

"Yes. So do I." Thomas cleared his throat, staring at Red Dress. "How did you ..."

Blue Suit held out the box and said, "This is our communication enhancement facilitator." Now that the aliens spoke again, Thomas realized the English words were coming from the box, while the aliens themselves were still producing the oscillating noises. "We connected it to your ship's wireless data transfer system and downloaded your language files. There were over one thousand of them! We were very pleased with such a find."

"So now the facilitator can translate between our two kinds," said Red Dress. "Let us try our initial meeting once more. Hello. Welcome to the World of Infinite Tones. I am Echo, third leader of the People of Tone, and this is my assistant, Note. We are in charge of greeting visitors to our planet."

"We are very pleased to meet you," said Note with a small bow.

"Um, my name is Thomas ..." Thomas blinked at the box as it began producing the noises of the aliens' language in time with his words. "Er, Captain Thomas Withers. We're from the planet Earth."

The two aliens' antennae tilted forward at an inquisitive angle. "The planet ... Dirt?" Echo asked.

"No. Earth."

"That is what I said. Dirt. You call your planet Dirt?"

"No." Thomas shook his head. What was wrong with the translator box?

"Actually, I think we do," Chris said. "Technically, earth is just another word for dirt. They probably only have one word that corresponds to it."

Thomas rolled his eyes. "Fantastic."

"What do you call yourselves?" Echo asked.

Before Thomas could answer, Chris said, "Earthlings."

"Hmm. Dirt People." Echo flashed a concerned glance at Note. "Well, I suppose not everyone is gifted with creative nomenclature. Your world still has more forms of speech than most we have encountered. We are very grateful to you for sharing them with us."

"We didn't really mean to do that," Thomas said, crossing his arms. Or trying to. The spacesuit made it a little difficult. "You hacked into our system. We'd usually take that as an aggressive act."

"Oh my." Echo's antennae drooped, and she bowed her head. "Our deepest apologies. We thought you wished to facilitate communication with us, and this is our usual method of doing so. We had no idea we had offended you."

This could work to his advantage. Thomas felt his confidence start to return as he slipped into the mode he used when he wheedled information out of criminals. "There is a way to make it up to us. We're trying to go back to Earth," *or Dirt,* he thought, "and we need some chrioladium to repair our ship. We thought your planet might have some deposits of it. Or of the minerals we need to make it, at least." He hoped the compound's name was in the language files these people had downloaded, or the conversation would get a lot more complicated.

Apparently it was. "Oh, yes, of course. We have a great deal of it." Echo bobbed her head. "We would be happy to provide you with all that you need. Assuming the Haxozin approve, of course."

"The who?"

She made a squawking sound that the box translated as "laughter." "You are a funny people. Imagine not knowing about the Haxozin."

Thomas exchanged blank glances with Areva and Chris. "No, we really don't know about them."

Her face turned serious. "Truly? Your world has not been visited?"

All three officers shook their heads.

Echo began speaking frantically. "Then you must go back there. Before they find you here. Go, quickly!" She planted two hands on Thomas's shoulders and one on Areva's and began trying to shove them back up the ramp. Beside her, Note pushed Chris backward in the same way.

"Hold on," Thomas said. "We still need the chrioladium. And just who are these Haxozin?"

"No time!" Echo glanced over her shoulder toward one of the buildings. "There are some here in the capitol. They have probably already sensed you. If you do not leave now, they will ..." Her voice died as the door to the building opened.

A group of five beings in full-body suits and helmets marched out in perfect lockstep. Thomas recognized military precision when he saw it and started to wish he'd brought Ivanokoff along after all, particularly when he spotted the cylindrical devices they carried on straps over their shoulders—weapons.

Though they each had two arms and legs, the marchers' actual appearance was completely obscured by their suits, which were dyed a deep shade of red. The suits were bulky, suggesting armor, but the soldiers' movement indicated it was made of flexible material. Their guns were shaped like miniature bazookas but carried like rifles, with gleaming metal barrels and handgrips worn from frequent use.

The group crossed the courtyard in seconds and came to a halt a meter from where Thomas was standing. Echo drew back and folded all three of her hands in front of her stomach, bowing her head and lowering her antennae.

Note hesitated, his hand still on Chris's shoulder.

Without warning, one of the soldiers raised his weapon and fired a blast of energy straight into the back of Note's leg. The man squawked in pain and collapsed, clutching at his injured thigh with all three arms and writhing on the ground. Echo turned her face away and took a shaky breath.

The translator box lay abandoned on the ground, but it still worked to convey Echo's words as she spoke up. "Venerated Haxozin, these strangers to our world claim not to know of your might. They attempted to leave without first meeting you. Note and I tried to stop them, but as you can see, they outnumber us." Her eyes flicked briefly toward Thomas as she spoke, then again focused on the ground.

Way to throw us under the bus, Thomas thought, his ambiguous feelings toward the People of Tone rapidly turning to dislike.

He raised his hands in what he hoped was a posture of nonaggression. "Look, we don't want to fight with you. We're just trying to get back to our own planet, Earth, and we needed some minerals you people have here."

"Planet Dirt?" One of the Haxozin stepped forward and studied Thomas. "The Haxozin Sovereignty has not heard of such a place. Where is it?"

A deep-seated instinct told Thomas not to answer that question precisely. "Several lightyears from here. And it's 'Earth,' not 'Dirt.'"

"That is what I said. Dirt."

Thomas sighed. "Okay, then, Dirt."

The soldier's helmet tilted upward as he gazed at the *Endurance*. "How did you travel so far in such a small ship?"

"You're asking a lot of questions," Thomas said. "I'd like to know who you are so that we can have this conversation properly."

In response, all five soldiers stepped forward and aimed their weapons at Thomas. He raised his hands but maintained eye contact with the lead soldier's helmet. *Never show fear to a bully*, he reminded himself. "Hey, we don't want trouble."

"You already have it," the soldier said.

He lifted the gun and slammed it across Thomas's spacesuit helmet. Thomas managed to get an arm up to defend himself, but the blow still sent him reeling to the ground, and his head smacked against the inside of the helmet as he hit the dirt. Stars blinked in his field of vision as a pair of Haxozin boots appeared in front of his face and another blow fell across his back. He grunted in pain and tried to push himself back to standing, but the Haxozin seized his helmet and began bashing his head against the ground. Someone screamed in the background as Thomas tried to free himself, but each impact with the ground sent more white stars flickering in front of his eyes.

The whiteness began fading to black, and Thomas felt his grip slip from his attacker's hands. His head contacted the ground again, and he dropped into darkness.

* * *

He glared down the sight of his gun, the scope trained on Pierre Callahan's head. Pierre held his own gun pointed back at Thomas. Thomas's eyes trailed over his opponent, looking for a weakness in the full-body armor the man wore. He couldn't see one. The only viable target was Pierre's skull.

"Lieutenant," said a voice in his ear. "Keep him talking. Reinforcements are on their way." He recognized Captain Liu's confident tone and nodded silently to himself. The motion wouldn't carry over the intercom interface, but Thomas felt reassured by it anyway.

"You're damaged goods, Pierre," he said, circling to edge the other man toward the ticket counter near the wall. The lunar plaza only had one exit to the surface, and Thomas currently stood between it and his target, but he wanted to keep the man away from the tram tunnels as well. He doubted they'd make a good escape route, but Pierre was slippery, and it had taken most of five years to finally catch up to him. No sense in taking chances.

"They'll take me back," Pierre said, matching Thomas's moves.

"You really think so? Knowing we found you? Knowing you could have led us the rest of the way up the chain? Face it, Callahan, even if you get out of here, you're done with the Uprising."

"Maybe. Maybe not." Pierre stepped back toward the counter. "Either way, I'm not giving myself over to you. And I know you're not gonna shoot me, because you need the information up here." He used his free hand to tap his head.

"That's good, Thomas," said Captain Liu via the interface. "Keep him going. We'll overwhelm him and take him alive. This one's in the bag."

Movement behind the counter caught Thomas's eye. Good lord, there were people back there. They must not have been able to get out with the rest of the crowd before the showdown started. He immediately stopped moving forward, not wanting Pierre to notice the potential hostages.

Pierre took another step back anyway. "I don't see you dropping your weapon, Lieutenant."

"That's not going to happen. In a few minutes, this place will be swarming with officers"

"In a few minutes, another train will come, and this place will be swarming with civilians, too. Plenty of targets, plenty of chaos. I guess we'll just play a game to see whose party arrives first, huh?"

One of the hiding people—from the sound of it, a little boy—whimpered.

It wasn't loud, but it was loud enough.

Pierre's head whipped toward the counter. "Don't move!" Thomas shouted, but it did no good. Pierre disappeared behind the counter and reappeared a moment later, dragging a dark-skinned woman with long hair. From her outfit, she was probably a mid-level businesswoman, here on her daily commute. She struggled against his grip, but froze when he pressed the gun to her temple. Tears began running down her cheeks.

Pierre's face lit up. "Looks like I don't need to wait for the train after all. You know how I deal with hostages. Don't make me perform a live replay for you. You can't shoot me, and your people won't be here in time. So let me go. Or she dies."

The woman let out a low moan that turned into a sob.

Thomas knew the situation was being transmitted through his intercom interface, but he reported it to convey the urgency. "Withers paging Captain Liu, be advised that this is now a hostage situation!" He didn't lower his e-gun.

"We're on our way. Do not let him leave."

"One chance, Lieutenant. For her, anyway. I've got more of them back here."

Liu repeated, "We'll be there in just a few seconds, Thomas. Do not engage."

Pierre shoved the woman to the ground and pointed his gun down at her. "Drop your weapon!"

"Don't touch her!" Thomas said. "Or I'll put an energy blast through your brain."

"Negative!" shouted Captain Liu in his ear. "Do not engage! We need him alive."

"Sir, he has a ..."

"Collateral damage, Lieutenant. This is an order: Do not engage."

The woman's sobs grew louder.

Thomas kept his sights centered on Pierre's head. "Let her go."

Pierre sneered. "I see I need to demonstrate my determination." He began to pull back on the trigger.

Thomas fired.

Pierre staggered backward. His gun went off, firing into the floor several meters away. The woman screamed. So did everyone else behind the counter.

Pierre Callahan crumpled into a heap on the floor, a hole in his head, right between his eyes.

Thomas stared down at the body. There was no going back from this.

"Thomas?" Captain Liu's voice rang out over the intercom. "Thomas, what happened? Tell me you didn't shoot him. Thomas?"

"Thomas. Thomas Withers. Captain of the UELE *Endurance*. How very interesting that you should come here today."

Thomas blinked the bleariness out of his eyes. His head felt like someone had driven a screwdriver into the side of it, and the bright light in the room wasn't making it feel any better. He squinted and took a look at his surroundings—stark, stone walls forming a room about three meters on each side, completely empty except for him and the high-intensity light panels lining the ceiling.

He tried to stand up and discovered that he couldn't move his arms. Or his legs. Or the rest of his body, for that matter. He frowned and looked down at himself. His limbs and torso were secured to a metal chair with a thick kind of wire. Apparently he'd been tugging against it during the dream, because the wire had left angry welts on his skin.

His *skin*.

Where was his spacesuit?

Thoughts of alien viruses invading his body and infecting him with all of their hideous maladies made him shudder, and he began trying to work one of his hands free from the wire around his wrist.

"Do not do that," said a voice behind his left ear.

Thomas would have jumped a foot out of the chair if he hadn't been tied down. "Who are you?" he asked. It came out a little squeaky.

"We are the Haxozin." Footsteps sounded behind him, and one of the red-armored soldiers walked around to stand in front of him. He held a translation box in his hand. The device took the sibilant sounds he was making and projected them as a deep man's voice. "And you are uninvited visitors to our territory."

"About that." Thomas fought the rise of fear in his chest. "We've never encountered an alien species before. We don't have any immunity against the diseases you might be carrying …"

"We have analyzed the computer files taken from your ship. You have no illnesses that are a threat to us, nor we to you."

Thomas peered up at him, which was difficult in the

bright light. "Then why are you still wearing your suit?"

The Haxozin didn't answer that. He paced around to stand behind the chair again and leaned in close beside Thomas's head. "Why have you infiltrated one of our conquered worlds?"

Thomas recognized the interrogation tactic—avoid the subject's sight, invade their personal space—and knew he was in for a rough time. "We're not infiltrating anything. We're lost. We need chrioladium to fix our ship and return home."

"To the planet Dirt."

"That's right."

"Where is this planet?"

"Far enough away that we won't bother you again." Thomas hadn't missed the word "conquered," and he didn't want the Haxozin to get any ideas about Earth. "Let me ask you a question. Have you hurt anyone on my ship?" There went that possessive reference again.

"Not yet." The Haxozin circled back into his view. "We have the loud one, but the female one evaded our capture. Where is she?"

So Chris had been taken, too. Thomas hoped he knew enough not to give anything away. But then, with his paranoid theories, Chris was probably used to keeping information a secret. The female one was obviously Areva, whom he assumed had gone back to the ship once the coast was clear. "I have no idea where she is."

The Haxozin studied his expression, then hauled off an enormous punch and struck Thomas across the face. The blow carried enough force to whip his head to the side and throw his entire body against the restraints.

"Hey!" he said. "I'm telling you the truth."

"I doubt that very much," said the Haxozin. "But let us talk about your ship instead. How does it travel faster than light?"

"I don't know."

"The captain doesn't understand the operation of his own ship? I also doubt that."

"It's true. And how do you know who I am?"

"The People of Tone told us everything you said to them." The Haxozin bounced the translation box in his hand. "And your computer system is not terribly secure. We were able to access a fair amount of your data."

"Uh-huh. Then why question me?"

"We were shut out of the system before we finished. Someone on your crew knows how to combat data thievery. And so far, we have been unsuccessful at opening the ship's airlock."

Thomas thought back to his first time entering the *Endurance*. "Yeah, that happens sometimes."

The Haxozin hit him again. "This is not a game. I want the code that will allow us to access your ship."

Thomas spat blood on the floor. "I'm not giving you that. And you have nothing to gain here. You can let me and the rest of the crew leave peacefully. We really don't have a problem with you."

"Anyone who challenges our power is a problem to us. Tell me how the Dirt People came to be able to travel faster than light."

The man was awfully interested in that particular topic. Thomas thought for a moment before replying, "Can any other species you've encountered travel faster than light?"

"Very few, and their systems are primitive."

"Can the Haxozin?"

"Of course. The Haxozin can do anything."

"Except get through an airlock, apparently." Thomas expected the next punch and turned his head with it to soften the blow. "Look, I'm guessing you're worried that we're some kind of threat to you. We're really not. We have no interest in encroaching on your territory. So why don't you just help us fix our ship, let us go, and we'll all pretend this didn't happen."

"It is too late for that." The man stalked out of Thomas's view once more. "The People of Tone have seen you. They have learned that you came from far away. They know we are not the only superior race in existence. We must bring you to heel in order to stop word of this from spreading and undermining our influence."

Understanding dawned on Thomas, and with it a chill as he realized how much he was in danger. "You're running an empire. You're afraid we accidentally touched off a revolution."

The Haxozin growled in answer.

Thomas's tone hardened. "If you're trying to conquer us to prove a point, then you're out of luck. I'm not giving you any information about my ship, about Earth, or about our species."

The chair suddenly tilted out from under him. Thomas found himself falling backward, landing with a crash on the stone floor. His head smacked painfully against the ground as he hit, and he had to fight not to black out again. The Haxozin loomed over him. "There are many ways to die, Captain. Some more painful than others. Shall I enumerate the options to you, or would you like to alter your intentions now?"

Thomas groaned in pain. "That was a really pretentious sentence. You're doing the interrogation wrong if the subject can't understand what you're saying."

The Haxozin snarled and lifted his boot over Thomas's head. Squeezing his eyes shut, Thomas prepared himself for a broken nose or worse.

Something made a loud noise, and then the Haxozin toppled over, sprawling on the ground beside the fallen chair.

Thomas opened his eyes to see Areva standing over him, one of the alien bazooka rifles in her hands. A small spark of residual energy discharged from the barrel and sputtered out in the air. "I like these," she said. "Can I keep this one?"

"Huh ...?" Thomas managed.

Areva set the gun down and began undoing the wires binding him to the chair. "I slipped out of sight when those soldiers showed up and started beating on you. Then I snuck up on one of them and took his gun. Then I followed another one in here. We're in the capitol building's basement." Thomas sat up and began rubbing life back into his limbs as she continued. "They have Chris in another room down the hall, but I thought I should get you first. Can I keep the gun?"

Thomas stared at the enormous hole in the Haxozin's helmet. "Yes. Yes, you can."

"Can we get another one for Viktor? He'd like them. The only energy weapons in his collection are too heavy for practical use."

"We'll talk about it." He managed to stand up, though the room spun for a moment as he did. "We need to rescue Chris and get out of here."

"What about the chrioladium?"

"We'll worry about that later. Right now, we need to get away before the Haxozin learn anything else about Earth. That's the top priority."

Areva shrugged and reclaimed the bazooka rifle. "Okay."

Thomas led the way down the hall, listening for any sound that they'd been noticed. Fortunately, the basement seemed deserted. Both sides of the hallway consisted of identical doors, presumably leading to identical stone rooms.

At a door about halfway down the hall, he held up a fist, signaling a halt. Raised voices came from inside.

"I'm serious. If you don't tell me who really abducted Elvis and prove that you aren't responsible for the 2103 Oslo incident, I'm not telling you anything!"

That was Chris.

Thomas placed a hand on the door and motioned for Areva to take out the Haxozin soldier once they entered. She nodded and positioned herself for a clean shot.

He opened the door and jumped aside, pressing his back against the wall next to it.

The Haxozin looked up and snarled at them.

Areva didn't move.

Thomas waved his hand impatiently. *Hurry up and shoot him.*

Areva shook her head. "Sorry, sir. I can't. He can see me."

"What?"

"He's looking."

"Why would that ..." Thomas was interrupted when the enormous form of the Haxozin soldier stormed out of the room and threw itself at Areva. He tackled her to the floor and began trying to wrestle the rifle away from her.

Thomas shook himself out of his confusion and jumped on the Haxozin's back, hoping to get an arm around the other man's neck. Unfortunately, it seemed the Haxozin had been trained for this kind of attack. Instead of trying to pull away, he threw himself backward and pinned Thomas to the floor beneath his superior weight. Though Thomas tried to tighten a stranglehold around his throat, the armored man elbowed him in the ribs and rolled to the side.

Then Areva shot him.

As the Haxozin slumped back to the floor, a hole burned in the back of his helmet, Thomas pushed himself back to standing. "What ... what was that?"

"He turned around. He couldn't see me. So then I could shoot him."

"That doesn't make any sense."

"That's what people keep telling me. It's just how I work."

"He could have killed us!"

"Hey!" Chris yelled from inside the room. "Can we maybe talk about this later? I'm tied up in here."

Thomas reminded himself that they were in the middle of an escape attempt, and that he was supposed to be in charge. "Right. I'll get him loose. Cover my back, Lieutenant."

"Yes, sir," Areva said, positioning herself in the doorway as Thomas went inside.

Chris was bound to a chair, too. As Thomas began undoing the wire holding him there, he said, "Captain! I've figured it out. The interrogation gave me time to think about it. The People of Tone are the Roswell aliens. I saw the blurry surveillance video from when they came back in 2087, and these are the same guys."

"Not now, Sergeant." He glanced over his shoulder at Areva. "Praphasat ..."

She was nowhere to be seen. He raised his voice as high as he dared. "Praphasat?"

"Here, sir." Her voice came from the hallway. "You can't see me, right?"

"No, I can't, but don't go anywhere. Do you know the way out of here?"

"Yes, there's a direct route to the surface. I came down through it."

"How well-guarded is it?"

"Not very. There are only ten Haxozin on the planet. There are a lot of those grey people, though."

"The Roswell aliens!" Chris repeated as Thomas finished releasing him.

"Ten armed enemies," Thomas said. "How do you know that, Lieutenant?"

"I asked Echo," Areva said.

"You *what?*" Thomas stormed out into the hallway to face his chief of defensives. "You talked to her?"

"Sir, I'm trying to hide!"

"I don't care. You asked a woman who turned on us in a heartbeat about how many enemies we're facing? Are you out of your mind?"

Chris appeared in the door behind him. "Captain, maybe you should take a deep breath …"

"Quiet, Sergeant."

"Yes, sir."

Areva took a moment to collect her thoughts. "I found Echo back inside the building after the Haxozin took you both down here and started trying to break into the *Endurance*. She said the Haxozin have ruled her people since she was little, and it had never even occurred to her that anybody could challenge them. Until we showed up."

Uh oh, Thomas thought. Maybe they *did* start a revolution.

"So she thought she'd give me some information to help us escape."

Chris grinned. "We inspired an alien revolt! This is great!"

Thomas studied Areva's expression. "Do you trust what she told you?"

"I can usually tell when someone lies, sir. I think she was telling the truth."

Thomas considered how much stock to put in her abilities. On the one hand, she was stationed on the *Endurance*, she had some strange habits, and there was a distinct possibility that she was missing a few of her marbles.

On the other hand, she was his chief of defensives—the person in charge of keeping him, his ship, and his crew safe. He was expected to trust her.

And he didn't have much choice. The other option was to run without a plan—always a bad decision.

"Okay," he said. "Ten enemies total. And you've taken out two of them already."

"Three, sir. One on the way in."

"Three. So seven left. Some of them are working on finding a way into the ship, so that leaves us with four or five armed soldiers between us and the *Endurance*. Praphasat, did you see where the other Haxozin stashed their bazookas when they came down here?"

"In a room down the hall. Close to the stairs to the surface."

"Great. Lead the way."

She hesitated. "If it's all right, could you lead? So I'm not, you know ..."

Chris nudged Thomas. "She doesn't like to be seen."

"I noticed. Keep your elbows to yourself, Sergeant. All right, I'll take point. Praphasat, cover our backs and tell me when we reach the door to the armory."

"Yes, sir."

"And if someone approaches from behind and sees you, hand me the gun. Don't just stand there with it."

"Yes, sir."

That about covered the contingencies Thomas could

think to prepare for, so the group set out down the hall, which proved to be rather lengthy. Most of the doors were closed, but one open door revealed a room of beds, while another led to an area of what looked like exercise equipment. "The Haxozin must have an entire barracks on this planet," he said.

"Then why are there only ten of them here?" Chris asked.

"I don't know." Thomas could just see the bottom of the stairs up ahead when voices arose and heavy footfalls approached. "Some of them are coming. Where's the armory, Praphasat?"

"There, sir." Areva pointed to the next door.

With his back against the wall, Thomas pulled the door open and leaned around the jamb to look inside. The room was the size of a large closet, filled with racks and racks of the bazooka rifles and a few smaller weapons that looked like projectile pistols. "In, quick."

Areva and Chris hurried into the room, and Thomas barely managed to duck inside and pull the door closed before the voices finished descending the staircase and passed by outside the armory.

Since Thomas wasn't carrying a translator box, he had no idea what the guttural, hissing noises coming from the Haxozin's mouths meant. He did know that they would notice their two dead allies within a few seconds, and their first impulse would probably be to arm themselves. He picked up one of the rifles from the rack and handed another to Chris. "We're going to have to make a break for the ship. Praphasat, take point. Sergeant Fish, in the middle. I'll take the flank. Everyone runs, and whoever gets there opens the airlock and alerts Ivanokoff that we need backup."

"Will we have time for that?" asked Chris. "The

airlock takes three tries to open."

"That's normal? I thought it was an error."

"Yeah. I'm pretty sure that someone at Dispatch rigged it that way as a part of the conspiracy to …"

"Okay, change of plans. Fish, you run for the ship and alert Ivanokoff. Praphasat and I will cover you."

Before anyone else could reply, shouts arose from further down the hall. The bodies had been discovered. "Go, now!" Thomas ordered.

The three sprinted out of the armory and up the stairs to the ground floor. Thomas inspected his new weapon on the way. The gleaming barrel flowed seamlessly into the stock of the weapon, which had a single-fire trigger and a dial that looked like it might adjust the size of the energy blast. Simple to use, point and shoot. Thomas appreciated that.

As he reached the top of the stairs, a blast of energy flew past his head and blew a dent in the wall. He whirled to see a pair of Haxozin crouched at the bottom of the stairs, aiming to shoot again. He fired his own bazooka rifle down at them, and a ball of energy about the size of his fist shot out of the barrel and shattered half of the bottom step. The Haxozin sprang back with yells that were probably curses, buying Thomas enough time to follow his two officers down a short, carpeted hallway.

They finally emerged into a functionally furnished lobby, with a black ceramic tiled floor and tall windows taking up the entire wall around the front entrance. Through the windows Thomas could see the central courtyard, deserted, and the *Endurance* still parked on the far side of it.

"Almost there," he urged his team, turning to keep his eyes on the hallway behind them. "These windows were reflective from the outside, so if there's anyone waiting out there, they can't see us. We can sprint out the doors and hopefully make it to the ship before they spot us."

"Or you could stop where you are," said someone up ahead. Thomas recognized the sound of the translation box, and the hisses and grunts of the Haxozin language. "Before I kill this hostage I have here."

He froze and heard the other two officers do the same. His heart rate sped up. *Underground, at the lunar plaza. Pierre Callahan with a gun in his hand. Loretta Bailey's tears.*

Thomas fought off the memory and the accompanying wave of nausea. *Deep breaths, Thomas. Deep, deep breaths.* That was then. This was now.

Slowly he turned around to take in the situation.

One of the Haxozin stood on the opposite side of the lobby. His dark red armor bore a line of silver diagonally across the chest, marking him as Somebody Important. One of the translation boxes sat on the floor at his feet. He carried another of the bazooka rifles, its muzzle pointed at the bound form of Echo, kneeling on the ground beside him. Her antennae drooped over her face, but her alien features showed the frozen terror of someone who knows they are about to die. Areva and Chris took a few steps back to stand behind Thomas, clearly expecting him to take the lead.

The Haxozin spoke. "It seems this Tone-person has betrayed her masters. Obviously we have grown lax without anyone to challenge us. I think it's good that you Dirt People came along. It will remind us how we need to treat those we rule."

"Who are you supposed to be?" Thomas asked.

"My name is Nervik. I am the tribute collector for this area of our territory."

"Good for you." Thomas raised his rifle to target Nervik's chest. "Let her go."

"You can shoot me if you dare, Dirt-Person. But I warn you that killing a Haxozin collector who is in the middle of performing his duties will be taken as an act of sabotage against our sovereignty, and an attempt to seize what is our rightful territory. It may lead us to declare war on your people."

"The interrogator seemed to think you were already declaring war on us. He's dead, by the way, so you're a little late with your warning."

"He doesn't matter. I can write that death off as a misunderstanding. And he was presumptuous in his threats. Our problem, for the moment, is not with your world, but with you. So here is what I propose. The three of you lay down your weapons and surrender. I spare this woman's life in exchange for yours, and we let the rest of your ship return to your Dirt planet. We will tell the People of Tone that we have beaten you in battle, and that you ran. This will prevent them from doing something ridiculous and rash."

"I think you need more damage control than that, Nerv. It's never that simple to stop a revolution."

"Perhaps not. Your choice, however, *is* simple. Either you die, or she dies. And then you die anyway." He laughed—a harsh, grating sound. "Or you fire on me, and we declare war on your people. It's your choice."

Obviously surrendering wasn't an option, even if Thomas thought the Haxozin really would allow the *Endurance* to leave. He didn't think he could incapacitate Nervik—a shot to the leg might not penetrate the armor, and it would leave him with plenty of opportunity to execute Echo if it failed. And something in the way these people carried themselves told him that Nervik's threat about declaring war on Earth was not idly made.

Of course, they could run for the ship. With Nervik's attention on Echo, they could make it to the courtyard, and with so much open space, he probably wouldn't be able to shoot them accurately. Once aboard, they could find an out-of-the-way area to dig up the chrioladium, or perhaps find it on one of the other planets. The strategy would cost Echo her life, but it would save the three of them, as well as keep the Haxozin away from Earth.

Collateral damage, Thomas thought, an echo of Captain Liu.

He braced himself, prepared to give the order to run, and to hear the Haxozin fire his rifle into Echo's brain. It was the sensible thing to do, the choice with the fewest negative consequences. It was the choice Dispatch would expect him to make.

But it wasn't the right choice.

"Sorry," he told Nervik.

Then he shot him in the face.

Nervik dropped just as quickly as Pierre had, crumpling into a heap on the ground. Echo flinched as the rifle went off, then stared in confusion at the dead form of her captor.

Another pair of shots went off in rapid succession behind him, and Thomas turned to see that Areva had taken out one of the Haxozin pursuing them. "Hah!" she said. "He should've looked up."

A second Haxozin appeared from the hallway and immediately dropped to one knee to fire. Thomas aimed his rifle at it, but Chris beat him to the punch, clipping the alien in the leg. The blast didn't break the armor, but it did distract the Haxozin long enough for Thomas to finish him off.

The lobby of the capitol building subsided into

silence.

"Hurry," Thomas said, crossing to untie Echo's three hands. "That's six of them, but there are four more somewhere. We have to get back to the ship."

"You ..." Echo said slowly, her antennae swaying. "You saved my life. You killed the tribute collector."

"Yes. I did."

"Why?"

Why indeed. "Because I took this job to protect people, and I'm damned well going to do it." Thomas finished freeing her and helped her back to her feet, then turned to his two officers. "Let's go."

They sprinted out the glass door and across the courtyard toward the ship, but before they made it even halfway, the remaining four Haxozin marched down the *Endurance's* airlock ramp and formed a firing line.

Thomas skidded to a halt, flanked by Areva and Chris, all three of their weapons pointed toward the Haxozin. Thomas swallowed. He hadn't expected all four to be out here, and he certainly hadn't thought they'd all be standing in the middle of the escape route. "Praphasat," he whispered, "you take the one on the left ..."

"Can't, sir. He's looking."

"Seriously?"

"It's her thing," Chris said. "You should've had her sneak around the edge of the courtyard to get them from a sniping position."

"Okay, how's your marksmanship, Sergeant?"

"With these guns? Bad, sir. When I hit that guy's leg earlier, I was aiming for his chest. I think it's the rifle's fault."

So it was more or less Thomas against four Haxozin soldiers. How could he get out of that?

The airlock behind the Haxozin opened and Viktor Ivanokoff, a gun in each hand and four more attached to his belt, marched outside and opened fire.

The Haxozin pivoted and tried to readjust their aim, but Ivanokoff blew two of them away before they finished turning, and eliminated the remaining two just as they raised their own guns. Four armored bodies collapsed on the stone walkway, four bazooka rifles clattered to the ground, and Thomas's eyebrows shot toward the sky.

His first officer calmly re-holstered his weapons and looked down at the bodies. "What a terrible thing, war is." From his tone, it sounded like a quote. The big man paused, then continued, "Fortunately, I am very good at it."

"That ..." Thomas wasn't quite sure what to say. "... was impressive."

"Thank you, Captain. Perhaps now you understand my fondness for Dickens and Dante." Ivanokoff patted the two pistols in a loving manner.

"I ... I suppose I do."

"Then perhaps you will allow me to carry them, as before."

In his current adrenaline rush, Thomas was ready to agree to almost anything his first officer suggested, but he had the presence of mind to put off the decision until he hadn't been about to die and his head wasn't nearly splitting open at the seams. "Maybe. We'll talk later."

Ivanokoff pursed his lips. "Very well, sir."

A voice spoke up from behind Thomas. "You finished them."

He turned to see Echo, translation box clutched in one hand, a bazooka rifle in the other two. "You finished them," she said again. "All of them. The Haxozin are gone from our world."

"Put the gun down, please," Thomas said, not sure what to make of the wild expression in her eyes.

"Oh, of course." Echo dropped the rifle and wrapped her hands around the translation box. "How did you defeat them?"

"Luck," said Chris.

"Skill," said Thomas.

"Better weapons," said Ivanokoff.

All at the same time.

Echo's antennae shifted from side to side. "I'm sorry. I didn't understand that. I suppose it doesn't matter." She turned toward the capitol building and waved a hand. "Come out! Come meet them. The discord is over."

Dozens of the People of Tone began flooding out of the capitol, and then out of the buildings on either side of the courtyard as well. Thomas tightened his grip on the rifle out of instinct, but the people moved in too orderly and controlled a fashion to be dangerous. Areva ran up the airlock ramp to hide behind Ivanokoff. Chris stood watching the approaching crowd with Thomas, then murmured, "It's a xenobiologist's dream."

The swarm of grey people stopped a few meters away, except for two of them, a man and a second woman, who came to stand with Echo. "Is it true?" asked the man. "The Haxozin are defeated?"

"They are!" Echo shouted.

"Don't get too excited," Thomas said. Goodness, it was like the lunar plaza press frenzy all over again. "There were only ten of them. I'm guessing more will come, especially when these ones don't report in."

"Then you will defeat those who come, too," Echo said.

"That's … not really on the agenda. We're only here by accident. And even if our world wanted to get involved with this Haxozin Sovereignty, they wouldn't send us to do it."

Echo tilted her antennae. "Why not?"

"Because …" Because they were incompetent? The fact that they were still here proved otherwise. As Thomas tried to answer the question, the only response he could justify was, "Because we don't play by the rules."

Maybe he did belong with them after all.

Echo's face lit up. "Then we will stop playing by the rules as well." She turned to face the woman and the man standing with her. "First Leader, Second Leader, I propose that the People of Tone secede from the Haxozin Sovereignty. Clearly, they are not as all-powerful as they have led us to believe. With the weapons and technology we can salvage from the tribute collectors, I believe we can defend ourselves from any counterattack."

"Now hold on," said Thomas.

"You may be right, Echo," said the woman, apparently the First Leader. "We will discuss it in our next meeting, but in the meantime we will take an inventory of the technology the Haxozin have left here. I imagine we can learn to use it all, given enough time." She then faced Thomas. "We like to be hospitable, as far as allowed by the Hax …" She stopped herself. "So sorry for that. Years of habit. We like to be hospitable. Is there anything we can provide for you?"

Thomas could see nothing he said would make a difference in the political movement now happening on the planet. It was probably just as well; if it was this easy to start a revolution, something would have triggered it soon anyway. "We'd like some chrioladium to repair our ship."

Echo wiggled her antennae. "Of course."

"May we keep the guns?" Ivanokoff called from behind him. "I like them."

"Certainly."

"And we could probably use any information you have about the Haxozin Sovereignty," said Thomas. "They're going to be mad at us. We should be prepared in case they start looking for Earth. I mean, Dirt."

"Yes, that is a wise precaution. I will have all of our files transferred, along with a program that will translate them for you. That is," Echo smiled, "if we may have permission to access your computer this time."

"You may."

Second Leader stepped forward, took the translation box from Echo's hands, and passed it to Thomas. "Please also take this," he said. "I imagine, with the ability to travel faster than light, you will see many more worlds and encounter many more people than we ever could. If you could download their language files and bring them to us the next time you visit, it would greatly further our studies of sound."

Thomas accepted the box, but hesitated. "We aren't really planning to travel around."

Second Leader shrugged. "Then consider it a gift that we hope you might one day use to assist us. We are patient in our studies. The thousand languages you already gave us will provide our researchers with work for quite some time."

Thomas nodded and tucked the translation box under his arm. "Thank you."

"I imagine you are tired," Echo said. "Do you have accommodations on your ship, or would you like a place to stay?"

"No, we'll be fine on the *Endurance*. But thank you."

The thought of resting on his bunk brought Thomas's headache back with a vengeance.

"Then we will speak again once we have collected the materials you need."

"That sounds good. Let's go, people." Thomas and Chris joined Areva and Ivanokoff. Ivanokoff entered his access code—three times—and the door opened to allow them through.

Most of the crew was waiting on the other side. "What happened?" "Did we win?" "Did he use both Dickens *and* Dante?" "They look pretty beat up. Are they okay?" "We won, right?" "Somebody get Maureen." "The captain's a hero in the corps. Of course we won."

That last one turned Thomas's head, but he couldn't see who had said it.

Ivanokoff pushed his way into the crowd and raised his booming voice. "Everything is fine. We won the fight. The nice grey aliens are going to help us fix the ship. We are going home. Please return to your duties."

Cheers and applause broke out, and everyone began high-fiving one another. "Making history!" someone shouted. Thomas spotted Chris engaging in an intense discussion with Joyce, probably explaining how he was right about aliens wanting to conquer Earth. Areva had disappeared.

Ivanokoff strode back to where Thomas was standing. "You should have your head examined, sir."

Thomas gave him a sharp look. "What?"

"Your head, sir. There is blood. You should have Maureen inspect it."

"Oh." Thomas pressed his hand to his skull and felt the wound. "Yes. Thank you."

"Just doing my job, sir."

The first officer started to move away, but Thomas

caught his arm. "Lieutenant. I owe you an apology. You were right to call me out earlier."

Ivanokoff shrugged. "As I said, sir, I am big." But he smiled as he said it. "Does this mean you will change your mind about the new rules?"

"Probably not. But who knows? Give me enough time, and it might happen."

They went their separate ways—Ivanokoff toward the bridge to ensure the data transfer and repairs proceeded properly, Thomas to the medical bay to see to his injuries. As he passed Matthias in the hallway, Thomas handed him the translation box. "I have a side project for you. See if you can figure out how that works. Don't break it."

"Okay. What is it?" the engineer asked, already turning the box on each side to inspect it.

"It translates between languages."

Matthias's face lit up. "Ooh! Can we call it the talky box?"

"No."

"But …"

"I have a headache the size of a small country right now, so this conversation is going to have to wait until later." Thomas paused. While he was giving apologies, he could afford to be nicer to the engineer. "But I look forward to hearing what you learn about that box. You're good at your job, Lieutenant."

Matthias grinned. "Thanks, sir! Did we get the chrioladium?"

"It'll be on board by the end of the day."

Matthias whooped and turned to head back to the reactor room. "I'll have us back on Earth before you know it!"

"Glad to hear it."

The pounding in his head was becoming too much to bear, so Thomas hurried the rest of the way to the medical bay. After Maureen inspected him, cleaned up the blood, concluded that he might or might not have a concussion, and handed him a container of painkillers, he headed back to his berth.

After he finished changing out of his dirtied and bloodied uniform, the computer access console on his desk caught his eye. *You just walked on a new planet, started a revolution, and declared war on an alien species,* he thought to himself. *The big problems are over with. Time to deal with the smaller ones.*

He took a seat at the desk and opened the computer, then keyed in his access code. A list of his messages popped up on the screen, and he clicked to open the unread one from Loretta Bailey. He steeled himself against what was sure to be another letter of thanks and praise, congratulating him on his "well-earned" promotion, and began to read.

Dear Thomas Withers,

I know this is a little weird, but I felt like I needed to write to you. I'm the woman you saved from that gunman at the lunar plaza. I can't imagine how hard it was to make the decision to shoot him, but I'm grateful that you made it anyway.

My brother is a United Earth Law Enforcement officer stationed on Mars, so when I heard how they'd promoted you and assigned you to that ship, I knew what it meant. I've heard the stories. I'm sorry that they're punishing you for saving a life. Rumors are flying that the gunman was a key player in the Uprising, so maybe if you hadn't saved me, a lot more good could've been done. I don't know. All I know is that I was going to die, and you stopped that from happening. For that, you are my hero.

I'm not sure how often you get leave time, but if you find yourself around Lunar Dome Three any time in the future, I'd love to meet you for coffee or lunch or something. Don't feel pressured; I'd just enjoy the opportunity to say my thank-you in person.

Hoping you are well, and that they let you out of that dead-end job soon.

Sincerely,
Loretta Bailey

Thomas took in a shaky breath. She understood. She wasn't gushing, she wasn't fawning, and she wasn't ignorant of what had really happened that day. She got it. And she was at peace with it.

After the events of the past week, so was he.

He pulled the computer closer and began to write out a reply, to be transmitted as soon as they returned to their own solar system.

Dear Ms. Bailey,

I can write with complete honesty that, even knowing the consequences of my actions, I would make the choice to save your life again in a heartbeat. It would be a pleasure to meet you for lunch …

* * *

Less than a day later, Thomas sat in his command chair and looked at the World of Infinite Tones from orbit once more. The D Drive had been fixed, the files on the Haxozin uploaded, and the People of Tone had waved many three-handed farewells as the *Endurance* took off and headed back into space.

"Two minutes until the D Drive is ready for the jump," Ivanokoff reported from the defensives station. "And Matthias says he will have a schematic of the talky box in the next few days."

"We're still not calling it that," Thomas said.

"Whatever you say, sir." Ivanokoff crossed the bridge to stand beside the command chair. He lowered his voice. "You know, sir, the Haxozin may yet declare war on Earth."

"I know."

"And the circumstances of our disappearance will no doubt raise questions at home."

"I know."

"Dispatch will not be pleased. They will probably launch a full investigation into our conduct."

Thomas smiled and shook his head. "Let them. We have nothing to hide. Besides, what are they going to do? Send us to direct traffic around Neptune?"

Ivanokoff snorted. "You have a point, Captain."

Thomas's intercom interface beeped. "Matthias Habassa paging you."

He tapped it. "Answer."

"All ready to go down here, Cap!" Matthias's voice announced. "Just say the word, and we'll be back in our own solar system in under a minute."

"Thank you, Lieutenant. You'll get the signal from the helm station shortly."

"Sounds good. Engineers out!" A chorus of cheers arose from the other engineers, then the intercom line went dead.

"Under a minute," said Ivanokoff. "And then fireworks start."

"We'll handle it." This time, the "we" didn't feel like

such a foreign word to Thomas. "Back to your station, Lieutenant."

Ivanokoff nodded. "Yes, sir."

As his first officer returned to his seat beside Areva, Thomas tapped his intercom interface. "Page all personnel." He waited a few seconds for the crew to tune in to his announcement. "We are about to engage the D Drive. Fasten your seatbelts and hang on. We'll be home soon." He nodded at the helm. "Whenever you're ready."

Seatbelts clicked as the bridge crew strapped themselves into their chairs. The pilot tapped out a series of commands into his computer console. Thomas secured himself and held onto his armrests, not wanting to wind up sprawled on the ground like last time.

The ship lurched forward, and the viewport suddenly became a mass of swirling streaks, starlight bending in impossible ways, space shifting and rolling and folding in on itself until Thomas had to look away to keep himself from getting sick.

When he looked back, his own planet's sun shone in the distance. He could just make out a small blue dot in the upper left hand corner of the viewports.

Engineering paged him again, and Matthias announced, "Jump complete, Cap! We're back home. And the D Drive is still perfectly functional."

"Good work, Lieutenant."

"You too, Captain."

Thomas knew he was in for a grilling. He knew his ship would be examined top to bottom and his story checked and rechecked and his crew debriefed until they were exhausted. He knew he was further than ever from winning back Dispatch's trust.

But for the moment, he didn't care. He'd gotten them home alive, and that meant he'd done his job.

Maybe this post wouldn't be so bad after all.

Then a panel on the back wall exploded.

A Numbers Game

A Short Story

Thomas Withers groaned as he walked into the spacious office. "That was a *long* press conference. Can we hold the debriefing till morning?"

"No." Commissioner Wen slammed the door shut behind them. She dropped down into the big leather chair behind her desk and started turning on her computers with more force than was necessary. "If facing the reporters is too tough for you, maybe next time don't go off and pick a fight with extraterrestrials." She seemed like she was going to end her criticism there, but then muttered, "You really screwed the department on this one, Captain Withers."

"What, with the press?" Thomas asked. "The media loved what I said. I made the department look good! Hell, I made all of law enforcement look good."

"Yes, the press is all over you, but that doesn't

change the fact that the rest of us are playing catch-up and pretending we knew what you were doing from the beginning, before you went off on your little adventure. You can't just do whatever you want, Withers. We have rules. We have a chain of command. They exist for a reason."

Thomas watched her for a moment before crossing his arms. He could sense a fight was coming. "I get the feeling I'm in trouble with the department again."

"Oh?" Wen stopped what she was doing and narrowed her eyes at him. "Why? Just because you let your chief engineer test some new tech and leave the solar system without permission …"

"Technically he'd gotten it approved beforehand."

"… ran into a bunch of hostile aliens …"

"Technically only one species was hostile. The other one was nice enough."

"… and started a war with them …"

"Technically they only *threatened* to start a war; they didn't actually do it."

Wen glared at him. "Fine. Technicalities aside, that's the gist of what happened. And you want to know why you *might* be in trouble?"

"I did the best I could under the circumstances."

"I'm sure you did. Unfortunately your best might have long-term consequences that you weren't expecting. Like, I don't know, a war with aliens. Or something worse. Use your imagination." Wen huffed and turned back to her computers.

Thomas felt his muscles tensing. "This isn't just about the aliens."

"What else could it be about?"

"Maybe some latent anger about the *other* time I disobeyed orders and you couldn't demote me?"

Wen propped her elbows on her desk and rubbed her face with her hands. "Don't bring that up right now, Withers."

"This is that same thing all over again, isn't it? You and the rest of headquarters are upset because once again, the media is on my side, and you can't punish me for doing what was right."

The commissioner's face suddenly darkened with fury and she bolted up from her chair. "Excuse me? Doing what was *right*? Do I need to remind you that you're talking about killing a man?"

Thomas met her anger with his own. "A man who had a hostage, yeah."

"A man we needed alive!" Wen's voice rose until she was shouting. "A man who was our best possible source of information for what the Uprising criminals are planning to do next! If you had done what you were told, we'd have gotten that information and we'd finally be a step ahead instead of running neck and neck! And then who knows how many of their attacks we'd be stopping?"

It was after hours, so hardly any other officers were around to hear the confrontation, but Thomas wouldn't have cared if the entire floor was listening. It was time to get this all out in the open. "The department keeps saying more people would have been saved if I'd let Loretta Bailey die," he countered, waving his hand in the air to punctuate his point, "but that's all speculation!"

"Word is you're chatting with Ms. Bailey regularly since you saved her from Callahan. I realize you're getting personally attached to her, but you have to see this by the numbers, too!"

"Screw the numbers! Those other people were just possibilities, Commissioner. She was a living, breathing person right in front of me. She has a name, a face."

That sentence seemed to trigger something in the commissioner's demeanor. Her jaw muscles clenched and her hands tightened into fists. "You want faces, Captain?" she demanded. "Is that what it takes to make the numbers real to you?" She jabbed at the touch screen embedded in her desk and pulled up a file, then rotated the image to face Thomas. Pointing a finger down at it, she spat out, "These people had names and faces, too. All twenty-eight of them."

The screen showed a series of driver's license photos, along with the subjects' names, ages, professions, fingerprints, DNA analyses—all of the information in a typical police report. Darnell Adams, 36, account manager at a bank. His biceps showed that he worked out, and he obviously put a lot of effort into maintaining a polished smile. Miranda St. Clair, 42, stay-at-home mother of four. Big, curly hair and callouses on her fingertips. She probably sewed or played the guitar. Or both.

"They were all on a routine flight last night from Shanghai to L.A. Uprising operatives did an orbital jump and broke in from above. They didn't care about the people. They just wanted the ship."

Harry Intarnia, 79, retired/carpenter. A face that had seen a lot in his life. He probably would have fought long and hard against anyone who crossed him.

Kyla Fitzhou, 28, law student. She had green eyes that defied the world to give her a challenge she couldn't handle.

Thomas glanced up at the commissioner, a frown creasing his face.

Wen was still glaring at him, but delivered the news in a flat tone. "They depressurized the cabin and dropped all of the passengers over the Pacific. None of them survived."

Thomas felt like he'd just been punched in the stomach and knew instantly that he'd lost this argument. His eyes dropped back down to the list of the dead. "I get the point," he said quietly. He knew what was coming next. He didn't need to hear it out loud.

It didn't stop her from continuing. "We could have stopped them. We could have found out when, where, and how they were attacking. We could have gotten all of that information from Callahan. But you killed him."

The commissioner paused for a moment, though Thomas could feel her eyes still boring into him. "Those are the lives that *we* were trying to defend, Captain. The lives that your superior was considering when he ordered you not to shoot. That's the choice *he* had to make, and it wasn't your prerogative to second-guess him. So don't you dare stand there and act like you've got some kind of moral superiority over the rest of us. We all have to make tough choices in this line of work."

She paused, glanced once more at the list of names and faces—the list of people—and closed the file. "And we all have to live with the consequences."

Thomas found himself staring at the United Earth Law Enforcement logo on her computer background, unable to look her in the eye. He could argue that they didn't know for certain that they could have saved those passengers. That they couldn't be sure they could break Callahan in time to learn what the Uprising was planning. That there were a million other factors to consider. But he felt in his gut that there was some truth to what the commissioner was saying. He'd saved one life, yes, but he'd likely condemned several others in doing so.

Was it worth it?

Having asked himself that question a thousand times since the department transferred him to the *Endurance*,

Thomas thought he knew the answer. And he'd thought he was finally at peace with it, but it seemed that moral questions were never so easy to settle. "I still think I did the right thing," he admitted.

"I know you do."

"But you don't agree."

"No."

"Are you telling me …" Thomas knew he was pushing his luck, but if the department hadn't fired him for botching an investigation and provoking a war with aliens, he doubted that antagonizing his superior would be the last straw. He looked up. "… that you could have stood there, where I was, looked Loretta Bailey in the eye, and let Callahan kill her? Not knowing who these other people were yet, just thinking of them as statistics. Could you have made that choice?"

The commissioner went perfectly still, and Thomas watched as she considered the question. Finally she looked straight at him and answered, "Yes."

That admission had cost her something. Thomas had intended to point out that she didn't exactly have the moral high ground either, but he could see from her reaction that she already knew that. He dropped his gaze back to the desk and responded simply, "I couldn't."

"I know."

Silence filled the office.

Both of them seemed to have lost the will to argue, so Thomas thought it would be best to leave. Before he did, though, there was something he needed to ask. "Those twenty-eight people … do their families know? That they might have been saved?"

Wen shook her head. "No. They have enough what-ifs going through their minds already." She paused, then asked, "Are you going to tell Ms. Bailey?"

Thomas thought about his answer before replying. "No. She doesn't need to carry that."

The commissioner nodded. "At least we agree on something."

Thomas turned to go, but Wen's voice stopped him. "I'm sure you're going to go over this conversation in your head a million times, trying to decide if you were right or not. I meant it when I said we all have to live with the consequences of our choices." She paused. "But you don't have to let them drag you under."

He looked back at her over his shoulder, surprised by the sudden show of empathy. They stared at each other for a few seconds, and Thomas decided that, much as he didn't like her or her way of doing things, he at least understood her position. And he got the feeling that she understood his. That was enough to merit some respect. "Thanks," he said.

She nodded once, then looked back to her work. "See you in the morning for the conference debriefing."

"Yes ma'am."

He shut the door quietly as he left the office.

Book Two

Mightier than the Sword

Suffocation. Viktor's lungs burned for air, but the toxic atmosphere of the ship gave him no reprieve. He again checked the time and wondered when it would finally be his turn to don an oxygen mask and escape this hell. True, the air tanks would only prolong the crew's torment, but by breathing in shifts, they might survive long enough to ...

"What are you reading?"

Annoyance. Why did people always ask that question at the most dramatic part of a chapter? Viktor Ivanokoff looked up from his computer tablet, ready to chew out whoever had dared disturb him while he was off duty. "I do not do interrupti ... oh, hello, Areva."

Areva Praphasat leaned on his open door hatch, her dark-haired head tilted to the side with her question. "Can I come in?"

"Certainly."

She stepped through the hatch and entered Viktor's berth. Like every personal compartment on the UELE *Endurance*, the room was small, with a lofted bed over a desk and a set of drawers, all constructed of the same grey metal. The walls were a boring shade of off-white, but Viktor had covered them with his mounted gun collection and a set of shelves that held an assortment of hard-copy books. Some texts just read better when he could feel the paper and smell the ink. He also had a cushioned folding chair that he'd "borrowed" from the rec room and placed in the one unoccupied corner to serve as a reading spot. He sat there at the moment. His long legs took up most of the empty floor space.

Areva seated herself on Viktor's desk chair, which she rolled to one side so that she couldn't be seen through the open hatch. She looked troubled, and Viktor had one guess about why. "The captain should return soon from his latest meeting with Dispatch," he said.

She sighed. "Hopefully with good news."

"I doubt that. They will send us back to Neptune. You will see."

"But it's been a whole month, and we're still all over the news." Areva leaned forward. "They have to let us do something more useful than traffic duty in the middle of nowhere!"

"Dispatch hates the *Endurance*, Areva. They will never trust us with anything important."

"But we were the first ship to discover an alien species. *Two* alien species."

"Which made them hate us more. The trip was not exactly planned."

"You're such a pessimist, Viktor." Areva sat back. "You'd think the threat of alien invasion would at least make them want to explore what else is out there."

"The threat is not real. The tech team said that the Haxozin did not find the location of Earth when they accessed our computer. Aliens will not invade us today. Or any day, so long as they do not know where we are."

"Still. They should organize more exploration."

"If they do, they will not send us to do it."

Areva paused. "Then I guess you're not planning to meet the captain at the airlock to hear about his meeting?"

"I do not do airlocks."

"You should probably compromise this one time. If you're right about Dispatch still not assigning us a new job, the captain's going to be in a bad mood. It won't help to make it worse."

Viktor remembered Captain Withers's first few days on the ship and felt inclined to agree. Though the ire of a superior officer didn't bother him personally, it tended to ruin the morale on the ship, and as first officer, he was supposed to avoid causing such problems. Besides, Areva had asked him, and he didn't like to turn her down. "Very well," he said. He stood up and placed his computer tablet on his desk.

Areva glanced down at the active title. "Jules Verne?"

"Da. Unfortunate that this meeting is scheduled during one of the only interesting parts of the book."

"It'll still be there when you come back."

Viktor waved a hand. "I have lost my momentum. It will not be the same. I may just start the chapter over again." He turned toward the hatch just as Matthias Habassa, the *Endurance*'s chief engineer, capered by. "Lieutenant," Viktor greeted him.

Matthias stopped and grinned at him. "Hi, Ivanokoff! Are you going to meet the captain at the airlock?"

"Yes."

"Stellar. We can walk together. Is Areva here, too?"

Viktor glanced over his shoulder and saw that Areva had vanished from the chair. He squinted and looked around his berth more carefully until he noticed a slight movement near his desk. Areva had ducked beneath it. He caught her eye and inclined his head toward the hatch in a silent question. She shook her head, but smiled at him.

Viktor stepped out of his berth and closed the hatch. "No," he told Matthias, "but I imagine she will meet us there."

"Okay. I just thought she might be here since you two spend so much time together." Matthias resumed his route down the corridor, his quick stride almost outpacing Viktor's longer legs. "Do you think the captain has good news this time?"

"No."

"I think he does."

"You said that last time."

"I know. But I have a feeling. You've got to keep a positive mindset, sir."

They reached the airlock shortly and found Chris Fish, the chief scientist and head of the scanners team, leaning against the wall.

"Sergeant," Viktor said.

"Lieutenants." Chris turned his pointy nose toward the other two officers with accusatory force. "Any idea what this is about?"

"It is probably just another delay in Dispatch re-assigning us," Viktor said.

"That's not what I think. Want to know what I think?"

"No," said Viktor, just as Matthias said, "Yes."

Chris glanced both directions down the corridor and lowered his voice. "I think the captain's gone over to *them*."

"I see," said Viktor. He actually had no idea which "theory" the scientist was referring to this time, but he'd learned a long time ago that questions only drew out the conversation, and he did not want to listen to another of Chris's conspiracies. Not with Jules Verne's tipped iceberg scene still so dramatically fresh in his mind.

Chris, however, didn't seem to care about Viktor's preferences. "The government's not happy about what we found in the galaxy, not at all."

"You mean the aliens? The government's mad about that?" Matthias asked.

Viktor rolled his eyes. "Habassa, stop encouraging him."

Chris huffed. "I obviously mean the aliens! They threatened to invade Earth! That's a big deal. And the only reason they did that is because we didn't surrender to them." He leaned in closer. "I think Dispatch wants to send us back to them as a peace offering to stop this war from happening. And I think the captain's working with them to save his own skin." He nodded again to emphasize his point. "All I'm saying is, if we're sent out of the solar system again, watch your backs."

"Aw, come on, Chris," said Matthias. "You're still mad because the captain suspended your side research for a week."

"That's not what this is about!"

Beep beep! The noise announced that someone had entered their authorization code—incorrectly—on the other side of the airlock.

"I think it is. You need to let that go, buddy. Here, take a deep breath."

"It won't help."

Beep beep! A second failure.

"You don't know that. Just try it."

"No."

Beep! On the third attempt, the airlock accepted the code and opened the external hatch.

All four officers—as Areva had surreptitiously joined them at some point—stood at attention to greet their CO. Captain Thomas Withers walked on board the *Endurance* and started to head toward the bridge, but halted when he saw the group waiting for him. His dark brow furrowed. "You're all actually here."

"Yes, sir," said Viktor. "You made it clear you wanted all of us present."

Withers shook his head, probably to clear the sense of astonishment away. "Well, good. This'll be more efficient than trying to find each of you individually. I had a talk with Commissioner Wen right before I caught the shuttle back up here …"

"Sorry I'm late!" Maureen, a young woman in her early twenties, darted around the corner and came to a halt. "I only just heard about the meeting. I was looking for my brother in the reactor room, and Grace told me all department heads were supposed to be up here." She waved to Matthias. "Hi."

"Hi, sis! What do you need?"

"Figure that out later," said the captain. "Officer Habassa, while I appreciate your enthusiasm, you're not a department head."

"Yes, I am," Maureen said. "I'm the *Endurance*'s chief medical officer."

"You're its only medical officer."

"And that technically makes me the head of the department."

"Whatever the case, you weren't invited."

"But I came prepared!" She produced a small notebook and ink pen from one of her uniform's pockets. "I'm ready to take notes!"

Chris snickered. "Who uses paper and pen anymore?"

"I do." Maureen put a fist on her hip. "It's more reliable. For instance, yesterday my computer deleted changes I made to a dozen different files. Paper never does that."

"Did you save the changes?"

"I thought that happened automatically."

"Every twenty minutes. You have to tell it if you want it to save more often."

"Oh. Oops. That explains a lot."

"Getting back to the point," Captain Withers said, "you're not supposed to show up to meetings for senior officers when you aren't one."

"But I am one."

"Not officially. And this is an official meeting."

"Oh." Maureen flushed and tucked her notebook back into her pocket. "I guess I'll, uh, just go, then."

Viktor thought it was rather silly of the captain to dismiss her after so much ado. "Sir, whatever you tell us will spread through the ship anyway. Perhaps it would not hurt for her to hear your news directly from you?"

Withers pinched the bridge of his nose, and Viktor prepared for an argument. To his surprise, the captain shrugged and nodded. "Fine. Officer Habassa, you can stay."

Viktor frowned and paid closer attention to the captain's tone and movement. Was something distracting him?

Withers straightened his shoulders and looked each

officer in the eye. "I just talked with Commissioner Wen. The department of Oversight and Investigations has officially cleared us of any wrongdoing involving the Haxozin."

That was good news, particularly for Viktor, who had shot four of them. His use-of-force reports had taken ages to fill out, but at least his thoroughness accomplished something. He smiled. Matthias whooped.

"But they're still refusing to assign us anywhere."

Viktor's smile vanished. "Not even our regular patrol? What reason did they give this time?"

"They want us to land at headquarters for a full systems checkup before they send the *Endurance* off into space again."

"Didn't they do that already?" asked Matthias. "You know, when they were inspecting it to see if our story was true and find out what information the Haxozin downloaded and …"

"They want to do it again. I'm just as upset as the rest of you, but there's not a lot I can do about it."

The captain didn't quite meet anyone's gaze as he said this, and Viktor grew suspicious. Before he could start asking hard questions, though, Withers adopted the tone he used when issuing orders. "I hoped to have better news when I called this meeting, but it is what it is. You're all dismissed to start prepping the ship for landing."

Areva, Chris, Matthias, and Maureen dispersed in various directions. Viktor waited, unwilling to abandon the issue so easily.

It seemed the captain had a similar idea, but he waited for the corridor to clear before speaking. "Lieutenant Ivanokoff, I'd like a few more words with you."

"Good, because I have some words I would like to share. What are you and Dispatch hiding from us?"

Withers glared at him. Viktor was a few inches taller than his captain, so the effect didn't intimidate him as much as probably intended. "Is that what everyone's thinking? That I'm conspiring against the rest of you?"

"Since we returned, you have not spent much time on the ship. You have had multiple private meetings with Dispatch. Now you will not even make eye contact when discussing the issue. It appears as though you are working with them to keep the *Endurance* in dry dock forever."

"That's not what this is about."

"Then explain what it is about, sir, because morale among the crew is plummeting. They need something to do. *We* need something to do."

"They'll have to wait until Dispatch figures out how to handle everything. They're still not happy about having the *Endurance* in the public eye, and with what's happened now ..." The captain's voice trailed off and his shoulders tightened. He ground his teeth for a few seconds, as if unsure how to proceed.

Apparently this wasn't the same political song and dance that the *Endurance* crew had, well, endured for so long. No, this was something new, and from Captain Withers's demeanor, it was significant. Viktor asked, "What has happened?"

Instead of answering, Withers studied the wall. "You worked in the organized crime division for almost a decade, right?"

"Yes, sir." Viktor didn't know what his service record had to do with anything.

"You probably had some run-ins with the Uprising crime group?"

"Yes."

"They murdered a UELE officer two nights ago."

Viktor's jaw clenched in anger at the news—outcast or not, he was a part of the United Earth Law Enforcement corps, and an attack on one was an attack on all—but he still didn't understand where the captain was going with his story. "That is terrible news, sir, but what does it have to do with us?"

"Not us, Ivanokoff. You." Withers took a deep breath. "The officer they killed—it was Adwin Soun. Your captain from the organized crime unit."

Viktor's stomach dropped. "Captain Soun? Murdered?"

"Yes, but that's not the only reason this affects you."

"I would think that would be enough."

"Unfortunately, there's more. Whoever did it left a note on the body. A list of names. The first one was Soun's, and it was crossed off." Withers paused. "The second one was yours."

Viktor exhaled slowly. "A threat."

"Looks that way."

"Do they know who wrote it?"

"If they do, they didn't tell me."

"How do they know it was the Uprising?"

"I didn't have time to ask, but I'm sure it's in the case report. Since we're stuck here for a while longer, they've asked you to consult."

Viktor raised an eyebrow. "Is this the real reason they are keeping us here for another inspection? To coerce me into helping?"

"I honestly don't know. It's possible." Withers took a deep breath. "I'm sure you and Org Crime didn't part on the best of terms …"

"That would be an understatement."

"… but despite the bitterness I'm sure you have, you

can't get out of …"

"I have no problem with working the case, sir."

Withers stopped in mid-sentence. "You don't?"

"No."

"Huh." The captain stared at him. "Here I was, thinking I'd need to deflect a thousand excuses before you'd be willing to work with those people again. From what I've heard, Captain Soun was the one who kicked you out of Org Crime and got you assigned to the *Endurance*."

"That is true."

"Is it some kind of literary justice thing? You want to catch his killer to make up for not reconciling with him?"

"No." Viktor shook his head. "It is simple. If we are to be stuck here without an assignment, I would like to have something to do. I do not do boredom."

"What, running out of things to read?"

"Never. But as I expressed earlier, the crew is tired of inactivity, myself included. If they are indeed keeping us here to secure my help, then the sooner I give it to them, the sooner they will give us a real assignment. I am doing this for the good of the ship. Also …" He shrugged. "I would not mind the opportunity to outperform the organized crime team."

"I see." Withers nodded, and then a smile of understanding crossed his face. "Oh, I see. You want to look good by showing them up? Get some brownie points with Dispatch?"

Viktor frowned. "What do you mean?"

"I get it. You do well on this investigation, and maybe you get yourself off the *Endurance*."

"That was not quite what I …"

"Lieutenant, don't worry. Nobody on the ship is going to think less of you if you try to secure a transfer.

In fact, I'd think you were crazy if you didn't take advantage of the opportunity."

Viktor honestly hadn't considered that angle. While the thought of staying on the *Endurance* didn't trouble him as much as it would others, he realized that Withers had a point. "I intend to do my best work, sir. If Dispatch takes notice of it, then I suppose that is an added benefit."

The captain, who Viktor knew had his own transfer request on file, clapped Viktor on the shoulder. "Then report to Commissioner Wen once we land tomorrow. The ship will be serviced by the Median engineering team, so if we need you, you'll be right next door."

"Good to know."

"Best of luck, Lieutenant. Here's hoping for a positive outcome."

* * *

The *Endurance* suffered a shaky re-entry into Earth's atmosphere and a bumpy run onto the landing pad, probably due to the way the Haxozin had poked around the ship's machinery. Or just due to the pilot. Viktor debarked as soon as the ship taxied to its parking space in the Dispatch service lot. Fortunately he didn't have to deal with a quarantine before getting down to work; the entire crew had undergone an embarrassing number of medical tests after returning to the solar system.

He keyed in his code and waited for the middle deck airlock to slide open. A blast of fresh air scented with salt water blew into his face. It always smelled like sea salt in Median City, the capital of United Earth. Viktor had lived and worked in Median until his mid-thirties, but after spending the last six years mostly in space, he'd started noticing the scent whenever he returned. Amidst the salt he could pick out the aromas of various restaurants wafting through the air, offering cuisine from every corner of the world.

He paused to breathe deeply of the sea air, and despite the morbid event that brought him here, he had to smile. He loved this city. Built on an artificially-constructed island in the middle of the Mediterranean, equidistant from the shores of Europe, Asia, and Africa, Median had eagerly shaped itself around its identity as a crossroads. It wasn't unusual to see a family dressed in Yoruba apparel eating sushi in a building styled with Corinthian columns while conversing in Spanish, and so on. The scents, sights, and sounds blended into something that was simultaneously a mess and a work of art. Like any metropolis, Median had problems, but it was a destination that everyone had to visit at least once in their lives.

After his moment of reverie, Viktor checked his belt for his two favorite guns, and then he stepped through the airlock, leaving it open to vent the ship's interior. He descended the long metal staircase that had been set up to allow passage to the ground. While the *Endurance* had its own loading ramp on the lower deck, deploying it took a while, so the crew used the smaller, middle-deck airlock whenever possible. This meant they needed to use the parking lot's portable stairs. Viktor noted that the parking crew put the *Endurance* all the way at the end of the lot— no doubt on purpose.

Dispatch headquarters lived in a ten-story, square-shaped building constructed of gray blocks of stone. Viktor took the stairs up to the fourth floor, the home of Oversight and Investigations, and approached the division's reception desk. "Lieutenant Viktor Ivanokoff," he said. "I am here to see Commissioner Wen."

The young man sitting behind the desk looked up. His mouth dropped open when he saw Viktor's height, but he quickly collected himself. "Ivanokoff. From the *Endurance*, right?"

Of course, he had to announce the name of the ship to the entire room. At a nearby desk, a sergeant nudged his partner and muttered something, then both started laughing. Viktor lowered his voice as he replied, "Yes."

"You're late," said the desk officer. "She had you down for 0900."

Viktor's eyes narrowed. "That is not my fault. My ship has only just now landed."

The man shrugged. "You can tell her that, but the commissioner doesn't like excuses."

"That is an explanation. I do not do excuses."

"Everybody does excuses." The young man hit a button on his desk. "Your 0900 is here, Commissioner."

"Good," said a female voice. "Send him in."

The man waved Viktor toward the corner office and returned to whatever he'd been doing on his computer. *Probably playing cards*, Viktor thought.

He passed the still-snickering sergeant on his way to the commissioner's office. The sergeant's desk had a computer tablet on it, open to a digital library. Viktor twisted his neck to see the title of the active book. "Ah, I enjoyed this one."

"Oh?" The sergeant had tensed when Viktor stopped at his desk, but relaxed at the comment. "Yeah, I like it, too. Seems very deep. When did you read it?"

"When I was in the second grade." Viktor turned a stony expression to the man. "That was also when I learned that it is rude to laugh at other people."

The sergeant spread his hands. "What, you can't take a joke?"

"I can. But I do not want to. So keep your mockery to yourself next time."

The sergeant sputtered something, but Viktor knew better than to continue the argument until it became a fight. With his size, he'd definitely be the one charged with instigating, and he didn't want to get kicked off of this case before he even started work. He continued toward Commissioner Wen's office.

The commissioner's door opened on a nicely furnished room. Four computer displays covered the huge desk—three of them upright and one built flat into the surface. Of the remaining desk space, one corner held a couple piles of paper, and the other displayed one of those laser-pointer desk toys that showed the alignment of the solar system in real time.

Behind the desk sat the commissioner. Wen herself was a tiny woman with a tight bun of black hair and a glare that could melt titanium. "You're late," she told Viktor as he walked in. "I expected you twenty minutes ago, especially since you didn't even need to take the shuttle down from space dock. Shut the door behind you."

He obeyed. "Our ship was ..."

"I don't particularly care at this point, Lieutenant. There's work to do. I assume Captain Withers briefed you on what's going on?"

He nodded.

"Good. Then I want you to report to Lieutenant Okoro on the eighth floor. He's running the investigation into Captain Soun's murder. He'll fill you in on the details and tell you what he wants you to do. Also, in light of your name being on the list we found, I'm assigning someone to watch your back."

"That is not necessary," said Viktor. "I had a perfect

score on my last marksmanship test, and I am well armed."

"That's not good enough." Wen paused. "Although I admit I was impressed by the report of how you took down those aliens. I understand you used guns that you customized yourself."

"I call them Dickens and Dante." Viktor patted the weapons on his belt.

"Cute. You brought them with you?"

"Da."

"Tomorrow, don't. Bring your service weapon, and only your service weapon. The uniform may seem like a suggestion to you, but at headquarters we take it seriously."

Viktor's eyes narrowed. He hadn't yet convinced Captain Withers to let him carry the two guns on the ship, but he'd hoped to sneak it past the people here at headquarters. He hated leaving his favorite weapons in his berth, but he wanted even less to be left there himself. He nodded his understanding of the rule.

"Also," continued the commissioner, "I'm still going to insist that you have backup." He grimaced, and she rolled her eyes. "Everyone on the list is getting a bodyguard. I don't know why all of you act like it's a big inconvenience. They're just keeping an eye out for you."

"May I at least request the officer assigned to me?"

"If they're available, I suppose so."

"She is available. Areva Praphasat."

Wen cocked an eyebrow. "From the *Endurance*? Are you sure?"

"I am from the *Endurance* too, Commissioner."

"Of course, but from what I've heard, she's not the best person to have with you in a firefight."

"With Areva around, the other side will not have a

chance to fire."

Wen folded her arms. "Are you only making this request because you don't want to deal with anyone from headquarters?"

"No. I am already comfortable with Areva, and we have a good working relationship. She will provide less of a distraction than someone else. Also, she has nothing else to do at the moment, so you will avoid reassigning one of your own people."

The commissioner regarded him for a moment, perhaps gauging his honesty, before she uncrossed her arms and waved her hand in agreement. "Fine. I'll page the *Endurance* and have her come meet you upstairs."

"Thank you."

"One more thing before you go." Wen looked up at him, though somehow she made it feel like she was looking down. "You and the organized crime team are working on this together. I know there's some bad blood between you. Am I going to have to deal with problems coming up later?"

"If Lieutenant Okoro will play nicely," Viktor said, "I will do so, too."

"That's not what I asked, Lieutenant. Am I going to have problems because of this assignment, or are you all going to act like adults?"

Viktor forced his expression to stay neutral as he spoke. "No, Commissioner. There will be no problems."

* * *

Viktor headed to the eighth floor and contemplated the officer running the investigation. Lieutenant Okoro had been Sergeant Okoro when Viktor last knew him. They'd worked in the organized crime division together for several years under Captain Soun, and while they were never exactly friends, they did work on many of the same cases.

More importantly, Okoro had been running backup the day Viktor got into a bar fight and broke a suspect's arm, the act that eventually led to his dismissal from the Org Crime division. Neither Okoro nor any of the other officers present bothered to stick up for Viktor at his disciplinary hearing, allowing Captain Soun to get rid of the problem by simply firing him and having him reassigned to the outskirts of the solar system. Easy fix for the captain, no inconvenience for the other officers, and complete ruination of Viktor's career.

At least it wasn't all bad. He had more time to read out there.

He arrived on the eighth floor and located the investigative team in one of the meeting rooms. Four officers sat in a semi-circle of chairs around a gigantic touchscreen displaying the known information about the case. Lieutenant Okoro himself stood at the board, in the middle of saying something while the rest of the team took notes.

Viktor took great pleasure in barging into the room during the lieutenant's speech. "I am Lieutenant Ivanokoff. I was told to report here as a consultant on the investigation."

Okoro turned to face Viktor and put on a forced smile. "Lieutenant. You're late."

"My ship did not arrive on time."

"Oh, right. The *Endurance*, wasn't it?"

The other four officers exchanged glances with each other, and Viktor knew he'd already lost any appearance of dignity he might have gained from his entrance. But rather than give Okoro the satisfaction of a verbal acknowledgment, he simply nodded.

Thankfully, Okoro didn't prolong the discussion. "That's fine. Take a seat. I was just going over who's going to be doing what, before you interrupted."

Viktor seated himself on one end of the semicircle and avoided eye contact with the others in the room.

Okoro pointed to an image of a house on the screen. "Quick recap. We found a laser-hacked lock on one of Soun's basement windows, which was probably the murderer's point of entry. No security system, no dog, nobody else at the house—Soun's divorced, and his kids are all grown up. From what we can tell, the hit was quick. They found him in his bedroom and shot him twice, chest and head, with an illegal energy gun. Based on the wounds and the type of weapon used, it was a professional hit. He didn't even wake up."

Viktor closed his eyes in a silent moment. Antagonist or not, Soun had deserved better.

"We canvassed the neighborhood, and nobody saw or heard anything, but the list on the body makes the motive pretty clear," said Okoro. "Somebody wanted revenge on the department."

"Do we know who wrote the list?" Viktor asked.

Okoro shook his head. "No, but we're ..."

"Were there any DNA traces at the crime scene?"

"Not so much as a skin cell. We're ..."

"And the names on the list, are they ..."

"Ivanokoff." Okoro glared at him. "Shut up until I'm done."

Viktor wanted to argue that these questions were important, but he remembered Commissioner Wen's admonition to avoid making waves. He crossed his arms and nodded.

Satisfied, Okoro went on to answer his next question

anyway. "The names on the list all belong to people who worked or work in Org Crime. Soun, Ivanokoff, myself, and six others. I cross-referenced our employment dates in the department and found thirty-one cases where we all had some input. We then narrowed it down to cases where we were all heavily involved, and where no other currently-living officers played major parts in the investigation. We came up with six cases, all of them Uprising-related."

Though he wouldn't admit it, Viktor was impressed. That was a lot of productivity for one day of work.

"At the moment, we have two goals. One, figure out which case motivated the murder. Two, keep the rest of the officers on the list alive. You two." He pointed to the first pair of officers in the circle. "Talk to everyone on the list about the six cases. See if they remember anything that could point us in the right direction. Also, check up on everybody mentioned in the case reports, and especially look for recent prison releases or status changes among Uprising members. There's a reason this happened now, and not earlier. You two," he said, indicating the other pair, "talk to Soun's ex-wife, his kids, his friends, and everybody else in his life. Get alibis and look for other possible explanations. Even though the murder style has Uprising written all over it, it could still be a cover to throw us off. I'll go over the six old cases and see if anything makes one of them stand out from the others as a possible motive. We'll check back this afternoon. Any questions?"

Everyone shook their heads, except Viktor, who started to speak. "I think ..."

"Good," Okoro said. "Get to it."

The two teams headed out of the room, and Okoro turned to Viktor. "Now you can talk."

"I assume I am to be paired with you?"

"That's right."

"What made you think that would be a good idea?"

"We both worked with Adwin Soun for a long time, and we're both on the list. I thought if we went back over that time together, we might stand a better chance of figuring something out."

Viktor tucked his thumbs into his belt near his guns. "And it was not just so that you could keep me under your control?"

Okoro looked away. "Look, I know we didn't part on good terms."

"You did not have my back when you should have, and then Soun sent me to the *Endurance* to keep me out of the way. If that is the way things still are, I do not need to be here."

"Ivanokoff, I need you on the team. Your knowledge of the previous cases might prove helpful, and the division is low on manpower. I'm losing two of my people to another case tomorrow, so there'll only be four of us left. That said, I'll settle for three if you're not going to pull your weight. You're a decent investigator, Lieutenant, but if you're too bitter to think objectively ..."

"I am not bitter."

"Good. Then let's leave the past in the past and solve this murder. All right?" Okoro held out a hand.

"Fine." Viktor shook the man's hand, though he made a point of showing off his tighter grip.

"Who knows?" said Okoro once they let go. "Maybe this case will be the catalyst that lets you finally get off of that ship."

Several comments about the reason he was on the *Endurance* in the first place came to mind, but Viktor ignored them in the interest of not prolonging the conversation. Instead, he said, "You mentioned that you were on the list of targets. I thought Commissioner Wen assigned all of us a bodyguard."

"She did. Mine's out on the floor. Some big guy from O&I. Where's yours?"

"She will arrive soon. If she has not done so already." Viktor thought it entirely possible that Areva had slipped into the room unnoticed and secluded herself behind a bookcase.

"Someone from the *Endurance*?"

"Yes."

"Oh." Okoro made a face.

"She is good."

"Right. I believe you." Before Viktor could call Okoro out on the obvious lie, he changed the subject. "We should begin looking at those cases. Take a seat. We're going to be here for a while."

* * *

Nothing popped out as they pored over the old investigations. Neither of the other two teams turned up anything either. This didn't surprise anyone, given the sheer amount of information to sift through. At the end of the day, Viktor bid farewell to the others—well, he grunted in their general direction as he left the floor—and headed back to the ship to continue working on his own.

The parking lot was still half empty as he crossed to the *Endurance*. Even at night, most of the UELE's hover cars stayed out on patrol, and its spaceships always had too much work to do to sit around idle on the ground. Dispatch stationed most of the fleet near Earth, Mars, and Venus, though a dozen or so ships took care of the area around Jupiter and the asteroid belt. One or two made it out to Saturn and Uranus, which each had a few populated moons and space stations, and the *Endurance* was the only one ever assigned all the way out to Neptune's unpopulated orbit. During a good month the crew would hand out one speeding citation and check up on a handful of college students who'd gone out that far in order to party.

A murder investigation was far more interesting, and Viktor's thoughts delved into the case as he walked through the parking lot. Industrial floodlights illuminated the area, and a brick wall protected it from the surrounding streets, but Viktor could still hear the traffic on Market and Park and see the skyscrapers stretching upward. It was too bright to see the stars, though.

He'd climbed two of the stairs to the airlock when Areva appeared from behind one of the ship's landing struts. "Hey."

"Hello. Where were you today? I did not see you in there."

"I moved around a bit. Under desks, in unoccupied rooms. I found a stack of old equipment in one of the corners where I could see the whole floor, so I spent some time there. Don't worry; I had your back."

"I was not worried."

Any further conversation they might have had ceased when someone screamed on the other side of the parking lot wall. The two officers exchanged a quick look and then ran toward the sound.

"Two and a half meters," Areva said as they arrived at the wall. "Can you boost me?"

Viktor folded his hands and held them out to make a platform for her. She climbed up onto his shoulders and lifted herself onto the top of the wall. She turned to offer him a hand, but he jumped and grabbed the ledge, then pulled himself up under his own power. They both dropped down to the other side of the wall and looked around for the source of the screaming.

It came from a young woman standing under a rain shelter across the street. Based· on her casual attire and the city map in her hands, she was a tourist, and she was alone.

Viktor waited for a break in the traffic before sprinting over, followed closely by Areva. He unfolded his pocket computer and activated his police badge, then held it out for the woman to see. "What happened?"

She glanced down at his badge and then back up at his face, probably making sure he matched the photo on his ID. Most people didn't look beyond that before trusting the officer in front of them. "H-he had a gun!" she said. She pointed toward the wall of the police lot.

"Who did?"

"The man who was there a minute ago. He ran when I screamed, but he totally had a gun attached to his belt!"

"Carrying a gun is not a crime." Viktor suppressed a sigh. This was probably just another easily spooked student on her first trip alone in the big city. He'd worked traffic in Median for several years, and this sort of thing happened on a regular basis.

"But it was an e-gun! You know, the kind that can blow up a building, like in the movies?"

"Energy handguns cannot actually do that," Viktor said, but he felt a rise of alarm.

E-guns cost a lot to produce, so they were rare, and they were difficult to maintain, so few people owned one. (Viktor was part of the exception—he had three.) But their accuracy and longevity made them a favorite of snipers and contract killers, and they were illegal to carry on the street in Median.

Adwin Soun's murderer had used an e-gun. Now, two days later, someone with a similar weapon showed up just a few blocks away. Viktor thought that an unlikely coincidence.

He stepped under the rain shelter, where he presented slightly less of a target, and looked to see if Areva had picked up the significance of what the woman said. Areva had ducked behind a nearby trashcan, but her eyes were wide. She nodded to Viktor and put her hand on her service weapon. Her wary eyes scanned the area.

Viktor turned back to the woman. "How do you know it was an energy weapon?"

"I saw the bubble thingy on the front."

"The energy focus?"

"Yeah, that thing. I took a self-defense class one time, and they said to watch out for those."

"And this man, what was he doing?"

The woman pointed to the wall again. "Just standing there. He was watching the main street, so maybe he was looking for someone."

"Or listening for someone," Viktor said. He and Areva had been talking on the other side of that wall just before the woman screamed. Perhaps the killer listened in, trying to gauge their position so he could take a shot. Knowing that he could be in the crosshairs at that very moment, Viktor spoke with more intensity. "Did you see which way he went?"

"Yeah, over there." The woman pointed toward Market Street.

"Can you describe him?"

"No, I didn't notice his face. But I think he had a gray jacket on. Like a windbreaker, maybe?"

Viktor nodded. "It is a start. Would you be willing to

look at some photos to see if one of them is the man you saw?"

"What, you know who this guy is?" the woman asked.

"No, but we have some suspicions." Viktor didn't want to tell her about the probable Uprising connection. Discussion of crime organizations tended to spook people, and he really needed her to look at the images of known Uprising members to see if she could identify any of them. An ID could narrow down which of the six cases provided the impetus for the murder and the list.

The woman hesitated for a moment between the fear of getting involved and the excitement of helping the police catch a criminal. Excitement won. "Sure, I can do that."

"Thank you." Viktor beckoned to Areva, who reluctantly emerged from her hiding place. "This is Lieutenant Praphasat. She will take you to UELE headquarters." With that, he started walking toward Market Street.

"Wait, I will?" asked Areva. "Where are you going?"

"To see if I can find him first," Viktor called over his shoulder.

He knew it was unwise to go out alone, but the chance of identifying the killer, and maybe even collaring him, made the risk worth it. He patted his sides and felt the reassuring presence of Dickens and Dante, which steeled his resolve. He'd just look around to see if he could spot the man, and then he'd return to headquarters.

He rounded the corner onto Market and scanned the passersby for any sign of Mr. Gray Jacket. This time of evening saw most people eating dinner or preparing for the nightlife, so few pedestrians populated the streets. He passed a few businesspeople heading to the hover train and gave directions to a group of tourists who had gotten lost, but saw no sign of his target.

He had just decided to head back to headquarters to see if Areva and the woman had found anything when a sudden movement in one of the side streets caught his eye. He turned his head fully and saw a man sprinting away while tucking something into the back of his belt.

He wore a gray jacket.

Viktor took off after the man, dodging hover cars as he darted across the road. "Stop!" he yelled. "UELE!"

The fleeing man didn't obey, and instead rounded a corner to head down an alleyway. Viktor followed, his heavy footfalls pounding the pavement as he built up momentum. He took the turn wide so he didn't lose any speed, but came to an abrupt halt as he entered the alley.

The man was gone.

Viktor jogged ahead and searched for places the man could have made another turn and escaped, but all of the connecting streets were deserted. He looked upward, in case his suspect had somehow climbed the side of a building, but saw no sign of him. He'd either entered one of the buildings through the back doors that faced the alley, or he'd taken a side street and evaded Viktor's view. In either case, he left no way to pick up the trail.

A chill began creeping up Viktor's back as he looked down the empty roads. The assassin could also have lured him here for an easy kill. After all, he was next on the list, and if this man did in fact work for the Uprising, he had enough experience with law enforcement to predict how Viktor would behave. Viktor shivered, though it was a warm night, and turned to head back to headquarters.

On the way, he tapped his intercom earpiece. "Page Areva."

"Paging Lieutenant Praphasat," the earpiece's voice

responded.

A few seconds later, Areva answered the page. "Viktor, are you all right?"

"I am fine. I saw the man in the gray jacket, but I have lost him. Tell Okoro to have people canvass the area around Aldan Avenue, between forty-seventh and forty-eighth. That is where I last saw the suspect."

Areva cleared her throat. "You can tell him yourself. He wants you to report back in right away."

"He is upset?"

"Probably."

Viktor grumbled a curse. This was not his day. "Then I will see you in a few minutes."

* * *

Okoro met Viktor at the entrance to the Org Crime division floor. "You chased a suspect without calling it in? A suspect who is probably trying to kill you? Are you out of your mind?"

"I did not have time," Viktor said. "To be honest, I did not think I would actually find him."

"But you did, and you chased him into an empty area without calling it in. For crying out loud, Ivanokoff, you're not even in your own jurisdiction."

"If I had caught up to him, we would not be having this conversation."

"No, we'd probably be discussing your funeral arrangements because you went somewhere without backup and got shot!" Okoro threw his hands up. "You're supposed to help me solve this case."

"I am doing so."

"By not reporting your movements?"

"I informed you as soon as I had something to

report. And I sent the witness we found directly back to you." Viktor nodded to where the female tourist sat poring through digital photographs. "Even if she does not identify anyone, we have learned something important."

"And what's that?"

"That the murderer is still in the area."

"Assuming the man you saw really was the killer."

"The witness saw him with an energy weapon, and he fled when I tried to speak with him. I doubt very much that this was a coincidence."

"Even if you're right, that proves what, exactly?"

"That the list was not fake. That we are on the right track in our suspicions."

Okoro begrudgingly nodded. "All right, I'll give you that. The other teams didn't come up with anything to implicate someone else from Soun's life, so this does give more credibility to our working theory. And I admit it took guts to run after him. Though it doesn't get us any closer to finding the killer, or to figuring out who's targeting us and why."

"Then we will have to hope our witness recognizes one of the Uprising members in the photos."

Said witness chose that moment to look up from the computer. "I'm done. None of them jumped out at me. Like I said, I didn't get a good look at him. Sorry."

Okoro raised an eyebrow at Viktor, who amended his previous statement. "Then we will have to hope we find a link between the list and one of the previous investigations."

Okoro nodded. "We'll all keep looking. It'd be easier if we had more people, or hell, if we just had more security recorders in the area. We could've gotten a look at that guy's face and be done with this already."

"Those were private homes and businesses. You could not put recorders there even if you had the budget for them."

"Unfortunately, you're right." Okoro sighed. "In any case, tonight's work gave us some movement in the case, unproductive as it was. Tomorrow we'll try to find something more useful. Now get out of here before the department has to pay you overtime."

Viktor took that as an obvious dismissal. He collected Areva and headed back to the ship.

* * *

After returning home, Viktor seated himself at one of the long tables in the *Endurance*'s rec room and continued to study the old case files and drink coffee by the liter. The rec room was almost empty—most of the crew had left the ship to take advantage of being on Earth for the inspection. Chris Fish and his wife both sprawled on the rec room's couch, reading digital books, and a handful of other officers passed through, but the room remained essentially silent.

That changed when Matthias Habassa arrived, the pants of his black uniform streaked with dust from crawling around in the reactor room's network of machinery. He headed to the coffee maker and poured himself a cup of decaf. "Hi, Ivanokoff! How'd the investigation go?"

Viktor looked up from his computer pad. "I see the rumor mill has not slowed down at all."

Matthias shrugged. "It's not classified. Somebody on the ship inspection team is friends with a bunch of the Org Crime people, and he told Officer Lee that he saw you up there this morning, and then Lee told the rest of engineering, and now the whole ship knows. I think the captain was mad that it all spread so quick, but he's probably over that by now."

"Why?"

"He went out with Loretta Bailey tonight. Hard to stay mad when you're on a date."

"Ah."

Matthias seated himself at the table, across from Viktor. "So how's the investigation going? Is it true you're on some kind of list of Uprising targets?"

"Uprising targets?" Chris Fish looked up from his digital reader. "Who else is on the list?"

"Not you," Viktor answered. "Only a few people from Organized Crime."

Chris pocketed his book and crossed the room to join them at the table. "Do we know why it's these specific people? What's the connection between them?"

"Chris, it's none of your business," his wife said from the couch. "Just leave it alone."

"You never know when my knowledge might be useful," Chris said. "Or yours, for that matter. Come over here and help us figure this out."

"I do not need help," said Viktor.

"So you know who did it and how to catch them?"

"Not yet."

"Then you need help." Chris leaned forward and grabbed Viktor's computer. "What do you have so far?"

Viktor took the computer back, but admitted to himself that a unique perspective might prove useful. And though Dispatch liked to ignore the *Endurance* crew, they had uniqueness in spades. "We believe everyone on the list was involved in one of six previous Uprising investigations. The first person—the murder victim—was crossed off."

"How are they going to keep the rest of you safe?" Matthias asked. Before anyone could answer, he said, "Ooh, I have an idea! We can pick everybody up on the ship and then use the D Drive to take you all out of the solar system so the Uprising can't get to you!"

Chris snorted. "That's called kidnapping."

"Only if we do it without permission. What if ..."

"Dispatch has already assigned each of us a bodyguard until we find the killer," Viktor said. "Also, I doubt they would like us to show such weakness by running away from the Uprising."

"Bodyguard?" Chris looked around the room. "Where's yours?"

"I'm here." In one corner of the room, a hand appeared from behind a potted plant and waved.

Matthias waved back. "Hi, Areva!" To Viktor, he said, "I thought you'd pick her."

Viktor frowned. "Why?"

"You guys do everything together."

"No, we do not."

"Gentlemen, can we get back to the important matter?" Chris said. He pointed at the computer tablet. "Somebody is trying to kill our first officer. We need to figure out who it is and why before they target the rest of us, too!"

"Why would they do that?" asked Matthias.

"I don't know yet. That's why we need to figure it out."

Viktor relinquished the computer across the table. "You are welcome to look for any connections, but I see nothing to make one case stand out from any other. All six seem equally plausible, and at least one person in each case has motive to eliminate everyone on the list."

"What about the order of the list?" asked Chris.

"What?"

"The names on the list. Were they in any particular order? Alphabetical, age, rank?"

Viktor thought back over the list, which he'd read enough times to memorize it. "No."

"Then why put them in that order? There has to be a reason."

Matthias bounced in his seat. "Ooh, maybe it's a code!"

Chris scoffed. "Calm down. We need to look at this logically."

"Occam's razor," said his wife, still engrossed in her book.

"What?" asked Matthias.

"Occam's razor," said Chris. "It's a principle of logical reasoning. It says that you should go with the simplest solution to a problem, unless or until a more complicated solution presents better supporting evidence."

"I like that," said Matthias. "So what's the simplest explanation for the order of the names in the list?"

Viktor thought about it for a moment. "If the murderer chose his targets based on who worked on his case, he probably consulted the official UELE write-up to determine who was involved. Perhaps the names go in the same order as one of the reports."

They spent a few minutes looking at each case's official write-up, but none of them contained the investigating officers' names in the same order as the list.

"So that's not it," said Matthias. "What else? How would you go about making a list if you wanted revenge on a group of people?"

"Alphabetical order," said Chris's wife. She still didn't look up from her book.

"I'd make mine as convoluted as possible to throw people off the scent," said Chris.

"Ease of eliminating them," Areva said from behind the plant.

Viktor thought over famous revenge stories from literature. *Moby Dick, The Count of Monte Cristo, Hamlet* ... the characters in each story went about achieving vengeance in a different way, but they all targeted their wrath specifically at a few people. If they had bothered to make lists, how would they have organized them?

Then Viktor thought about his transfer to the *Endurance* and how he would arrange the list of people responsible for it. The man whose arm he'd broken (whose lawsuit had led to the disciplinary hearing) would definitely go toward the top of the list. Viktor's partner at the time was a female officer who called Dispatch for backup instead of intervening to help stop the fight before it got out of hand. She'd be up there, though below the man himself. He'd include all of the other Org Crime officers who hadn't stuck up for him at his hearing, including Okoro. Commissioner Wen from O&I would go toward the bottom. She'd assigned him to the *Endurance*, but she could just as easily have fired him completely. She, at least, had heard his side of the story, so while he harbored some resentment toward her, he didn't think of her as a huge target.

The first place on the list would have to go to Adwin Soun for signing the order that kicked Viktor off the organized crime team. Others had contributed to his fall, but Soun had overseen the entire process.

"How involved they were in the event that I wanted to avenge," Viktor finally said.

"That makes sense," said Matthias. "Sounds like the simplest solution to me!"

"Good." Chris leaned over the computer tablet. "Then we can eliminate it."

Viktor frowned. "I thought you said the simplest solution was most likely correct."

"No, Occam's Razor says that. I say the simplest solution is too easy and should be rejected outright. Now, if I rearrange the letters in the names of each person on the list ..."

An idea occurred to Viktor, and he pulled the tablet back over to himself, eliciting a protest from Chris. He pulled up one of the six probable cases and began reading the investigation overview.

It had been a tough one. A key player in the Uprising crime organization had stolen a shipment of body armor intended for a UELE base on Mars. Because of the Uprising connection, Org Crime took the lead. They eventually recovered the stolen armor, and though the leader of that particular group of operatives escaped, they arrested some of his subordinates and shot and killed his number two, who also happened to be his nephew.

The nine people on the list played the key roles in the case. The bottom two discovered the connection to the Uprising operative and figured out his hiding place. The five above them, including Okoro at number three, manned the strike force that recovered the stolen goods. Viktor, second on the list, led the strike team and fired the shot that killed the leader's nephew. Adwin, at the top, oversaw the entire operation and approved the use of lethal force in the first place.

A simple explanation. It made sense.

Viktor looked across the table at his crewmates. "This is the one."

* * *

"Killian Yang." Okoro tapped the digital photo to enlarge it on the projection board. It showed a tan, bald man somewhere in his sixties. Despite his age, he had a strong cut to his chin and toned musculature, and he looked at the camera with bored indifference. "I thought the Uprising dumped him after he failed to get that shipment of armor."

"Apparently not." Viktor handed him a computer tablet with a list of recent flights into Median Interplanetary Airport. "I found this flight record from the day before Adwin Soun's murder. It is for a man named Darwin Yang. While his fingerprint scan and identification initially seemed in order, I ran a comparison to all existing Darwin Yangs who are the same age as this passenger. The fingerprint record is a fake, and so were the identification cards, but facial recognition matched the passenger to one of Killian Yang's associates—an Uprising contract killer known as Cassius. I believe he flew in under the name Darwin Yang in order to eliminate Soun."

"Darwin Yang. That was the name of Killian's nephew. The one you killed in the strike."

"Yes." Viktor tucked his thumbs into his belt, missing the presence of Dickens and Dante. His service weapon just wasn't the same. "They want us to know why they are doing this. We were meant to find this information."

Okoro frowned at him. "How *did* you find all of this?"

"I consulted with the other officers on the *Endurance*." Viktor allowed himself a small smile. He and his team of washouts had outperformed the acclaimed

Org Crime division, and he enjoyed the opportunity to rub Okoro's face in it.

"You went outside the investigation team?"

"You did not tell me not to."

"You should've asked."

Viktor raised his eyebrows. "Very well. Next time I will check with you before solving all of your problems."

"Not all of them." Okoro tapped the flight record. "We may have found a suspect, but that doesn't help us figure out where he is now, or prove that he was hired by Killian Yang."

"We can check security footage from the area for facial matches to Cassius."

"True, but there aren't nearly enough of them for it to be a sure thing. If this guy kills for the Uprising, he knows enough to keep himself off the grid. We don't have enough infrastructure in place to track him everywhere."

"We will not need to track him. There are other names on the list. We know he stayed in the area to finish his job. Eventually, he will make a mistake, and we will either catch him, or follow him back to Killian Yang."

Okoro paused. "If he shows himself again, he'll be trying to kill you."

"I know."

Another pause. "I'll do my best to make sure that doesn't happen."

Viktor cocked an eyebrow. That had sounded like an attempt to make amends. "That would be appreciated, as is the sentiment, although it is a bit late."

"Nothing's too late 'til you're dead." Okoro bit his lip and winced. "Poor choice of words. The point is, you know what you're doing, as you showed yesterday by finding that witness, and again just now by finding this connection. You're a good officer."

"Not good enough, apparently. I work on the *Endurance*."

"Maybe not for long." Okoro waited until Viktor looked at him to continue. "I know the new captain they're bringing in to head Org Crime. He's against having too big a police force, but he values my opinions. If the rest of this case goes well, I'll put in a good word with him and suggest that you return to the team. Consider it a way of making up for everyone abandoning you before."

Viktor hoped Okoro missed the look of shock that crossed his face before he forced it back to neutrality. "And what do you want in return?"

Okoro chuckled. "Seriously, this isn't a hostage negotiation. I'm being up-front with you, Ivanokoff. All I ask is that you do the same with me. Let me run the investigation without you questioning my every move. Prove to me that you can be a team player again. You do that, and I'll do my best to see that your move here is made permanent. Deal?" He held out his hand.

Viktor hesitated. "What makes you think I wish to leave the *Endurance*? We recently made history."

"That was a fluke, and everyone knows it. By this time next month, that ship will be back at the edge of the solar system with nothing to do. Hell, you're only still here because we needed your input on this case."

Well, that confirmed one theory, though Viktor couldn't shake the feeling that Okoro's offer was less than genuine. Maybe he thought the job opportunity would make Viktor easier to work with until he could get rid of him again. On the other hand, maybe he was telling the truth. Maybe he did want Viktor back on the team.

But did Viktor want to return to that same team?

Everyone knew the *Endurance* was a dead end, and no one in their right mind would actually enjoy working on it. While everyone on the ship would understand if he took a new job, something felt smarmy about getting reinstated into the position he had before his fall from grace. Could he do that to them? Could he do that to himself? Or should he wait until something else came along? That would mean more time on the *Endurance*. The thought might fill another person with dread, but it didn't bother Viktor. And Okoro's offer didn't excite him as much as he thought it should. That meant he needed to think long and hard before he made a decision.

He ignored Okoro's hand, but smiled to show that he appreciated the offer. "I will consider what you have said."

Okoro nodded. "Good enough." He turned back to face the board and pointed to the photos of their two suspects. "We should keep running security footage to see if either of these two showed up near the crime scene, and also see if either of their communication records are on file. If they're talking to each other, that could help us pinpoint their locations, as well as prove a connection between them. I'll get the other two officers on it, and hopefully something turns up. In the meantime, you watch your back. I don't want you getting shot just before you rejoin the team."

* * *

Areva met Viktor in the Org Crime break room for lunch, appearing behind him as he poured himself a cup of coffee. "I heard your conversation," she said.

Viktor finished filling his mug and turned calmly to face her. "What do you think?"

"I think you should do it."

"Accept the transfer?"

She nodded. "You don't like being on the *Endurance*."

"Does anybody?"

"Matthias does."

"Good point."

"And Okoro was right. This might be your only chance before we're sent out to the edge of the solar system again. You're still at least twenty years from retirement. You don't want to spend all of them out there doing nothing. Not when you could do more good here."

Viktor took a sip of coffee. "Why were you put on the *Endurance*, Areva?"

She wrinkled her nose. "I thought it was obvious."

"I would like to hear your own explanation."

"There's not a lot to tell. I was in a different department. An investigation went bad. It changed me. Changed the way I worked. I wouldn't shoot at anyone who was looking at me. Started staying out of sight whenever possible." She shrugged. "I didn't fit into the mold anymore, so they kicked me out. I think everyone has a similar story."

"Most likely. If they offered you your old career again, would you accept it?"

She shook her head. "No. That's not me anymore. I'd be no good to the department in that job. Besides, I have friends on the *Endurance*."

"So do I."

"Besides me? No, you don't."

"Yes, I do. I play Wordsmithy with Officer Varma."

"Over the ship's network. You don't even meet in person."

"It still counts."

"My point is, you don't have anything to keep you on the ship. Not really. So why shouldn't you take the opportunity to go back to making a difference, even if it is the position you had before?" Areva met his eyes with hers, and for a moment Viktor forgot to answer as he stared at them.

"I do not know," he finally said.

She smiled. "So you'll take it."

"Perhaps."

"I'm happy for you." She patted him on the back. "And don't worry. I'll stop by and say hi to you whenever we visit Earth."

"I would like that."

The conversation turned to other topics as they headed down to the cafeteria, though Viktor still felt distracted by the other ideas turning around in his mind. He had enjoyed working on the Soun murder case so far. So why didn't he jump at the thought of doing this every day? Was it Okoro? Did he not trust him? Was it Org Crime? Did he not want to work for the division that had dumped him before? Such a big decision to be made. So many questions to be answered.

* * *

The shot came as Viktor crossed the shipyard to return to the *Endurance* after an afternoon spent screening security footage and communication records. He passed a pair of patrolmen returning to the headquarters building after their day's route and nodded to them. He'd done his own years as a traffic cop in Median before he was picked up by Organized Crime, and while he had doubts about returning to the latter job, he never wanted to return to the former. It was exhausting. In fact, returning to any job in Median would require him to move. He considered the annoyance of removing his entire gun collection from the walls of his berth. Did he really want to go through the hassle? He was just calculating how many boxes it would take to hold all of the weapons when something slammed into his back and threw him forward, face-first onto the pavement. He gasped as the landing knocked the wind out of him.

The two patrolmen quickly reacted to what happened. "Officer down!" one of them shouted into his intercom interface. "Shots fired into the Dispatch service lot!"

"Suspect sighted on a neighboring rooftop! We need hover squads up there!" said the other.

Viktor heard a set of running footsteps approach and looked up to see Areva, her eyes wide. She dropped to her knees next to him. "Are you all right? Where did it hit?"

Viktor groaned and reached behind his back to feel where the shot had struck him. It had burned a hole in his black uniform shirt, which annoyed him because he'd have to replace it, but more telling were the frayed layers of his under-shirt body armor. "It was an energy gun," he said, gingerly sitting up.

Areva breathed a visible sigh of relief when she saw that he hadn't been injured. "As soon as you went down, I spotted a guy up on a building on Market. He cut and ran right away. I would have tried to get in a shot, but …"

"But he was looking," Viktor finished. He pushed himself to his feet and took a tentative step forward. He could walk; that was good. The shot probably hadn't burned him, though he'd have to check with a medic to make sure.

Areva looked at the ground. "Sorry."

"It is all right. He was foolish enough to try to shoot me here at headquarters. He will not go far." Viktor looked over at the two patrolmen, who were now engaged in coordinating the manhunt. This was probably the most excitement they'd seen this year. If he and Areva hadn't encountered the aliens last month, it would be the same for them. Viktor again felt the burned edges of the back of his shirt. "He must have thought I was not wearing armor, or he would have aimed for my head."

"Good thing he didn't. It would be hard to miss a target that big." Areva looked toward the rooftop again, where a UELE hover car already circled the area. "They'll get him."

"Yes, they will." Neither of them voiced the thought that if they didn't, the assassin wouldn't make the same mistake twice.

* * *

"They didn't get him." Okoro minimized the digital photo of the rooftop and brought the profile of the assassin Cassius to the front of the screen.

Viktor closed his eyes to contain his frustration. "Why not?"

"Same reasons as always. Insufficient resources. Too many civilians in the area. He lost them in the crowd." Okoro shook his head as he studied the profile. "If we used a better way of tracking people, this wouldn't happen."

"Freedom and security. It is always a tradeoff." Viktor crossed his arms. "What *were* we able to learn?"

Okoro tapped the photo. "An off-duty sergeant saw Cassius run out of the building shortly after we lost eyes on him on the roof. Got a good look at his face and everything. And we matched the energy burns on your armor to the ones that killed Soun. This is our guy."

"Is there any indication of where he went?"

"No, but he gave us something else we needed. Since we knew he was on that rooftop, we checked satellite telemetry from the time when he was there. We got the ID of his pocket computer."

Viktor raised an eyebrow. "He is not still carrying it, is he?"

"No, he deactivated it shortly after we spotted him. But we pulled up the records of his past transmissions and found one that was sent just after Captain Soun was killed. I have a tech team tracing it now. We had to pull records from every satellite in the system. He bounced it off of half of them on its way to wherever it went. At the moment it looks like he sent it toward the outer planets."

"Do we know what the message said?"

"No, we'd need to check the receiving station for that. But whether it went to a satellite or a ship, it gives us a place to pick up the trail, which might lead us to the man who hired him."

"Killian Yang."

"Yeah. If we find Yang, we can make him tell us where Cassius is, and we'll nail them both." Okoro glanced over at Viktor. "Don't worry. We'll get him before he has a chance to attack you again."

"I am not worried. Areva has my back."

"She didn't exactly do a bang-up job the first time. You sure you don't want someone else? Someone, you know, not from the *Endurance*? Or hell, someone who can handle being in public?"

"Do not mock her," Viktor said. "Her idiosyncrasies make her good at her job. And she is a close friend."

Okoro gave him a skeptical look. "Close is the right

word, though I'm not sure about friend."

"I do not know what you mean."

"I saw your face when I offered you your old job. You had doubts. There's something or someone who could keep you on that ship. Is it her?"

"You are imagining things." Viktor said. "There is nothing to keep me on the *Endurance*. Areva and I are simply friends, nothing more. But I still insist that you respect her, as well as the rest of my current crewmates."

"Fine. I will."

"Good."

Okoro turned back to the board. Satisfied, Viktor followed suit.

"So she's single?"

Viktor whirled on Okoro, who held up his hands. "Just a joke. Calm down."

"Your sense of humor needs improvement."

One of the tech team members chose that moment to run into the conference room. "Got it!" she said. "We finished tracing Cassius's message from the night of the murder. Guess where it went?"

"I do not do guessing," said Viktor.

"A ship in far orbit," said Okoro.

"Nope." The techie shook her head. "The signal was received by a civilian research station orbiting Saturn. Number twelve, to be exact. It was built by the Lunar University system, though they rent it out to private firms, too."

"Lunar University." Okoro shook his head. "Seems like everything belongs to the moon these days."

"Who was on the station when the signal arrived there?" Viktor asked.

"A team from Breakthrough Technologies," said the techie. "They were experimenting with some new kind of gravity plating that's supposed to work better in orbit of a planet or something. I don't know. The important thing is, they're still there." She grinned at them. "Maybe one of them remembers seeing the signal come through."

"Or maybe one of them passed it on to Killian Yang," Okoro said. "Good work."

The tech left. Okoro turned to Viktor. "Saturn has over an hour of lightcomm delay. We'll have to travel out there to interview them. I also want to bring a technical team to take apart the station's signal receiver to look for anything suspicious. It's possible the Uprising bugged it and the satellite team isn't even involved."

"We will need a ship," Viktor said.

"Yes, we will. I don't know how quickly Dispatch can get one to us. We're stretched pretty thin. If I submit the request this afternoon, we might manage a departure tomorrow at best, or over the weekend at the latest."

Viktor grinned. Irony was delicious. "I happen to have some authority aboard one of the UELE's ships, which does not have an assignment at the moment."

"What, the *Endurance*? Isn't it being serviced right now?"

"Only as a ruse to keep us occupied. You stated as much the other day. Dispatch will probably approve the mission. Unfortunately, Lieutenant Habassa's D Drive is not precise enough to let us jump straight to Saturn, but we can still travel there in good time."

Okoro tapped his fingers on the projection board. "I don't know if this is a good idea. We'll be in an area with few other UELE ships, and the local police departments are tiny operations. That's probably why the Uprising people are out there in the first place. If something goes wrong, your ship might be the only one around."

"We did recently win humanity's first battle with

aliens. We may not be Dispatch's favorite people, but we are still trained UELE officers. I am confident that we can handle it."

* * *

"I don't think we can handle this," said Chris Fish as he paced nervously around the rec room.

"Why not?" asked Matthias.

"This is the Uprising we're talking about. They're organized. They're everywhere. They have a good supply of resources. United Earth has been trying to get rid of them for almost a century, but they're still here. We weren't trained for this!"

"Actually, I think this is exactly what we were trained for," Matthias said. "Fighting the bad guys. Stopping crime. Catching killers." He punched the air. "Feels good to act like a real cop, doesn't it?"

"Oh please, we're not the real cops here." Chris pointed at Viktor. "He's the only one doing anything on the mission. The rest of us are just here to give him a lift."

"Then why are you worried?"

"Because the Uprising has a habit of stealing ships. They're going to see us arrive at their station, where they've probably butchered the entire science team, and they're going to sneak aboard, kill us all, and take the *Endurance* for themselves."

"The *Endurance* is an old ship," Viktor said. "I do not think they would want her."

"What?" Matthias looked personally offended. "Why not? What do you mean, old ship?"

Fortunately, the captain entered the rec room at that moment and distracted Matthias, who said, "Hiya, Cap!"

Captain Withers nodded at each of the three officers. "Lieutenants. Sergeant. Where's Lieutenant Praphasat?"

"I'm here." Areva stuck her hand up from behind the plant in the corner.

"Okay, that's a start, but I'd like you to stand here with everyone else. We're meeting a representative from another division. I want to make a good impression."

Everyone went quiet for several seconds. Then Areva asked, in a small voice, "Do I have to?"

"Yes."

Another pause, then a sigh. "Okay."

Areva came out from behind the plant and joined the group. Captain Withers appraised everyone. "Good, you all look professional. Now keep in mind, this is our chance to impress Dispatch."

"You'd think discovering aliens would have done that already," said Chris.

"Well, it didn't. So be on your best behavior. Especially you, Mr. Fish. I don't want you accusing him with any of your wild theories."

"They aren't ..."

"Fine, your theories, wild or otherwise. Don't talk about them to the lieutenant. In fact, don't talk at all."

Chris crossed his arms. "Fine. If he does turn out to be the assassin in disguise, I'll keep my mouth shut and let all of you get shot."

"Much appreciated." The captain then turned to Viktor. "Is Okoro here yet?"

"He is on his way," Viktor said. "We have been cleared for departure once he is aboard."

"Hey Cap, how was your date?" Matthias asked. "You went out with Loretta Bailey last night, right?"

Withers shook his head. "It wasn't a date."

"But you went to a fancy restaurant."

"Yes."

"At night."

"Yes."

"With a woman whose life you saved only, like, a month and a half ago."

"Yes."

Matthias shrugged. "Sounds like a date to me."

"It wasn't a date! Loretta had some business deal on Earth. We just got together for dinner."

"I think it sounds like a date," said Chris.

"Me too," said Areva.

"It wasn't a date. It was just dinner."

Viktor agreed with the others. What the captain had wasn't just dinner; it was a date. "Just dinner" was when two friends shared a casual meal, like Viktor did with Areva all the time. It occurred to him that if he accepted the position at Org Crime, they wouldn't be able to do that anymore. That would be a heavier loss than Viktor wanted to admit.

Okoro and his bodyguard—the big guy from O&I—appeared in the hatch to the rec room. All of the *Endurance* officers turned to greet him, and out of the corner of his eye Viktor saw Captain Withers smile broadly, no doubt hoping Okoro would notice how he'd reshaped the *Endurance* crew.

He didn't. "We're about ready to go," said Okoro, barely looking at each of the officers as he stepped into the room. "The tech team is on board, and they're putting away their bags. I'm going to need somebody to link my computer to the ship's network right away. I'm waiting on some paperwork from Dispatch, and I want to receive it immediately when it comes in. As soon as we're done here, I'd like one of the ship's engineers to report to my room."

"This is a ship," Matthias said. "We call them berths, not rooms."

"Berths." Okoro crossed to where the rest of the group stood. "Don't interrupt me, Lieutenant ...?"

"Habassa." Oblivious to the correction, Matthias took Okoro's hand and shook it. "Chief engineer. Nice to meet you!"

"Lieutenant Habassa." Okoro freed his hand. "Listen up. I know I'm not the highest-ranking officer aboard, but Dispatch put me in charge of this mission. I don't know what kind of laxity goes on here on a regular day ..."

At that comment, every person in the room stiffened, and Captain Withers lost his welcoming smile.

"... but I'm going to insist on following all of the rules while I'm aboard your ship. I don't have time to waste making sure people are doing their jobs right. Understood?"

Silence answered him. Viktor tried to work up a properly scathing reply. Before he could do so, Captain Withers smiled again, this time with an undercurrent of venom. "You must be a hit at parties. Don't worry. We have no intention of messing up your mission, and I've enforced Dispatch standards since I took command here. I think you'll find that the *Endurance*'s reputation is going to start changing."

Okoro cast a disbelieving glance at the captain, but nodded. "I hope to see that. It'd be good to have another ship contributing to the UELE's goals."

"Fantastic. Now, can I introduce you to the crew and give you a tour as we get ready to leave?"

While Captain Withers smoothed over the situation, Viktor glared at Okoro's back. So much for showing respect to the *Endurance* crew. Hopefully this mission would change Okoro's opinion of them. If it didn't, then Okoro clearly couldn't overcome his own biases, and Viktor wouldn't want to work for him. If that meant he had to stay on the *Endurance* instead of accepting the Org Crime job, so be it. Of course, he wouldn't be happy about it, but he could definitely live with it.

* * *

Viktor watched in horror as the other ship exploded, its contents bursting and destroying the outer hull. He could do nothing but stare helplessly through the port as the ship foundered and dragged its helpless victims to an untimely death. He shuddered with the knowledge that this was murder—his own ship had been the cause of their ...

"What are you reading?"

Why did people only intrude upon the good parts of this book? So much of it was completely interruptible. Why did nobody ever want to talk to him during those sections? This time Viktor didn't bother to hide his annoyance as he looked up and saw not Areva, but Okoro. "Jules Verne. Twenty Thousand Leagues."

"Haven't read it. I just wanted to let you know we're approaching the number twelve Saturn station. Your captain thought you might want to be on the bridge for that."

Viktor set the tablet down on his bookshelf and stood. "You spoke to him? It seemed you avoided the entire crew during this trip."

"Not on purpose," Okoro said—an obvious lie. "I didn't want to get in the way while they repaired that panel that blew out yesterday. Plus, I was working. I had to get the warrant to search the station and dismantle their communication relay to look for wiretaps, so I was glued to my computer for the whole trip. It took a while to come through. Short-staffed, you know."

"For all the complaining you do about the UELE's lack of resources, you are surprisingly reluctant to use those at your disposal," Viktor said.

Okoro's eyes narrowed. "They're legitimate complaints. It seems like every year they make up new rules that limit what we can do. You know how frustrating it is to try to track an organization as decentralized as the Uprising with all these hoops we have to jump through? And then they keep cutting our budgets, eliminating the people we have available, shrinking the size of the space fleet. What are we supposed to do if a bigger threat comes along, huh?"

Okoro's voice rose in pitch as he spoke, and Viktor suspected he'd touched a nerve. Since he didn't want to debate the merits and drawbacks of limited police power, he tried to redirect the conversation back to his point. "If that is how you feel, you should utilize the *Endurance* and its crew, not ignore us."

"I am utilizing you. I'm here, aren't I?"

"And yet you were annoyed when I consulted with the rest of the crew about the old case files, you resisted taking the ship on this mission, and you have not given any of the crew members, besides myself, a task to help further your goals."

Okoro tried to laugh it off. "Ivanokoff, come on. It's just the *Endurance*."

"They will surprise you if you give them the opportunity."

"Why do you keep defending them?"

"I am not defending them."

"Sure you are." Okoro paused as another member of

the crew walked by. He waited for the other man to round the corner before continuing. "Look, if you don't want the transfer, you can just say so."

"I did not say that."

"Good. If you did, I'd think you were crazy. No offense." Okoro clapped Viktor on the shoulder. "I'll think about what you've said if you think about what I've said. Now come on. We need to get up to the bridge. I asked your captain to avoid sending any messages to the station before we talk to the scientists there. If they're involved in this, I don't want them getting their stories together before we question them."

* * *

Viktor stood to one side of the command chair as the research station grew larger in the ship's ports. It took a few seconds for one of the scientists to answer their page. "Hello?" a nervous voice asked over the ship's speakers.

"This is Lieutenant Okoro from United Earth Law Enforcement," said Okoro. "We'd like to dock at your station for a little while so we can ask you some questions."

"About what?"

"Nothing about your research. We have reason to believe that the Uprising may have tampered with some of your equipment."

"Tampering?" The man's voice went up an octave. "How could they do that? When could they do that? Is it dangerous?"

"We don't think there's any danger," Okoro assured him, "but it could interfere with your work. And it's very important to our current investigation that we have a chance to look around. Will you let us dock?"

The scientist apparently covered his speaker, because muffled sounds of conversation came from the background. A moment later, he took his hand away and said, "Yes, that's fine. There's only one docking port, and our supply ship is making a run to Earth, so it's free. You can use it. I'll send you our network access code so you can sync up with it and guide your ship in automatically."

"Thank you."

The communication channel closed. Captain Withers turned to Chris, who manned the scanners station. "Mr. Fish, transmit the last five minutes of audio to Dispatch. It'll take a few hours to get there, but I'd like them to know we had a warm welcome."

"I wouldn't call that warm," Chris muttered. Nobody answered.

"Here's the plan," Okoro said. "Ivanokoff and I will speak to the scientists individually while the tech team inspects the communications relay. Captain Withers ..." Okoro glanced at Viktor before continuing. "... I'd like you to have a team search the entire station. Hopefully one of us will find something to show why Cassius sent his message here and what the message said."

Withers looked as surprised as Viktor felt that he was being included in the investigation. "Sure," he said, "we can do that. Lieutenant Praphasat ..."

Areva popped out from under one of the bridge's work stations. "Yes, sir?"

"Assign some people to the job."

"Yes, sir."

Areva darted through the hatch into the corridor. Okoro and Viktor followed, then headed to the airlock so they would be ready to board the station once they docked. Viktor wondered if Okoro had taken his advice to heart, or if he was just short-staffed enough that he had to utilize the *Endurance* people. Whatever the case, the crew would enjoy doing something useful. Already Viktor could feel the energy level increasing on the bridge. Hopefully that meant things would turn out well.

* * *

The head scientist for the Breakthrough Technologies team did not look at all happy about having his station turned upside-down by law enforcement, particularly after they explained the Uprising connection to him. "Look, we've only been here for a week or so," he said. His hands fluttered as he spoke, punctuating every syllable in the air. "Even if you find something, it was probably here before that. We just rent the space from the Lunar University; they do all the maintenance. We're only supposed to be here for another week, anyway." He settled into a chair on the other side of the coffee table from the two UELE officers. "Can I get you some coffee?"

"Not right now, thank you, Mr. Mehra," said Okoro.

"Doctor, if you please. I did earn the title."

"Sorry. Dr. Mehra, has anything unusual happened since your team came aboard the station?"

"Yes, as a matter of fact."

Viktor and Okoro shared a look. Neither expected to stumble upon a promising answer so quickly. Near the opposite wall of the office, Areva and the big guy from O&I—both here on bodyguard duty—shifted position. Maybe this wouldn't take as long as they thought. "What was it?" Okoro asked.

"One of the sinks in the bathroom doesn't work. There are only three of us here, so it's not a huge problem, but it is a minor annoyance."

Viktor shook his head. "That is not what we meant. Have there been any unexplained signals, unexpected visitors, ships that passed too closely?"

"No, nothing like that."

"Suspicious behavior by anyone on the station?"

"Are you suggesting a member of my team is involved with the Uprising? That's preposterous."

"Why?"

"I've worked with these two other doctors for over ten years. No, if it was one of them, I would know."

"We understand that," Okoro said. "Just for the sake of argument, though, could one of them relay a message without your knowledge? Do you monitor your communications?"

"Of course. We tied our computer systems directly into the station's relay network. Any time a communication is received, someone checks it immediately."

"Were there any messages you weren't expecting, either incoming or outgoing?"

"Besides yours?" The scientist laughed. "No, I don't think so. All of our communications have been official business from the company, random marketing spam, or personal messages for members of the team."

"Do you monitor the personal messages?"

"You mean spy on my coworkers? No." Dr. Mehra waved a hand and rolled his eyes. "That's for you people to do."

"We don't do that, sir," said Okoro. "And even if we did, it would only be for your own safety."

"Of course it would," said Mehra. He shook his head. "But no, I don't check on their personal messages. Breakthrough Technologies does, though. Everything we receive here is automatically copied to them. We send out a mass report twice a day. So you see, even if something suspicious was sent or received by a member of my team, our company would know about it shortly afterward. They would report it, and you'd know about it already. Check with the company if you don't believe me." Satisfied with his answer, Dr. Mehra leaned back in his chair.

Viktor sat up straighter. "These copies, they are sent automatically?"

Mehra looked confused. "Yes."

"Is it possible that a second copy was sent elsewhere?"

"You mean at the same time?" The scientist considered the question. "I suppose that's possible. We wouldn't detect an additional transmission if it was simultaneous. But someone would have had to access our computer system to program the additional destination. How could they do that without breaking into the station?"

"They could have done it before you left Earth," said Okoro.

"We're from Mars."

"Sorry, before you left Mars. With so many people involved in a research project like this, I'm sure there were ample opportunities for someone to sneak in and rewrite the program."

"We will have to wait for the tech team to confirm it," said Viktor, "but it is likely someone has been using your computers as a relay station for Uprising communications since you arrived."

"But, but I already told you that the company receives copies of every communication! How would they not notice this?"

Okoro glanced at Viktor and waited for him to respond. Viktor gestured to Dr. Mehra's computer, sitting on his desk a few feet away. "You mentioned marketing spam?"

* * *

The *Endurance* senior officers stood around the desk in Captain Withers's office, watching the end of a five-minute "documentary" about some get-rich-quick scheme involving a totally legitimate terraforming project on Pluto. Viktor observed their reactions, having screened the video himself several times already. Okoro was still on the research station with the tech team, which left Viktor to fill the rest of the crew in on the plan.

The video image panned across a digital rendering of the supposed final result of the project as the narrator said, "Contact us today about sending in your investment! Transform both your finances, and our solar system!" Contact information popped up on the screen, the image faded out, and the film ended.

Matthias looked at Viktor. "Why are you showing us this? Ivanokoff, did you get scammed?"

Maureen cocked her head. "It's a scam?"

"Clearly!" Chris said. "People will believe anything these days. There's no good reason to try terraforming Pluto. It's a dead hunk of ice. For crying out loud, the Martian project isn't even finished yet, and the Venus one is only in its planning stages!" He pointed at the screen, then at Viktor. "If you believed this, sir, you're a lot dumber than I thought."

Viktor sighed. "No one believed the film."

"I did," Maureen said in a small voice.

"No one on the investigation team," Viktor

amended. "This was received by the Saturn station's communication relay the day after Adwin Soun's murder, at the exact time we expected to see Cassius's message arrive from Earth." When no one reacted, he said, "It appears to be junk mail."

"It IS junk mail," said Chris. "It's about a project too far away to visit, from a company you've never heard of, doing something with results you wouldn't see for centuries, which isn't even possible in the first place."

"And they want your money," Matthias said.

"Yeah, and that."

"Incorrect." Viktor tapped the computer screen to reset the video to an earlier point. "Watch closely."

He hit play, and a quick stream of images flashed by, none lasting more than half a second: trees, rivers, mountains, and so on. The narrator gleefully announced, "The results are positive!"

Viktor stopped the video again. "Do you see?"

"Bad editing?" asked Matthias.

"I liked the duck," said Maureen.

"I thought I saw the illumasonburg symbol," said Chris.

Captain Withers, who had been silent until now, said, "Someone edited a quick shot of something into the video. Couldn't catch what it was, though."

Viktor nodded. "It was this." He pulled up the time code of 3:14 and froze the playback.

The image showed a list of names on a sheet of paper. The names themselves were gibberish, but the first one was crossed off. "It is only on the screen for a tenth of a second, but that is enough time to make the point."

"'The results are positive.' The hit was successful," Withers said.

"Yes. The message is short, but they used the rest of

the video to mask it from the scientists on the station, as well as their company. Okoro and I questioned each of the scientists, and none of them appear to be involved. They did not even know they were being used."

"I agree," said Withers. "None of our teams found anything suspicious elsewhere on the station."

"Then who sent the message from here to the Uprising?" Chris asked.

"More importantly, *where* did they send it?" Withers said.

Okoro appeared in the hatch between the bridge and Captain Withers's office. "I think I can answer that." He stepped into the room. "By the way, I bumped into your janitor on the middle deck. I think he needs a new vacuum."

Captain Withers shook his head. "You're welcome to try telling him so."

Chris snickered. "I'd love to see that." He nudged the captain. "I wish I'd thought to record it when you tried …" The captain flashed him a disapproving look. He stopped talking.

Okoro waited for a moment, but nobody explained the conversation to him. "Anyway," he said, "I just finished speaking with the tech team. The communications relay itself was fine, but the program that automatically copied everything to their home office was …"

"Ooh! I bet I know!" Matthias stuck his hand in the air. "It was rewritten to send an additional copy to the Uprising!"

"Yes." Okoro looked a bit miffed at having his thunder stolen, but surprisingly he didn't call Matthias out on it. "The modifications happened over three weeks ago, before the scientists had even left Mars. I let Dispatch know, but I doubt we can catch whoever did it after so much time."

"Fortunately, we do not need to catch them," Viktor said, "as long as we can trace where they sent the copy of the message."

Okoro smiled and held up a data drive. "And fortunately, we can." He stuck the drive into Captain Withers's computer and pulled up a transmission log. "Enceladus."

Everyone around the desk leaned in. "Saturn's fourteenth moon?" asked Chris.

"Does anyone actually live there?" asked Maureen.

"Yes, and yes," Okoro said. "Enceladus has a small population, all living in underground domes. About 100,000 people during the last census."

"I tend to forget about everybody on the smaller moons except during election years," Chris said. "It takes forever for their votes to come in."

"The point is," said Withers, "we probably traced the transmission to a particular area of the moon. So we have a much smaller search grid than before."

"Correct." Okoro nodded. "We can't determine exactly where the receiver is located, but we've narrowed it down to an outer region of one of the domed cities. There's a good chance the Uprising has a post there, where Killian Yang waited to receive Cassius's message. With a population this small, it's hard to hide your activities, so someone must have seen him in the area. We'll need to canvass door to door. I've also requested all records of spaceflights leaving the moon, so we'll know if Yang has gone elsewhere."

Viktor stared down at the image of Enceladus rotating on the screen. "I doubt he would leave. I think he is waiting for us to find him."

Everyone in the room looked at him. "What do you mean?" Okoro asked.

"We followed a clear trail of breadcrumbs—the list, the false name, the pocket computer, and now the ability to trace the message from its origin all the way to its destination. We may have been lured here."

"What for?"

"You and I are both on the list. The next two names, to be exact. Perhaps Mr. Yang wanted to take his revenge more personally."

"That ..." Okoro looked around the room. "That's ridiculous. How could he know Dispatch would assign us to the case?"

"You still work in the organized crime division, and you are on the list. It is obvious that Dispatch would include you in the investigation, if only for your knowledge of previous Uprising cases. And the *Endurance*'s presence at Earth has been on every news source for the past month. It would make sense for you to ask me to consult, since I was in the area and also on the list."

"I don't know." Okoro scratched his chin. "It seems a little far-fetched."

"I buy it," said Chris.

"The reason I bring this up is because we can use it to our advantage." Viktor tucked his thumbs into his belt. "Whether or not this was part of Killian Yang's plan, he will not let the opportunity pass him by. We can lure him out by letting him know that we are present on Enceladus."

"Use you as bait?" Withers asked. "I don't like that. Cassius already tried to shoot you."

"He succeeded," Areva said from beneath the desk. "I don't like this either, Viktor."

Okoro seemed more open to the idea. "How do you plan to let him know we're here?"

"A man this high up in the Uprising does not settle down somewhere without ensuring he knows everything that happens in the area. We will conduct our investigation as we would normally. If he is here, he will find us."

"You'll wear armor, I assume," said Withers.

Viktor nodded. "We will also set our intercoms to an open channel with the ship, to make sure we stay in contact. With your permission, I would also like to bring Dickens and Dante with me. I know they are not part of the uniform, but they are the weapons with which I am the most comfortable."

He was ready for an argument, but the captain only hesitated for a moment before he agreed. "That's fine. I've seen your marksmanship, and I want you well-armed if we run with this plan. I know you've got Areva and that big guy from O&I watching your backs, but I want every other qualified officer on this ship organized into teams to keep an eye on you, too. We'll form a perimeter, and when Yang's men move in, we'll get them before they can get you."

* * *

Ten hours later, Viktor and Okoro walked away from yet another home and headed back down the street. They were in one of the tunnels that made up the suburban area of Portsmouth City on Enceladus. Viktor could smell salt water and assumed they were near one of the moon's subterranean oceans. They'd chosen their position on purpose; they could maintain a more secure perimeter here than they could in the tightly packed city proper. The low ceiling of the suburban tunnel and its limited number of exits left few opportunities for someone to sneak up unnoticed. The road could potentially cause a problem, but the officers on the perimeter should spot any approaching vehicles in time to warn Viktor and Okoro of a drive-by. Viktor doubted Yang would try to kill them with such an imprecise method anyway. No, whoever came would come on foot, giving the perimeter enough time to close in and arrest them.

The big guy from O&I sat on a bench on the opposite side of the street, keeping an eye on them over the top of his computer. Areva was out of sight, which surprised no one. The rest of the ship's officers who had a Defensives ranking of two or higher (except Captain Withers, who stayed behind to coordinate everything from the ship, and an officer named Nina, who had food poisoning) were dispersed throughout the neighborhood to maintain the perimeter around Okoro and Viktor. The local police department had insisted on putting some of their own people on the team as well, and as a gesture of cooperation, Captain Withers had agreed.

"Still nothing," said Okoro as they approached the next house—a medium-sized home styled with swooping lines and soothing colors. "Nobody's seen anything, and Yang hasn't showed. We might be wrong about our presence luring him out."

"There is still time." Viktor rang the doorbell, and a few moments later an older man, probably in his nineties, answered.

The two officers flashed their badges at him. He looked unimpressed. "Can I help you?"

"Yes." For what felt like the hundredth time that day, Viktor pulled up the pictures of Killian Yang and Cassius the assassin on his pocket computer. "Have you seen either of these men?"

The old man studied the photos for a few seconds. "No, can't say that I have. What'd they do?"

Okoro answered that one. "We traced a transmission between them to this area of Enceladus. Did you receive …"

"What, sending messages is illegal now?"

"No, the message was …"

"Seems like every time I turn around, the government's got its nose in something new. I moved out here to avoid those kinds of intrusions."

"Sir, the message itself isn't …"

"Tell me, do you read my mail now, too?"

"No, sir. I promise you that the UELE respects your privacy."

"Good. Then leave." The man shut the door in their faces.

Okoro sighed. "I really don't think Yang is coming, Ivanokoff. We should head back."

Viktor looked back at the bench across the street, where the big guy from O&I still sat watching them. "We may have alerted them. Your bodyguard is not being very subtle."

"At least mine is here. Where's yours?"

"Here," Areva said from the bushes to the left of the door.

Okoro jumped. "Seriously, that's creepy."

Viktor kept watching the big guy on the bench. Was it just him, or had the bodyguard held that same pose for a long time? His pulse quickened as a disturbing possibility occurred to him. "Areva, watch from here," he said. He headed down the driveway toward the street.

Okoro caught up with him halfway across the road. "What's wrong?"

"I think your bodyguard is dead."

They reached the bench and looked down. The big guy still didn't move. Viktor checked for a pulse, but felt nothing. He circled the bench and saw a small, neat hole burned in the back of the bodyguard's head—a zap from an energy rifle. He hadn't felt a thing. In his sitting position, death hadn't even made him drop his computer.

"They must've figured out he was with us." Okoro looked up and down the street. "Can't tell where they shot from, but they aren't going to show up now. I'll call off the perimeter. The local force is going to want to run the investigation on this one."

Viktor studied the corpse. Something didn't make sense about it. "Why kill him?"

"What?"

"If they saw that he was part of a surveillance team, why would they kill him? Why not simply leave the area? Why let us know they were here at all?"

"I don't know. They're Uprising. They don't always make sense."

"No, but they usually do." Viktor looked toward the row of houses lining the street. "What was unique about this man?"

"I didn't get to know him."

"Neither did I. If we assume he was not personally a target, what was unique about him?"

"Ivanokoff, you're not Sherlock Holmes."

"Perhaps not, but I have read all of his stories. He was positioned near the street."

"What?"

"That is the uniqueness. He was the only one on the surveillance team positioned near the …"

The whirring sound of a low-altitude hover vehicle rose from around the corner, just as Viktor heard his earpiece chirp with an incoming page from someone on the team. He didn't need to answer the call to know it was a warning. He drew Dante from his belt. "Okoro, move away from the road!"

The next few seconds blurred together. Viktor shoved Okoro toward the houses, but the other man didn't move quickly enough. A black hover vehicle rounded the turn and came to a sudden stop in front of the bench. Three men in full-body armor and face masks jumped out of the vehicle, right next to the two officers. Viktor brought Dante up but only had time to fire one round before the assailants moved in. His bullet hit one of the men in the chest, but it only elicited an annoyed grunt as it struck his armor.

The man he'd shot aimed a small energy pistol at him and fired, but Viktor saw it coming and dove behind the little protection offered by the bench. The lance of energy impacted harmlessly into the pavement.

Viktor crouched in a combat stance and raised Dante to fire again. He peered over the top of the bench and saw the three men hustle Okoro, who looked unconscious, into the hover. The door slammed shut behind them, and the vehicle sped off. Viktor stood and aimed at the retreating car, but with Okoro inside and so many civilian homes around, he didn't want to risk ricocheting a shot.

Areva appeared at his elbow. "I'm sorry, it was all too fast. I hit one of them in the back, but it didn't even slow him down."

"They took Okoro."

"I saw."

"We must follow them."

"How? We're on foot."

Viktor looked toward the house of the old man he'd

interviewed not five minutes earlier. More specifically, he looked at the driveway. "Follow me."

* * *

"We just stole a car," Areva said. She slouched down a bit further in the passenger seat and looked over at Viktor. "We stole a car, Viktor."

"Commandeered."

"That's stealing."

"But legal."

"Barely."

Viktor executed a sharp turn and continued following the black hover that had abducted Okoro. It had no identification number, but the back fender bore a distinctive dent that made it recognizable. Also, the driver was speeding and weaving through the tunnels of Enceladus like a madman. That made him stand out a little.

Viktor kept his eyes on the road and his target. "If we had not left immediately, they would have escaped. We will return the hover once we are finished."

"We could have at least brought backup."

"The other officers were dispersed throughout the neighborhood. We had no time to wait for them." Viktor tapped the intercom interface attached around his ear and said, "Subject is heading back toward the center of the city. He may be trying to reach the spaceship parking lots."

"Understood," said Captain Withers's voice. "I'm keeping the local office updated. I still can't believe you stole a car, Lieutenant."

Viktor ignored the comment as he increased the altitude on his hover in order to hop over a slower-moving vehicle. In the rearview, he saw the other driver gesticulating furiously at him.

"Dispatch is going to be livid," Areva said.

"They already hate us."

"They'll hate us more than usual."

"It was technically legal. They cannot punish us."

"Not officially. But they can do something else."

"We already work on the *Endurance*, Areva. What else could they possibly do?"

"Not let you transfer back to Org Crime," she said quietly.

The thought of losing that opportunity gave Viktor myriad conflicting emotions, but he shoved them aside. "That may never have been an option."

"Why not?"

"The abduction of Okoro does not make sense. If Killian Yang wanted revenge, the hit men should have simply shot him. They should have shot both of us."

"I thought one of them did shoot you. The second time, I mean."

"He missed. And he was too preoccupied with Okoro to try again."

"Maybe Yang wants to take revenge himself."

"Then why not take both of us? Why leave me behind? I was the one who killed his nephew. Okoro was just a member of the team." Viktor shook his head. "There is something else afoot."

Areva chuckled. "Did you really just say 'afoot'?"

"Okoro made a Holmes reference. It is on my mind." Viktor wove around a caravan of hover bikers and hit an empty stretch of tunnel. He increased his speed, hoping to get in front of the other hover and cut it off before the road cluttered up again, but it seemed the Uprising operatives had the same idea. Viktor only closed the distance between them by a small amount before the tunnel ended in the underground dome that contained the downtown area of Portsmouth City.

As far as cities went, it was tiny. The tallest buildings only reached three stories—nowhere near the grandeur of Median or Tokyo or New York. The stone ceiling only cleared the buildings by about three meters. Even the domed cities on the moon dwarfed it by comparison. But the dome's small size and the tightly packed buildings somehow produced the same claustrophobic effect as the biggest metropolises on Earth. Strange what effect proportions could have on the senses.

Captain Withers's voice came through the intercom after Viktor again reported their position. "Local law enforcement has set up barricades around the spaceship lots, and they're blocking off some of the major streets, too. We should be able to stop them from getting away. Just don't let them lose you, or they might double back."

"Understood, sir."

They chased the Uprising vehicle up and down the city streets, although they couldn't tell whether the other car wanted to lose them or simply reach its destination. "We are turning from Eighteenth onto Wood," Viktor said into his intercom as he caught sight of the unfamiliar street signs.

"That's right near the lot where we parked the *Endurance*," Withers said. "If they head down Sixteenth next, they're going straight for it."

"You don't think they'd try to steal the ship, do you?" asked Areva.

"The *Endurance*?" Viktor shook his head. "Our security system is too good. They would never get past the airlocks."

"Tell me about it," Withers said over the open

intercom channel. "Even the people who are supposed to be on the ship have trouble with those."

"It is more likely that they have their own ship waiting to take off. But the local barricade will stop them."

"It'd better," Withers said. "I don't have anybody on the ship to send out to help. All of our defensives people are still stuck at that neighborhood where you left them."

"Sixteenth!" Areva said, pointing out the window. "They turned on Sixteenth!"

"You were right, sir," said Viktor into his intercom. "They are coming straight for you."

He peeled around the corner, following the other vehicle as closely as possible. Far ahead, he saw a standard three-level barricade blocking the road—concrete walls and a ground car on the street, as well as two pairs of police hovers occupying the air above. Behind all the hullaballoo, he could see the spaceship parking lot, crowded with vehicles.

The Uprising hover didn't slow down. If anything, it sped up and began increasing its altitude.

"What's he doing?" Areva asked. "He's going to ram the barricade! Probably at the third level!"

Viktor watched the hover's trajectory. "No, he is ..."

"Aiming for the rooftops," Areva finished his realization with him.

Viktor nodded and began increasing his own altitude as well. "I will follow him."

"You'll have to switch altitudes fast. The dome ceiling only looks about three meters up. If the car is still set to a ten-meter height when you put it on top of the building ..."

"We will die. I know." He glanced at her. "Do not worry. This will work. If it does not, at least it will be quick."

Areva exhaled a short breath, but nodded. "Good luck."

Both hovers climbed past the second and third stories of the buildings, rising until their tops nearly brushed the roof of the dome. The barricade continued to come closer and closer, and Viktor began to worry that the Uprising men did, indeed, plan to crash into the vehicles ahead and go out in a blaze of glory. He could see the police hovers positioning themselves to absorb the impact with the least amount of damage possible, for all the good that would do.

At the last second, the Uprising hover swung to the right and hopped onto the tops of the buildings lining the street. They shot straight up for a fraction of a second, and Viktor feared they would crash into the roof and destroy themselves, but whoever was in control had quick instincts. They shifted to a ground-level altitude, and the hover evened out, zooming forward a foot or so off the tops of the buildings.

Viktor took a deep breath. "Our turn." He jerked the controls in a hard right and followed the other hover's path to jump on top of the row of buildings.

He felt the jolt as the hover sensed ground immediately beneath itself and shot into a rapid ascent. His stomach flew down into the floor as he punched at the hover's altitude controls to set it back to the lowest flight level.

For a moment, he didn't think he'd done it in time. The ceiling took up the entire view through the front windshield. Its smooth, domed surface threatened an imminent impact. Then the front of the vehicle tilted downward, and he saw the row of buildings extending in front of him. The top of the hover grazed the dome, but the impact only caused a slight bump. The angle of the hover evened out, Viktor's stomach returned to its proper place, and he knew that he'd done the maneuver properly.

Areva looked up at the ceiling, then over at Viktor. "Good thing we stole a short car."

Up ahead, the Uprising vehicle shot over the edge of the last building in the row and dropped out of sight. It briefly looked as if the driver forgot to change altitudes and plummeted into the ground, but a second later the car reappeared at a high hover, flying over a row of spaceships in the parking lot.

Viktor hit the accelerator and followed them, adjusting from rooftops back to ground far more easily than he had done the reverse. He set the vehicle back to a low hover altitude and threaded his way between the ships instead of going over them. They quickly passed out of earshot from the street and disappeared amidst the jungle of parked ships.

"I am letting them think they lost us," he explained to Areva. "They will have to board their spaceship from the ground. With the barricade in place, no civilians can access the lot, so if we find a ship prepared for takeoff, we will know it is theirs and can wait for them."

"Like that one?" Areva sat up enough to point out the window to a small, family-sized ship with its airlock open and a boarding staircase situated next to it. Then she slid back down in her seat.

"Da. Like that one." Viktor brought the hover to a stop a few spaces down from the ship in question. He opened the door of the hover, hopped out and drew Dante from his belt, and tapped his intercom interface. "Sir, we believe we have found their escape ship. Have the local authorities meet us at spot ..."

A bright flash lit up the area, and the intercom link

died. Before he could react, a voice came from behind him. "Set your guns on the ground, take off that intercom, and turn around slowly."

The voice made the hairs on the back of Viktor's neck stand on end. He knew that voice, though he'd never seen its owner in person before. "Killian Yang."

"A pleasure to meet you, Lieutenant. Do as I ordered, please, so that I don't need to have my men here shoot you. They have real weapons in addition to their EMP guns."

Viktor crouched and set Dante down. He removed his intercom interface and placed it beside the gun as well. Then he unholstered Dickens and set it beside the rest. He stood, raised his hands to shoulder level, and turned around.

Killian Yang was not an intimidating man. He was tall, slim, with no hair on his head or face. He had the muscle tone of someone who enjoyed an occasional jog, and he wore an unassuming pair of slacks and a sport coat.

The two brawny goons on either side of him, however, looked like they might have eaten semi-trucks for breakfast. Viktor had an inch or two on each of them, but they more than matched him in terms of muscle mass.

Also they had energy guns. Huge energy guns. Even his under-uniform armor wouldn't stop a blast that size. One of the goons kept his weapon trained on Viktor while the other headed over to investigate the hover.

"You lured me here," Viktor said to Yang. He avoided looking back at the hover; he didn't want to draw attention to Areva if he could avoid it.

Yang laughed. "To some extent. I can see in your eyes that you've realized this is about more than vengeance."

"If it was only about your nephew, your assassins would have shot me long ago."

"You're right. My nephew made some mistakes, and they cost him his life. Aggravating, yes, but not worth all this effort."

"Why did you take Okoro? What made him a target?"

"The information he carried."

"What information?"

"All the data your ship brought back about the Haxozin Sovereignty."

Viktor's eyebrows shot up. Whatever possibilities he'd expected, this wasn't one of them. "Why would you want that data? And why would Okoro have it?"

The goon searching the hover interrupted his questions. "Mr. Yang."

Viktor held his breath.

"There's nobody here. It's empty."

Viktor let the breath out. Areva had escaped.

"Good," said Yang. He glanced at a point somewhere behind Viktor. "I believe the rest of our team has arrived."

The Uprising hover with the dented fender pulled up alongside them. The three armored operatives hopped out, one of them pulling Lieutenant Okoro along by the arm. Okoro was alive and conscious, though he'd been relieved of his service weapon, and from all appearances, his body armor as well. Viktor tried to catch his eye, but Okoro fixed his focus on the ground.

The operative holding him removed his headgear and revealed himself to be Cassius the assassin. "We have him, Mr. Yang," he said.

"The data?" Yang asked.

To Viktor's great surprise, Okoro raised his head and answered the question himself. "I've got it. It's all downloaded to my pocket computer. I was tied directly into the *Endurance*'s network during the trip, so it wasn't too hard to access the files. I don't think they even noticed the breach."

One of the armored operatives pulled out Okoro's computer, unfolded it, and handed it to Yang. Viktor stared at his coworker. "Okoro. You work for them?"

Okoro shrugged and nodded. "For about a month now."

"Why?"

"You noticed how I'm always mentioning our limited resources? That's why. You discovered aliens, Viktor. Aliens who want to kill us. United Earth isn't strong enough to fight off an invasion from another solar system. They can barely even keep the Uprising at bay. Look at how long it took us to track Yang here, for crying out loud!"

"The solar system is big," said Viktor. "It is impossible to monitor all of it closely."

"Not impossible. The UELE just refuses to do it." Okoro shook his head. "We have the technology to track every movement of every person and every ship in the system. But we don't!"

"For obvious reasons. People would never stand for that."

"They'll have to, if they want to survive the Haxozin. The government will need to build up the UELE, keep a closer eye on things, remove the ridiculous limitations we've imposed on ourselves for all these years. And with the threat of an alien invasion hanging over their heads, people will accept it. No, they won't just accept it; they'll beg the UELE to get more involved!"

Viktor sighed. "The Haxozin are not invading. They do not even know where Earth is."

"Not yet," Yang said. He finished studying whatever was on Okoro's pocket computer and snapped it closed. "Now that we have this data, they will."

Okoro half-smiled at Viktor. "We're going to find a way to contact them and tell them Earth's location."

Viktor's eyes widened and he sucked in a breath. "Have you lost your heads? Why would you want to do that?"

"To make United Earth strong again," said Okoro.

"To give United Earth something to do besides interfering with Uprising business," said Yang at the same time.

Viktor looked from one to the other. "Your goals do not seem mutually compatible."

Yang shrugged. "The ends, maybe not, but the means, definitely. Alliances have been formed with less to go on." He handed the computer to one of the big goons and nodded toward his ship. "Take everyone on board and prepare to leave as soon as I join you. I have one more thing to do here. Cassius will stay with me."

The five other men, including Okoro, all headed up the boarding stairs and into the waiting spaceship. One of them remained at the top of the stairs to keep an eye on the situation. Cassius took up a place beside Killian Yang and leveled his energy gun at Viktor's head. A stray quote crossed Viktor's mind: *Yon Cassius has a lean and hungry look. Such men are dangerous.* Accurate, if not entirely helpful.

Viktor needed a topic to keep Yang talking long enough for the officers from the barricade to find them. "What are you going to do with Okoro?"

"Not kill him, if that's what you mean," said Yang.

"He suspected the UELE would catch him if he simply sent me the data, so part of our deal was that I provide him a way out. I keep my promises. Besides, we still need to work together to find a way to contact the Haxozin. Our collaboration isn't over yet." Despite Cassius's overtly threatening position next to him, Yang smiled at Viktor. "Inciting a war by simply sending a message. I suppose the pen really is mightier than the sword, isn't it?"

Viktor's eyes flicked between the assassin and his master. "You would use a computer to contact them. Not a pen."

"It's a metaphor."

"It is an inaccurate description. It is also a foolish plan."

"Maybe. I don't really want your opinion on that."

"Then what do you want?"

Yang spread his hands. "I've told you my strategy."

"Yes, I am not sure why you did that."

"Because it's important that you understand it in order to know what I'm offering you now. From what I've heard of your work over the past week, you came close to figuring it out several times. You've proven that you are smart. I would not mind having you work for me."

Viktor snorted. "I do not do treason."

"United Earth betrayed you first. Okoro's told me about you. How they assigned you to the *Endurance*. They don't appreciate your talents, and they certainly don't value them. They dislike you, and you dislike them."

"Perhaps," said Viktor, "but I like my job."

The words felt like an epiphany as he said them. After the week of mulling over Okoro's job offer, it felt good to come to the conclusion that he wouldn't have accepted it, even it if had been genuine. Much as he enjoyed working on a real investigation, he couldn't leave the *Endurance* to do it. The ship was his home.

Killian Yang didn't seem to believe him. "You must be joking."

"I do not do jokes."

"Hmm. Then perhaps you're too far gone for me to use after all. Oh well. I'll settle for the revenge you originally thought this was about. Goodbye, killer of my nephew."

"The word is 'nepoticide.'"

Yang blinked at him. "That is the worst last sentence I've ever heard."

He waved a hand at Cassius, who took on a cold expression as he looked down the barrel of his energy gun. Viktor's body went rigid with tension and his breath caught in his throat as he sensed he was about to die. But before the assassin could fire, the loud report of a projectile weapon drowned out all other sound.

Blood spurted from Cassius's head, and he collapsed to the ground, dead before he landed. Yang instinctively crouched to make himself a smaller target. The goon in the ship's airlock brought his weapon up and looked around for the shooter.

In the absence of another target, he opened fire on Viktor. Viktor dove for the hover vehicle and took cover behind it, hearing the lances of energy strike the vehicle's side. He could also hear Yang yelling something, and a glance around the side of the car showed the crime boss sprinting up the staircase toward the airlock. Viktor ducked his head back before an energy blast could remove it. He wished he'd had time to grab Dickens or Dante.

"Hey," said Areva's voice. A handheld projectile gun

slid out from under the hover.

Viktor picked up the weapon, then bent down and took a look beneath the car. Areva clung to the underside of the vehicle. She smiled at him. "Use my service weapon. I can't see their ship from under here, and if I come out, they'll see me."

Viktor chambered a round and returned the smile. "Thanks."

He leaned around the side of the hover and aimed up at the airlock, just as Killian Yang disappeared inside. Viktor instead fired at the remaining goon, but only grazed him as the man moved to trigger the airlock closed. Viktor emptied the gun at the door, but the bullets couldn't penetrate a hull designed to withstand the duress of space travel.

Yang's ship lifted off from the lot and soared toward the domed ceiling, heading to one of the airlocks to Enceladus's surface. Viktor hoped that the airlock would stop the escape attempt, but he had a sinking feeling that someone like Killian Yang wouldn't plan all of this and forget to ensure his ability to leave once he achieved his goals.

He was right. Apparently the Uprising members had a way to bypass the normal security procedures and let themselves out remotely, because the airlock's inner door slid open and allowed the ship to enter. A moment later, the inner door closed, the atmosphere vented from the lock, and then the other side opened to the blackness of space. The ship disappeared from sight, and Viktor knew he had lost them—Yang and Okoro both.

He sighed and leaned back against the hover. Areva crawled out from underneath it and joined him. "They're gone?"

He nodded.

"With the data?"

Another nod.

Areva blew out a breath through pursed lips. "That's bad."

Nod.

"At least we got the killer."

Shrug. Nod.

Areva leaned around the corner to look at Cassius's corpse and caught sight of all the energy holes burned into their commandeered hover. "Oh, great," she said. "This'll make our division's insurance premium go up."

* * *

It took a few days to clear everything up with the Enceladus police force. They matched Cassius's weapon to the one that killed the big guy from O&I. Since Cassius was dead and had murdered Adwin Soun first, Enceladus PD had no problem ceding jurisdiction of the case back to the UELE.

They couldn't find any traces of Yang's ship, and the few Enceladus spaceships patrolling the moon's perimeter hadn't seen it speeding away. The lead officers talked about system-wide bulletins and possible ways of tracking the ship, but realistically, everyone knew they wouldn't see Yang or Okoro again in the near future. Space was just too big.

They replaced the grumpy old man's hover car. Then they returned to Earth.

Ten days after the chase, and a little less than three weeks since he began work on the case, Viktor again found himself standing near the *Endurance*'s airlock, waiting for Captain Withers to return after another meeting with Commissioner Wen. The other department heads stood with him, though Areva kept herself mostly obscured around a corner.

Chris Fish was in the middle of a rant. "I'm just saying, you had a chance to save the world, and you missed it. That's pathetic."

"We did not fail to save the world," Viktor said.

"I disagree. You didn't get the bad guys, and now they're calling aliens to kill us all. If you'd gotten the bad guys, that wouldn't be happening. Ergo, you'd have saved the world. And you didn't. Do you know how rare an opportunity like that is?"

"I'm still impressed you survived at all," Matthias said cheerfully. "That stunt with the hover on the roofs? Amazing. I coded a simulation of it in my favorite CAD program, and some of the other engineers are beta testing it. We're thinking about making a video game."

The *Endurance*'s 104-year-old janitor walked by, dragging his vacuum cleaner behind him. "I'd play that," he said.

"I'll send you a copy," Matthias said as the old man rounded the corner and disappeared from sight. "What about you, Viktor? Want to relive the moment?"

"I do not do video games."

"We know." Chris rolled his eyes. "Because then you'd actually have to bother *saving the world*."

The airlock beeped twice.

"Oh good, the cap's here!" said Matthias. "I bet he has good news this time!"

"No, he doesn't," said Chris. "You just watch. At best, we'll be sent back out to Neptune."

Beep beep.

"What about at worst?"

"Kidnapped and sent to the Haxozin as a peace offering."

"You're still going with that theory, huh?"

"I'm not convinced it's wrong."

Beep!

The airlock slid open, and Captain Withers entered the ship. Unlike last time, he made eye contact with each of his department heads and smiled. "I have ..."

"Good news!" Matthias bounced on his heels and held out a hand for Chris to high five. When the other man refused, he high-fived himself and then resumed his attention stance. "Sorry, Cap. I got a little excited."

Withers collected himself, then began again. "Yes, I have good news."

"They caught Yang and Okoro?" Viktor asked.

"Okay, not *that* good. No, they're still under the radar."

"So we do not know if they have contacted the Haxozin or not."

"No. But bad as that is, it had at least one positive side effect. Dispatch finally gave us something to do."

"If it involves going back out of the solar system to fight the Haxozin, I'm out," said Chris.

"It doesn't."

"Good."

"It involves going back out of the solar system to figure out where the Haxozin are so we don't have to fight them."

Everyone stared at the captain blankly. "I'm confused," Chris finally said.

"Look," said Withers, "no one knows exactly how far the Haxozin Sovereignty extends. They could be hundreds of light-years away."

"Probably not," said Matthias, "since they were on the World of Infinite Tones, and that's practically next door."

"The point is, even if the Uprising manages to send them a message, we have no idea how long it will take to get to them. It could be years. Maybe even decades."

"Unless Okoro also stole the plans for building a D Drive," Viktor said. "Then they could simply go to the Haxozin in person. We do not know how much data he copied."

"True. The point is, United Earth isn't sure how big of a threat we're facing. So once they finish building the new D Drives, they'll send out some ships to do reconnaissance on the galaxy. Learn what's out there. How big the Haxozin Sovereignty is. How powerful they are. How likely they are to get any message the Uprising sends. There's a lot we don't know, and UE wants to find out."

"That sounds like a military thing," said Chris.

"It would have been. But it's been decades since the Lunar War, and the disarmament treaties mean our solar system's militaries are almost non-existent. No, this is falling to law enforcement. To us."

Matthias grinned. "Cool."

"And, because we were instrumental in solving the murder of Adwin Soun and identifying Okoro as a traitor, we get to be one of those ships."

No one could miss the captain's look of pride as he recounted their achievements, but Viktor frowned. "We played directly into Yang's plan. We went straight to him. We brought his messenger and message with us. And we stole a car."

"Or," said the captain, "you were skillfully manipulated by an enemy behind the lines, yet you still managed to uncover the truth, stay alive, and take down one of the Uprising's top assassins. And you used quick thinking to come up with a solution that wouldn't have occurred to most other officers. It's all in how you spin the story, Ivanokoff."

"Understood, sir."

"It'll take a couple weeks for Dispatch's engineering teams to install the other D Drives, but since ours is already built into our ship, we'll be the first out there. They want us to check in with the People of Tone and learn more about the Haxozin, then see if they know of any other planets we can check out. We're leaving in two days."

Even Viktor cracked a smile at that. This news was better than he'd hoped. His old job at Org Crime couldn't compare to serving on the first ship sent out to explore the galaxy. And this way he didn't have to move. "We will be ready, sir."

"Good." Captain Withers headed past him toward the bridge, walking with a new spring in his step. "Let's get to it!"

Chris and Matthias went the opposite way, toward the reactor room, and Chris began another rant. "If we're going out into space, I need to give everyone a list of things to watch out for."

"How do you know what's out there?"

"I've watched enough science fiction. First, there's going to be a planet-sized death machine somewhere in the galaxy, so we have to prepare for that. We'll also probably encounter evil clones of ourselves at some point, so I'll have to make up a code to determine which of us is the real us. There'll be a couple dozen alien species that live in the Stone Age, so we should make sure the whole crew learns hand-to-hand combat. And I'm still not convinced that this isn't an attempt to give us over to the Haxozin, so I think we should set up a security system ..." They passed out of earshot.

Areva came fully around the corner and smiled up at Viktor. "Good news."

"Yes, it is. Though I wonder how long it will last."

She tilted her head. "What do you mean?"

"At some point, we will no doubt annoy Dispatch again. Eventually they will not need us to do this. They will re-assign us to our old patrol, where we will be out of their way."

"You're such a downer. We can at least enjoy it while it lasts."

"True."

Areva looked at the now-closed airlock, behind which Viktor could picture the Dispatch headquarters building rising up in Median City. "Too bad about the other job. I know you would've liked to work in Org Crime again."

Viktor smiled. "Yes. Too bad. But there is nothing to be done about it." He headed down the corridor. "We should prepare the ship for departure, but later this evening, I know of a nice restaurant in Median that I would like to visit before we leave Earth. Would you care to join me?"

"Just for dinner? Sure. Sounds fun."

Too bad indeed.

Book Three

Under Cover

Death looked different on every person. Areva had seen it enough times to start noticing. Cassius the assassin had died just before he could murder another victim. He'd died cold, dispassionate, without any hint of emotion. His corpse didn't look much different than when he was alive. The four Haxozin soldiers had worn helmets that hid their faces, but they had each died in the middle of combat. They had died intent, focused. They hadn't even seen it coming.

The person Areva killed before that had died sad. Sad and afraid.

But that was a long time ago.

Areva shook herself out of her reverie and watched as the end of the funeral procession passed by her hiding spot. She didn't know the dead person. She didn't know how they'd died. To be honest, she didn't even know what species they were.

The aliens had six long, spidery limbs, four of which they used for walking, while two served as the equivalent of arms. They were taller than humans, though not quite as tall as the People of Tone, and from what Areva had heard, their language consisted of a lot of low-pitched hums.

She'd only been on this planet for a day, which was nowhere near enough time to learn an alien race's customs or recognize their most solemn rites. But Areva was a trained detective, and she knew a funeral when she saw one. The solemn expressions. The hunched postures. The way others moved out of the way to let them pass.

Oh, the body being carried by the four people leading the group was also a giveaway.

From her position behind a mountain of raked leaves, she watched the aliens round a wooden building and head toward the center of town. She reached a hand up to her ear, tapped her intercom interface, and whispered, "Sergeant Fish, the procession is heading in your direction."

Sergeant Chris Fish took a moment before he responded over the open channel. "I'm out of sight. They'll never know I'm here."

Another voice spoke up, this one female. "Chris, I can see your hand hanging onto that branch."

"What, this one?"

"Stop waving! You're going to attract their attention!"

"Joyce, I'm on the other side of the tree from the road. There's no way they can see me."

Joyce huffed over the channel. "Move your hand anyway. You can never tell who's watching."

"Mmm," said Chris, "I like it when you're paranoid."

"Um, excuse me." Sergeant Ramirez, the fourth

member of the surveillance team, spoke over the intercom. "I, uh, I think I see the funeral coming. Are they the ones, you know, carrying the dead guy?"

"Yes," answered Areva.

"Okay. Then yeah. I, er, I see them."

"And as I told you, they didn't see me," said Chris.

"Hey! Surveillance team! Cut the chatter unless it's relevant!" While the four team members had kept their voices quiet, Captain Withers's voice came through at a normal volume. Areva instinctively covered her earpiece, though the aliens couldn't possibly have heard it.

"Yes, sir," she answered. The other three gave similar responses.

The conversation died as the four-person team observed the end of the procession. Areva took a deep breath as the last alien rounded the corner away from her. "Well, we know they honor their dead," she whispered.

"Maybe," said Chris. "We can't be sure they're not taking him off to eat him or something."

"Honestly, Chris," Joyce said. "Nobody carries a meal with that much solemnity."

"You've, uh, obviously never had dinner at my, er, my mother-in-law's house." Ramirez chuckled uncomfortably as his joke fell flat.

"I'm just saying," said Chris. "Let's not make any assumptions. For all we know that guy was still alive, and they're going to ..."

The channel crackled as Captain Withers interrupted again. "Sergeant Fish, knock it off. You're trying to see if it's safe to make contact with them, not write a horror story."

The line went silent for a moment, then Chris muttered, "Sorry, Captain."

The captain didn't bother to acknowledge that. "Any

indication of what's causing those energy readings?" The alien city's pre-industrial society seemed on par with the other civilizations on the planet, but the captain had chosen this area for observation because of some heat readings that indicated they possessed more advanced technology. Like nuclear reactor-level technology.

So far, Areva hadn't seen any sign of it. "No, sir."

"From what I've seen," said Chris, "they don't even have the facilities to build that sort of thing. If they do have a reactor, somebody else probably gave it to them."

The captain grunted. "Hopefully it's not the somebodies we've already met. Have any of you seen any indication of Haxozin activity?"

"No," said Areva. The three other members of the surveillance team chimed in with similar replies.

"That's good, at least," said Withers. "If these people do have contact with another advanced species, hopefully they're friendly, and the spider aliens can put us in touch with them. We'll give it another day or so before revealing ourselves, just in case. For now, make your way back to the ship. By my count, you've been out for ten hours. I don't want anyone slipping up and getting caught because they were tired."

Three replies of "yes, sir," sounded over the channel. Areva added her own before she slunk back to the nearby wall and waited for an opportunity to hop back over it. Once on the other side, she had a clear line of hedges she could use to sneak her way back to the UELE *Endurance* without the locals spotting her.

She waited as a pair of the spider-legged aliens strolled past, humming at each other, and then hopped over the wall and dove under the hedge. She army-crawled her way forward, pausing every so often to listen for anyone approaching, but she'd picked her stakeout spot carefully. No one even noticed her presence.

The alien city had been built in a natural clearing in one of the planet's dense forests. The hedge led Areva to within a few meters of the tree line. She made sure no one was looking, then darted out from her hiding place and sprinted into the forest. The thick foliage obscured her sight of the city within seconds.

Once safely secluded among the trees, Areva unfolded her pocket computer and used its navigation system to make her way to the rendezvous point where she would meet the rest of her team. She stepped carefully through the terrain, keeping to rocks and solid ground where possible to avoid leaving a trail. She didn't know if these people were trackers, but it was best to be safe.

She spotted the rendezvous—a large banyan-type tree—and tucked herself behind a cluster of bushes to observe. Her p-gun rested in its holster, and she kept her hand on it as she listened to the wind and a nearby river and some bird that made a noise not unlike the laugh of a currently popular late-night comedian. She glanced upward and spotted the bird circling overhead. It had a purple tail with luminescent streaks, and its head was shaped like a pineapple. She wrinkled her nose and refocused on the ground level. Alien worlds were weird.

Within a few moments, she heard brisk footsteps approaching from the city. Then she heard a thud as the person tripped and muttered "aw, crap." She recognized the voice of Sergeant Ramirez.

The young officer himself came into view near the banyan tree a few seconds later. He looked around with wide eyes. "H-hello? Am I the first one here?"

Areva whistled softly, but Ramirez didn't hear her.

"Aw, crap," he said again. "I hate moments like

this ..."

"Ramirez!" she whispered.

He jumped and whirled in her direction. "Who said that? Lieutenant? Is that you?"

She raised her hand above the level of the brush and waved. "Yes. Get behind some cover."

"Why? There's nobody here. R-right?" He looked around nervously.

"I don't know, but do it just in case."

"Y-yes ma'am."

The young man hid himself on the other side of the tree, taking up a position so that he could see any areas that Areva wasn't already covering. That was part of why she'd picked him for this team—he knew how to form a perimeter, even if he did get jumpy.

They waited another five minutes or so before Ramirez broke the silence. "A-are Chris and Joyce back yet?"

"No. Be quiet. This isn't the intercom; people can hear us."

"But you said there's nobody here."

"I don't *think* there is."

"Why is everybody on our ship so paranoid?"

Areva didn't answer that question. Sure, Chris Fish was paranoid out of his mind, but her cautious nature was simply logical. If the enemy never saw you, you always had the upper hand.

"A-are you still there?"

Speaking of paranoid. "Yes."

Ramirez heaved a sigh of relief. "Oh, good. I thought you left."

"Where would I go?"

"I don't know, but ..."

The sound of footsteps pounding on gravel reached

Areva's ears, and she whispered, "Shh!" Ramirez fell silent, and Areva waited, hand on gun, and watched the clearing. A few moments later, Chris and Joyce Fish sprinted into sight, both panting. Chris took a look around. "They're not here," he gasped. He leaned over and putting his hands on his knees.

"Stand up straight!" Joyce said. "We have to keep moving!"

"And go where? We can't lead them back to the ship!"

Areva's heart started pounding. Someone had seen them.

"I don't know, maybe we can lose them in the woods!" Joyce looked fearfully over her shoulder.

"We're scientists, sweetie. We're not athletes. They're already gaining, and I've got a stitch in my side the size of Area 51."

"I seriously doubt that."

"What, that they're gaining?"

"No, that it's the size of Area 51. That place is huge."

"So is my pain level right now." Chris groaned. "They're going to catch us, so we might as well let it happen now rather than later."

Areva drew her gun, hoping Ramirez knew enough to do the same. She wanted to radio Captain Withers for input, but feared attracting the notice of whoever pursued the two scientists.

Of course she couldn't shoot the aliens; that would *not* be a good way to make friends with them. Maybe she could scare them off with some suppressive fire, assuming it was just two or three aliens who'd accidentally spotted the intruders and followed them out here. Her team could then escape to the ship and let the captain figure out what to do next.

She was about to signal Chris and Joyce to let them know her plan when not two, not three, but no less than twelve spider-people burst out of the foliage into the small clearing and surrounded the Fishes, who both went rigid with fear and put their hands in the air. The aliens wore green uniforms that identified them as some sort of law enforcement, and they carried little pointy weapons that sparked on the ends—probably stun guns. So much for them being completely pre-industrial.

Shit, Areva thought, ducking further behind the plants. So much for a small patrol, too.

She thought again of distraction fire, but rejected the plan immediately as too risky. With this many armed soldiers, she was more likely to draw their attention to herself than to get them to run away. The last thing she wanted to do was reveal her presence.

She watched as they did a pat-down on Chris and Joyce, grimacing when they found the box that translated between alien languages and English. Chris protested as they relieved him of it. "Hey, wait, we need that to ..."

The aliens didn't even look at him as he spoke. Instead they inspected the talky box itself.

Joyce nudged her husband. "They can't understand us. We didn't find a computer to download their language files yet."

"We didn't find a computer at all," Chris said. "And now they're going to haul us away and eat us."

"They're not going to eat us."

"I appreciate your optimism, dear. It's a bright spot in this gloomy situation."

The aliens finished whatever they were doing with the box, apparently deemed it not-dangerous, and placed it in a clear bag, along with both officers' guns, pocket computers, and everything else carried with them. Then they shoved them back toward the city.

Ramirez's voice crackled in Areva's earpiece. "Shouldn't we rescue them?"

Areva shook her head, though she knew nobody would see. "Too risky. Quiet."

"But they're taking them away!"

"I'll follow."

"What will I do?"

"Be quiet."

The group of spider aliens herded Joyce and Chris out of the clearing and back down the path toward the city. Once the last of them disappeared from sight, Areva began moving through the bushes, trailing them. Fortunately, the tall spider aliens' heads stuck out above the brush. They stayed on the path for about a quarter mile, but just as the city's stone buildings came into view through the tree line, they veered off on a different track, heading toward a small hill on the outskirts. Areva followed.

With the foliage thinning, she could maintain a greater distance and still see her targets, so she hung back until she was sure no one could hear her. She was about to tap her intercom interface and report the situation to the captain when something moved in the bushes behind her. She whirled and crouched in a combat-ready stance, aiming her gun at the sound.

Ramirez appeared from behind a plant that looked like a begonia. When he saw the gun, he jumped and fell straight back onto his rear. "Whoa! Don't shoot!"

Areva holstered the gun and ducked even further down. "Quiet, Sergeant!"

His face turned red. "Sorry. But you almost *shot* me!"

Areva turned back around to see if the aliens had

heard, and discovered that the group with Chris and Joyce had nearly reached toward the hill. Atop the hill sat a large, forbidding stone structure that looked very much like a prison.

"We can't let them get there," she whispered, half to herself and half to Ramirez. She looked back to where he'd fallen and saw ... nothing. The sergeant had vanished.

Areva crouched lower and drew her gun back out, starting to feel like she was playing with it like a yo-yo. "Ramirez?" she whispered.

No answer.

When Areva turned around again to check on the captive team members' progress toward the prison, she found herself facing the crackling energy of an alien stun gun.

She froze, her gun pointed uselessly at the ground. The alien behind the stun gun glared down at her with his gigantic spider eyes and gestured for her to drop her weapon.

There's only one, she thought. *I could shoot him.*

No, she answered herself just as quickly. *He's looking.*

She dropped the gun, raised her hands, and hoped Chris was wrong about the aliens eating them. She knew that when she returned to the ship she'd have to write a report about her decision to surrender. She'd put down that she didn't want to antagonize the aliens when the *Endurance*'s overall goal was to make friends with them. "I don't shoot people who can see me" wouldn't go over as well.

* * *

Areva's captor brought her to the building on the

hill. The building itself turned out to be not so much a building as a fortress—a rectangle of two-meter thick stone walls surrounding a dirt courtyard. The road led them through a thick metal door in the southern wall that clanged shut behind them with frightening finality.

The eastern wall extended into the courtyard and formed a square building, and it was into this building that the spider alien brought Areva. They passed a security checkpoint where the spider dropped off her gun, intercom interface, and equipment belt, and then he continued herding her through a short hallway.

Her thoughts ran with ideas of escape, but given how little she knew about these people, she wasn't sure how they would react to such an attempt. Would they stun her or jump straight to lethal force? Was this a hostile capture or just a precautionary measure? Maybe they were just curious about the humans and wanted to learn more about them. Maybe they would introduce her to whoever gave them their advanced technology, and the *Endurance*'s mission here would wrap up nicely and diplomatically.

Sure. And that room they were approaching at the end of the hall probably contained punch and cookies and balloons.

They entered the room, which Areva calculated to be under the eastern wall, and she heard a familiar voice.

"Oh, thank God!"

Chris and Joyce stood before her in a stone cell behind a wall of thick glass. To one side of the glass Areva could see a small hole in one of the stones with a wooden lever beneath it.

Chris ran up to the glass and pounded on it as the spider alien brought Areva over. "Hey!" he said to the alien. "I'm guessing she's explained everything to you, so let us out now!"

The alien ignored Chris. He (or she—to be honest, Areva couldn't tell) inserted a key into the hole and turned the wooden lever. The glass slid down into the floor, apparently connected to some sort of pulley. He pointed his stun gun menacingly at Chris and Joyce as he did this, and the two of them backed away from the front of the cell.

Areva had found her missing team members, and the alien wasn't looking at her. Time to get out of here.

She threw a hard elbow strike into the aliens' stomach, expecting him to drop his weapon and double over, after which she could hit him in the back of the head and knock him out.

Instead, her elbow struck something hard and chitinous beneath the alien's green uniform. Her strike landed, produced an audible thud, and more or less bounced off. She yelped and started rubbing her stinging elbow.

The alien, for his part, simply blinked at her, then shoved her into the cell and used the lever to raise the glass barricade back up. He then retrieved the key and headed back down the hallway, leaving them alone.

"Oh, good job," said Chris, rolling his eyes. "They're obviously insects; you should know not to use brute force to attack the exoskeleton."

"I didn't see you do any better," Joyce said.

"I'm not the security person here."

"Okay, I'll grant you that." Joyce looked over at Areva. "So I'm guessing you didn't succeed at explaining who we are, either."

Areva sighed and shook her head. She glanced around the furniture-devoid cell. No place to hide. She didn't like feeling this exposed. "Did they bring you both straight here?"

"Yeah."

"Were you able to communicate with them at all?"

"No. And we certainly won't now," said Chris. "They have the talky box. And our guns. And our way of contacting the ship. And everything else. And, oh, by the way, one of them licked his teeth as he looked at me." He shook his head in defeat and wrinkled his pointy nose. "We're dead. We're skinned, roasted, and devoured already. This is NOT the legacy I planned to leave behind."

Joyce huffed and crossed her arms. "Chris, stop it. He wasn't licking his teeth. I don't even think they *have* teeth. We're not in danger of being eaten." To Areva, she said, "I told the captain that we should've just come right out and met these people instead of sneaking around."

"This way was safer," said Areva. Sneaking around tended to be her go-to option, and she didn't like hearing it so casually insulted. She kept that opinion to herself, though, and tried to focus on the positive. "At least we're not in danger."

Joyce laughed humorlessly. "I didn't say that. I said we're not in danger of being eaten. I'm fully convinced that we're never getting out of here alive."

"At least we agree on something," said Chris.

Areva pointed toward the hallway that led back to the prison courtyard. "Ramirez is still out there. He'll tell everyone on the ship what happened. Then they can come and rescue us."

Chris snorted. "So much optimism." He and Joyce shared a look as if Areva was hopelessly naïve.

She took issue with that. "Look, both of you, I'm the senior officer here. I know neither of you like to think positively, but I'm ordering you to do that. No more talk about dying. We're going to be fine!"

One of the aliens chose that moment to re-enter the room. Carrying a gigantic fork.

Chris screamed. Joyce froze. Areva had already worked her way into the far corner of the cell during the conversation, but she shrank back a bit more into the shadows.

The alien with the fork took no notice of them. He crossed out of their field of vision, to one side of the cell. Areva heard him drag something across the stone floor. She thought about moving closer to the glass wall to try to see what it was, but she decided it was safer to stay in the shadows and observe.

She turned out to be right. After a few seconds, the alien came into view through the glass, hauling a large wooden desk behind him.

Areva's breath caught in her throat when she saw the object on the desk.

"They have a computer!" Chris said, pointing at the glowing screen with its various icons and attached keypad.

"Where'd they get it?" asked Joyce.

"Who cares? We can use that to get the talky box working!"

"We don't have the talky box."

"Then we have to get them to hook it up themselves!" He pounded on the glass again, his fear of being eaten apparently forgotten in his excitement. "Hey! We want to talk to you!"

The spider alien continued ignoring them. He positioned the desk and computer near the wall opposite the cell, looking upward as if trying to align it in a specific place. Areva craned her neck, but couldn't see anything on the ceiling to designate one area as better or worse for ... whatever the alien wanted to do. Maybe he didn't quite get how the technology worked.

He finished arranging the furniture and then grabbed the huge fork again. Chris immediately backed away from the glass, but before anyone could panic, the alien stuck the fork into a slot in the top of the computer. Areva couldn't see the screen, but she heard the device beep in acknowledgment of its new attachment.

All three captives breathed a sigh of relief.

"See?" Joyce said. "It's a wireless receiver or something. They're not cannibals."

"I'm still not ruling it out," Chris replied. "And are they technically cannibals if they're eating us? We're not the same species as them."

"Oh, shut up, you know what I meant."

While the married couple bickered, Areva stayed crouched in the shadows, observing and collecting information. She worked best this way: analyze the enemy first, and only then engage. And only then if she could control the whole situation. She knew from her previous job to never enter a situation unprepared. That was how people got killed.

She watched the alien in silence as he began entering some sort of information into the computer keypad. He worked slowly, checking his progress every few keystrokes. Whatever he was doing, it wasn't a familiar task. She watched his insectoid face and thought she detected some measure of anxiety in his expression, but maybe she was just reading too much into it. After all, she'd only observed these people for a day.

Just as the alien finished his work on the computer, he happened to look in her direction. Their eyes locked.

Areva diverted her gaze immediately and cursed herself for being dumb enough to leave her attention where that could happen. She never wanted to make eye contact with an enemy. The eyes revealed too much. When you looked in someone's eyes, you saw them, and they saw you. If you weren't in complete control of your thoughts, you could give away everything in the space of that one second.

If they weren't in control, you could see their thoughts, too. If they were dying, you could watch their life flash before their eyes. You could see them realize what was coming. You could see them realize you were the last thing they would ever see. Areva stopped that train of thought before it could derail her. She hadn't shot anybody who was looking at her in years. She wasn't the harbinger of death anymore. She wouldn't be that ever again.

She refocused on the present. Fortunately, the moment of eye contact had been short enough that Areva didn't glean any information from the alien, and she didn't think he learned anything from her either. That was good. In such an unknown situation, she didn't want to show vulnerability.

The moment passed. The alien looked away, too. He checked the computer screen again, and what he saw apparently satisfied him. He glanced at the prisoners once more and then left the room.

Areva let out a breath she didn't realize she'd been holding. When she glanced at the Fishes, she found both of them staring at her.

"The hell was that?" asked Chris.

"What?" she asked. She looked around the cell for a distraction, not liking how she was suddenly the center of attention.

"You freaked out. You were watching the guy, and suddenly you got really nervous, and then he left, and now you look like you've seen a ghost." Chris's face lit up. "*Can* you see ghosts? Was he haunted?"

"Or were you communicating with him telepathically?" asked Joyce.

"Good question!" said Chris. "Or was he ..."

"No." Areva cut off the rampant speculation. "Nothing like that. Just thinking."

"About what?"

"How to get out of here."

"Lies," said both Fishes simultaneously.

"You showed a tell. Your eyes went up and to the left," said Joyce.

"And you swallowed after speaking," said Chris. "You're a defensives officer. You should know not to give yourself away like that."

Areva sighed. For all their paranoia and brazenness, the two scientists were astute observers. She knew if she didn't give them an answer, whatever they came up with would be much weirder, and rumors would circulate around the entire ship within hours after they were rescued. She didn't want the rest of the crew thinking she had psychic powers or some sort of dark secret, so she answered, "I accidentally made eye contact with the spider-alien. It reminded me of something from my past. That's all."

"What, life before you were transferred to the *Endurance*?" Chris shook his head. "It is not a good idea to think about that. It'll depress you."

"Chris, you've never worked on a ship other than *Endurance*," said Joyce.

"Yeah, because nobody appreciates my expertise. Soon as I passed the police academy, they sent me straight to the armpit of the solar system. It's because the establishment is afraid of me. They're afraid of what I might find out. Science sees all, my dear."

"Can it see a way out of this cell?" Areva asked.

"Nope." Chris shook his head. "Walls are solid rock, and this glass is bulletproof."

"We think it's bulletproof, at least," said Joyce. "Obviously we haven't actually shot it. You should try to kick through it or something."

Areva frowned. "Why me?"

The other woman laughed. "Do you really think either of us has the fortitude to kick through a wall? You're the security person here."

She had a point. Areva got to her feet and walked over to inspect the glass wall. "If this does break, we're going to need to run for it."

"We're ready," said Joyce.

Areva gauged the distance and prepared to throw a side kick at the wall. In the middle of that process, Chris asked, "So, what about your past life were you remembering?"

She closed her eyes in a moment of frustration. She'd thought they finished with that topic. "Something I learned at work."

"Mind-reading through observing others' behavior?"

"No."

"What, then?"

"I don't want to talk about it."

"Can we guess?"

Areva decided to give them the short summary to appease them. "I was on a mission seven years ago, undercover, and I accidentally got caught. Someone I had become close to outed me, and they did it by reading my eye movements. So eye contact makes me nervous. That's it."

"Seven years?" asked Chris. "That's right before you came to the ship. Did you get in trouble? Were they mad that you were found out, so they sent you to a dead-end job? Is that why you won't shoot anybody who ..."

Areva interrupted the unwanted questions by throwing her hardest kick into the glass wall. The questions had stirred up quite a bit of emotion, so she released it through the assault, throwing her entire body weight behind the attack. It produced a loud thud, and shivers of vibration swam up her leg and set her nerves to stinging, but the glass itself didn't shatter. It didn't even dent.

She hopped on one leg, rolling her ankle to try and get the blood flowing back through her now-painful limb. She inspected the point of impact and shook her head. "I can't break it."

"Not for lack of trying!" said Joyce. "Damn, woman, you are scary!"

Areva blushed and headed back to the corner, where she could observe while trying not to be observed. She really disliked the cell's openness and visibility. "We're going to have to do something else."

* * *

"I say we blow them up."

"Stop *saying* that, Ivanokoff! We're not blowing them up!" Captain Thomas Withers paced in front of the conference table set up in the *Endurance*'s rec room. "We want to rescue our people, not kill them."

"My plan would only kill the aliens."

"We don't want to kill them either. We're here to make friends with these guys, not start another war!" Thomas rubbed a hand across his forehead. Meetings with his crew always made him sweat with frustration, but this time was worse because the rec room's climate controls had been out of whack all week. "Does anybody have an idea that *doesn't* involve murder?"

Matthias Habassa, the ship's chief engineer, raised his hand. "We break in, get the talky box …"

Thomas rolled his eyes. "I told you all that we aren't calling it that."

"… and tell the aliens that this was a big misunderstanding. And maybe we should bring them cookies. Everybody likes cookies."

"That's not a bad idea," said Thomas. "Just coming clean with who we are and what we're doing here. We were going to do that in another day or so anyway."

Matthias's copper-skinned face brightened. "And the cookies?"

"No cookies."

"Aww."

Viktor Ivanokoff, the ship's enormous first officer, crossed his arms so that his biceps bulged out and made him look even more intimidating than usual. "But how are we to get inside the prison to retrieve the box? Ramirez said they closed the door. It is completely sealed off."

Thomas chewed his lip. "There has to be another way in."

All three of them—captain, first officer, and chief engineer—turned to look at the fourth attendee at the meeting, Sergeant Irvine Ramirez, who looked like he'd much rather be anywhere else at the moment. Ramirez gulped audibly as all of the senior officers stared at him. "I didn't see anything else," he said. "L-like I said, I saw them, er, the aliens, I mean, take Lieutenant Praphasat, and I, um, stayed around just long enough to see. Where they went."

"And did not help her," said Ivanokoff.

"Leave him alone, Ivanokoff," said Thomas. "He would've been caught, too. And then we'd have no idea what's going on." He nodded to the nervous young officer. "You did the right thing."

"T-thanks."

For some reason Ramirez always seemed skittish around him, and Thomas couldn't figure out why. He'd worked on being patient with his crew, and while many of them had started to come around to him, Ramirez seemed constantly on edge. The other senior officers said that it was just the way the sergeant was. Maybe he had a fear of authority.

In any case, Thomas needed him to help plan a way to rescue his three missing people. "Sergeant, I need you to tell me everything you can remember about that prison. Take your time."

Ramirez gulped again and closed his eyes. His forehead wrinkled in thought. "Okay. It's big. It's stone. It has a thick metal door. Um ..."

"Any other entrances? Any possible ways of breaking in?"

Ramirez shook his head, eyes still closed. "No. It's just a solid wall, all the way around the courtyard."

Thomas picked up on what sounded like a promising piece of intel. "What courtyard?"

"The courtyard in the middle of the prison."

Thomas smiled. "Perfect."

"Indeed," said Ivanokoff. "If we drop an explosive into the courtyard just inside of the gate ..."

"Dammit, Ivanokoff, we're not blowing anything up! Stop suggesting that!"

Ramirez opened his eyes again and stared at the two of them in consternation. "W-why is it perfect?"

"Because it means the prison is open from above."

Thomas's smile broadened. "And we have a spaceship."

* * *

If it was a prison, Areva decided it was the least efficient prison in history. They'd sat in the cell for almost two hours without a single visit from one of the spider-aliens, excepting the guy who brought out the computer. She was thirsty, she was tired—after all, she'd finished a ten-hour shift right before all of this happened—and she had to use the bathroom. She'd thought that by now, somebody would have come to ask them who they were—and more importantly, *what* they were.

Also, Chris and Joyce were loud cellmates.

"That theory is bogus, and you know it!"

"If it's bogus, then why is Officer Varma's research getting more funding from the CPLA than your project on endothermic degradation?"

"Because his stupid chemical research ties into the popular thing right now! Just wait, next decade everyone will have forgotten about it and be on to some new buzzword."

Despite having a ferocious argument, the Fishes smiled at each other as if they were actually having fun. Their faces grew redder and their eyes more dilated as they bandied words until finally Chris said, "By god, sweetie, I love the way you argue."

Joyce laughed, though she still looked mad. "It goes both ways."

And then they started kissing.

Intensely.

Areva cleared her throat to remind them that they shared the room with her. Much as she liked going unnoticed, she didn't want them to embarrass themselves if they really had forgotten she was there.

The married couple split apart, though they kept throwing little impassioned glances at each other across the cell. It was common knowledge on the *Endurance* that the two of them argued all the time, and also that they both enjoyed it way too much. It was like a team sport, and they used each other as practice opponents. God help whoever brought down the wrath of both of them together.

Footsteps echoed from down the hall, and Areva stiffened. "Someone's coming." She rose from her seat against the wall, but stayed in a crouch. Hopefully now they would find out what the aliens wanted to do with them.

The spider alien who'd repaired the computer returned, carrying with him all of the team's gear. Areva smiled as she spotted the talky box—that was a step in the right direction. Now they just needed to get him to hook it up to the computer.

Her smile vanished when she saw the figures walking behind him. They walked in lockstep, their right arms cradling bazooka-shaped energy rifles, their bodies decked out completely in blood-red armor, their faces obscured by matching helmets.

She recognized them. She'd killed four of them a couple months ago. She had not wanted to kill any more.

"It's the Haxozin!" Chris said. Joyce, who had never seen the Haxozin in person, gasped. Areva stayed motionless and silent. Chris shook his head. "They must be the ones who gave these people their tech."

"Then why didn't we see any of them before?" Joyce asked.

"Does it matter? They'll recognize us now. We're doomed."

"Maybe not," whispered Areva. "The only Haxozin who saw us before are dead. And the People of Tone wouldn't betray us. These soldiers might not know what we are any more than the spider people do."

"That's assuming that the People of Tone are still around! They might have been obliterated after we helped them kick the Haxozin off their world! Who knows what they would have given up to try to save themselves?"

"Not to mention the message that the Uprising wanted to send to the Haxozin," Joyce said. "There's a good chance they know everything."

"And a good chance they know nothing. Just be quiet." Areva fell silent as the Haxozin and the spider person reached the cell.

One of the Haxozin stepped up to the glass and looked the three humans up and down. Then he turned to the spider-person and uttered something in the guttural language of his species.

The talky box, still held by the spider person, translated his words. Unfortunately, it translated them into the humming of the indigenous people, rather than into something the humans could understand.

The two aliens conversed back and forth—deep glottal words and low-pitched hums—for several minutes. The lead Haxozin grew angry. He lowered his weapon and pointed it at the spider alien, who dropped everything he carried and put up his hands, the universal sign for "holy crap, please don't shoot me." He continued making pleading hums, and the Haxozin finally retracted his weapon.

Without even glancing at the humans, the Haxozin jerked his head toward his colleague, and they both headed back down the hall.

All three humans let out a breath. "What was all of

that?" Joyce asked.

"No idea," said Chris.

Areva found herself watching the spider alien as he picked up everything he'd dropped. She felt sorry for him, having a gun pointed in his face.

Nobody should see death coming.

The thought came unbidden, and Areva immediately hushed it. She didn't want to revisit the memory of that mission—her last as an undercover agent. Technically it was a success; she made it out with the data she'd been sent in to retrieve, enough info to bring down the Tycho Crater drug ring. Dispatch was pleased.

Areva was not. She'd made a sisterly connection with a young woman in the ring and had wanted to bring her out of it. When the time of the heist came, though, her newfound friend realized who she really was and threatened to blow her cover. She killed the woman to save the mission. She served as the angel of death for one more person. *Nobody should see death coming;* those were the woman's last words. They'd stuck with Areva.

She ended up on the *Endurance* less than a month later. It was the last time she killed someone to their face. She'd thought it would be the last kill of her career, but fate seemed to have decided otherwise. She didn't think she could get out of this situation with the Haxozin without bloodshed.

The spider alien continued picking up the fallen equipment and glanced toward the prison cell every few seconds. Areva thought he looked nervous, but genuinely curious about the identities of his captives. Despite his apparent cooperation with the Haxozin, she didn't think he was hostile.

Her eyes fell on the pile of confiscated equipment. She recognized the value this opportunity presented. The talky box had translated into the alien's language; obviously someone had linked it to a computer, allowing it to download their linguistic files. That meant it could now translate between his language and English.

Areva didn't understand how the talky box worked—technically nobody did. Matthias had taken it apart and figured out the hardware, but the code that provided the translations was so far beyond anything Earth's programmers had seen that they were still trying to sort it out. There was probably an entire lab doing nothing but analyzing the spare devices they'd received from the People of Tone.

One thing Areva did know was that the box was supposed to automatically switch to any language spoken in its proximity. If her team didn't make a connection with their captors now, they might never have another chance. She didn't trust either of the Fishes to handle this diplomatically, which left the job to her. So she stood up, took a deep breath to steel her nerves, and walked to the glass. "Hello."

The alien didn't look up. He continued his cleanup duty.

Areva tried again. "Hello?"

Still nothing.

She'd spent so many years keeping out of sight that she actually had to think to come up with other ways to be noticed. Finally she pounded a palm on the glass. "Hello? Mister alien? We need to talk to you."

Still the alien didn't look up.

Chris walked up behind Areva and peered through the glass, too. "I don't think he can hear us."

"What are you talking about?" asked Joyce. "He's right there."

"No, I mean I don't think he can hear us. Literally. I

think his ears don't pick up the frequencies of human speech."

"That's …" Joyce stopped whatever retort she was about to give and "hmm"ed thoughtfully. "That's actually a pretty good explanation. I wondered why none of them reacted to you screaming about being eaten."

"Why isn't the talky box translating us?" Areva asked.

Chris shrugged. "Maybe we're not close enough."

"So we need to get him to come over here," Areva said. "How do we do that when he can't hear us?"

"You're sure you don't have hidden psychic powers?" Chris asked. "Because they'd be really useful right now."

"I don't."

"Damn."

"How about we just wave at him?" Joyce said.

Nobody had any better ideas, so when the alien looked up again, he was treated to the sight of all three humans beckoning him toward the glass as if they were advertising a used hovercar sale.

Areva felt ridiculous. If someone had told her that she was going to seek out new alien species and try to make first contact with them, she'd have assumed that meant dignified formal meetings and the type of espionage she'd been doing when all of this started. Not waving her arm like an old-fashioned traffic signal.

In any case, the spider alien seemed to decide that the weird behavior of his captives merited a closer look. He set all of his supplies on the desk and walked toward the glass.

All three immediately waved their arms back and forth, shaking their heads. "No," said Chris, despite the alien's inability to hear them. "Bring the talky box!"

The alien retreated toward the table. They nodded at him.

He picked up the supplies. More nods.

He began walking toward them again.

Very enthusiastic nodding and waving.

He stopped just outside the glass wall.

"Good," said Areva, glad the silliness was over. "Now what? We just talk and the box will detect our speech?"

"Only one way to find out," said Chris. He stood as close to the glass as he could without pressing himself against it. "Testing, one, two ..."

Joyce whacked him. "No! We don't want that to be the first thing they hear from us!"

Apparently they'd said enough words to activate the translator, because everything Joyce said was promptly re-emitted by the box in the form of the low hums used by the aliens.

Areva sighed. What a great first impression.

The alien's eyes widened. He blinked at them very slowly and dropped the pile of equipment. His hands came up to his mouth in surprise. He hummed, and a few seconds later the fallen talky box provided a running translation. Because of the way his language worked, his words came out sounding slow, and unfortunately, a bit dull-witted. "You ... you can speak? Why did you not say so earlier?"

"We tried!" said Chris. "But you guys were too busy to ..."

Areva stepped in before he could ruin the meeting. "We tried," she repeated. "It seems our voices are out of your hearing range."

"I see," said the alien. "Then ... what are you?"

Tricky question. If their identities hadn't been

exposed yet, Areva didn't want to give them away. "You don't know?"

He shook his head. "I showed our masters your technology—that you possessed a speaking box like their own—but they said all of their worlds use them. Even they are unfamiliar with your species."

Areva breathed a sigh of relief. Their cover was secure, at least for now. "Do your masters come here often?" She realized belatedly that her phrasing sounded like a bad pickup line, but she needed to know why they hadn't detected any Haxozin on the planet until just now.

The alien shook his head. "Oh, no. They stay up in space and watch over us from above. They only come down on occasion, or when we request their presence for a problem using the technology they have graciously given us. That is what we did when we found you." He smiled, flashing blue-colored gums.

Joyce poked Chris and whispered, "I told you they don't have teeth!"

Fortunately, the talky box didn't pick that up. Areva asked, "Where do they come from?"

The alien shrugged. "We have only ever seen a few, but they say they have a ship in space. Sometimes they take our leaders up there in their little space boat."

Areva assumed the "little space boat" meant the same kind of shuttle used by the first team of Haxozin they'd encountered. The spider alien's words suggested the presence of a larger Haxozin ship somewhere nearby. She didn't like the problem that posed for when the *Endurance* tried to leave.

She realized she was semi-interrogating this alien, and while the spider guy didn't seem to mind, she felt that she should be nicer, especially if they were going to convince him to let them go. "What's your name?"

The alien made a humming noise that the talky box didn't translate.

Areva frowned. "I'm sorry, could you repeat that?"

"My name is …" again the box stopped translating, and the alien said, "Humnumnum."

"Humnumnum?" asked Areva, trying to speak in as low a tone as possible.

Apparently she came close enough for translation, because the talky box emitted the same noise the alien had made himself. He nodded, pleased. "Yes. And what are your names?"

Areva had no idea how human names would translate, but she gave it a try. "My name is Areva. This is Chris and Joyce Fish."

The talky box made some more sounds, and the alien said, "I am sorry. I do not think your name translated. But I am pleased to meet the two aquatic swimming food animals."

Chris choked and began gesticulating wildly. "*Excuse me?* We are *not* food animals! We are definitely, completely, not edible in any …"

"I think that's the literal translation of our last name," said Joyce.

Chris stopped with his finger in the air. "Oh." He took a shaky breath. "Okay. That makes sense."

"Where are you from?" asked Humnumnum.

Dangerous conversation material. If the Haxozin found out they were humans—the same people who'd helped the People of Tone escape Haxozin oppression—things would not go well for them. "Another planet," Areva said. She tried to redirect the discussion. "Tell me, what are …"

Humnumnum made a face. "You have asked me many questions. I think now it is my turn. What planet?

Where?"

"You haven't heard of it."

The alien eyed them suspiciously. "You withhold information. Why?"

Areva knew she stood on thin ice and needed to be at least a little honest if she wanted him to trust them. "You seem nice enough, Humnumnum, but we've just met you, and we haven't met your masters at all. We don't usually like to discuss the location of our planet with strangers." *Especially since your masters want to invade it,* her mind added.

"You do not trust us?"

"No, it's not that."

"Then you do not trust our masters?" Humnumnum's face clouded. "A few weeks ago they told the entire Sovereignty to look out for subversives who attacked one of their teams for no reason. They said these people are a danger to any world on which they land. Were they talking about you?"

"No," said Areva.

"Nope," said Joyce.

"Definitely not," said Chris.

The alien blinked slowly at them. "Then you have nothing to fear, and you will be happy to tell me, and them, where you are from."

Crap. Humnumnum had proved to be more intelligent than he sounded. Areva knew she couldn't divulge the information he wanted, and she didn't know enough about the galaxy to make up a lie. "Very far from here."

"You evade my questions. I am growing annoyed with you. I will let the overlords decide what to do with you." He turned to go.

"Wait!"

The spider alien turned back to face them. "Yes?"

Areva suspected the Haxozin would want to interrogate them. That would involve separating them, and probably moving them, which would put them outside of any area where the *Endurance* could hope to find them. If they were going to escape, they needed to do it soon, and Humnumnum presented the best option she could see coming. She couldn't lose this chance. Despite all of her instincts screaming for her to wait for a more controllable situation, she knew she needed to gamble.

She pushed aside all of her training and instincts, then lifted her gaze and locked eyes with Humnumnum. "All right. We're not friends of your masters, but we're not your enemies. We've seen how the Haxozin oppress other species, like yours. We didn't want to start a fight with them, but they threatened to invade our world, so we had no choice. We liberated the People of Tone. If you let us out, we can help you get out from under their rule, too."

She continued to stare into Humnumnum's eyes, hoping she could transcend their brief acquaintance with the power of that connection. She poured out her honesty and vulnerability through the gaze, trying to connect with his emotions. She searched for some indication of his reaction—surprise, suspicion, alarm, and maybe just a little bit of empathy.

His eyes widened. "You would fight them? But they are so powerful!"

"We've done it before." Areva tried to convey confidence despite wanting to do nothing more than break eye contact and go hide in the corner again. "We can do it again. All you need to do is lower the wall."

He glanced toward the lever, then back at her. She

watched his eyes the entire time. He tilted his head to the side and ran his tongue over his blue gums; he was considering it. *Come on*, she thought, *you're so close.*

Because of the intense eye contact, Areva had a perfect view as his eyelids lowered and fear crowded out any other feeling. Her heart sank; she knew in that instant that she'd lost him.

"Wait," she said, but she was too late. He turned and ran back down the hallway, escaping the connection before she could sway him. She knew where he was going; she'd seen it in his face. She wished she could run away, too.

The last thing the talky box translated as he ran away was, "Masters, come back! They *are* the subversives!"

* * *

Viktor Ivanokoff did not do extreme sports. They were dangerous, reckless, and a surefire way to break a bone or find an early grave. As he descended through the air, he wished he could cross his arms in protest. Unfortunately, he needed to keep his grip on the harness in order to maintain his balance while the *Endurance* lowered him into the prison courtyard. He settled for simply scowling.

"Hey, Ivanokoff, isn't this fun?"

Viktor turned his scowl on Matthias Habassa, who hung from another cord a few meters away with an enormous grin on his face. "No."

"Oh, come on, I'd think you would like extreme sports!"

"This is a rescue, not a sport."

"It can be both."

"No."

"Why not?"

Viktor didn't answer, and the conversation was cut short by their imminent approach to the ground. He hit the brake on his harness and slowed to a barely safe landing speed just in time. He rolled forward to absorb his momentum and stood back up, his hands resting on his two holsters. He wanted to draw his guns, Dickens and Dante, immediately, but the captain had told him to play nice. He settled for glaring at the handful of spider aliens who'd gathered to watch them descend.

It was too bad the ship couldn't fit in the courtyard; Viktor would have liked to see them scramble in fear to get out of the way of its landing. He knew the captain wanted to form allies with these people, but he couldn't help viewing anyone who kidnapped UELE officers as the enemy. At the moment they just stood there looking surprised and non-threatening, but they had taken Areva hostage. And they had the two Fishes, too. He couldn't be objective about something like that.

Matthias landed safely beside him and looked around at the half-dozen aliens. "Hi!"

The aliens didn't move.

Viktor picked one who looked a little more sure of himself than the others and made eye contact. He raised his voice to be heard over the rumble of the *Endurance's* engines overhead. "Where is the talky box?" he asked, forming the shape of the device with his hands. First he had to establish communication with these people. Then he could demand the return of the missing crewmembers.

Fortunately, the alien seemed to understand his meaning. The spider-person made several low-pitched humming noises and then headed toward a stone building that jutted out from the eastern wall of the yard. He opened the metal door and disappeared inside.

Viktor tapped his intercom interface. "Captain, one of them has gone inside, supposedly to retrieve the talky box. I am watching the door in case he returns with reinforcements or weapons."

"Stay sharp, but think positive, Lieutenant," said Withers's voice in his ear. "I want to resolve this peacefully. Hopefully then we can find out who gave them their advanced tech."

"Hopefully first we will find out what they have done with the surveillance team," Viktor said.

"Obviously, Lieutenant. Keep your intercom open; I want to hear what's going on in case you need backup or we have to pull you out of there fast."

Viktor snorted. So much for thinking positive. "Yes, sir."

Matthias, who seemed to have the positive thinking angle covered, smiled at the aliens and pointed up at the sky. "Nice day."

The aliens stared upward to where the hovering bulk of the *Endurance* obscured most of the view. One spider person glanced at another, pointed up, and made more humming sounds. They both took several steps back and cast worried looks between the two officers and the ship.

Matthias dropped his arm. "I don't think they get it. We should have brought cookies to break the ice. Everyone understands food."

The door to the stone building opened, and the alien who'd left reappeared. In one of his hands he carried the talky box. His other hand was empty. Viktor breathed a small sigh of relief. At least they hadn't started a firefight.

The alien approached and held the box in one hand. "My name is ..." His next word didn't translate, but sounded like "Humnumnum." "You are like the others."

"Where are they?" Viktor demanded. Orders or no

orders, if these people had hurt Areva, he was going to shoot some of them.

"Gone," said the alien.

Viktor shook his head. "I do not believe you. Their equipment is still here." He pointed to the box.

Humnumnum blinked his bulbous eyes. "We would not dare lie to anyone who has flying boats, as you do. The overlords left this with us, as they already have one. We gave the captured subversives to the overlords, but if you had come first, we would gladly have given them to you." The other aliens nodded in agreement. Humnumnum handed the talky box to Viktor and spread his hands in a pleading gesture. "Please, take your speaking box and do not harm us. We were afraid. We did as we were told."

"Overlords," said Viktor slowly, passing the talky box off to Matthias. He didn't like the implications of this conversation. "They have our people?"

"Yes. They came in a flying boat, but it is smaller than yours. They returned to space."

While these overlords could possibly come from a completely new species who simply didn't know what the humans were, Viktor had a sick feeling. "Who are your overlords? Are they the ones who gave you the technology we detected here?"

Humnumnum nodded. "Yes, they give us what we need to serve them properly. I do not know your word for them, but the other subversives recognized them. On our world, we call them the ones in red armor."

The sick feeling turned into full-blown rage. "Captain, did you receive that?"

Withers's voice was tight. "Copy that, Lieutenant."

"They gave Areva and the Fishes to the Haxozin!" Viktor waited, hand on his gun, for orders. He hoped the captain would at least let him rough up some of the spider people.

Apparently the captain could guess at his thoughts. "Don't shoot them, Ivanokoff!"

"I am not shooting them, but should we not at least ..."

"Are they willing to cooperate?"

"Captain, they just *gave* our people over."

"Answer the question."

Viktor sighed and looked at the cowering spider aliens. "Yes, sir, I believe they will cooperate. They are terrified of the ship."

"Then ask them nicely where the Haxozin took the team, and get your ass back up here so we can go rescue them. Revenge isn't going to help."

Perhaps not, thought Viktor, *but it would help me to feel better.* "Yes, sir," he said grudgingly. He glowered at Humnumnum, who shrank back from his gaze. "Where did the ones in red armor go?"

"Into space."

He took a threatening step forward. He matched the aliens in height and more than matched them in weight, so he hoped he looked intimidating. "*Where* in space?"

"We do not know!" Humnumnum fluttered his upraised hands.

Viktor took another step and his voice rose. "That is not an acceptable answer. You must have some way of contacting them, which means you must know where they are."

"They gave us a computer to contact them! They come down and then leave. We do not know where they go or how it works, only that it does!"

"A computer signal?" Matthias asked. His face had lost some color as he watched the interrogation, but he brightened again at the mention of machinery. "I can trace that. If the Haxozin ship is in the same general area, maybe we can catch them!"

Viktor's eyes narrowed at Humnumnum. "Get the computer. You are going to send your overlords a message."

* * *

About ten minutes later, the *Endurance* shot into space at its maximum safe velocity. "Find me that ship!" Captain Withers ordered.

"Scanning the area where the message was directed," said Viktor. He willed the scanners to work faster. Finally they pinged a small object moving toward the destination of the spider aliens' signal at a leisurely pace. Mass and energy readings were consistent with a powered vessel. "I found them," he said. "A small ship, the same size as the previous Haxozin craft we encountered. They are rounding the planet's second moon, but they have not seen us; they are moving too slowly to be running away."

"Follow them," said Withers. "And be ready to shoot an EMP as soon as we're within range. I want them dead in the water!"

"I am always prepared to shoot," said Viktor.

The *Endurance* sped after the Haxozin ship, swiftly closing the distance between them. The captain issued orders on the way. "Once they're disabled, we're going to need to dock with them. I'll want every qualified person armed and ready to board. We'll try to avoid casualties, but if necessary we'll engage them. It's a small ship, so we should be able to outnumber the enemy and find our people without too much …"

The captain's voice trailed off as they rounded the

moon and saw the small Haxozin vessel's destination.

Viktor's throat went dry. He didn't often experience fear, but this … this scared him enough to make his stomach lurch. "What did you say about a small ship, sir?"

They stared out the front windows at what had to be a Haxozin mothership. It was the size of a skyscraper and shaped like a gigantic star, with a tall central hub and four prongs that tapered off to narrow points. Even at such a great distance, Viktor could count thirty decks on the main body of the ship with his naked eye, and twice that many openings in the hull to serve as weapons ports.

The captain cleared his throat, but his voice still sounded hoarse. "Back off on engines. Keep us under their radar. Get me everything you can on that ship."

Viktor checked the scanners. "It has energy output frequencies similar to the other Haxozin ship, but it is at least one hundred times the size. They do not seem to be running active scans; I do not think they know we are here. Weapons appear unpowered. Based on thermal readings, I believe they have engines located in the ends of each of the star points."

"Gravity on a stick," said Matthias Habassa from the secondary scanners station.

The captain looked at Matthias. "What?"

The engineer cocked his head and studied the thermal readings. "The Haxozin said they have faster-than-light travel when we first met them. I think they use gravity on a stick, where they turn one of the star points into a gravity well. That would bend space and let them travel faster than the light speed limit. It's not as good as our four-dimensional travel, but they don't have to jump to a completely new reality to do it."

Viktor only heard one salient point in the

explanation. "So they can travel away faster than we can catch them with our regular engines."

"Yeah."

That didn't give them much time. Viktor swiveled his chair to look at Withers in the command seat. "Captain, we must stop the shuttle before it reaches the mothership."

Withers checked the scanner readouts on the screens mounted above the forward viewports. He shook his head. "There's no chance. They're too close."

"We must do something!" Viktor said.

"I'm working on it!" The captain faced Matthias again. "Can't we just use the D Drive and jump after them?"

"Only if we know where they're going. Sorry," said the engineer. "The second they cross the light barrier, scanners won't detect them anymore."

"Is there any way to track them?"

"No, even if we tagged them with a signal broadcaster, it would take years for the signal to reach us from their destination."

Viktor watched the captain rub a hand across his dark forehead again. He thought he knew what his CO was thinking. Dispatch would not want the *Endurance* to fall into Haxozin hands, especially since it seemed the D Drive was better than the gravity-stick-bending thing. And the *Endurance* had no chance in a firefight against such a larger ship. The correct thing to do, by the book, would be to engage the D Drive and return to Earth before they could sustain any further losses. Of course that would likely mean the death of the missing crewmembers, but Dispatch would expect them to leave anyway.

He knew Withers had made some non-by-the-book

decisions in the past, but he doubted this would be one of them. The captain was too invested in the UELE method of doing things. Viktor began preparing arguments in his head against abandoning Areva, Chris, and Joyce to their fate, drawing from all the best literary quotes and argumentative techniques he could remember. If he had any influence at all, he would not leave them behind.

Though only a few seconds passed, it felt like an hour that the captain stared out the viewport at the enormous enemy ship. During his contemplation, the shuttle reached the mothership and disappeared into some sort of hangar. Viktor waited for the right moment to tell the captain he was wrong.

Finally Captain Withers stood up, his expression unreadable. "All right. Here's what we're going to do."

* * *

Areva expected dozens of eyes bearing down on her as the two Haxozin soldiers led her, Chris, and Joyce down the shuttle's boarding ramp and into an enormous hangar bay. After all, they were three prisoners from Earth, the world that had dared defy the Haxozin Sovereignty's authority. Surely they would put on some measure of fanfare as they captured their first example of their enemies. She dreaded that level of scrutiny, of being held under a microscope and stared at like a science project.

She closed her eyes to steady herself and refocus as she took the last few steps down the ramp. She couldn't let anxiety get in the way of doing what she had to do. This was just like when she worked in stealth ops. The mission—getting the three of them out alive—took priority. She could do this. She took a deep breath and opened her eyes.

The bay was empty. It contained a second shuttle, a few rows of cargo containers, and some repair equipment, but no people.

"Where is everybody?" Chris asked.

One of the Haxozin soldiers shifted his talky box to his other hand and shoved Chris toward the hangar bay exit. "Walk."

They strode through metal corridors designed for function over fashion. Areva tried to memorize their route and make note of any doors, twists in the path, or possible sources of weaponry.

Fortunately, the two Haxozin seemed more interested in getting to their destination than confusing their captives. They took a straight path with only two left turns and arrived at what appeared to be a cell block—a hall lined with solid metal doors evenly spaced along both walls, leading to a dead end.

The aliens took them to one of these doors, twisted open the hatch, and shoved them into a small, undecorated room. They then shut the door before the humans could ask any questions.

A door in a tiny, walled-off section of the room led to the alien equivalent of a bathroom. They each took care of business, and then Areva inspected the door holding them captive. She pressed her ear up against the edge, hoping that despite the seal, she might pick up something of what was happening outside.

"Why are there so few of these guys?" Chris asked. "I didn't see any others on the walk here, and we must have crossed at least a quarter of the ship. Did you?"

The two women shook their heads.

"Maybe there aren't that many members of their species," Joyce said. "It would explain why there were only ten of them on the People of Tone's planet, and only two here."

"If their ships are this big and mostly automated," Areva said, "it doesn't matter if their army is small. I saw how many weapons ports they have. There's enough firepower on this ship to destroy Tokyo in five minutes."

"Why is it always Tokyo?" Chris asked. "Have you ever noticed that about disaster movies?"

"Those are monster movies, Chris," said Joyce.

"No, there's a lot of disaster movies about Tokyo, too."

"I bet you can't name three."

"What do I win if I do?"

Areva hushed the two before they could start an argument. "I think I hear something outside the door," she whispered.

They dropped their conversation and pressed themselves up against the door on either side of Areva, listening intently.

Indeed, the two soldiers seemed to have decided to take a break after delivering their prisoners to their cell. They carried on a barely audible conversation, and apparently they'd left their talky box nearby, because it continued to translate.

"I just don't believe that *these* are the subversives that helped steal the Tone-People's planet. They look pathetic," said one in a voice that wheezed a bit as he spoke the guttural language.

"Maybe they're tougher than they look. They killed an entire occupation team," answered the other in a deeper voice.

"So we think. I still find it more likely that the Tone People did that. They're the ones who killed the follow-up team we sent."

"Using the weapons they stole from the first team. Weapons they wouldn't have had if the subversives hadn't helped them in the first place. You don't really believe any of our subjugated people would think of rebelling on their own?"

"Well, no."

"Exactly."

The two fell silent for a moment, and Areva feared that they had left before providing any useful information. Fortunately, the conversation had merely paused, and it started up again.

"What does the Sovereign plan to do with them?" asked the wheezy one.

The deep-voiced one laughed. "The Sovereign? I doubt he cares."

"But they're the subversives."

"He's got too much else to think about. The Sovereignty won't run itself. We'll probably execute these as an example and send their decapitated bodies to the Tone People as a warning. If they keep refusing to pay tribute, he might send a ship to blow up some of their cities, but we don't have the time to do more."

"We should blow up the subversives' cities. That's the real way to send a message!"

"Yeah, if we knew where their world is. I'm sure the interrogators at the base will be able to get that information out of them. Maybe once things calm down in our own territory, the Sovereign will send a few ships."

A third voice, this one gruffer than the first two, entered the conversation. "Hey! You two! What do you think you're doing?"

Despite the wall between herself and the soldiers, Areva could picture their postures straightening as their voices took on a more professional tone. "Taking a break after securing the prisoners, sir," answered the wheezy one.

"Is your shift over?"

"No …"

"Then get back to work! We just received another message from the planet. You need to take your shuttle back and investigate; something sounded off about the way they spoke. We'll retrieve you once we return from the homeworld."

The wheezy Haxozin groaned. "We're stuck here for that long? I was supposed to cycle off-shift in two days!"

An audible punch and a grunt of pain sounded, and then the gruff Haxozin spoke again. "I am the third in command of this ship, and you *will* respect me, soldier!"

"Yes, sir," said the wheezy one. "Sorry."

Satisfied, the third Haxozin began to leave, as evidenced by his retreating footsteps. "Back to the shuttle!"

The other two Haxozin followed him, but just before they passed out of translation range, the deep-voiced one mimicked their superior in a whiny tone. "I am the third in command!"

The wheezy one snickered. "Yes, out of what, twenty-five?"

The two laughed. After that, the talky box no longer provided translation.

Areva realized she was sandwiched between the two scientists, and she immediately felt claustrophobic. She broke away and crossed to the other side of the cell. "Do you know what this means?"

"Yeah, we're going to be brutally interrogated and then decapitated and our mangled corpses mailed to our allies," said Chris. "Best day ever."

While that carried frightening implications, Areva

focused on something she deemed more important. "No, the part about their numbers. They said there are only a handful of them on this huge ship. All this time we've thought they have an army, but it sounds like there are only a few of their species running the entire empire. That's why nobody was there to see us brought aboard."

"Well, that's great," said Joyce, "but it only means we don't have to worry about a land invasion. They still have the technology to cause serious damage, even with only a handful of people operating it."

"Like destroying Tokyo," said Chris.

"Or Median. Or New York. Or an entire lunar dome. There's no reason it would be Tokyo."

Areva continued trying to look on the bright side. "At least it doesn't seem like attacking Earth is a priority for them right now."

"That doesn't help us be, you know, *not* decapitated," said Chris.

"Would you stop worrying about imminent death?" asked Joyce. "We've got Areva with us. I'm sure she'll think of a way to escape before then." She looked at Areva. "Right?"

"Um ..."

"Oh God, she doesn't have a plan," said Chris. "We have the ship's chief of security here, and she doesn't have a way for us to survive. We're doomed."

"Look," said Areva, "we have to survive in order to let the rest of the crew know what we've learned. I'll think of something. I've been in worse situations."

Both scientists looked at her with utter disbelief.

She spread her hands. "All right, maybe not. But close."

"What, before you were transferred?" said Chris as his eyebrows rose to impressive heights. "What the hell department were you in that put you in situations close to being sentenced to death by aliens?"

Oh dear. She'd accidentally brought them back to this conversation. She fumbled for words for a minute. "Um ... you know." Her voice dropped to almost inaudible. "Special operations."

"Spec ops? You were in the department's freaking undercover team? With your problems?"

"Chris, be nice," said Joyce. "Call them 'issues,' not 'problems.'"

"I don't have issues *or* problems," protested Areva.

"You stay out of sight all the time, and you refuse to shoot anyone who's looking at you," said Chris. "I'd call those issues."

"They're not issues! They're choices."

"Didn't those choices almost get Lieutenant Ivanokoff killed a few weeks ago?"

Areva drew in a short breath. "Don't bring that up."

"Why? It's the truth."

She dropped her gaze to the ground. "He survived."

"Only because you got a second chance to shoot the guy. The story's all over the ship. Everybody knows it, even if Ivanokoff won't come right out and say it. If you won't shoot the enemy, how are we supposed to get out of this alive, huh? My aim sucks, and Joyce's isn't much better."

Joyce sniffed. "I managed a headshot the last time we were at the range."

"On *my* target, sweetie."

Areva felt so low that she hoped they started an argument with each other and forgot about the current topic of discussion. She wasn't so lucky. They both returned to staring at her, waiting for some sort of explanation that would make everything okay.

She didn't have one. "I'm sorry. I don't have an answer. Maybe we can overpower them when they come to get us out of the cell. Maybe we'll find another opportunity that shows up. We'll have to take things as they come." She looked up. "But I promise that I'll do everything I can to keep you both alive."

Chris raised an eyebrow. "Even shoot at the Haxozin?"

That was an interesting question, wasn't it? She'd failed twice before to shoot at enemies who posed a threat to her crewmates, and things had turned out all right. But here, now, in the center of an enemy stronghold, that same choice posed a strong likelihood of getting all of them killed.

No one should see death coming. Areva had come to believe that as firmly as she believed anything.

Could she violate that belief now, if it meant saving her team?

She didn't know the answer. She doubted she would know until she had to make the choice. "I'll try."

Chris inhaled and exhaled slowly. "I guess we have to take what we can get."

* * *

Captain Withers took a deep breath and tried not to look out the bridge's viewports, which currently showed nothing but blackness. They were moving too fast to see the passing stars. It didn't make him sick the way the twisting, swirling maelstrom view did when they were in D Drive, but somehow this empty nothingness felt almost worse. "What's our position?" he asked the bridge at large.

"We're still anchored to the bottom of the Star

Ship," said Matthias. "The seal between our hull and theirs is holding strong."

"No, not our *literal* position. I mean, where are we in space?"

"That *is* a literal position," said Ivanokoff from his position at the defensives station.

Thomas rolled his eyes up. Sometimes it took so much effort to get a simple question answered. "Is there any way to tell where the Haxozin ship is taking us?"

Matthias shook his head. "Nope. Not until we get there."

Thomas stood up to pace around the row of consoles at the front of the bridge. "I want that EMP to fire the second we return to normal space."

"Yes, sir," said Ivanokoff. "As I said, I am always ready to shoot."

Thomas ignored him. "That should buy us at least fifteen minutes before they restart their ship's systems. That's how long we have to get in, get our people, and get out. Does everyone remember their part of the plan?" Heads nodded. "Good. Hopefully it won't be much longer."

* * *

It took another few hours before Areva felt the motion of the ship change. "I think we're slowing down," she said. "We must be here."

"Oh good," said Chris. "Time for torture."

As if on cue, military footsteps echoed outside of the cell. "Here they come," Areva whispered. "Be ready."

Metal clanged on metal as the Haxozin unlocked the cell hatch and pulled the door open. Areva had poised herself on one side of the door to strike them by surprise, but instead of stepping inside, the Haxozin stayed outside the cell and ordered, "All of you, out."

Chris met Areva's eyes and jerked his head toward the door. *Go attack him*, was the silent message.

She felt her heart flutter. She had no idea what waited outside the room, what sort of weapons the Haxozin carried, and whether or not they'd be staring at her when she emerged. If she jumped out and broke one of the soldiers' necks, he'd probably have a firsthand view of his own death. Alternatively, the assault would fail miserably, and she'd get herself killed.

Likelihood of failure. It was a solid reason not to attack.

She shook her head at Chris and stepped out of the cell, right into the mouth of a bazooka rifle pointed at her chest. Good thing that she didn't strike blindly. Chris huffed and followed her, and then came Joyce.

There were only two Haxozin soldiers, though their head and body armor made it impossible to tell if they were the same two as before. One of them picked up the pile of confiscated equipment, which had apparently been left on a table outside the cell the whole time, and headed back down the hall. The other brandished his weapon and pointed after him. "Follow."

Areva was closest to the lead Haxozin, so she obeyed. Chris and Joyce trailed behind her, and the armed Haxozin soldier brought up the rear. Areva knew he had his weapon pointed at them to keep them in line.

She thought quickly. Chris and Joyce were relying on her, and she felt like she had to do *something* to try to save all of their lives. She didn't know where the Haxozin were taking them, but it couldn't be safe.

The Haxozin ahead of her faced forward, away from her. She could jump on him and incapacitate him before he had any idea what had happened. Of course, that might result in the soldier behind them opening fire, so she'd need to get Chris and Joyce out of the line of fire before doing that.

And of course, the soldier behind them would see her.

Areva's thoughts wandered back to that moment, that sentence that made her rethink everything: *Nobody should see death coming.* Before that, she had done her job without thinking too hard about the consequences of her actions. About what each mission meant for the people who didn't survive it. Yes, most of them were scumbags and probably would have been killed by somebody within a year, but it wasn't just somebody who shot them. It was Areva. She was the last thing they saw before they died. She didn't like being the final vision seen by so many ghosts.

She'd killed since making that choice so long ago, more than most officers killed in their entire careers. But at least those people hadn't known they were about to die. They hadn't had a chance to experience the fear, the dreadful anticipation, and they hadn't stared into Areva's eyes as she gunned them down. She could live with that.

She didn't know if she could live with herself if she went back to the way it was before.

The Haxozin in front posed no problem—she could take him by surprise. But the one behind would see her attack coming, no matter how she played it. Either she retrieved her gun from the first soldier and shot the second one in his face ... or he'd have free reign to eliminate all three of his human captives.

She didn't know if she could pull the trigger.

She wouldn't know until she got there.

She did know that she had to try. At this point she

had no other choice.

She waited until the lead Haxozin rounded a corner. She followed him and turned her head just enough so that she could see when Chris and Joyce came around. She waited for the split second when the corner stood between them and the soldier behind them.

Joyce rounded the corner.

Chris rounded the corner.

"Drop!" Areva shouted. She lunged forward and wrapped her arm around the lead Haxozin's neck. She didn't see if Chris and Joyce obeyed her, but she heard two thuds and assumed they hit the deck.

The Haxozin dropped everything in his hands and reached back to pull Areva's arm off his throat, but he was too late. She tightened her grip and yanked the soldier around so that he faced the corner, serving as a living shield. In a few seconds, he'd pass out, alive, but out of the way, and then she'd have to deal with his comrade.

The other soldier appeared around the corner with his weapon ready. He'd heard the skirmish. He barely glanced at the situation before he raised the rifle and fired an energy blast toward Areva.

Straight through his ally's head.

The soldier went limp in Areva's arms as he died, and she jerked away from his body by instinct. She stared down at the corpse and only barely remembered to dive into a forward roll to evade the Haxozin's second shot.

She grabbed her gun from the pile of fallen equipment as she came out of the roll, and she aimed it at the enemy.

Time seemed to slow down as they stared at each other.

Her finger tightened on the trigger.

You have to fire, she told herself. *You have to save Chris and Joyce.* A darker part that she'd thought she'd suppressed added, *It's only one more.*

Her hands trembled, and she saw the Haxozin adjust his aim to shoot again and kill her. It was now or never.

Her fingers felt clammy on the gun.

The Haxozin began to fire.

Areva closed her eyes.

Time returned to its normal pace as the crack of the Haxozin's bazooka rifle filled the corridor. Areva expected to feel searing pain as the blast tore into her chest, but to her shock, nothing happened.

She opened her eyes to see a smoking hole in the wall to her left. In front of her, the Haxozin soldier crashed to the floor, with Chris Fish's arms wrapped around his knees in a sloppy tackle.

The soldier struggled to bring his weapon around to aim at Chris, but the scientist managed to get his hands around the barrel of the rifle and began wrestling for control of it. The soldier had him hopelessly outmatched, but before Chris could lose his grip, Joyce jumped into the fray and tried to yank the Haxozin's hands away from the weapon.

Between the two of them, they wrested it away from him and stood back up. Chris pointed the rifle down at the enemy, his face pale, and fired without really aiming.

He was close enough that it didn't matter. The shot hit the Haxozin's faceplate, and he slumped back, dead.

They all stood there in frozen silence for several seconds.

Then Joyce squealed, sprang over at Chris, and wrapped him in a hug. "That was *hot,* husband!"

Chris dropped the bazooka rifle, his eyes the size of saucers. "T-thanks." He swallowed audibly. "That was s-stupid. W-what if it was rigged to backfire on me?"

Areva finally realized the danger had ended. She lowered her gun. Her hands shook as she bent to pick up her holster from the fallen pile of gear. She forced her breathing to return to a normal rate. "Thanks," she said quietly.

Chris swallowed and nodded. "Uh-huh. Thanks for getting the other guy."

"Oh. Sure." Areva looked down at the soldier she'd strangled.

"S-sorry for tackling this one before you could shoot. I just … I just reacted. It all happened too fast."

Areva placed her gun back in its holster and reattached the rig to her hip. "Yeah. It was too fast." She could make herself believe that explanation, at least for now. Once they returned to the ship safely, though, she knew she'd need to think more about what she'd done—or more accurately, failed to do. "Come on, get your stuff, and bring the Haxozin rifle, too. We need to get out of here."

* * *

They ran back toward the hangar bay, keeping toward one wall of the long hallway for cover. "If they have any kind of surveillance, they know we're escaping," said Chris, his voice and paranoia now returned to normal.

"Hopefully there are too few of them to do anything about it," said Areva.

No sooner had she spoken than she heard voices up ahead. She swore and veered off down one of the side corridors. "This way."

The other two followed. "Do you know where we're

going?" asked Joyce.

"No, but we have to get out of sight." Areva didn't know if she could handle another firefight. She led them into another branch of the hallway network, and then through an open hatch into a room filled with a few stacks of boxes and an empty conference table. She put her back against the wall near the door and listened to see if they were being followed. Chris crouched on the other side of the door and peered anxiously out. Joyce headed further into the room.

The Haxozin voices came closer, and Areva's breath quickened. She tightened her grip on the gun. If they approached, she had to shoot. She had to. And yet she didn't know if she could.

The voices passed the cross-corridor, but instead of turning toward the room, they continued to fade into the distance. Apparently they hadn't noticed the escape.

Areva breathed a sigh of relief and looked over at Chris to give him a reassuring nod.

Behind her, she heard Joyce whistle and breathe, "Oh, shit."

Chris closed his eyes. "Let me guess. There's a whole bunch of Haxozin waiting for us right here."

"No," said Joyce. She cleared her throat, but apparently couldn't resist correcting him. "And how would they know we'd hide in here, anyway?"

"I don't know," said Chris. He stood and turned to continue the argument. "But what if ..." His voice trailed off. "Oh, shit."

Now deeply worried about what had silenced them both, Areva turned around. She didn't know what to expect, but she thought it would involve enemy soldiers, or weapons, or maybe a bomb with a timer counting down. Something out of an action movie.

Instead she faced a window.

Outside the window, she had a clear view of a big, brown planet. With no lights on the surface, it didn't seem inhabited, but in orbit around the planet she could see dozens and dozens of floating metal structures. They were too far away to make out the details, but they were all roughly star shaped.

One of them moved away from the planet. It picked up speed until it seemed to stretch into an elongated plane, and then it simply vanished from sight.

Areva's eyes widened. "It's a ship."

They watched in silence as another of the star-shaped objects jumped into faster-than-light travel. "It's not just a ship," said Chris. "It's an armada."

Joyce voiced what they were all thinking. "If they have a fleet this size, and they're still too busy to spend much time with us ... how big is their territory?"

A third ship took off to some unknown destination

"Big," said Chris. "Really, really big."

Areva finished the implication. "Too big for us to fight. We have to get out of here, now."

They ran back down the hallway, retracing their steps until they again headed toward the hangar bay. "There's no way Earth could hold off a fleet that size," said Joyce breathlessly.

"Good thing they're not interested in us," said Chris.

"Not yet," said Joyce. "Who knows when they'll change their minds?"

"We can't let them know where our solar system is," said Areva.

Despite being out of breath, Chris snorted. "Obviously. That's why we're escaping, isn't it?"

They finally reached the hangar bay at the end of the corridor. Areva covered the door as the two scientists went through the hatch into the bay, then she followed them. They all ran toward the second Haxozin shuttle. No doubt the first one had already returned to the spider-people's planet.

"Can you turn the ship on?" she yelled to Chris as he reached the boarding ramp.

Chris stopped and gave her an incredulous look. "I have no idea! Why do all of you command officers think that being a scientist means I know everything?"

Joyce reached the ramp and slapped him on the back. "It's okay. Between us, we probably do."

The two disappeared into the shuttle, and Areva trailed behind them, checking over her shoulder every few seconds for pursuit. She took up a position near the door and kept an eye on the hatch to the rest of the mothership. She could hear the Fishes arguing somewhere in the forward section of the shuttle. "Well?" she called. "Can we fly out of here?"

The argument broke for a second as Joyce yelled, "Working on it!" Then the two resumed chattering.

A few seconds later, Chris's voice rose to audible. "The People of Tone have been working on their captured shuttle for over a month, and they don't even know how to fly it! How are we supposed to do this in the space of ten minutes?"

A humanoid form appeared in the hatch to the hangar bay—an armored Haxozin soldier, leaning in to take a look around. Areva froze. *Move along,* she thought. *Move along. Nothing to see here.*

For a moment she thought luck might favor them. The soldier took a few steps into the hangar and then turned around to head back toward the hall.

Chris chose that moment to shout a particularly loud expletive.

A. C. SPAHN

The soldier whirled and raised his bazooka, looking straight toward the shuttle.

Unfortunately for him, he looked toward the bridge, not the ramp. Areva fired once and felled him.

Another soldier poked his head through the hatch. When he saw his comrade collapse, he yelled something and turned to run. Areva aimed, but her shot missed and hit the side of the hatch. The soldier disappeared from sight. She had one guess about where he was going.

"You don't have ten minutes!" she yelled to the Fishes.

Chris swore again. "Best day ever!"

Areva heard shouts as the Haxozin approached the hangar. If she assumed there really were only twenty-five soldiers aboard the ship, and subtracted the three her team already eliminated and the two who'd returned to the planet, that left a score of fighters bearing down on their position. Way too many to take by herself.

"Time?" she called, hoping Chris had deciphered the shuttle's controls.

"A month or two!" he yelled back. "This is alien technology, Lieutenant. I can't just interface with it and figure out how it works!"

The first Haxozin soldier appeared in the hatch. Areva fired, and while her shot missed, it convinced him to duck back to the side. She could keep them pinned down that way for a few minutes, but then what? Two more soldiers appeared in the opening, and while she sent one scurrying back, the other dove through and took up a position behind some cargo containers.

The two Fishes appeared in the shuttle's hallway and crouched near Areva, who continued to fire at the hatch. She'd need to reload in a couple more shots. Fortunately, the Haxozin were keeping their heads down, which meant they weren't looking at her and she could shoot without compunction. Unfortunately, that wasn't helping. They were too quick to kill.

Joyce stared out at the fray. "Are we going to die?"

Areva fired again. "We can't let them recapture us."

"I guess that's a yes."

Chris blew out a breath. "Well, that stinks."

"You're taking this awfully calmly," said Joyce, glancing at her husband. "Weren't you the one freaking out about cannibalism earlier?"

"This is just an energy blast to the chest. That was being eaten, possibly alive. Big, big difference."

Areva fired her last bullet and held her pistol out toward Chris. "Give me your gun and reload this one." During the space between shots, another pair of Haxozin came through the hatch and took up cover closer to the shuttle.

Chris handed her his service weapon. "Don't you want the bazooka rifle?"

"I'm more accurate with a p-gun."

"Oh." Chris reloaded the second gun. "How many have you taken out?"

She took aim with the new gun and fired. "One."

He made a choking sound. "Then what's less accurate?"

"It's not my fault. They're keeping covered, and their armor is too thick." She fired again, and her bullet grazed her target's faceplate. "Two-ish. They'll overwhelm us before long."

One of the soldiers behind a cargo container presented her with a perfect shot, but he was also staring right at her. Instead of firing, she ducked behind the wall to avoid his aim. By the time she looked out again, he had returned to hiding.

Chris brandished the bazooka rifle and began firing with her. All of his shots went wild and only served to distract the aliens. Areva took down two more enemies, one dead and one wounded, but another five swarmed through the hatch.

Will this ever end? she wondered.

That's up to you, another part of herself answered.

She felt a weight settle on her heart. She'd been thinking about the current battle, but she realized the question applied more readily to her struggle between her self-imposed limitations and her job. Would it ever end? The answer really was up to her.

Or at least it would be, if she survived the day. At the moment that looked unlikely. But even as she felt the futility of her internal debate settle in, she realized that she already knew the solution to it. She'd thought she could have both—her career and her conviction—but she couldn't keep fooling herself. The struggle had to end. She needed to choose, and she knew which one had the higher priority. That choice carried some implications for her future, but at the moment it looked like she wouldn't live to see them through.

Bazooka rifles fired right and left, and Areva had to duck back more often than she could look out and shoot. It wouldn't take long before the soldiers overwhelmed their position.

Before she died, she felt she owed the Fishes an honest apology about her inaction in the corridor. "Chris, Joyce, I want to let you know that ..."

Her deathbed confession was interrupted when all the lights went out and the hangar plunged into darkness.

Areva looked up, startled. "What just happened?"

"Power loss?" said Chris. "Maybe somebody tripped a circuit breaker."

"Or severed one of the power conduits with stray fire," said Joyce.

Clanking and rumbling sounds came from the enormous pair of airlock doors at the external end of the hangar. Areva feared another Haxozin ship was about to enter and blast them to pieces. She crouched further behind the shuttle's bulkhead and listened. The Haxozin soldiers shouted at each other, but she couldn't tell if they knew what was going on or not.

The internal door clanged to its open position, and a bit of starlight filtered in through the glass plate in the airlock's external door. It illuminated vague outlines of the cargo containers and repair equipment providing cover for the Haxozin, but didn't give enough visibility to see any of the actual enemies, nor the exact shape of the ship entering the bay.

Areva peered around her hiding place to get a better look. She assumed the new ship would come in slowly for its landing.

It did not.

Instead the ship's running lights snapped on, illuminating the bay and giving her a clear view as a huge, white object with backswept wings careened into the hangar, landed with a thud right next to the Haxozin shuttle, and opened fire on the Haxozin soldiers.

"It's the *Endurance!*" shouted Chris. The ship's two forward guns fired round upon round at the hiding enemies.

Areva caught sight of the ship's loading ramp lowering, and she waved the two scientists toward it. "Get aboard, while they're pinned down!"

The three ran down the ramp of the Haxozin shuttle, ducking to avoid any stray fire the Haxozin might unleash. They needn't have bothered. The ship's machine fire provided plenty of cover, and the darkness had disoriented the Haxozin too badly to regroup. They made it to the *Endurance*'s rear ramp without any trouble and entered the ship's airlock. Areva triggered the ramp to close and then followed the Fishes into the ship.

Viktor met her there. "Did they hurt you?" he asked.

She shook her head. "No, we're fine."

He grinned. "Did you hurt them?"

"Kind of." She couldn't quite return the smile.

"Good. We will leave now. The captain will want you on the bridge."

"Right."

The two left Chris and Joyce to hug each other and exclaim their good fortune—and no doubt start arguing about it a few minutes later—and headed to the front of the ship.

Captain Withers nodded to Areva as she entered. "Welcome back, Lieutenant."

"Thanks," she said. She assumed a spot near the back where she could keep out of sight. It felt good to hide again, to return to her natural state of being. The adrenaline of her ordeal began to wear off, and she suddenly felt exhausted.

Viktor stood near her, since someone else currently manned the defensives station. She took advantage of his proximity and hid herself a little more behind his impressive size. "Viktor, we're lightyears from the planet where we were captured. How did you get here?" she asked.

He didn't turn around to look at her as he answered, which she appreciated. "We anchored the *Endurance* to the bottom of their ship before they activated their gravity stick."

She blinked. "What?"

"Never mind. We would have rescued you right after they returned to normal space, but the method Matthias used to anchor us took some time to undo. Also we did not think about how we would get into the hangar once we disabled their ship, and we had to send someone out in an EV suit to open the airlock manually."

Areva nodded at the explanation. "Thanks for coming for us."

"Of course." He turned and met her eyes. "I would never leave you behind."

She smiled at the phrasing. Viktor was sweet, despite his outward appearance of antagonism. Her smile grew sad as she thought of the realization she'd reached in the hangar bay, when she thought she wasn't going to survive.

She watched through the forward viewports as the ship's guns continued firing on the Haxozin. She also felt the engines kick in as the *Endurance* took off and hovered slightly above the hangar floor. Through the windows she saw the ship's angle yaw to port, and they headed back toward the exit. The hangar's external airlock door loomed ahead, sealed shut.

With the power off, she had no idea how they planned to open the path without sending somebody outside. That might have worked to let them *into* the bay, but they didn't have time to repeat the strategy now. "How are we getting out of the hangar?" she asked.

Viktor grinned. "Easy."

In front of him, Captain Withers ordered, "Fire."

An enormous torpedo shot out of the *Endurance*'s forward launcher and sped straight into the airlock door. A second later, there was no airlock door.

The *Endurance* zoomed out of the hangar and back into open space. Areva avoided looking at the scanners and external camera feeds. She didn't want to see the Haxozin bodies flying out of the depressurizing bay.

"Get us out of here," ordered the captain.

In the viewports, space began to spin as the D Drive activated and jumped the ship into four-dimensional space. Areva averted her eyes from the dizzying view and looked at the floor.

A few seconds after that, the ship re-emerged into normal space.

They were safe.

* * *

It took the ship's computer about an hour to determine their exit point from D Drive and calculate the necessary travel plans to return them to Earth. Captain Withers used that time to debrief Areva, Chris, and Joyce and hold a staff meeting about what they'd discovered.

"So they're not actually interested in attacking us?" asked Matthias. "That's great!"

"Not *yet*," said Chris. "They're short-staffed, but once they get around to it, I think we can expect them to look for Earth."

"And when they do come, they'll come in force," said Joyce. "We saw the size of their fleet."

"Were they orbiting their homeworld?" asked Captain Withers. "That dead-looking planet?"

Areva sat slouched in her seat so that her head just barely peeked above the table, but she knew she should answer this one. "It's possible," she said. "They were bringing us to see their Sovereign, whoever that is. It would make sense for him to be at their base of operations."

"Wonder what they did to turn it so lifeless," the

captain said.

"Whether or not it is their base, it makes little difference," said Viktor. "We cannot fight them."

"No, but we can't just wait around for them to get ready for us, either," said Withers. "Especially now that they know for sure that we're out here."

"So what do we do?" asked Chris.

Withers placed his palms on the conference table. "If Dispatch takes my advice, the same thing we've been doing. We get out there and explore. We look for allies and try to liberate some more of their worlds. We keep an eye out for the Haxozin home, assuming we haven't already found it. And we keep Earth safe from them."

"Ooh," said Matthias, "that's like capture the flag!" When nobody agreed, he explained, "You know, we're looking for their base, but trying to protect our own at the same time, and whichever team finds the other team's base first wins, and ..."

"In any case," Withers interrupted, "I don't think we'll have to worry about any reprimands for what happened here today. With our new intelligence, Dispatch will want all hands out there looking for possible ways to defend ourselves. They'll be willing to overlook minor breaches of protocol."

"Yay!" said Matthias, which actually made the captain crack a smile.

Areva did not smile, and she didn't know if her breaches of protocol could be overlooked. Maybe Dispatch would ignore them, especially since Chris and Joyce seemed to think she'd overcome her neurosis about shooting.

But she couldn't ignore them.

Viktor invited her to his berth for a drink after the meeting, and she accompanied him with anxiety in her heart. She'd made her decision, and she knew that as her closest friend, he should be the first to know. She also knew it would hurt him, but she had to do what was best for everybody.

"To you," said Viktor, raising his glass in a toast after he'd poured them both a shot of vodka. "Based on what the Fishes said, you are quite a hero."

He downed his drink, but Areva set hers quietly on the table. "Viktor, I have to tell you something."

Her serious tone made him sit down in his desk chair. She remained standing. "What is it, Areva?"

She swallowed. "I couldn't do it."

"Do what?"

"What Chris Fish said, about taking out the guards who were escorting us out of the cell. I choked the first one out, but when it came time to shoot the second one … I couldn't do it. I couldn't pull the trigger."

"Right," said Viktor, "because you did not have time."

"I had plenty of time. I just couldn't do it. I looked straight into his helmet's faceplate, and I couldn't bring myself to shoot him."

Viktor exhaled slowly. "That is understandable."

"But it's not excusable!" Areva sank into a sitting position on the second chair. "If Chris hadn't killed the guy, we would have all died."

"Areva, it is all right. You are still here."

"And what about the next time? Or the time after that? I've been through three firefights in the past three months, and every single time, someone nearly died because I couldn't shoot an enemy in the face. I'm a liability, Viktor."

"That is not true!"

She sighed. "Did I ever tell you why I wound up on

the *Endurance*?"

"Da. You were in spec ops, and when you could no longer kill the way they wanted, they transferred you here."

"That wasn't completely true. They didn't transfer me." Areva took a deep breath. "I requested the move."

His eyebrows rose. "You asked to be placed here? On the ship where nobody wants to go?"

"I wanted it. I thought that being in a remote assignment, with little to no action, I could live with my eccentricities and yet still feel like I was making a difference." She looked at the floor. "And now our remote assignment has turned right back into the thick of things."

Viktor pulled his chair closer and took Areva's hands. "You will adapt to what is happening now. You simply need to trust yourself."

She shook her head. "I'm fighting against myself, and it doesn't make sense to keep doing that."

"Sometimes the most important things do not make sense. That does not mean we should give up."

Viktor spoke with an earnestness Areva had never heard from him before, and she looked up into his eyes in confusion. "What do you mean?"

"You put limitations on how you will fire a weapon, and yet you are a UELE officer. From the outside, this makes little sense, but from the inside, we see that you have done a lot of good." Viktor kept staring into Areva's eyes as he spoke, and she grew uncomfortable with the intensity, but she couldn't tear herself away as he continued. "You and I are very different, and yet our relationship is very deep. From the outside, this makes little sense, but from the inside …"

Areva feared where this conversation would lead.

Maybe a month ago she would have been happy to go there. But not now. She stood up, broke eye contact, and pulled her hands out of his grasp. "Viktor ..."

He stood and spoke quickly. "Areva, I ..."

"Viktor, I'm resigning from the UELE."

She stepped out of the room and turned down the corridor, not wanting to see his reaction, nor wanting him to see the tears threatening her eyes.

Book Four

Preferred Dead

The police didn't have a code for zombie infestations, so Lieutenant Ivanokoff made one up. "Captain, we have a large number of one-four-sevens who are one-twenty-three."

His EVA suit's intercom was silent for a moment, and then his commanding officer's voice filled his helmet. "Repeat that, Ivanokoff? It sounded like you reported a bunch of dead bodies being drunk and disorderly."

"That is correct."

More silence. Then, "Lieutenant, this is not a good time for jokes."

"I do not do jokes."

"Then explain why you just said there are dead people walking around out there."

"Because there are." Ivanokoff watched a corpse shamble past his hiding place in a fire-gutted building. Its milky pink eyes were sunken into its head, its skin stretched taut over dry bones, and the few remaining strings of its hair clung limply to its skull. The being had once looked something like a human, although it had a much larger nose, pale orange skin, and the vestiges of extra fingers on each hand, from which protruded thick, overgrown nails. It was an alien. A very dead alien.

Ivanokoff shifted his position to lean against the charred rock wall and keep his head out of sight from the street on the other side, a difficult task given his height and muscular build. "As far as I have seen, there are no living beings left on this planet. I believe their entire population was killed by whatever turned them into these—"

"Don't say zombies."

"Corpses. I was going to say corpses, Captain."

"And you're sure they're dead?"

"Yes. They do not produce any heat readings on scanners, and I saw one walking with a projectile wound in its torso. They are definitely dead."

He heard a sigh and knew Captain Withers was adjusting to this curveball. "Just once I'd like to encounter a normal planet," the captain muttered. "All right. So the entire species is dead. Any guesses about what killed them? Or why they're still, er, mobile?"

"No information yet. I will try to find a government building, which may have records on …" Ivanokoff heard movement on the other side of the wall and silenced himself. While he doubted his words would carry through the transparent faceplate of his helmet and he had the external speaker on his EVA suit turned off, he didn't want to attract the zombies' attention. He hadn't seen anything to suggest they were hostile, but caution had kept him alive in the past.

He peered over the damaged wall. On the other side, he spotted a female zombie who seemed to have crashed into the wall by accident. Blue scraps of fabric hung from her emaciated frame. She shook herself, looked quizzically at the remains of the building, and then turned ninety degrees to meander down the road.

Ivanokoff continued his conversation with the captain. "As I was saying, I will locate an official building to learn who these people are and why this happened to them. I saw a probable location a few blocks away, past what used to be a factory."

"All right. I'll have team two converge on your position to provide backup. Don't stay out too long, Lieutenant. Your suit only has a few hours of air left, and I don't want you breathing the atmosphere here in case it has something to do with what happened to the zombies."

"I thought you did not want to call them zombies."

"Shut up, Lieutenant."

* * *

On the United Earth Law Enforcement Starship *Endurance*, Captain Thomas Withers silenced the communication channel with the surface teams and turned to face the pair of suits standing behind his command chair. "We'll have a full briefing once they all get back. In the meantime ..."

"Your first officer seems to think he's a comedian, Captain," said the suit on the left in a snooty accent. Bradshaw, Thomas remembered his name. The man had a buzz cut and a mild twitch in his left eye that constantly drew Thomas's attention.

He tried not to look at it. "Believe me, he's no comedian. He's serious."

"He reported zombies. And you played along." Bradshaw took out his pocket computer, unfolded it, and made a note in a file. "This is not going to look well on your review."

Thomas folded his arms and flexed his own not-unimpressive muscles. He was no Ivanokoff, but he still knew how to look intimidating. "I know you Oversight and Investigations people don't get out of the home office very often, but this isn't a joke. My people don't give false reports. If he says there are dead people down there, then it's the truth."

"You'll forgive us if we're skeptical."

"No, I won't. We're dealing with things humanity never imagined existed. We're finding invaluable resources and technologies to bring home. That is the goal, isn't it?"

Bradshaw gave a noncommittal grunt.

"It's not easy being the first ship to leave the solar system. While Dispatch may not like everything we've done out here in the past few months, we're doing our best."

Bradshaw looked at the other suit and then back at Thomas. His good eye narrowed, while the twitchy one continued spasming. "Depending on how we grade you, you might not need to do your best any longer. I know your engineer invented the engine that allows four-dimension travel, but R&D has installed the devices on several other ships, with dozens more on the way." His lips formed a thin smile. "Soon, plenty of real officers will be out here exploring, and your unique status will no longer apply. So I suggest you impress me on this review,

Captain. Otherwise you'll shortly be returning to a nice, quiet patrol route around Neptune."

"Heh," said Bradshaw's partner.

Thomas's gut clenched. "They're a good crew, no matter what Dispatch says."

"Of course they are. That's why they're assigned to the Dead End-urance." Bradshaw didn't bother to lower his voice. A rookie officer at the scanners station looked up, offense coloring her face.

Thomas growled "follow me" at the two suits and ushered them into his coat-closet office to one side of the bridge. He banged the hatch shut behind them. "This ship may be the Dead End of the corps, but it's still mine, and they're still my crew. Screw ups or not, you're going to stop talking about them like they're not people."

Bradshaw looked supremely unimpressed. "Perhaps when they stop making up stories about zombies—"

"They're not making it up." Thomas's heart fluttered a moment as he hoped that was true. While he could name a few members of his crew he wouldn't believe if they reported the undead rising, Ivanokoff tended to be reliable and factual. The problem with him was that he might try to re-kill all the zombies single-handedly if one of them pissed him off.

Thomas pushed all of that anxiety away and raised his chin at the suits. "You'll see. With any luck, we'll figure out what did this to them and use it to discover some new branch of medical science. Bet Dispatch will love that." He forced a grin onto his face. "Might even have to give us a commendation."

Bradshaw glanced at his partner while the twitchy eye threatened to tear itself off his face and hop across the deck. "We'll see," he finally conceded. He then wrote something else down on his pocket comp and let himself and his partner back out onto the bridge without asking permission to leave.

Thomas glanced down at his desk, immaculately organized with his computer panel open in the middle, a photo of himself and his girlfriend in one corner, and a copy of *War and Peace* his first officer kept trying to get him to read in the other. "Don't screw this up, Ivanokoff," he muttered to the book.

* * *

"I think Areva's going to die first."

"No talking." Ivanokoff glared over his shoulder at the space-suited man following him past rows of rusting machinery. The factory had once produced some sort of carbon fiber reinforced polymer, formed into what appeared to be lightweight chassis for personal hover vehicles, and they passed multiple bins half-filled with the sculpted parts. The production lines stretched into shadow on either side, and dim light filtered in through dirty skylights. Overhead pipes and claws of automated machinery played tricks with the illumination and cast twisting patches of darkness on everything.

The speaker, Sergeant Chris Fish, had a pointy nose that nearly touched his helmet's faceplate and blond hair that looked unkempt even in the suit's controlled environment. "I'm just saying," he said in a lower tone, glancing through a mesh of twisting pipes to his left. "She's two days from retirement."

Behind the pipes, a humanoid shadow hunched as it followed them. "Eleven days," Areva said, her voice carrying through her spacesuit's speaker. "And it's not retirement. I quit."

"Same idea, though," said Chris.

"No, it's not."

"I'm just saying. You're supposed to be our security guard, and you're the most vulnerable."

"Horror movie logic isn't real."

"Tell that to the zombie that eats your bone marrow."

Areva hunched a bit more as she darted to the next bit of cover, though Ivanokoff knew it wasn't because of the gruesome mental image. She didn't like being in public.

He tried to avoid looking at her in those moments of visibility, despite the beauty of her dark hair curling around her ears and falling to shade her soft features. She was lovely, even if he'd never found the words to tell her so. Or the words to properly convey his respect for her marksmanship and espionage skills. Or the words for half a dozen other important thoughts he couldn't seem to express. No quote he'd read had ever seemed quite good enough.

"He has a point, Areva," Viktor said. "If you were not retiring, you would have less to fear."

"Not you too. We've been over this, Viktor. Just leave it alone."

Viktor had fought with Areva about her imminent departure from the corps at least half a dozen times, but she was convinced she didn't belong anymore. Something about her refusal to shoot any enemy who could see her coming. As if that mattered.

They rounded a freestanding wall of maintenance and diagnostic tools for the machinery. Everything hung neatly in place in spots delineated by taped outlines.

"Look," said Viktor, pointing to the tools. "They are organized. There was no panic when this happened."

"Or it happened at night and nobody was at work," said Chris.

Boom! In the darkness to the left, something heavy and metal crashed onto the concrete floor. All three jumped, and Viktor whipped his wristlight around, his other hand clasping the butt of his gun. The light glinted off the unrusted bits of the machines, showing him a row of huge, rounded structures that looked like ovens. The doors gaped open, daring him to investigate the darkness inside.

One second passed, then two. The echo of the crash died, and nothing else stirred in the silence.

Viktor finally relaxed. "Keep moving."

Chris Fish exhaled through his teeth. "What if it was a zombie?"

"We avoid going closer to it."

"What if it's following us?"

"We move faster."

Chris picked up his pace, heavy footfalls thumping on the factory floor. "Looks like this place was completely automated. These people were just as advanced as us. Maybe more. Too bad they're all dead. It'd have been great to collaborate with them."

"'Would have been is the enemy of is,'" said Viktor.

"Who said that?"

"Sekrin Nandor. Lunar philosopher, early twenty-second century."

"Yeah, well, 'would have been' is the friend of 'don't repeat what these people did to get their whole population killed.' I bet you anything the government is behind it. Some sort of conspiracy to implement mind control or make everyone live forever. They screwed up, and everybody died. If we want to survive, we have to be cautious. My wife and I, especially. No sex until we're away from this planet."

Despite his lifelong stoicism, Ivanokoff choked. "What?"

"Do neither of you watch old films? Having sex in a horror story is like a guaranteed death sentence. Especially if the couple is happy."

"Then you and your wife have nothing to fear."

"What's that supposed to mean? We're happy!"

"With each other, perhaps, but you berate the rest of us so often, I would not call you happy."

That silenced the scientist for a while, though he muttered, "Yeah, well, if I'm wrong and we find an ancient evil talisman that wakes the dead, I'm putting it in *your* backpack."

They made it halfway across the factory floor before another bang froze them. This time it came from the right, and it didn't stop. Another bang followed, then another, and a moment later hums and whirrs rose from all directions as the production lines came to life. Automated arms placed stripes of polymer tape crisscross on a thick metal mold. More arms lifted the completed structures and flew them overhead to slide smoothly into the black maws of the ovens. Foot-thick doors closed, and waves of heat rolled from the autoclaves as they baked the structures. Somewhere, Viktor imagined completed chassis being assembled into working hovercars that would never seat living passengers.

"This all still works!" said Chris. "You know what this means? Either this species was way better than us at building things, or they haven't been zombies for that long." He paused. "Or another species has been maintaining the machinery. Maybe all of this happened because some unknown people wanted to produce comfortable vehicles with virtually no overhead cost." He leaned over a series of display screens, still hypothesizing to himself.

From one moment to the next, Areva appeared at Viktor's side. "Do you think they did that on purpose? Turned everything on to scare us?"

Viktor watched the machines work, hand still on his gun. "No. The best time to ambush us would have been just after activating it. This was an accident."

"I hope so. I may not believe this 'two days from retirement' nonsense, but I don't want to die here."

"Neither do I. 'I have never died in all my life.'"

Areva thought for a moment. "Cervantes?"

"Da." He grinned at her. "I see you are making your way through my recommended reading."

"It helps me understand you. I'm just sorry I won't finish the books before I leave."

Something twisted in Ivanokoff's gut. "You can borrow them, if you wish. Return them when we see each other next."

"Really?"

"Or you could stay aboard longer. Postpone your resignation."

Areva went quiet, and he worried he'd upset her. She finally said, "'Before the government threw me over, I preferred to throw the government over.'"

He recognized the quote from the same book he'd just referenced. "They are not going to fire you, Areva."

"They should. I told you what happened on that Haxozin ship. They were looking at us, and I froze. If it weren't for Chris, they would have killed us."

"What?" called Chris from the back of the group. "If it weren't for Chris, what?"

"We would have much less inane conversation," Ivanokoff said.

"Oh, that reminds me, try not to sound too intelligent while we're here, because it will make your brain seem tastier. Can we get out of the haunted factory?"

Ivanokoff looked at Areva, hoping his words might have made her reconsider, but she'd disappeared behind a tool rack.

Viktor collected Fish, who had dismissed his economic takeover theory as "too probable" and had returned to postulations about government conspiracies. The trio picked their way toward the crumbling back wall of the factory without talking. Viktor kept his senses attuned to any irregular movement that might betray the presence of a zombie, but only the whirring and turning of the technology broke the stillness.

They reached a patch of wall that had rotted away, exposing metal support pylons and providing access to the outside. Viktor peered upward into the sunshine to where a towering skyscraper with an ornate rotunda sat prominently on its own concrete island encircled by roads.

Chris opened his mouth again. "See? Even on an alien world, the government is easy to find. I bet you anything they were responsible."

* * *

Thomas was in his office when somebody knocked on the door in the rhythm of a popular ad jingle. "Come in, Habassa," he called.

The ship's chief engineer came in, his immutable smile warming his copper-skinned face. "Hiya, Cap. Got a second?"

"Not really, I need to—" Thomas cut himself off as Matthias spun the chair opposite his desk and straddled it. "What's on your mind, Lieutenant?"

Matthias snatched a stylus from the desk and twirled it between his fingers. "I heard about these zombies."

Thomas closed his eyes and pinched the bridge of his nose. "They're not zombies, and how did you hear about them already?"

"Rupin told Natalie Chao when they switched shifts, and Natalie told Lee during her coffee break, and Lee told Grace, and she told me. Is it true? Are there zombies?"

If Thomas stayed tight-lipped, by the end of the day the whole ship would believe they'd found super-powered mutants with tentacles for hands, or worse. "There are ... unusual beings on the planet who appear to be dead," he said.

"Cool!"

"But there's no definite reason to believe they're actually deceased, or if they are, that they're, er ..."

"Undead?"

"Look, don't inflate this, Habassa. There's no such thing as the undead. It's a mortal coil, not a mortal yo-yo."

Matthias's smile shrank by approximately two millimeters before growing again. "But isn't a coil a spring? And those bounce back when you squash them, so according to your metaphor—"

"Lieutenant."

"Yes, Captain?"

"Stop."

"Sorry, Captain."

Thomas rose and paced toward the viewport currently revealing a metal wall of the warehouse where they'd hidden the *Endurance*. "The point is, we don't know what we're dealing with, and since the O&I people are here, I want to maintain professionalism."

Matthias nodded eagerly and tapped the pilfered stylus against the desk. "No problem. That's actually why I came up here. See, if these aliens actually are zombies ..."

Oh, good lord.

"... then maybe we can cure them."

That ... was actually an interesting idea. Thomas turned from the window and rubbed his chin thoughtfully. "What do you mean?"

"It's probably some kind of disease that did this to them, right?"

"I suppose."

"Well, diseases can be cured."

Thomas studied the engineer. Matthias had the energy and attention span of a caffeinated hamster, but the man was also a genius, single-handedly responsible for inventing interdimensional travel and deciphering the various technologies acquired from alien species. "Do you have any idea how to do that?"

"Not yet. But if we could get a sample of their blood, we could analyze what's in it."

"You're a chemist now?"

"I dabble, but the rest of my team can help. And Maureen's the medic, so I'm sure she'd want to be a part of this. Don't worry. She's been taking correspondence courses. She's learned a lot, I promise." Maureen Habassa was Matthias's sister, and where he built supercomputers out of spare parts for fun, she once diagnosed the entire ship with a dangerous contagion that turned out to be the common cold. She only held the chief medic's position because Dispatch didn't want to assign an actual physician to the ship.

"We'll see how it goes," Thomas said. "No promises, though. If the search team doesn't find evidence to suggest what caused this—"

"Zombieism?"

"—phenomenon, we're going to leave and let Dispatch decide whether to send another ship. That's procedure."

"Aw." Matthias dropped the stylus back on the desk. "Procedure's no fun."

Thomas smiled in spite of himself. Sometimes he was tempted to agree.

* * *

"This is a LOT of stairs," Chris said.

Viktor grunted and rounded the landing to continue up yet another flight. It really was a lot of stairs, though he'd never give Chris the pleasure of agreeing with him.

A whole flight ahead of them, Areva scouted ahead, using the bannister to keep out of sight.

"Couldn't these people have invented elevators before dying off?" Chris asked.

"We are almost there," said Viktor.

"How do you know?"

"Because Areva has stopped ahead. I can see her."

Areva squeaked in his earpiece. "Viktor, you should have *said* you could see me!" The exposed toe of her EV suit boot vanished behind the bannister to hide with the rest of her. "Better?"

"Yes," he said.

"Next time tell me sooner."

"I will. Next time." If there was a next time. If he could find the words to convince her to stay. Or even just to express how he felt.

They found Areva half-secluded behind a decaying bookshelf on the top floor of the rotunda. They'd started out by searching each floor of the building for rooms containing important records, but after three floors of nothing but vacant offices, they left the two backup teams to do that and headed for the top floor, intending to meet the other teams in the middle. Viktor reasoned the records would be kept either on the bottom floor, for easy access, or the top, to be ignored.

He was not disappointed. The third door on the left opened to a large room stacked floor-to-ceiling with shelves containing boxes of papers.

He held the door open for Chris and Areva. "Here. Look for the most recent—"

"Found it," Chris said, pointing to a box that had been hastily re-shelved next to a writing desk opposite the door. The box had split, and half the papers had spilled onto the floor. "It looks new, and whoever put it back was in a hurry."

Viktor hauled the box out and spread its contents on the desk. It took a moment before anyone voiced the imminent problem.

"How do we read it?" Chris asked.

Viktor stared at the unintelligible markings that could be letters, but could also be pictographs, for all he knew. "I am uncertain."

"Maybe they made audio recordings," Areva said. She'd taken refuge behind another stack of shelves.

"How will that help?" asked Chris.

"The talky box might be able to translate their verbal language."

Viktor shrugged. "It is worth a try."

They spent another several minutes wandering the room before they located a section of collections of light blue chips of glass. Beside each row of the glass sat a metal device with a slot the right size for the chips to be inserted. They retrieved one of the machines, picked a glass piece at random, and inserted it.

A second later, vocal chattering sprang out of the machine. Chris yanked the chip out of the slot. "It works."

Viktor nodded and tapped his helmet to activate his intercom. "Ivanokoff to all teams, we have found the records room. Proceed toward the top floor and meet us in the open room halfway down the hall."

Affirmations sounded in his ear, though Viktor didn't expect the other teams for quite a while.

It really was a lot of stairs.

"Prepare the talky box," he told Chris.

Chris retrieved the palm-sized cube from a pack strapped to his EV suit and set it down next to the audio player. Matthias Habassa had taken it apart and figured out how to duplicate the technology, but nobody was entirely sure how the software inside the talky box managed to translate between languages so rapidly and fluidly. But it worked, so they just copied the program to each new box and hoped for the best.

Viktor picked another chip out of the tray and inserted it into the alien player. The chattering started up again, but this time the talky box provided a running translation through their intercoms.

"Wogogo Palunu is a child and a fool! True citizens of Thassis will cast their vote for Pogogo Dulayu, a real patriot and protector of—"

Viktor removed the chip. "Campaign ads."

"At least we know the name of their planet now," said Chris. "Thassis. Sounds like the sort of place zombies would devour a team of explorers, doesn't it? Thassssss-isssss. Like a snake. Hey, do you think they eat their victims alive, or—"

Viktor inserted another chip.

It was the same voice as before. "I told them, I did, that Wogogo would be the end of our society. Did anyone listen to me? No. Now his administration is keeping who knows what secrets from the Thassian public, but we have a right to know! If it is to be the end of our people, we must face it squarely."

He removed the chip.

"Sounds like Wogogo screwed up," said Areva.

"You don't know that," said Chris. "Maybe Pogogo is just running a smear campaign. I didn't hear him offering any better suggestions."

"I hope you realize you are taking sides in an alien political debate," Viktor said. He picked the last chip in the tray and inserted it into the player.

This time a different, deeper voice boomed out of the speaker. "It is with great regret that I must announce that the recent plague is the direct result of government fallibility. For reasons I hope are clear to most of you, we had no choice. I apologize for those breathing in this air who do not understand why this is happening, but this is the way it must be. Do not resist; it will be easier that way. This is Chief Administrator Wogogo Palunu, wishing you a peaceful transition."

The recording ran out. A click announced the end of the data on the chip.

All three humans were silent for a moment.

"So it was the government," Areva said softly.

"Yes. Fish, for once your conspiracies were correct," said Viktor.

Chris frowned through his faceplate. "I'm not so sure."

"What?"

"If it was a conspiracy, why go public with it? You don't just expose all your secrets like that."

"They were all about to die," said Viktor.

"Which just means history doesn't need to remember how badly you screwed up. If you're hiding something, there's no reason to admit it at the end. Especially when the people you hurt are about to become flesh-tearing monsters."

"Maybe he felt guilty," said Areva.

"A politician? Never."

Viktor snorted.

"I'm just saying," Chris said. "It doesn't make sense. Play some of the ones in the middle. That might clear all of this up."

Viktor returned the last chip to its storage slot and was about to pick one a few rows before it when something thumped near the door.

All three officers jumped to their feet. Areva disappeared behind a desk. Viktor knew she'd already have her service weapon out and armed.

Chris slunk behind Viktor. "Oh no."

"Stay calm," Viktor said. He tapped his intercom. "Backup teams, report your locations."

Nothing but static.

He tried again, but the intercom had gone dead.

Chris moaned. "We're gonna die. I'm never going to kiss my wife again."

"Be glad you have kissed even once," Viktor said, glancing toward Areva's hiding place. "Now silence yourself. They may track their prey through sound."

He had no idea whether that was true, but it would make Chris shut up, which was motive enough to say it. The scientist clamped both hands over the faceplate on his helmet, for all the good that would do, and said nothing else.

They held completely still as another thump sounded from the shelves one row over. Something was coming down the aisle, bumping into boxes of papers as it walked. Crash! Folders and files spilled. Smash! Audio chips flew into the air and shattered on the wooden floor. The cacophony was even with their position now, on the opposite side of the shelves.

Viktor edged toward the dividing shelf. There was a small space between the boxes. If he could look through, he could see what they were facing.

A flash of stringy hair, a pattering of bare feet as something flashed by the space.

Viktor let out a slow breath. It was just one zombie.

He turned to tell the others everything was all right.

"Viktor!"

Areva's scream and pointed finger wrenched his attention behind himself.

The bookshelf was falling. Boxes split and files flew in every direction as the enormous shelving unit leaned precariously over Viktor's head, tipping slowly toward that point of inevitable collapse.

He dove toward Chris and Areva. "Run!"

They fled, hopping over fallen boxes and dodging shards of glass as the shelf crashed against its twin on their other side. The wooden beams groaned under the impact, and then planks of broken wood joined the rain of other detritus. Chris held the talky box over his head like a shield while Viktor grabbed the scientist by the arm and pulled him faster after Areva.

The second shelf began to fall as well, and soon the entire room became a blur of thunder as everything broke and crumbled around them. The distance to the end of the aisle seemed longer than it had before, and Viktor risked a glance upward to see if they could make it out before being crushed to death.

The zombie was on the ceiling.

Unfair.

It wasn't just hanging onto the ceiling fixtures, but clinging to the decaying roof itself, apparently with the long-nailed extra digits of its hands and bare feet. It scrambled after them, vacant eyes staring down, mouth open to reveal rows of sharp incisors.

Even more unfair.

Tumbling boxes and trays of glass slips hailed around them, and the shelf loomed only a few feet overhead as Areva cleared the end of the aisle. Viktor shoved Chris stumbling after her. He dove forward, arms outstretched, and hoped his lower body cleared the wreckage before his legs were crushed.

He overshot.

As the bookshelf's impact shook the floor, Viktor banged his helmet on the opposite wall and brought his flight to an abrupt and painful stop. He grunted, but he would not tarnish the impressiveness of what he'd just done by saying "ow."

Areva was there the moment he sat up, her gloved hands fussing about his helmet. "Are you all right, Viktor?"

"Yes."

"You hit your head."

"Not badly."

"Too bad," Chris muttered. "Might've given you a sense of humor."

Viktor ignored that and pushed himself up to survey the aftermath. Every shelf had fallen, and the shaking it gave the room had caused some of the ceiling to cave in on top of what was left. An enormous pile of scattered files, splintered wood, and broken glass blocked their way back to the stairs.

"Huh," said Chris. "I guess we have to find the emergency exit."

Viktor checked his EV suit's monitors. One hour of air left.

He lagged behind the others and chanced a second look at the ceiling. Only gouges in the wood remained. The fanged zombie was gone.

* * *

After reporting their predicament and ordering the other teams to return to the ship, they took the back exit from the library, which led to a maintenance catwalk. Rusted railings lined the metal mesh walkway, which was suspended a few feet above a damp concrete floor. A dull light filtered through cracks in the walls and ceiling.

At the back of the group, Areva said, "Ooh." Both men turned.

"No, don't look at me. Look up."

Viktor did.

They were in the rotunda. Overhead, metal trusses crisscrossed to form a lattice supporting an enormous, high dome. Though a few patches had worn through from time and weather, the skin was mostly intact, and consisted of only four large sheets welded together over the superstructure. This planet's industrial capacity had to have been enormous to create and move such large panels.

Chris whistled. "How many people do you think it took to build that thing?"

"Many," said Viktor.

"Bet some of them died in the process and haunt this building."

"If so, they are fortunate to have escaped the zombie plague."

Chris didn't have an answer for that. Viktor smirked in his helmet.

He led the way along the catwalk to a zigzagging set of metal stairs that ended about three floors up in another catwalk that circled the inside of the rotunda. He pointed across the space to the far side of the dome. "There. Another set of stairs. We will take the catwalk around and climb down those to return to the main building."

"Best hurry," said Chris. "Forty-seven minutes."

They mounted the stairs in good time and circumnavigated a quarter of the dome before Viktor glanced back and saw that Areva had frozen. "What is it?"

"I heard something," she whispered.

Chris leaned over the railing and peered at the murky floor below. "Rats? Ghosts?"

"Footsteps."

Viktor's heart skipped a beat. "The library. The corpses heard the shelves fall. Move faster."

They ran toward the escape stairs, spacesuits pounding the metal floor in rhythm—thump, thump, thump. Viktor's heart beat the same tempo, and his eyes darted here and there, scanning for signs of danger. He made sure to check the rotunda roof as well; he would not be ambushed again.

Halfway there, he slid to a halt, staring at the path ahead.

A section of the catwalk had fallen away, corroded too badly to hold its own weight.

Worse, he could now hear the footsteps, too.

Chris spotted the broken flooring and swore. "Can we jump that?"

"I can," said Areva.

"I do not know," said Viktor.

"If you can't, I definitely can't," said Chris.

Pound, pound went the footsteps behind them. Fearing what he'd see, Viktor glanced over his shoulder.

Shadows moved near the base of the stairs from which they'd come.

People.

Lots of them.

Viktor tried to ignore the dryness in his mouth and the fear hammering against his ribs, and peered into the darkness ahead. At the foot of their escape stairs, more shadows twisted and jumped.

Both sides, cut off.

His hands formed fists. "We are trapped."

Chris gulped and made a whimpering sound in the process. "Oh, come on! I'm not supposed to die like th— hey, what's that?"

Viktor turned toward the scientist's voice and found him pushing against a door recessed into the skin of the rotunda.

His heart leapt again. They had another way out. He whacked his intercom interface. "Ivanokoff to *Endurance*, engage engines and head toward us. We are going onto the roof."

The captain's voice cracked through his ear. "Repeat, Ivanokoff?"

"The zombies have cut us off. We are going outside. Pick us up atop the building."

He didn't hear the captain's reply, as Chris screamed a swear. "It's locked! Quick, Areva, kick it down."

"I can't," she said.

"Sure you can! If you don't, we're going to be eaten alive, so at least try to—"

Areva didn't answer, but pointed at the hinges of the door. The *interior-mounted* hinges of the door.

"Oh," said Chris, and he pulled his standard issue utility knife from his suit pocket and began prying out the hinges.

"Two minutes, Captain," Ivanokoff advised.

Static answered him.

Viktor frowned and re-tapped his intercom. "Captain?"

"I warned you guys," Chris said, "but nobody wants to be genre savvy." He finished prying out the hinges and shoved the door from its housing.

Empty sky loomed on the other side, beckoning from across a ledge just wide enough for one person to walk.

Viktor glanced back. The roiling zombie hordes had made it up the stairs to shamble along the catwalk. He could see the ragged clothes and gaping mouths of those in the front. If their eyes had been alive, he'd soon see the whites.

"Go," he ordered, and Chris skittered out onto the ledge. Areva followed, then Viktor.

Viktor's enormous size gave him the most trouble picking his way along the narrow ledge. Chris kept a hand on the rotunda and walked in almost a straight line, well away from the edge. Areva navigated the treacherous space with ease, her footing sure. Viktor, in contrast, felt like half his body was already sticking out over the edge. He regretted some of his exercise regimen. Fewer muscles and more balance would have served him better here.

The first wave of zombies poured through the open door behind them. Heedless of the perilous drop, they ran along the ledge after the escaping humans, or dug their long nails into the rotunda and clawed along like insects. A few fell in the crush, but they latched on below and climbed back up.

"Faster!" Viktor ordered, but no sooner had he spoken than Chris came to an abrupt halt, arms flung wide to arrest his momentum.

"Go back!" he screamed as more zombies poured through a hole in the rotunda.

Viktor scanned the horizon for any sign of the *Endurance*, but saw nothing. He swallowed and drew his two personalized guns from his belt. He would not surrender. "Scientist, get between us. Areva, fire at—"

"They're looking, Viktor."

"No. They are dead. They cannot look."

Areva drew her service weapon and aimed it at the encroaching horde. "Already dead," she muttered to herself. "Already dead."

Viktor set his weapons to rapid fire mode and leveled them at the decaying bodies closing in. "These are my guns, Dickens and Dante. Welcome to the inferno."

"Dammit, Ivanokoff!" said Chris. "You can't spout cool catchphrases and survive! Am I the *only* one who's seen a zombie movie?"

"Yes," said Viktor.

He opened fire.

Dickens and Dante spewed a dozen tiny projectiles every second. The grips warmed in Ivanokoff's hands, but he kept firing. Wave after wave of zombies swarmed toward them, and wave after wave stumbled back under his assault. Many tumbled off the ledge, but more simply blinked at the holes in their bodies and resumed the attack. His wrists began to ache from the relentless firing and the weapons' kickbacks, but he gritted his teeth and continued tapping the trigger panels as fast as he could. No need to aim; enemies were everywhere.

Behind him, he heard Areva firing just as rapidly, and the scientist shooting haphazardly and spewing a curse for every bullet he spent.

Three meters divided them and the horde.

Then two.

Then one.

Still no sign of the ship.

We cannot win, Ivanokoff thought. He had never put those words together in that order before, but they were true. Against a foe who shook off weapons fire and attacked in limitless numbers, he and his two allies stood no chance.

Still he kept firing.

He didn't see the ambush until it was too late. A hand lurched out from beneath the ledge and grabbed his ankle. He stumbled and aimed downward to fire at his assailant. One of the zombies had used the ledge as cover to crawl all the way to them unseen.

His shots severed the zombie's arm, freeing his leg, but the horde seized the opportunity to swarm over him, pressing him back and dragging him down with the sheer weight of their bodies. Chris screamed and Areva shouted. Viktor's back hit the concrete ledge and he nearly rolled off, but more zombies crawled up from below and shoved him back. One of them dove onto on his helmet, blocking out his sight. Though he strained until fire burned in his muscles, he couldn't budge. Still they kept piling on.

As mounting pressure from the pile crushed the air from his lungs, Viktor had one thought:

That zombie had planned its stealth attack.

These things could think.

* * *

He woke on a table.

He sat up in panic, Chris's warnings of cannibalism echoing in his mind, but he quickly realized this was an examination room, not a dining room.

Areva and Chris were already awake, the former hiding under an identical metal table against a wall, the latter pacing the area before the only door in the small, windowless room. The floor was chipped tile, the walls a generic shade of tan, and a counter topped with dozens of sealed containers lined one wall.

"A hospital," Viktor said. "This is a hospital." He realized his two companions still wore their spacesuits and checked to make sure his own helmet was still sealed. Then, afraid of what he might see, he looked at his wrist monitor.

Eight minutes of clean air.

"We are so dead," Chris said. "They're going to eat us."

"You said that the last time we were captured by aliens," said Areva.

"I know, but this time I mean it. They brought us to a hospital, as our good catchphrase-spewing tank so intuitively informed us. They're going to make sure we don't have any hideous diseases, and then eat us."

"Or," said Viktor, "they do not know what we are, and brought us here to investigate."

"Great. Death by dissection instead of digestion. That's so much better."

Viktor rolled his eyes and hopped off the table to study the room's contents. The jars on the counter were of a strange, twisting design probably unique to this culture, but they were all empty, a few of them shattered or their airtight seals popped.

"They were kind of like us, weren't they?" Areva said from her hiding place.

"Yes."

Chris waved his hands. "If you're about to suggest that this could happen on Earth, then I've beaten you there. In fact, back in 2063, something like this almost—"

The door in front of Chris opened, and a quintet of zombies shambled in.

The scientist leapt backward with such force that he upended one of the metal tables. "Gyah! I'm not tasty! Eat Ivanokoff; his brain's full of literature!"

Viktor strode forward and positioned himself between Chris and the zombies. The leader of the undead had been a tall man, a little portly, with liver spots on his bald orange head. The remnants of some sort of tan jumpsuit clung to his frame, with multiple pockets on both breasts and hips. Various tools protruded from the pockets, including something that looked vaguely like a stethoscope.

"You are a doctor," Viktor said to the alien zombie. It didn't appear to understand. And why would it? "Fish, get the talky box."

Chris scrambled at his suit for several seconds before he found the box. "Tell them we taste like asparagus."

"What if they like asparagus?" asked Areva.

"Enough!" said Viktor, whirling on Chris. "You have a PhD and a commission from the UELE. If any of us is qualified to figure out how to reach these people, it is you. Help, or shut up."

Chris froze in shock. Then his terrified expression melted into indignation, as Viktor had known it would. "No need to yell at me, Lieutenant. One of us has to be the voice of reason here." He brandished the talky box and took a step forward, though he stayed well behind Viktor. "Hey, uh, zombies. Mind if we walk out of here?"

He mimed walking toward the door, then slapped his forehead and actually walked toward the door. However, one of the zombies stopped him, placing a dead hand on his suit. Chris flinched away, but to his credit, did not run screaming into a corner.

"Okay, then can you turn off whatever's blocking our communications?" He pointed to the area of his suit helmet that contained the non-working intercom. "In-ter-coms. We want to talk to our people. We're kind of running out of air, and while you all wear the grave look wonderfully, it would look terrible on us."

Viktor checked his monitor. "Five minutes."

"Yes! Pressure makes things magically go faster!" Chris's lip curled. "I swear they tell you that in command school. Don't deny it."

Movement in the back of the zombie group caught Viktor's attention. While all five seemed content to simply stare at their captives, the two in the rear were not entirely motionless. One of them had been another doctor, presumably, since she wore the same tan jumpsuit as the leader. The other looked like he'd been wearing some sort of professional attire, multiple layers of expensive-looking fabric.

They were holding hands.

Viktor might have assumed their dead fingers got tangled together by accident, were it not for the way they mingled their hands, thumbs rubbing against each other in a gentle, comforting gesture.

He knew that kind of movement. He'd tried to use it on more than one occasion to communicate to Areva what he could not seem to find words to say.

This changed everything.

"Sergeant," he said to Chris, who was still babbling to the lead zombie, "look."

Chris took notice of the hand-holding zombies. His mouth dropped open. "Oh. Oh my."

"What is it?" asked Areva.

"The two in back," said Viktor.

A pause. A gasp. "They're holding hands."

"They still have feelings," said Chris. Viktor watched the change in demeanor as his inner scientific curiosity took over his fear. He stepped forward, right between some of the zombies, to the two lovers. "Can you understand me?" He held up the box, which translated his words into the alien language from the library.

They stared blankly at him. Their interlaced fingers tightened.

Then, slowly, the female one nodded.

Chris leaned forward. "Do you know what's happened to you?"

Blank stares.

"We think this undead thing was caused by your air. So you see, we can't stay here. Our suits are about to run out of oxygen. We have to return to our ship." To highlight his point, he waved to the numbers counting down on his arm display. Four minutes.

Pause.

The zombies all shook their heads.

"Uh, no, see, we don't have a choice here. We need to leave, right now."

Shake, shake.

Viktor strode forward. "Move."

More shaking.

Three minutes.

A movement to Viktor's left caught his attention. Areva was trying to take advantage of the conversation's distraction to slip past the zombies. The second she tried to pass through the door, the lovers in the back grabbed her and forced her to retreat.

Viktor flexed his arms. There was no more time. "We will not be captives. Release us. Now."

Shake, shake.

That left no choice. Without Dickens and Dante, Viktor felt far less confident of victory, but the guns hadn't exactly helped on the rooftop. He popped his knuckles. "'Once more unto the breach.'"

He grabbed the lead doctor by the collar and threw him across the room.

Two minutes.

The zombie doctor crashed through one of the metal tables, but before Viktor could remove another alien from his path, the remaining four swarmed him, as they had on the roof, each one taking a limb and using their entire body weight to pin it in place. He struggled through a few halting steps, but then the doctor leapt up. Areva lunged onto the back of one of the zombies holding Viktor's legs and began strangling it. The zombie didn't even notice his lack of airflow. She snaked her arm through his and twisted her hips to pry him off Viktor. The zombie smashed to the floor, and Areva followed, but just as quickly the undead man tried to fight his way back. Chris Fish grabbed the empty jars from the table and threw them at the walking corpses, but even when the glass shattered against their skulls, they barely flinched.

The lead doctor righted himself and grabbed the stethoscope-like object from his pocket. He banged it on the metal tables, sending clanging sounds echoing through the walls and shaking the floor. Backup would be coming immediately, Viktor knew. Even if they abandoned him, Chris and Areva wouldn't get far. "Go!" he shouted.

The scientist bolted out the door, but Areva shook her head, still valiantly holding the zombie away from him. "I won't leave you."

One minute.

The doctor zombie came to stand before Viktor, ignoring Areva and the escaping Chris.

A scream sounded from the hall. The scientist had been caught. "No, no, don't do that!"

The doctor paid the noise no mind. He blinked dead pink eyes at Viktor's face, then reached up to fiddle with the clasps binding his helmet to his EV suit.

"No!" Viktor choked, fighting to free his limbs. The zombies' wispy frames belied their strength. "No, the air is …"

Click.

Shhhhhhhhh.

Viktor gasped as the planet's atmosphere seeped into his helmet and filled his lungs.

* * *

"Your people are dead."

Thomas's dark complexion darkened further at the O&I man's bluntness. "You don't know that."

"They were captured by the planet's inhabitants," said Bradshaw, eye twitching away. "Surely you don't dispute that. You heard the reports from the other two teams. There was evidence of battle on that rooftop."

"Yes, but captivity doesn't equal lost in my book. They might still be alive."

"Their suits' air supplies will have run out by now. Even if they survived the fight on the rotunda, they've inhaled whatever is in the atmosphere."

"We're working on a cure for that." Thomas wasn't technically lying; teams two and three had procured several samples of DNA from the dismembered zombie parts on the rooftop and ground below. His people were studying them on the middle deck at that very moment.

"Dispatch is awaiting your report, Captain," said Bradshaw. "According to procedure, you should cut your losses and return home."

"Tell me, which subsection of the police code covers zombie infestations? I missed it at the academy."

"Your sarcasm is a blunt weapon. My point stands."

"So does mine." Thomas rose from his chair in the center of the bridge, conscious of the eyes of his three bridge crew members. "I'm not leaving my people behind until I know what's happened to them."

"This will reflect badly on you in our report," said Bradshaw.

"I'm sure it will." Thomas straightened his uniform shirt and strode toward the hatch that led to the corridor. "Now, if you'll excuse me, I'm going to check on actual solutions to our problems."

He found Matthias and Maureen Habassa in one of the labs on deck two, with three scientists, two engineers, and for some reason, the ship's janitor. "Mr. Cleaver," he said, nodding to Archibald.

The ancient janitor waved a liver-spotted hand at Thomas. At his side lurked his equally antiquated vacuum cleaner, stinking of must and industrial soap. "Cap'n. Just helping Mattie with some figurin'."

"Arch is great at calculus," said Matthias. "I've got him double-checking my automated math on some of these reactions we're doing with the mitochondrial—"

Thomas held up a hand. "I don't need the details. Just tell me if we have a chance of curing this thing. Ivanokoff, Fish, and Praphasat have been out for twenty minutes longer than their air supply, and from their reports, this plague might be in the atmosphere."

A woman across the room laughed. She had a dark complexion and short curls of hair and sported a three-stripe science patch on her uniform sleeve. "Don't worry. My husband will refuse to breathe out of sheer stubbornness." Joyce Fish finished whatever she was doing with a bunch of phials and a microscope and came over to join the group. Her brazen humor faded as she asked, "Is ... is there any word from them?"

"Not yet," Thomas said. "We're monitoring all channels and sending a constant ping to each of their radios. If they come back into receiving range, we'll find them. And if they come with friends, I'd like to have a way to deal with them."

The chief engineer grinned at him. "Actually, we're there! I mean, not *there* there, but we've got a working idea of what happened here."

He waved at Joyce, who folded her arms as she spoke. "These aliens are physically dead. From what we've seen in the tissue samples, their cells don't process oxygen anymore. They don't need to breathe, eat, drink, or sleep, and we don't think they can reproduce."

"That's still gross," muttered Maureen Habassa.

"But we can't tell if this is reversible unless we examine a whole zombie. We're theorizing that their brains still have some neurons firing to account for them being, well, mobile."

"Neurons," said Thomas. "They can still think?"

"Yes. Most likely at a very basic level. If we could observe that process, we might be able to learn more about how that system stayed active despite the body ceasing to function."

Thomas chewed his lip. "Good work. Keep on it. I'll check in again once we locate our missing people, but don't count on getting one of the zombies to inspect. I don't want to bring one aboard if we can avoid it."

He headed back to the bridge, bracing himself to tangle with the O&I suits again. He hoped that when they found their people, they wouldn't *be* the zombies to be brought aboard.

* * *

Chris Fish paced faster than a racing hover on a straightaway. "How long?" he asked for the eighty-fourth time.

"Twenty-five minutes," said Viktor from his seat on the floor, leaning against the wall.

"You didn't even check the chronometer!"

"You last asked only seconds ago. It is still twenty-five minutes."

Their spacesuits lay abandoned in a pile next to one of the upended metal tables. Viktor breathed the planet's air, wondering if even now it was rewiring his body, causing untold horrors to his internal organs. He wasn't a biologist; he had no idea how long it would take for the zombie plague to take effect. But so far, despite the initial panic all three had felt when their air ran out and the zombies removed their helmets, they seemed fine.

Areva crouched almost out of sight behind one of the tables, but from time to time her hand would reach out, pull one of the suit's wrist monitors to herself, and check it.

"Twenty-six," she said.

Ivanokoff ignored Chris's huff of indignation. "How do you both feel?" he asked.

"Fine," said Areva.

"Nauseous," said Chris. "On the brink of hyperventilation. Bad headache. I think it's starting to affect me." He shivered and rubbed his arms, despite the blue UELE uniform providing more than enough warmth in the temperature-controlled room. "If it takes me, if I start to turn, what do you plan to do?"

"Kill you," said Ivanokoff without missing a beat.

The scientist's horrified expression made him laugh.

Chris's face melted into indignation. "That was mean."

"Yes." Viktor stifled his chuckles and shook his head. "The zombies have not harmed us. If we turn, we will not become hostile."

"Maybe I won't, but both of you are trained killers!" Chris said. "How do I know your baser instincts won't suddenly take over and make you try to eat my delicious, science-filled brain?"

"You told them to eat my brain for its literary knowledge."

"I'm serious!"

"We will not eat your brain, Sergeant." Viktor wondered what *would* happen if zombieism brought out his suppressed instincts. He doubted he'd attack anyone. More likely, he and Areva would wind up like that hand-holding couple from the group of doctors. He smiled. As zombie plagues went, that might not be so bad.

On the topic of the zombie doctors, Viktor wondered where they had gone. After ensuring the three had ample time to breathe the planet's air, the doctors hung around to watch them for ten minutes or so, before wandering from the room. They'd heard the magnetic lock on the door buzz, trapping them inside.

Chris paced to the door and tried the handle for the forty-seventh time. "They're waiting for it to take us," he said. "I just know it."

"If we were going to turn, wouldn't we have started already?" Areva asked. "We're not the same species as them. Maybe we're immune. That could be why they locked us in here, to see if we're unaffected."

"If so," said Viktor, "that may be why they captured us. If we are immune, they may wish to make themselves the same."

"Great," said Chris. "We're back to the dissection theory."

"They may simply ask for help," said Viktor.

"What is it with you people being so optimistic? It's like I'm working with a roomful of Matthiases here."

The magnetic lock on the door stopped humming. Viktor rose. A moment later, the liver-spotted zombie doctor entered and shut the door behind him. The humming lock resumed.

"What do you want?" Viktor asked. The zombies had left the talky box on the counter to translate their words.

It took several seconds, but the doctor appeared to understand. He pointed to all three of them, then to himself, and then waved his hand between them in a negative gesture. The effort at communication appeared to strain his capacities.

"Correct," said Chris, "we're not like you. We don't want to become like you, so please let us go back to our ship."

Blank stare.

"Our *ship*. Shiiiiiip." Chris pointed up and mimed flying.

Still no clear sign of comprehension, but one of the doctor's hands drifted up to point a claw at the roof.

"Up?" Viktor asked. "The ship is here?"

More blank staring.

"The shiiiiiip," said Chris, flapping his arms like wings, "is a-bo-ve us." He pointed up, eyes wide, head nodding.

The zombie stared some more, then made another negative gesture with his hand.

"Not the ship," said Viktor. "Something else is above us?"

Relief spread on the zombie's face, and he nodded.

"Right, the thing that made you undead," Chris said.

Negative.

"No, you didn't understand. The thing that made you all into zombies, it's in your air."

Negative, this time more forceful. Something glimmered in the doctor's vacant eyes. Viktor sensed that he was trying very hard to make a point. Given the absent-mindedness inherent in the others, it must be taking all he had to focus. They might not have long before he forgot what he was doing here and wandered away again.

"You pointed up," said Viktor, doing so. "That was to show that you breathed in the disease?"

Nod.

"So you are corpses because of something in the air."

Negative.

Chris threw up his hands. "This makes no sense."

Viktor's frown deepened. "If not in the air, where is it?"

That sentence proved too complicated for the zombie, so Viktor ran through a litany of possibilities. "Are you zombies because of your food?"

Negative.

"Radiation?"

Negative.

"Water?"

Negative.

"Infection?"

Pause. The zombie lifted his elbows in an uncertain motion.

"Was it a disease?"

Negative.

"An accident?"

Negative. Forceful negative.

"You infected yourselves on purpose?"

Nod.

Excitement began to pump through Viktor as he gathered momentum. There was more to this story than they had assumed. "Your government claimed responsibility. Did they organize the infection of your people?"

Nod.

"You are a doctor. Was it a medical treatment?"

Nod.

"An injection?"

Nod.

"If you injected the infection that killed you, then what is in the air?"

Negative, nod, negative. Frustration creased the doctor's sallow, tattered face.

"Does he mean there are two plagues?" Areva's voice asked from behind the table.

Chris stopped his pacing, one finger poised in the air, mouth open. "There are *two* plagues!"

"I just said that," said Areva.

Viktor, now thoroughly intrigued, approached the doctor. "Is the problem in the air related to your people being undead?"

A pause. Then a nod.

"Did one problem lead to the other?"

Negative.

"But they interact in some way."

Nod.

Chris fluttered his hands excitedly. "And you're holding us to see if the thing in the *air* is affecting us!" He mimed breathing, then pointed to his companions.

Nod.

A slow breath seeped through Viktor's lips. "That is it. They are confused because we have not died from the air, and they want our immunity." He did his best to use gestures to communicate this to the doctor.

Nod, nod, nod.

Pieces of the information they'd gathered fell together in Viktor's mind. He turned to Chris and the table hiding Areva. "The recording we found stated that the plague was the result of government fallibility, but he did not say which plague he meant. Perhaps the government made an error that caused the problem in the air, and they distributed the zombieism to combat it."

"Dumb way to do that," said Chris. "Dying doesn't really solve a plague."

Viktor held up a hand. "What is the most important mechanism on the *Endurance*?"

"The coffee maker," said Chris at once.

"No."

"The D Drive."

"No."

"Archibald's vacuum cleaner."

"No. The air recycler."

Chris huffed. "Technically that's a subsystem of the environmental mechanism, which is interdependent with …"

"The air recycler allows us to live on the ship," Ivanokoff continued. "It filters contamination, the way trees do on planets."

"Look who passed high school biology," Chris said.

"Whatever contagion is in the atmosphere, their trees could not correct it. What would happen then, if the air was bad and the people had to breathe it?"

"They'd die," said Areva, poking her head around the edge of the table in curiosity.

"Death by disease," Chris said. "Thanks, I needed another pleasant outcome to consider."

"Correct," said Ivanokoff. "Now suppose the people did not need to breathe …"

Chris's eyes widened. "They could go on living, even on a contaminated world!"

"Da."

"The mayor was apologizing for whatever situation brought about the air problem, not the zombieism. They had everyone injected with the zombie virus to protect them!"

"By killing them," said Areva's voice, her face hidden once more.

"They still have emotions, and some semblance of society," said Chris. "That's better than mass extinction." Now heedless of his germophobia, he grabbed the doctor's arm. "We're immune to whatever's in your air! Don't give us the zombie drug!"

The doctor merely blinked at them, apparently content to let them talk. Maybe he'd already forgotten why he came.

"Good," said Chris, letting go of the zombie. "Now, time for solutions. If we get a few samples of atmospheric content, we might be able to fix their air, and then we can reverse the zombieism and set this entire planet back to normal. How's O&I gonna like *that*?"

"I don't think they will," said Areva.

"Decidedly not," Viktor agreed.

Chris sighed. "The two of you have the combined sense of humor of a nihilist joke book."

"Thank you," said Viktor.

"That wasn't a compliment."

"You have clearly not read a nihilist joke book."

Chris waved his hands. "Whatever. The point is, we know what we're dealing with, and we can do something about it." He grinned broadly at the zombie. "So how about it, Doctor Decay? Can we go back to our ship and try to fix your society?"

* * *

Thomas grew tired of his O&I shadows, but he didn't think it would help their report if he confined them to their berths.

Matthias had asked to fiddle with some bridge controls to scan for their missing people. Now half an entire console lay in pieces on the floor, and Thomas could hear the two suits making scathing notes on their pocket comps behind him.

"Whoops, that shouldn't be wired like that." Matthias's chipper voice filled the bridge, only slightly muffled by his position beneath the console. Something went *zap*, and something on the other side of the bridge went *fzzzzBANG*! The engineer emerged, grinning. "Fixed it. You know, I bet with enough rewiring, I could make these things detect the cold bodies of those undead people. Could prob'ly make it find ghosts with enough experimentation."

Tap, tap went the two suits' note-taking fingers.

Thomas tried to ignore them. "There's no such thing as ghosts, Lieutenant."

"Sure there are, Cap!" Matthias bounced to his feet. "When I was a kid, my family went to stay in these ruins of this ancient pyramid—one of those package tourist trips, you know—and I got up to use the bathroom in the middle of the night, and on my way back in, I heard these footsteps coming from inside the room where we were all sleeping, so I hid. The footsteps stopped, but when I got back to the main room, *no one was there*."

"Your family was gone?"

"No, no, they were there. But no one else was. So …" Matthias widened his eyes, and his voice dropped to a spooky hush. "Who was making those footsteps?"

Thomas was spared from having to answer that question when an alert message began flashing on one of the bridge consoles. "One of the EVA suits just pinged."

The officer currently stationed at scanners slid her chair back into position and brought up her displays of the area outside the warehouse. "It just appeared, sir. Probably left a building shielded by a jamming field to block radio signals. Or they turned the field off. Or something. I've got all three of them now, heading this way."

"Visual?"

"Buildings are in the way, sir. I've only got thermal."

"Let's see it."

A moment later, one of the screens suspended over the bridge's front window ports switched from its normal display of engine output to a multi-colored wash. In the dull greys of the lifeless buildings and decrepit roads, Thomas made out three distinct warm bodies moving in the center of the screen. There was also a dark form partially obscuring them—a decidedly humanoid figure that shambled along in front of the others, clearly heading to the same destination.

"Correct me if I'm wrong," he said, "but that looks like *four* people."

The officer squinted at her own display of the same data. "Confirmed, Captain. We've got four incoming."

"Maybe they brought a zombie with them," said Matthias.

"We're not calling them zombies," Thomas said absently, rubbing his forehead with one hand while his other clutched an armrest for support. Surely Ivanokoff wouldn't be that stupid, or Areva that reckless, or Chris that, well, brave.

The orangey figures grew on the display as they approached the ship, proving Thomas wrong.

He slowly raised his hand to his intercom interface. "Page medical."

"Paging medical," confirmed the ship's automated voice.

A moment later, Maureen Habassa's soft soprano answered. "Chief medic responding, Captain. Can I help you?"

"Our people are coming back, and after this long, they've got to have breathed the planet's air. Worse, they've got one of the locals with them. I know you're no doctor, Officer Habassa, but we're going to need whatever training you've got."

To her credit, Maureen didn't panic, or even raise her voice. "I'll do my best, sir. I've got some good reference materials on respiratory function that I'm sure will help."

"We're going to have to keep them in isolation, so set up one of the empty berths as a ward. I don't want anyone coming into contact with them without protective gear."

"Understood."

Thomas took a deep breath to still his racing nerves. If the most junior member of his crew could handle this calmly, so could he. "I think we're about to get some answers."

Bradshaw the suit glanced up from his pocket comp. His twitching eye narrowed to a slit. "I hope they're good ones."

* * *

It took over an hour and a full medical examination by every remotely qualified scientist on the ship to convince Captain Withers that Viktor, Areva, and Chris were not infected with the zombie plague, and therefore humans were likely immune to the air contagion.

Ivanokoff considered that a victory, especially since it had been achieved with so little shouting.

The zombie doctor was another matter.

Withers refused to allow him into the ship until Maureen admitted she couldn't perform an examination of the doctor while wearing an EV suit, and the science posse ganged up to argue that since humans were immune to the plague, there was no reason to fear bringing the doctor aboard. The captain finally agreed, but the zombie still had to pass three rounds of decontamination in the airlocks and be escorted to the isolation ward, which no one could enter without full surgical gear.

Chris performed the introductions. "Doctor *Decay*, meet Captain *Withers*. Heh heh."

The zombie took this without reaction.

Viktor stood with the captain to watch Maureen take samples of hair, skin, and blood from the zombie and place them carefully in slides. "She is improving."

The captain gave a grudging nod. "She took some correspondence courses."

Maureen moved the slides to a microscope she'd borrowed from the science team and peered at them.

"So you convinced them to let you go?" the captain asked.

"Da. We discovered our immunity. We realized this zombie—"

"Don't call them that."

"—undead state was protecting them from breathing the plague in their air. We offered help."

"And they believed you?"

"It was truth."

"Yeah, but they believed you?"

"Why not?"

The captain shrugged. "Most of the people we've found out here aren't the trusting types."

"Death has slowed their higher thought processes."

"So they had to be half brain-dead to trust you?"

Viktor grimaced. "I did not say that."

Maureen made an "aha" sound and leaned forward, keying various commands into the microscope control pad.

"So," said the captain, "who did this to them?"

That same question had been needling Viktor since he realized the true reason behind the zombieism. Why was the air contaminated by that deadly plague? Given the nature of the recordings in the library, he doubted these people did it themselves.

The not-a-doctor stood up and twirled away from the microscope, her ponytail of long curls dancing with the movement. "Well, I think I've learned all I can from that analysis."

Withers leaned forward. Viktor did not.

Maureen nodded to Doctor Decay. "This man is definitely dead."

They waited for more.

That was it. Maureen smiled pleasantly.

"We knew that," said the captain. "He's not breathing, and he has no pulse, and, I mean, look at his flesh."

"True," said Maureen, "but now it's proven. Scientifically."

"Is there anything new?"

"I can confirm that he's a corporeal being."

Viktor's lip curled. "How does that help?"

"Well, he's not a ghost, even though he's clearly dead and mobile."

"Ghosts are not real."

"I think they are," said Maureen. "My parents used to take us on these cultural enrichment trips, and on one of them we went to a ruined pyramid for an overnight stay. In the middle of the night, I woke up in my sleeping bag and heard footsteps coming down a hallway from the outside. I stood up to investigate, but when I came to the hall, there was no one there, so I went back to sleep."

"You slept despite thinking you heard ghosts?"

"Why not? They weren't hurting anything."

"Wait," said Captain Withers. "Was this the same trip where—"

Viktor interrupted. "Can these people be cured?"

"Maybe. The biologists will want to take a look at him. The cells aren't producing energy, but the membranes are still intact. The textbooks say that's impossible, but it's like the aliens halted the decay partway through."

"Suspended animation?" said the captain.

"More like the opposite, halting death processes instead of life processes. Suspended ... un-imation. The point is, he's not damaged. Just dead. It's weird, but we might be able to fix it." She paused. "Please note that I am not qualified to give medical advice."

The captain waved his hand. "Yes, I know."

"Sorry. The textbook says I have to say that if I discuss treatments with anyone in an official context."

"So the question is," said Withers, "should we try to fix them?"

All eyes went to Doctor Decay.

He blinked vacantly back over his protruding nose.

"First we'll have to cure the plague in their atmosphere," Maureen said. "If we don't, and we force them to breathe the contaminated air, we might kill their entire species." Her soothing voice managed to make the possibility sound like a minor inconvenience.

Viktor folded his arms. Such an act would be reprehensible. Not only that, it would completely ruin the

O&I review. "Recommend we try. These people would make excellent allies against the Haxozin."

"I've thought of that," said Withers. "Considering that their society is so similar to ours, and their incredible medical technology, it's believable that they have more advanced tech here, or at least the capacity to build it. Most of the other species we've met are behind us technologically, so this is a rare chance."

"We should at least investigate the plague in their air," said Maureen. "That can't hurt."

"Carefully," said Viktor. "Caution is the best defense."

The captain glanced at him. "Sun Tzu?"

"No. Areva."

"Ha. She say that when you two were on a mission together?"

"No. Over dinner."

This time Withers's look held more significance. "Dinner? The two of you? Together?"

"It was just dinner, sir."

"Does this happen often?"

"Da."

To Viktor's discomfort, the captain shared a knowing look with Maureen before speaking again. "Take a hint from me and Loretta, Ivanokoff. That's not just dinner."

A flush crept into Viktor's cheeks. He humphed and fled the berth before they could tell him any other things he already knew and preferred not to admit.

* * *

The atmospheric samples went straight to Chris and Joyce Fish and their team on deck two.

From the cacophony echoing up the ladders, Thomas thought they must have brought aboard some howler monkeys as well.

He entered the designated lab area, an interconnecting series of converted berths alongside the starboard hull, to see half a dozen officers, each wearing two or three science certification stripes on their shoulders, yelling at one another.

"That chemical balance might be the result of the plague!" a red-faced Chris shouted at Officer Varma, who worked scanners on the night shift.

"Or," countered Varma, "it could be perfectly normal for this planet!"

Joyce had one hand on her hip, the other gesticulating furiously at a woman with three engineering patches beneath her two science stripes. "I don't care how well you understand theoretical physics; this is a *chemistry* problem!"

"Chemistry is just applied physics!" argued the engineer, folding her arms.

"Physics is just applied math," said another engineer-scientist wearing reading glasses and doing two different things on two different computer screens at once.

Thomas had broken up enough scientific debates on his ship to know not to bother with subtlety. "HEY! LISTEN UP!"

The arguing stopped, except for Chris finishing his sentence: "... breathing it, if not experimental verification?"

Once he had their attention, Thomas asked, "What have we got?"

Half a dozen voices spoke at once, and he held up a hand and pointed to Officer Varma.

Varma gave Chris Fish a triumphant look before holding up a finger and declaring, "This planet has a higher oxygen-to-nitrogen ratio than our own, as well as a fractionally higher amount of argon and—"

"I don't need all the details. Can we cure the plague that almost killed these people?"

Varma deflated at the interruption, but then shrugged and spread his hands. "There is no plague."

"What?"

"We found no unexpected chemicals, compounds, or even organisms in our study of the samples. The atmosphere is quite close to Earth-normal. It appears that whatever was in the air, it is now gone."

"*Appears*," said Chris, "but who knows whether that's actually—"

Again Thomas held up a hand. "You're saying we can cure their zombieism right now, and they'll be fine?"

"Theoretically," said Varma. "But I strongly recommend testing in order to observe any complications."

"Right, right," said Thomas, a grin coming to his face. Pulling unlikely achievements out of certain doom seemed to be his crew's specialty. *Take that, Bradshaw.* "I want you all to work with Officer Habassa on a way to revive the zombies."

"I thought we weren't calling—" began Chris.

Thomas talked over him. "In the meantime, I'll talk to our ... guest about the situation."

The arguing resumed, this time about the best way to resuscitate the dead, before he'd even left the compartment.

* * *

Doctor Decay sat unnervingly still on the exam bed in the medical compartment. Maureen was trying to get him to do some sort of breathing exercise, perhaps hoping that sheer willpower would overcome his undead state. Thomas dismissed her and remained alone with the zombie.

"Hi." He focused on a point somewhere between the vacant eyes, rather than look directly into them. "So, I'm sure this is very unnerving for you. Honestly, I'm not even sure how much you understand of what I'm saying right now."

Blink, blink, nod.

"That's good, keep nodding when what I'm telling you makes sense."

Nod.

"So ... we think we've got a solution to your problem. The plague that someone released in your atmosphere to wipe all of you out—it's gone."

The zombie cocked his head to one side.

"That means you're safe. It can't hurt you anymore."

A tentative nod.

Encouraged by this progress, Thomas continued, "That means all we have to do to restore your society is, well, revive you. I've got my people working on that, but I'm guessing you could be a big help. It sounds like your government planned this out pretty well, and your medical sciences are years beyond anything we can do. Did your people create a cure to this ... state?"

Blank stare.

Too many words, Thomas decided. He slowed his tone and used his hands to supplement his words. "Cure. Do you have one?"

More staring.

Thomas decided to drop the topic. If his own people failed to think of an idea, he could always send a team to search the hospital where Ivanokoff and the others had been held. "Okay, let's try something simpler. If we find a cure, we'll need to test it on someone." Again he gestured. "We need a volunteer."

A long pause. Thomas wasn't sure if Doctor Decay was even listening. Then, slowly, the zombie lifted a thin hand to point at himself.

"Thank you," said Thomas. "Given that you're dead right now, I don't think anything we do can make you worse."

Blank stare.

"So ... you agree to let us test the cure on you?"

Nod.

"I promise we won't let you down."

Pause. The alien made a shrugging motion, but with his elbows.

"I know, you seem like you're all more or less happy this way, but trust me. Things will be better when you're alive and functioning again."

Blank stare.

Thomas had more questions, but they would wait until they found a way to revive the doctor. It'd be easier to discuss the origin of this plague and possible alliances when he was sure the conversation was understood.

* * *

It took another day before any news came from the science team. Thomas started writing his report to Dispatch for when the Endurance returned home—he still had a few days before they were scheduled to report back, and he hoped they were able to resolve this problem before leaving. Once the zombie folk were restored to their proper mental capacities, maybe they could even bring one to Earth to talk with human scientists about their impressive medical technology. *That* would be an invaluable help in just about every sphere of life.

Maureen Habassa rapped quietly on the bulkhead around his office hatch before stepping inside. He glanced up and set his pocket comp on standby in hopes this would be a lengthy conversation containing many usable solutions. "Come in. Anything to report?"

She arranged herself in the chair across his desk and crossed her legs. "The scientists stayed up until two a.m. debating ideas, and it wasn't until Officer Lee pointed out that whatever we do has to be massively applicable to the population that they started actually working together. But they think they have something, and it's even something I have enough training and qualifications to implement."

"What is it?"

"Revixophin."

Thomas waited for more, but she just smiled pleasantly.

"What's that?" he finally asked.

"It's a virus-based stimulant that was created a few decades ago." She smiled, and Thomas wondered if she was proud of using such science-y words. "They use it on Earth during major surgeries, when they have to shut down people's hearts or other organs. The Revixophin virus goes in and kick-starts the body processes again."

"You're talking about people who are still alive, just undergoing surgery. Is this going to work on dead people?"

"In high ... one second." Maureen pulled out her pocket comp and checked a page of notes. "Highly concentrated viral colonies. In those, sometimes the virus makes people's bodies keep functioning for hours after they're technically dead. These zombies' internal organs aren't working, but they're still there, and Doctor Decay's don't seem to have suffered any damage. Assuming they're supposed to look like the textbook pictures of human organs, of course. If not, he could be a mess and I wouldn't know. But the basic functions of his brain are still working, so if we turn the other parts back on, it should set him back to normal. Like waking up a device from standby." She nodded toward his pocket comp on the desk.

"What about those with worse injuries?" the captain asked. "Bullet holes won't just disappear."

"I imagine some of them will be too hurt to survive. Others may need medical intervention. But if we cure them in controlled groups, with the help of their own doctors, we should be able to avoid most problems."

"You want to give these undead aliens a viral infection to revive them. That seems like it's moving in the wrong direction."

The young woman shrugged. "Isn't it worth a try? You said we need their help."

"Do we have any of this stuff on board?"

"Just a little, but Varma and the Fishes said they can breed more of it super fast."

"What are the risks?"

Maureen ticked them off on her fingers, the same mannerism her brother used. "It could not work, leaving them as they are. Or it could damage the organs so that they can't be fixed in the future. But that's very improbable."

"How improbable?"

"Very." She blushed. "You could ask Chris Fish for the actual math."

"I'll do that." Thomas had no doubt it would check out. "How soon could you have this ready to go?"

"Half an hour to set up the medical devices. The science team had to build a few pieces of equipment out of spare parts, since the ship doesn't have a full medical lab."

"They did all this last night?"

Nod.

"When do they sleep?"

"They don't." Maureen grinned as she stood to leave. "Why do you think the ship's coffee pot is always empty?"

* * *

After confirming with the scientists that the Revixophin would do its job, and was unlikely to kill Doctor Decay (again), blow anything up, or otherwise ruin the week, Thomas okayed the project.

Bradshaw and the other O&I suit, predictably, did not approve. But *Endurance* was still Thomas's ship, and he was still the final authority. He overrode them. They made little notes on their pocket comps and insisted on observing the treatment.

He allowed it. If it worked, he wanted to see their faces as they realized his crew was indeed competent. If it didn't work, they'd find out about it sooner or later anyway.

Doctor Decay lay on a medical bed, his empty eyes staring at the tan ceiling panels. Multiple contraptions and machinery sat around the bed, covering dents in the metal floor plating and almost filling the tiny medical bay. There was a large wheeled cart holding a sealed tub of hazel-colored goo, labeled in fine print. Next to it sat a paintbrush. Maureen's usual comfy chairs, exercise equipment, and stretching gear were piled in one corner.

Maureen herself stood over the devices, with Matthias, Chris, and Joyce hovering over her shoulders to give advice and ensure the machinery worked properly. Thomas stood on the other side of the bed, his own shadows peering over him and tap-tap-tapping notes into their comps.

Maureen glanced at a textbook displayed on a computer screen her brother held up in front of her, then checked the pulse and respiratory monitors she'd attached to her patient. Her mouth moved silently as she counted them and cross-referenced against the book.

Tap-tap went the suits' fingers on their computers. Thomas wanted to break the stupid devices.

"That looks right," Maureen said. "Next book. The one about applying Revixophin." Matthias tapped a few controls on the screen and held it up before Maureen's face again. She read carefully, drawing her finger across each line. When she finished, she raised her arms over her head, stretched, and then switched out her surgical gloves for a fresh pair. "Ready."

Matthias whooped. "Let's do this!"

Smooth as a practiced surgeon, Maureen lifted the paintbrush, dipped it in the goo, and began spreading it on Doctor Decay's prone form. The zombie didn't seem to feel anything at first, but a moment later his mouth split in a lopsided grin, and he wiggled.

"You're tickling the zombie, sis," said Matthias.

"Sorry," Maureen said, continuing to paint the goop over the undead skin.

Doctor Decay seemed to enjoy the whole procedure, and a moment later Thomas was treated to a surprisingly cool sight when the Revixophin gel began disappearing before his eyes.

"As it evaporates, the virus goes into the skin," said Maureen. "From there it's supposed to search out organ tissue, move in, and start reviving it."

"I love science," said Matthias.

"You keep your engineering nose out of my field of expertise," said Chris.

"Engineering is science."

"Is not."

"Quiet, please," said Maureen. "My patient needs to rest."

Everyone stopped to look at her. "He's dead," said Chris.

"And if he's going to get over that, he needs rest. All the textbooks say rest is the number one healing factor for most injuries or illnesses."

"Not if you're *dead*. You can't—"

Before the argument could commence, Doctor Decay's chest rose, and the sharp intake of breath filled the silent room.

Chris Fish promptly screamed, "It's alive!"

Joyce pinched his ear.

"Come on, honey, *somebody* had to say it."

In and out the zombie doctor breathed, his chest expanding and contracting as his lungs filled with the *Endurance*'s air. Thomas may have imagined it, but he thought some faint orange color came back to the alien's skin as well.

Maureen studied her readings against her textbook as everyone around her congratulated each other. "This is starting to look good," she said. "The numbers are all way off from normal, but that could just be because he's not human." She switched the textbook off and beamed at them. Her sunshine smile filled the room. "I think we did it!"

Matthias whooped again, squeezed his sister in a hug, and then went around high fiving everyone in the room. When he reached the suits, they refused to set down their pocket comps, so instead he high-fived the devices.

Thomas watched them stare at the once-dead, now-alive doctor. *Take notes on that*, he thought. He had a feeling his crew had just earned the ship a passing mark on its evaluation.

Maureen cocked her head as the zombie doctor's face began regaining color. "I don't know how long it's going to take for him to wake up properly. We'll need to keep monitoring him."

Thomas nodded. "Take whatever resources you need. Well done, everyone. This was an excellent first step."

* * *

The zombie doctor woke while Viktor Ivanokoff was enjoying a newly released murder mystery. The second the captain summoned him to the medical bay, he switched off his pocket comp, re-buttoned his uniform shirt, and headed out of his berth.

Doctor Decay was sitting up on the medical bed. The various equipment used to revive him had been moved to one side of the room. The zombie's flesh was now a (presumably) healthy orange, his eyes no longer milky, but red. The claws on his extra fingers had turned from pallid grey to deep amber. The liver spots on his bald head remained a dark brown, but even that color looked healthier. His frayed tan jumpsuit had been replaced with a shirt and slacks that looked like they'd been donated by Archibald Cleaver. Only the memory of the shambling corpse reminded Viktor that the man had been dead not a day earlier.

The doctor's red eyes widened as Viktor entered, and he took a raspy breath. "You," he croaked, in words that sounded like rocks simmering in a pot. The talky box on the bed next to him translated. "I know you."

Viktor looked at Captain Withers, Maureen, and Chris Fish, the only other people in the room, noting the absence of security. He suspected Areva was hiding somewhere behind the equipment, and gave the captain credit for not making their patient uncomfortable with obvious armed officers around.

"Yes," he answered. "We brought you here."

The zombie lifted his orange hands and stared at them. "You cured it. You revived me."

Maureen smiled. "You weren't completely dead. Your brain was still functioning. We just turned the rest of you back on."

"But the plague, the one the knights of the blood armor dropped on us—"

"The *what?*" asked Chris.

Viktor felt a chill. "Do you mean the—"

Captain Withers shot them both a sharp look. "The plague appears to be gone," he told the doctor.

"Gone?" asked the zombie.

"Yes. It must have dissipated once all your people had been infected. By then, though, you'd all taken the zombie drug. None of you were coherent enough to realize it was safe."

"Ah," said the alien doctor, staring at his hands again. "That makes sense."

"We found some of your records," said Viktor. "Your planet is called Thassis."

"Yes."

"What are you called?"

The doctor inhaled, exhaled slowly. "Drugugo," he said. "That was—is—my name."

Withers nodded. "Drugugo, how much do you remember of your time as a ..."

"Zombie," finished Chris.

"Infected," the captain said with another glare.

Drugugo shook his head. "It all feels like a blur. I remember sensations—vague recognitions of people, distant thoughts about what had become of us, half-conceived plans to repair the damage, but my mind was empty. It felt like floating. I was not capable of any real action."

"Your people attacked us," Viktor said. "That is active."

Drugugo frowned. "Did we? I must apologize for that. In the initial stages of the drug's influence, patients are driven to spread it to others, either by injecting them or by transferring bodily fluids, but that side effect should have worn off long ago. Perhaps some dormant aspect of it was triggered when you arrived." He peered at them. "You're immune to it, aren't you? And to the plague that was in the air."

"Yes," said most of the humans in the room.

"God, I hope so," said Chris.

"What did the plague do?" the captain asked.

"It killed us," Drugugo answered. "Forced our bodies to shut down, slowly, with unimaginable pain. It drove a tenth of our population insane before we managed to distribute the drug. We treated all of the patients in our hospital before injecting ourselves. Other hospitals around the planet did the same. It spread from there."

"That is a rather extreme measure," said Viktor.

"The blood armored ones wanted us dead. We found a way to let them have their way, but retain some semblance of our society."

"Who are they?" asked Viktor. "These 'knights of the blood armor.' Your records said the plague was caused by government mistakes. It made no reference to invaders."

Drugugo shuddered. "They came from the stars, their bodies all in red armor. I don't know what demands they made of the government, but the Wogogo administration refused to surrender. So they tried to wipe us out. Some of our people infiltrated their warships and learned what they intended to do. They were captured and killed, but their valor gave us the chance to develop the, as you call it, 'zombie' drug to save our society. There was no mention in the records because there was no need. Everyone saw the star-shaped ships in the sky. Everyone knew what had happened."

Viktor knew of only one spacefaring species with star-shaped ships, red armor, and the technology to come to Thassis and unleash this kind of destruction. "We know these invaders."

The captain's posture was stiff. "Yes, we do. They call themselves the Haxozin Sovereignty. How long ago did they attack you? Have they been back?"

"I had no sense of time under the drug," said Drugugo, rubbing the largest of his liver spots. "But given the state of my clothes when I awakened, I would guess no more than a year ago. As for coming back, I do not think so. If they had, I doubt my people would still be here."

The captain's face was grim. "This isn't the first time we've encountered them. Hell, it's not even the second or third. They're a menace."

"It seems so. I dread the thought of what they will do if they rediscover us."

Viktor seized the opportunity. "We are at war with them. You can help."

The captain shot him a warning look and then said the exact same thing, if a bit more delicately. "It's not an open war. We scrap with them whenever we find one of their outposts. But their technology outmatches ours. Frankly, so does yours, and it seems we share them as a common enemy. We'd appreciate any help your people can give, especially seeing how advanced your medical science is. You're the closest thing we've seen to people who've foiled their plans. Besides us, I mean."

Drugugo nodded. "Of course. We would love to see the blood armored ones defeated. You are welcome to any help we can offer." He peered toward the door, red eyes squinting. "Did you revive the others? Where are the rest of my people?"

"Still outside," said Withers. "We wanted to make sure this cure worked on you before trying it on a larger scale."

"Ah, of course."

"We're about due to report back to our home. You're welcome to come with us, and once we let our people know what's going on here, they'll send more ships and we can—"

"No." Drugugo's orange features abruptly turned a darker shade. "I will not abandon my people in this state. Teach me what you did to revive me, and I will start curing them while you are away."

"We used a topically-applied viral stimulant," said Maureen. Every eyebrow rose to hear her use those words that confidently.

Drugugo's face fell. "That will take a great deal of time to administer to each individual."

"Exactly," said the captain, "which is why, if you're willing to wait, we can come back with more helpers—"

"Can you not cure a few more of them before you leave? I know if my staff were restored to themselves, we could study your drug and perhaps supplement it with our own. We did not finish a cure for this before the drug took effect, but we made significant progress. I know I could make substantial headway in reviving my species if I had the help of my staff. You would not need to cure a large area—perhaps just the clinic." Seeing the captain's frown, the doctor continued, "Please. I know you have done much for me already, but this would not take your crew too long. I am only one man. The sooner my people begin to recover, the sooner we can aid you."

"He is not wrong," Viktor murmured to the captain.

Withers chewed the inside of his cheek. "We don't have time to treat that many people one by one."

"Perhaps a larger scale solution is in order," said Drugugo. "You said this healing virus works topically, through the skin. The hospital is equipped with a chemical fire suppression system. Were we to switch your cure for the normal chemicals and then trigger the system—"

"Everybody would get an anti-zombie bath," said Matthias, grinning. "Good idea!"

"You could make this work?" asked the captain.

"If we can make enough of that Revixothing, sure, Cap."

Drugugo watched them with earnest eyes. "Please, Captain. I only want to speed the recovery of my people. As a physician, I'm sure your doctor understands."

Maureen smiled blankly before realizing he was directing the comment to her. "Oh! I'm not a doctor, and I am not qualified to give medical advice. I just followed the instructions on the label."

"Oh." The alien pursed his lips, but then elbow-shrugged. "Then, as I seem to be the medical expert present, I hope you understand my desire to help the ailing."

The captain sighed and rubbed his forehead with one hand, the other anchored to his waist. "We can't guarantee it'll work."

"Of course not. I am prepared to take that risk. And you can hardly leave them in a worse state than they are now."

Viktor thought that a fair point, and apparently so did Captain Withers. He dropped his hand and nodded. "All right. We'll give it a try."

Drugugo broke into a sharp-fanged smile. "Many thanks, Captain! My people will not forget this."

* * *

Revixophin turned out to procreate like, well, a virus, and the scientists had enough to fill the hospital's fire suppression system in short order. In the meantime, Drugugo returned to the hospital and checked his own vital signs with his own medical equipment. He pronounced himself perfectly healthy, confirming that the drug worked.

Viktor assisted the alien in locating the injured hospital personnel and escorting them out of the building so they could avoid being revived and bleeding out from their wounds. He disliked seeing the undead faces again, especially those that had participated in capturing the team on the rotunda. Aware of their actions or not, he'd thought they were trying to kill him, and had responded in kind. Reunions could get awkward.

Fortunately, none of the zombies paid them any mind. It seemed Drugugo's presence reassured the undead aliens and countered their "spread the drug" instinct.

As one last safety measure, Drugugo located a large cache of the zombie drug on the first floor of the hospital. Viktor watched him remove a long plastic cylinder divided into eight tiny compartments, each filled with an equal amount of pale blue fluid. Attached to the cylinder was a pneumatic injection tube that could slide from one compartment to the next for easy treatment of multiple people in a row. Drugugo nodded his approval. "These were kept sealed, so they should still work. If we missed any of the injured, or if some have internal injuries we couldn't detect on sight, I may have to re-treat them until we can properly care for their wounds." He replaced the drug cylinder and closed the cache. "Thank you again for your help. I don't know how long my people would have remained like this if you hadn't come along."

Viktor muttered some polite words and escorted Drugugo to check the progress of the fire suppression system team.

They were nearly finished. Matthias and a few of the scientists had disconnected the regular fire suppression tank and replaced it with the Revixophin. They ensured a tight seal in the intake valves, and then headed down to the ground floor, where Drugugo ordered the building's main control unit to activate the sprinklers on every story.

("I still think my fireworks idea would have been cooler," said Matthias.) As the verdant goo began spraying from the ceiling, the team darted out the door and headed back to the secluded warehouse.

Once everyone returned to the ship, Viktor escorted Drugugo to the bridge. "If this works," he said as they climbed the ladder to the top deck, "we will see them appear on thermal sensors as they revive."

Drugugo accepted Viktor's hand to help him off the ladder, then followed the bigger man through the corridors to the bridge hatch. "I cannot thank your people enough. I look forward to our long and fruitful collaboration."

Viktor didn't answer, but his thoughts did. *Chris Fish would say that guarantees our failure.*

He hoped the paranoid scientist was wrong.

The captain was in his chair in the center of the bridge when they entered, the curving row of stations along the front viewports staffed by the three officers of the afternoon shift. The officer in charge of the shift sat in one of the extra seats along the back wall, ready in case the captain should turn the bridge back over to her.

"Nothing yet," Captain Withers asked as Ivanokoff came into view. "We're keeping an eye on it."

Viktor noticed the captain's two O&I shadows were relegated to the back wall seats as well. Their pocket comps were uncharacteristically stowed at their belts, their faces impassive. He wondered what they were thinking.

"Still no readings," reported the scanners operator.

"Let's give more computing power to thermal," the captain said. "Might let us pick up fainter readings."

"Routing power," said the defensives crewman.

"I've got it," said scanners.

"Restart scan ... now," said the captain.

Viktor thought the pause unnecessary, though dramatic.

A few tense minutes passed. The beeps and hums of the control consoles intruded into the stillness like alarms. Any second, Viktor expected some report of disaster.

Instead, the scanners officer looked up. "Reading a few faint heat signatures inside the building. We did it, sir!"

Cheers erupted, and the captain's features melted into relief and excitement. Viktor allowed himself a small smile and turned to Drugugo. "Congratu—"

The words died in his throat. "Doctor?"

Drugugo's red eyes had faded to a flushed pink, while his orange skin contained patches of pale peach. He clutched his sides with both hands crossed in front of his body, and his breath seemed labored. "What ... why is this ...?"

Viktor wasted no time in draping the doctor's arm over his shoulders to support him. "Captain, a problem!"

Withers had already noticed and was out of his chair, barking orders into his intercom for Maureen and some of the scientists to hurry to the bridge.

"Pain," Drugugo hissed in Viktor's ear. "The pain, I remember, so bad ... feel it now ..."

A vice tightened around Viktor's chest. "The cure may not be holding," he told Withers. "He feels pain."

He saw the impact of his words on the captain's face. In a dark corner of the bridge, the two suits pulled out their pocket comps and begin tapping notes again. The one with the twitchy eye formed the shadow of a grim smile.

No time to worry about that. Viktor began hauling Drugugo toward the hatch to meet the medical people halfway. The doctor kept rambling. "You said it was gone ... said the plague was gone ... so much pain ..."

"This is not our fault," Viktor said.

"Why? Why kill us?"

"We wish you no harm."

"So much pain!" Drugugo suddenly seized up as a tremor shook his entire body. He wrenched free of Viktor's grasp and stumbled back against the wall, spasming violently. His fanged mouth opened in a scream that resonated through Viktor's bones.

When the seizure subsided and the doctor again opened his eyes, the whites had been replaced by bloodshot pink. The sharp teeth bared, and he pointed an accusatory orange-splotched finger at Viktor. "Finish what you started, red ones! Just end it!"

It took Viktor a second to realize what he meant. When he did, his skin went cold. "Captain, he thinks we are the Haxozin."

Another scream and spasm of pain, and Drugugo launched himself at Viktor, hands shaped into claws, jaws snapping.

Viktor leapt out of the way, his own hands coming up to defend himself as he spun to one side. Drugugo followed, moving jerkily as pain twisted his body, his sharp teeth aiming for Viktor's jugular. He lunged again, and Viktor stumbled back against the bulkhead. The sharp extra fingers sliced toward his throat.

Quick reactions trapped the alien's wrists in Viktor's larger hands, but still the lieutenant struggled to fend off the snarling man. "We are ... not ... your enemies!" he grunted.

Drugugo didn't respond. Viktor doubted he even heard.

He vaguely made out shouts from the other officers and hoped they were scrambling to help. His arms shook with the effort of holding back Drugugo. Older and less muscular the doctor might be, but his pain, or his rage, gave him immense strength. Viktor's heart pounded in his throat, his vision entirely filled with the gnashing teeth, the pink eyes. He let out a yell and shoved Drugugo back, giving himself space to move away from the wall.

The doctor leapt for him again.

Splitting reports shattered Viktor's eardrums.

He winced, bringing a hand up to his head. He struggled to regain his breath and looked around the bridge.

Captain Withers, the helmswoman, and the defensives officer all held standard-issue p-guns. All three had clearly just fired.

Drugugo dropped to the deck, three holes in his chest. Rocky breaths wheezed in and out of his damaged lungs.

The captain tapped his intercom interface. "Habassa, do you have the zombie drug samples we took from that hospital?" He paused. "Good. Bring them to the bridge. We need to re-kill the doctor to save his life."

* * *

Thomas stood over Maureen as she injected the zombie drug into Drugugo's arm. The doctor had lost consciousness quickly after being shot, and Thomas could see his breath becoming shallower. He hoped his idea worked, or he'd be responsible for killing this man. Twice.

"I don't understand," said Chris Fish. "We *checked* the air. There's no plague up there, I'd bet my life on it.

In fact, I *have*. Doctor Decay himself said his vital signs were fine! So why did he succumb to it again?"

Maureen shrugged. "Maybe the plague affected something he didn't check. Like DNA."

"Great," said Chris. "Just great. Can we check my DNA to make sure it hasn't been rewritten?"

"Not now, Fish," Thomas said quietly, staring down at the dying man. Maureen finished the injection and stood. "Will this work?" he asked the room at large.

"I think so," said Maureen. "But please note that I am not a licensed physician and—"

"Yes, I know," said Thomas. "Let's just hope the drug makes his body stop working before he dies, brain and all. Get a stretcher and take him back to the medical bay. We owe it to him to see this through."

Near the wall, Bradshaw and his partner tap-tapped away. After a moment, the O&I man looked up and made eye contact with Thomas. His eye twitched once, twice, and then flicked back to the notes on his comp.

There'd been accusation in that stare, and Thomas couldn't help feeling it was warranted.

As Maureen and another officer prepared Drugugo to be moved, Thomas faced the viewports. One of the overhead display screens showed a thermal reading of the medical building. The initial traces of heat had grown in both size and number, and now read as dozens of humanoid shapes walking, or in some cases, running through the halls.

It had worked. They'd revived the other zombies.

He swallowed. "Time until they go nuts?"

The scanners operator shook his head. "Based on how much faster they revived, it could be minutes, sir. Definitely under an hour."

Thomas rubbed his forehead. That wasn't enough time to find every confused alien wandering the building, confine them to hospital beds, and turn them back into zombies before they started trying to kill everyone.

"We need to reverse what we did," he said to the bridge at large. "Give me options."

No one moved.

"Is there a way to distribute the zombie drug through the entire building quickly?"

"No," said Ivanokoff, rubbing the bruises on his arms. "If the drug could be made airborne, the aliens would have done so."

"We didn't bring enough aboard to treat everyone. We need to get to the hospital's stash without any of them noticing."

"Areva can do it."

Thomas nodded. "Then we can start covertly re-drugging them before they start having symptoms."

Ivanokoff arched an eyebrow. "There is not enough time. When the plague begins affecting them, they will succumb to intense pain and attack anyone nearby."

Tap, tap went Bradshaw's notes, no doubt listing Thomas's sins as a commander. Thomas's lips formed a thin line. He had to correct this before "accidental genocide" became his latest failure.

"When that point comes," he said, "we'll just have to fight our way through the rest."

* * *

Ivanokoff paced outside the hospital, Dickens and Dante holstered at his sides. No spacesuits for him and his team—they'd need to move fast to rezombify the aliens without getting bitten or clawed. They weren't sure yet if the zombie infection could spread to human tissue, but he had no desire to find out. In either case, those fangs could still deal lethal damage.

He regretted recommending Areva for the initial infiltration. He should have volunteered himself. Yes, she was better at stealth—a lot better—but Chris's "two days from retirement" comment kept running through Viktor's mind.

He tapped his intercom interface. "Areva, report."

His headset crackled with Areva's breath as she whispered. "Viktor, are you going to ask me that every sixty seconds?"

"If I wish. I am the senior officer."

She sighed. "Okay, Lieutenant with seniority, everything is fine. I'm nearly to the lab where you saw the cache of zombie drug."

Viktor checked the time on his pocket comp. Ten minutes had passed since the conversation on the bridge. That left a maximum of fifty minutes for Areva to pick up the drug and administer it to as many aliens as possible before they attacked.

"How's the doctor?" Areva asked, her voice still a whisper.

"Dying, but in the way we prefer," said Viktor. "His organs are shutting down and his brain is returning to the zombie state. Maureen thinks the plan is working."

"Good. I'd hate to shoot all these people for no reason."

"Are you all right?"

"Yes. Why?"

"You talk about shooting people."

"I'm fine. Really," said Areva in a businesslike tone. "Like you said, they were already dead, so I'm just re-killing them. And if I do it right, none of them are going to see me anyway."

"True." He hoped that last part was true. The zombies had easily found them in the library and on the rotunda.

But Areva was alone now, able to utilize her sneaking to its utmost potential. She would be fine.

She *would* be fine.

A few minutes passed, during which Viktor paced some more and fought his urge to check in again.

His communicator crackled. "I've got the drug. Filling the pack now."

This part of the plan was questionably moral at best. They had armed Areva and the rest of the strike team with bazooka rifles—handheld directed energy weapons that they had received from another alien culture, which had stolen them in turn from the Haxozin. The plan was to stun each alien and inject them while unconscious. Viktor had proposed simply coating bullets in the drug, but the captain deemed that too likely to kill some of the aliens before they, well, died.

Another few minutes later, Areva spoke again. "Just made the dropoff at the main entrance. I left enough of those tube things for everybody to take three. That's twenty-four zombies each. Thermal scans show about a hundred in here, so we have plenty of spare injections. I'm heading back in to start shooting."

"Understood." Viktor paused. "Areva, be careful."

He could hear the smile in her voice. "I always am."

He could also hear Chris Fish's voice in his mind: *Saying that guarantees something will go wrong.*

Sergeant Ramirez snuck into the hospital to retrieve the pneumatic cylinders and bring them out to the strike team. "Uh, got them," he said as he returned with a standard-issue backpack dangling from one hand. "They're kind of, um, heavy, sir. So, uh, yeah."

Viktor and the other officers on his strike team took them with gloved hands and stored them in pouches alongside their gun holsters.

Viktor eyed Ramirez as he checked to make sure Dickens and Dante were still at his sides. "No one saw you. You are sure?"

The young man bobbed his head. "Positive. I'm, uh, not as sneaky as Areva, but I can sight out of seen. I mean stay out of seen." His youthful face flushed crimson, and he murmured, "Stay out of sight."

Another member of the team, the woman who worked bridge defensives at night, frowned at him. "Calm down, man. You're never this jumpy on the night shift."

Ramirez flashed a look at Viktor. "I know."

Viktor was familiar with the sergeant's tendency to get nervous in front of senior officers. He made a point of looking elsewhere. He had ample practice at that with Areva.

Her voice came into his ear again, and he tensed, fearing bad news. But all she said was, "Got three. Tracking a fourth." A sizzling rifle shot echoed through the channel. "Four."

"Are they aggressive?"

"Not yet. Most of them are just wandering around looking confused. The hospital's too big for them to have found each other yet." Zap. "Five."

Ninety-five to go, thought Viktor.

She reached nine before the problems began. "Tracking number ten," she reported. "He's having a few minor convulsions. I think it's starting." Zap. "Got him. But it looks like you should come in now."

Viktor motioned his team toward the airlock. "Move in pairs. Check your thermal monitors to avoid surprise attacks. Do not let them get close. Shoot, inject, and repeat."

All eyes stared at him, as if waiting for him to say something else.

"Go."

As the teams spread out to enter through the building's various doors, Viktor heard Ramirez say, "Rousing speech, yeah? I know I'm inspired." His night shift colleague laughed.

Viktor headed for the front. His pocket comp, mounted on a strap around his forearm, pinged Areva's position, guiding him to her. "Areva, I am on my way."

"Waiting for you."

Viktor hefted his bazooka rifle and yanked open the door. *Ten soldiers wisely led*, he quoted, *will beat a hundred without a head.* Euripides.

He wondered if only a fool would enact the battle plan of a tragedian.

* * *

The first alien attacked when Viktor was halfway up a flight of stairs. Thermal scans showed several bodies on the next floor, a safe distance away, but then an entire section of the ceiling caved in and a shrieking, clawing body flung itself at him. He shouted in alarm and raised his bazooka rifle, balancing the barrel in the crook of his arm, and fired. The white energy blast zipped out of the barrel and struck the zombie, fizzling out along his limbs and neck. He trembled in paralysis for one heartbeat, two, then collapsed. Viktor inoculated the alien with the first compartment on one of the pneumo-injectors.

On the second floor, a pungent odor assaulted his nose as he approached the heat blip that represented Areva. His pocket comp showed no other heat sources nearby. Whatever stank, it wasn't the aliens.

He found Areva crouched behind a tank of water filled with the desiccating remains of alien fish.

"Good hiding place," he growled at the one boot and tip of the bazooka rifle that wouldn't fit behind the tank.

Areva's voice answered, "Thanks. The aliens don't seem to like the smell."

"They are not breathing."

"Scents come straight through olfactory receptors in our noses. If those are strong enough, the aliens could smell particles that just drift up into their nostrils."

"How do you know that?"

"Some book." Areva laughed. "Honestly, Viktor, don't you ever read?"

He grinned. "Come. We should move on."

As he turned, the fish corpses caught his eye. One had a row of lobster-like claws protruding from its head and was lying on its back at the bottom of the tank. The rest of the fish floated in pieces, a fin here, a head there, a tentacle there, some cleaved right in half. "The clawed fish killed the others," he said. "The plague spread to the animals."

Movement at his elbow told him Areva had emerged. "Vicious."

"Yes." A glance at his pocket comp showed Viktor a pair of heat blips moving erratically through the rooms further down the hall. "Two there," he said, pointing.

"You lead. I'll cover."

They advanced as one entity.

Those two aliens went down easily, followed by half a dozen others scattered around the building. Viktor and

Areva worked their way up the stairs, sticking to the western wing and coordinating with the other teams through intercom. An hour into the fighting, sixty-one aliens had been stunned and injected. Forty-some-odd to go.

The difficulty increased on the fifth floor. After injecting yet another alien, Viktor checked his pocket comp and saw a heat blip moving along somewhere below them. He tapped his intercom interface. "Teams two through five, are any of you on the fourth floor?"

A round of negatives came back. Viktor glared at the heat blip. One of the aliens must have snuck through the lines. "Areva and I will eliminate the readings down there. Keep moving upward."

They headed back down a flight of stairs to the floor below, but the heat reading kept moving, plunging deeper into the facility. "It is trying to escape," Viktor realized.

"If it does, it'll die," said Areva.

"It does not know that."

They tracked their quarry all the way to the first floor of the facility. The heat signature spread out as it moved, and Viktor came to another realization. "There are multiple targets."

"Confirmed," said Areva, monitoring her own pocket comp. "I count four."

"They are moving to that large room. What is there?"

"I don't know. None of us have been through here."

They passed a wall-mounted sign, and Viktor wished he could read the alien print inscribed on it. No doubt it would tell them exactly what part of the hospital they'd discovered.

The heat signatures stopped in the room.

"They are lost. They must have expected an exit. Hurry."

"Right behind you," said Areva.

They crept down the hall, their footsteps treading lightly on the cold and cracked tiles. Light filtered in through the large windows on either end of the hall and the few plasma bulbs still shining in their recessed domes, but most of the artificial lighting had burned out. Shadows covered the area surrounding the door to the aliens' hiding place. Viktor put his hand on the handle and made eye contact with Areva, who blushed at the gaze but gave a nod.

In one fluid movement, Viktor flung open the door, brandished his bazooka rifle, and charged in.

They'd miscounted.

There were five aliens.

And they were ready.

Viktor had hoped to fell one, maybe two by surprise, but the aliens reacted at once, as if they knew the humans were coming. If Areva was right about their noses, perhaps they *smelled* them coming. Five fanged mouths opened in roars as Viktor burst through the door, and five sets of orange hands shot toward his throat.

He raised his gun and realized too late that the aliens had armed themselves. Clutched in the orange fingers he spotted glints of metal, and his first shot went wide as he leapt aside a thrust from a surgical tool. Three of the aliens broke off to follow him, while the remaining two went after Areva. She fired, taking down one, but the other careened toward her, waving a jagged bit of pipe.

Viktor fired and brought one of the aliens to the ground. This gave him enough breathing space to take note of the rest of the room. In the center sat some sort of large diagnostic machine shaped like a full-body imaging scanner from Earth, with a patient bed that could insert itself into a transparent sphere of glass.

Areva's opponent pressed her back toward a booth in the corner shielded by a half-height wall and another pane of glass connecting to the ceiling. Viktor took his two opponents away from her, toward the sphere and bed. He slipped a thrust from the scalpel-wielding alien and rolled backward over the diagnostic bed, putting it between them as a barrier. The blade-wielder hesitated, but the other one, armed with a length of thin plastic tubing, leapt over the bed and swung the tubing toward Viktor's throat. He ducked and dodged, but the alien spun moved with him, too agile to outmaneuver. While Viktor struggled to keep the scalpel wielder in his sights, the alien with the tubing darted behind him and threw his weapon over Viktor's head. The thin plastic line wrapped around his neck and dug in.

Viktor raised his rifle and fired forward just as the scalpel wielder scrambled onto the bed. The alien toppled forward and crashed to the floor, and the scalpel skittered away. Viktor tried to aim another shot behind to target the strangler. The bazooka rifle proved cumbersome, and the alien dodged the attacking end of it with ease. The only part of the alien Viktor could see were his hands. Veins popped out of them, and the orange knuckles tinged white as he twisted the tubing deeper into Viktor's flesh.

Air and blood both stopped flowing, and Viktor's body panicked. Dark spots flickered in his vision. Every heartbeat throbbed in his temples. Raw skin chafed where the tubing cut into it and his lungs began to burn. The dark spots in his eyes edged forward, crowding out the rest of the room.

He dropped the rifle and flung himself backward, ramming the alien against the wall. The alien grunted but clung to his back, and Viktor's fingers clawed uselessly at the tube. He threw himself backward again, with no results.

Someone screamed his name, but the sound came to him as through a long tunnel. His muscles began to flag, and tremors wracked his knees. His legs and arms both felt distant, detached. The urge to give up, to sleep, blanketed his thoughts. Darkness engulfed everything but a narrow spot in the very center of his vision, and he stared through blood-rimmed eyes at the glass sphere around the bed.

With one last burst of effort, he wrenched his body around and threw himself backwards through the sphere.

Glass shattered and the bed creaked as the full weight of Viktor and his opponent landed sideways across it. Something sticky sprayed Viktor's right arm. The dark spots crowded out all sight. His grip slipped on the alien's hand.

A moment later, the pressure on his throat lessened, and Viktor choked in a gasp of air. His head cleared rapidly, and he smashed his skull backward to where he hoped the alien's face lay beneath him. Bone crunched on bone, and the alien shrieked. Something began beeping in a complex rhythm, and strange bursts of light erupted from every direction as miniscule fibers running through the remnants of the glass sphere came to life.

The dark spots receded, and Viktor yanked the tubing away from his throat. The alien still clung to the other end of it with one hand. His other hand dripped blood from glass wounds all along the arm. Viktor used the tube to yank his opponent toward himself, spearing him in the gut with his free hand. He then seized the injured alien in a headlock, grabbed the pneumo-injector from his belt, shoved it against the other man's neck, and activated the cylinder.

The alien fought him for a few more seconds, then went still as the zombie drug flooded his veins.

Viktor dropped him and looked around for Areva.

She stood in the control booth behind her own wall of shattered glass. The fifth alien lay unconscious on the bank of buttons and screens behind the little wall. "Are you hurt?" Viktor asked.

Areva shook her head, breathing heavily. "You?"

"I am fine."

"Good." She ducked beneath the controls, staying out of sight once more.

Damn, he thought. That would have been the perfect moment to cross the room and take her hands in a gesture of reassurance and allow all the buried feelings to come out.

But he hesitated, and she disappeared.

He turned to survey the damage he'd done to the glass sphere and was surprised to see the remains of the structure alight with symbols and diagrams and more of the alien writing. The section he'd broken lay strewn across the bed and floor, bits of it ground to dust beneath the struggle, but the majority of it was intact.

The sphere must have activated when Areva's attacker fell on the controls. He circled the display, trying to comprehend it. Something about the rows of symbols and the shapes of the diagrams felt familiar.

Halfway around, he halted before a recognizable shape. "DNA."

"What?" asked Areva, still hiding.

"This machine. It scans DNA. This is a double helix."

Areva popped her head over the booth and peered out. "What do they use this for?"

"A DNA map would allow much more precise medical treatments. This is likely how they created inventions such as the zombie drug."

He continued circling the machine, puzzling out different parts of the readings. "The scans are stored on the hospital's main computer."

"So that the doctors can access it more easily. That makes sense."

"Yes. Easy access." Ice crawled down Viktor's spine. "Areva, the Haxozin plague only infected this planet's native species. It may have specifically targeted their DNA."

"True. You think the Haxozin used a similar scanner?"

"No. I think they used *this* scanner."

Areva poked her head up and saw the remote computer uplink display to which Viktor was pointing. She said, "I suppose it makes more sense to hack the hospital computer and take the data than try to create it on their own. The Haxozin do seem to be scavengers. So they used the DNA scans to try to kill everyone, and then the Thassians used them to find a way to survive. It's horrible, but I don't understand why this seems to trouble you so much."

Viktor's face was grim. "I fell while fighting. Inside the machine. It turned on."

Areva gasped. "If it scanned you …"

"A map of human physiology is now stored here." Viktor lifted the butt of his bazooka rifle and smashed it through the scanner sphere. It shattered, raining bits of glass on the already strewn floor. He repeated the movement, destroying every standing bit of the machine, until the scanner lay in bits at his feet, a few fragments still connected by fraying sensor wires. "That removes the data from this device, but it was likely already uploaded to the hospital mainframe."

"The ... the Haxozin don't look like they've been here recently. Maybe they won't find it."

"Do you wish to take that risk?" She didn't answer. "I thought not. When we finish drugging the aliens, we will escort them from the building and destroy it."

"The machine?"

"The building."

Areva's hand popped up in a "wait" gesture. "Or, we could have Matthias access the computer and erase the data."

That would be easier, if not as thorough. Viktor grimaced. "My way is better."

"You just like blowing things up."

"Explosions are effective."

"Sometimes subtlety is best."

"I do not do subtlet—" The words stuck in his throat. There was one gaping example of subtlety that he had done, a little too well. "Areva, I need to tell you ..."

He met her eyes, and for a brief instant, they connected fully. He saw her concern for his safety, her amusement at their banter, her determination to succeed at the mission. He knew his own expression was full of regret and longing. He'd tried to convey those same feelings before, to say with that connection what he could never seem to find the words to express, when she announced her impending resignation. He'd tried, and she'd fled.

He tried again now.

She fled again. A wrenching movement tore her gaze away, and she headed for the door. "When ... when we get back to Earth, we can go to the shooting range and you can destroy as many targets as you want. It'll be my going-away party."

She disappeared around the edge of the door.

Viktor stood where she'd left him. Again he'd hesitated, let his lack of the proper words render him mute. But in that instant when their eyes met, he thought he'd seen something beneath her confident veneer. The same vulnerability he'd tried to show, trying to break through.

He glanced at his pocket comp. Heat readings on the upper floors continued to dwindle as his teammates located the aliens. The lower half of the building was cold, except for his own thermal signature standing in the middle of the room, and another one just outside it, leaning against the wall.

She hadn't fled too far. "After we shoot things," Viktor said, "I will take you out to dinner."

A long pause. "I'd like that."

At dinner, Viktor told himself. At dinner he'd find the words. It wouldn't change her decision to quit, and it wouldn't fix his silence over the past years, but at least he would have told her how he felt.

And if he didn't, if he let the lack of the right words paralyze his tongue again, at least they'd have one more night of just dinner together.

* * *

Viktor and Areva met the other teams on the ground floor once every heat signature in the building had been located and treated with the zombie drug. By the time the final team arrived, the first zombies had begun stirring on the floor.

"Hurry," said Viktor. "We must leave before they notice us."

The teams sprinted out of the hospital, heading back toward the warehouse.

It took only seconds before the sounds of pursuit echoed behind them.

The zombies had risen, and instinct had taken over once more.

Viktor chanced a glance over his shoulder and spotted at least a dozen of the faded orange bodies sprinting after them, fangs bared, claws outstretched.

"Faster!" he yelled. His leg muscles burned as he dug his feet into the pavement, propelling himself forward, heedless of caution.

They made it almost all the way to the warehouse. Only a single street stood between them and the ship's hiding place, a narrow road between two skyscrapers that overlooked the alien city's port. The warehouse stood at the other end. Viktor could see pieces of its fallen roof littering the ground alongside its walls.

He could also see a mass of moving bodies swarming into the street from the other side.

"Turn!" he shouted, and executed a quick pivot that swung his momentum to the right. The others followed with a minimum loss of speed. No one questioned him. If they went down that street, they'd be overrun in seconds. Without the protection of spacesuits, Viktor had no doubt at least one of his people would be cut or bitten, and if the drug could spread to humans, it would do so.

The sounds of pursuit seemed to have attracted every zombie in the city. Wherever they tried to turn, hordes of undead appeared to cut them off. Viktor had begun to despair of finding an escape route when he spotted a decrepit wall fallen around metal pylons, right across the street from the capital building.

The hovercar factory.

A plan formed in his mind.

"Follow!" he called, and turned his steps toward the crumbling wall.

The officers clambered into the darkness of the factory. The machines were still running. Sound dampening technology muffled the bangs and clangs to a tolerable level, but the air conditioning appeared to have failed. Heat from the giant autoclaves filled the building. Viktor began to sweat as soon as he entered, but he couldn't spare any thought for the discomfort. He led his people straight down the main walkway through the center of the factory.

Halfway through, he skidded to a halt next to a bin of finished chassis. "Keep running!" he ordered the others.

Most obeyed, but Areva hesitated. "What are you doing?"

"You noticed they have sensitive noses." He spun the dial controlling his bazooka rifle's output all the way to its maximum setting and took aim at the bin. Armies of zombies closed in behind them.

He fired.

A high-energy blast struck the polymer chassis and burned a hole straight through them before dissipating on the bin's far side.

Nothing else happened.

"Dammit!" Viktor yelled, and fired again with the same result.

He could make out the individual limbs on the lead zombies now.

"They're gaining on us!" Areva screamed.

"Composite polymers release toxic fumes when they burn," Viktor said. "If we ignite these chassis, the zombies will avoid them like they did the dead fish."

He spotted one of the tool walls, equipment still neatly arranged inside tidy tape lines. He grabbed a plasma welding torch, rattling the wall and sending other tools crashing to the floor. "Look away, Areva!" He shut his eyes, squeezed the activator on the welding torch, and thrust it toward the bin of polymers.

The worst stench in the world exploded a second later.

Plasma from the torch ignited the chassis, and billows of acrid green smoke poured out of the bin. Viktor could taste the poison in the air even as the ash began to burn his lungs. He dropped the torch and grabbed Areva's hand. "Come!"

As they sprinted after their team, Viktor glanced back to see the zombie hordes pouring back through the hole to the safety on the other side of the building.

* * *

They made it back to the warehouse only slightly ashy, though very out of breath. Viktor felt the ship lift off as the airlock's decontamination process swept them for diseases.

No one had been bitten. The zombieism would stay on this planet, where it belonged.

After clearance from decon, Viktor climbed the ladder two rungs at a time to the bridge. "Captain," he said, "the DNA scanner ..."

"Already on it," said Matthias Habassa from the bridge's scanners station. "If it has wireless transmissions engaged, I should be able to pick them up and trace them to the hospital's main computer."

"And then?" asked Viktor.

Captain Withers sat in his chair, a grim expression on his face. "We blow it up."

The *Endurance* soared over the decrepit city. Through the front viewports, Viktor could see smoke pouring from the skylights on the old factory. The horde of zombies fleeing the stench had dissipated through the city, and nothing moved near the building. The polymers would burn themselves out without any casualties.

The hospital came into view as the ship rounded the rotunda on city hall. Here more unlife could be seen, zombie bodies milling around in the sunshine. Many stopped to stare agape as the ship flew by.

Matthias smiled. "They look happy."

"They look dead," Viktor said.

"Yeah. And they seem happy this way." The engineer tapped one final control on his console with a flourish. "Got it. Third floor, northwest corner of the building. All wireless connections map to there as the central hub. Can't hack into it, though. Our operating system won't interface properly."

"Any sign of movement?"

"Clear on thermal, obviously. We'll have visual in just a moment."

The ship stabilized in a hover just outside the designated room. The curtains were pulled back, showing a deserted, yet well-furnished office with a single, slim computer core on the desk. Lights shone from various surfaces, indicating the activity within, and a blank screen on one side awaited a user. It contained the records and operating systems for an entire six-story hospital, and the whole thing was the size of a paperback novel.

Matthias sighed wistfully. "Seems a shame. That looks like some real advanced tech. We could use it."

"So could the Haxozin," said Viktor.

"Agreed," said the captain. "Let's get rid of it."

A moment later, a low-yield torpedo from the *Endurance*'s main guns ripped through the window and curtains, blasted through the fancy desk, and turned the computer core and everything in a two meter radius into a blackened disaster.

"Wireless network is gone," said Matthias. "Nobody's getting any data from this hospital ever again."

Captain Withers stood and rubbed his forehead. "Helm, get us out of this city center and find a place we can accelerate enough to break orbit. I'll be in my office." He headed into the little room just off the bridge.

Viktor glanced around and noticed the two O&I officers were nowhere to be seen. He followed the captain and pulled the office hatch shut. "Your friends are gone."

Withers pressed a button to open one of his desk drawers and pulled out a bottle of headache medicine. "They've 'seen enough to make their decision.' They're in their berths, finishing their reports." He popped the canister open and downed two pills.

"It will be bad."

"Yeah. It'll be bad." The captain massaged his forehead again and replaced the medication. "We killed those people, Ivanokoff."

"They were dead before."

"That's not the point. I gave an order to exterminate a civilian population. They were attacking us, but they wouldn't have been doing that if we hadn't interfered with them in the first place. There's no way we come out of this looking good. At best, we can clean up our own messes and pick up some useful stuff like that zombie drug on the way, but that's not going to be enough for Dispatch. They're going to take us off interstellar patrol."

Viktor let out a slow breath. After the previous months of exploring unknown parts of the galaxy, thinking on his feet and facing threats no one had imagined, the thought of returning to the Endurance's former Neptune patrol felt like cutting off a limb. "The Haxozin threat remains. This planet proves the extreme methods they will use against us."

"We obliterated that computer. They won't get your DNA scan."

"That is not the point. They steal technology and research from those they encounter. We know their fleet outnumbers their personnel. Perhaps their very ships were scavenged from their victims. They do not need the DNA scan. They will have other weapons to bring against us."

Withers sank onto his chair. "And so we need all our ships out searching the galaxy for those same advantages so we're ready when they come, is that your point?"

"Yes."

"I agree. Unfortunately, since the Haxozin likely don't know where Earth is, that threat isn't going to seem as pressing to everyone at home."

"The message the Uprising sent…"

"Could take decades, or even centuries to reach them. The Haxozin are a problem, Ivanokoff, but a distant one. To the people at Dispatch, *we* seem like the more immediate issue. They won't want renegades screwing around with alien societies, away from their control. I realize I'm being pessimistic, but from the attitudes of those two suits and my own confrontations with the brass, I'm pretty sure I'm right."

Viktor couldn't argue. *Ten soldiers wisely led* ... From Dispatch's perspective, the *Endurance* crew must seem like part of the headless hundred.

"I will warn the others to expect disappointment," he said.

"No. Let them keep their hopes up. Goodness knows, Habassa is going to look on the bright side no matter what we say."

The captain's desk computer beeped. "Bridge paging you," said the computerized voice.

Withers winced and tapped a control on the screen. "Go ahead."

Matthias's voice came over the line. "We're over a park and gaining altitude. Just thought you'd want to know. In a few minutes, we'll be gone like the wind."

"*With* the wind," Viktor muttered.

"Good work, Lieutenant," said the captain. "I'll be right out." Withers closed the line and rose from his chair, stretching his back with the movement. His seat squeaked, and Viktor wondered how Withers managed to get anything done while sitting in an uncomfortable old chair. He spotted a few novels he'd lent his CO on the shelf behind the desk, the largest of which had a bookmark about a tenth of the way through it. "One good thing may come from reassignment to Neptune."

"What's that?"

He jutted his chin toward the shelf. "You will finally finish *War and Peace.*"

The captain mumbled something noncommittal and let himself out through the hatch. Viktor was about to follow when movement next to the bookshelf caught his eye.

Areva Praphasat emerged from behind a stack of old equipment that had found its way into the office and never been moved. Viktor didn't bother asking how she'd snuck in and secluded herself without the captain noticing; she didn't like to discuss her gifts. "You heard," he said.

She nodded. "Neptune again."

A strange glimmer in her eye gave Viktor the impression she was waiting for him to say something. He thought back to that moment on the planet, when he wanted to speak up, and she'd hidden too quickly.

She wasn't hiding now, and Viktor realized if he waited for dinner to say anything, he'd never speak up at all.

"Areva, do not leave," he said. "You are a good officer."

She flinched. "Good against zombies, but against the living …"

"We will not be fighting anyone around Neptune." He crossed to her, and she didn't back away. "Please, Areva. It is not only the ship. I want you to stay."

She swallowed, and the expectation in her eyes deepened. "Why?"

Where were the right words to express it all? He'd read a thousand books, and yet the sentences that would best serve this moment, best capture everything he wanted to say, eluded him.

At his silence, the intensity went out of her gaze. "It's okay. I'll just—"

Eloquence be damned. "I love you." There were. The words that spawned a thousand romances, a thousand wars, and a thousand really sappy novels. Viktor ignored the urge to quote one of a dozen classic poems and instead just spoke without filtering himself. "You are the only person I have ever met who is so fascinating, so self-reliant, and so deadly. You follow your convictions, and you seek to understand before you act. You do not just look at situations, you *see* them, and you make others around you do the same. You are incredibly unique, and you have become my closest friend. I cannot imagine life without you. I love you, Areva Praphasat. I have loved you for a long time. I want you to stay."

Areva's eyes shimmered ever so slightly before she blinked them dry. "I think those are the most words you've spoken in a row since I've known you."

"This is the proper moment for them."

"If ... if hypothetically, I felt the same way about you ..."

"I would be a happy man."

"You're a stoic man."

"I would be stoically happy."

The corners of her mouth curved upward. "I think I would be stoically happy, too."

Viktor's heart pounded like it had never pounded before. He took her hands in his own. "Areva, please stay."

She inhaled, exhaled slowly. "If ... if the ship does get reassigned to Neptune ..."

"It will." Now Viktor hoped for the boring patrol.

"If it does ... I'll stay." Her smile finally reached her eyes. "And if it doesn't ... I'm sure we can work something out."

Viktor's own smile grew and he seized the moment. He leaned down and pressed his lips gently against Areva's. It was a chaste kiss, quiet, but the heat thrumming beneath the light touch zinged through his entire body.

They didn't need outrageous displays of passion to communicate through that moment; this was who they were.

When they separated, Areva's smile remained. "Are we still going out for shooting and dinner?"

"Yes," said Viktor. "But now it is not just dinner. Now it is just a date."

"That sounds just right."

He turned to head through the hatch, but her voice stopped him. "I guess this explains why I came through the fighting without injury."

Viktor frowned. "What?"

She slipped her hand into his and squeezed. "I wasn't two days from retirement after all."

They returned to the bridge separately. No one commented on Areva's surprise appearance from the captain's office. Viktor wondered if they knew what had just happened. Then he decided they could mind their own business. This was one of the happiest moments of his life, and he would enjoy it.

Though the decaying city loomed on every side, the park over which the *Endurance* made its ascent was still moderately pretty. Overgrown grass and weeds choked it, but the greenery remained. Even the Haxozin couldn't kill everything.

One of the external camera views on the bridge screens caught Viktor's attention. "Zoom there," he said to the scanners operator.

Amidst the wilting flowers and misshapen shrubs, a pair of zombies shambled.

They were holding hands.

Viktor smiled inwardly. Mistakes may have been made, both today and in the past, but at least everything was now as it should be.

* * *

Systems away, a five-pointed star ship hung in orbit over a lifeless planet. A burst of light erupted nearby, and a second, smaller star emerged into regular space, braking thrusters firing all across the front of the vessel. It assumed a synchronous orbit alongside its sister.

A small craft slipped from a docking bay on the newcomer and darted across space to the larger ship. Its occupants, a pair of red-suited and helmeted soldiers, sat at the controls as if perfectly at ease, but small twitches in their movements belied the veneer of calm.

They landed in the star ship's bay and hurried from their shuttle through the winding corridors to the bridge.

The star ship's control room sat in the very center of the five prongs, protected by multiple layers of bulkheads and shielding. It had no windows, but the display screens on all four walls and the ceiling showed exterior views of the surrounding space. One screen held a visual of the sister star ship. Another focused on the dead planet. The others shifted between scanner telemetry of their current system and diagrams of other solar systems throughout the galaxy.

The control stations along the walls were unmanned, but on a short dais in the center of the room sat a single chair, turned away. The back of a red helmet could be seen over the seat, and red armored hands lay on the armrests.

The two soldiers halted at the door.

"Displays to default," said the man in the chair. His voice was monotonous, cold, dispassionate. Deadly.

All screens reverted to a three-hundred-sixty degree view of the space outside the star ship. The planet and sister ship remained, and in the distance one of the screens revealed the ball of light that was the system's star.

The chair swiveled to face the door. The seated man wore the same blood-red armor as the two soldiers, but where one of theirs had a silver patch running diagonally across its chest and the other bore no markings at all, the man in the chair wore a thick silver line trimmed with two stripes of gold. The same markings ran along the sides of his helmet.

Both soldiers spread their open hands and bowed. "Sovereign," said the one with the silver stripe, "one of our outlying scouts received a broadcast message from a system in one of the galactic tendrils. They relayed it to us, and we have come here as quickly as possible." The sound of his breath resonated out of his helmet. "We found the enemy's home world."

The chair swiveled silently as the sovereign turned to study the display screen showing the ruined planet below. "Recall the fleet," he ordered in the same dispassionate tone. "Tell the rest of our brethren to prepare for war."

Just Desserts

A Short Story

In retrospect, it seemed only natural that their first date would include a gunfight.

Even seated, Viktor Ivanokoff towered over the back of the restaurant booth, making Areva Praphasat look smaller by comparison. It didn't help that she shrank into the far corner of her seat and slouched so low that half her torso disappeared beneath the table.

"I am sorry," Viktor said, watching her slide down another centimeter. "I thought this establishment was dark enough."

"It's okay." Areva tossed her head so that her short, black hair covered the restaurant-exposed side of her face. "Nobody's looking."

Someone at a table across the tiled floor suddenly glanced at them, and Areva disappeared the rest of the way. The white tablecloth rippled to show her point of exit.

Viktor grimaced and lifted his own side of the cloth to peer beneath. "You can sit between me and the wall. Then nobody will see you."

Her face brightened. "Thanks."

Half a second later, she'd slipped into the booth next to him, protected by his colossus of muscles, able to observe the environment without risking it observing her back. Too many years in interplanetary undercover work had a way of making one jumpy.

"Guy in the white shirt," she whispered.

Viktor glanced across the room. A man in a suit that cost three months of Viktor's United Earth Law Enforcement salary sat in his shirtsleeves at a central table, boasting loudly to a slightly-less-well-dressed man about his purchase of some real estate. "An entire sub-island!" he said. "Just two kilometers off Median's coast. Great Mediterranean weather, close to the capital city. Luxury condos there are gonna be a hit. Building starts next week."

"I see him," Viktor said to Areva.

"He's lying. He's broke."

"How do you know?"

"His pinkies twitch every time he talks about the construction."

Viktor paid closer attention, and sure enough, the next comment about "superlative contractors and materials" came with a nervous jitter through the man's hands.

"Also I've seen that island, and there was a big sinkhole in the middle of it. Whoever built it did a lousy job. He'd have to have spent a fortune filling it in, or the first storm is going to flood the place."

Viktor smiled and found Areva's hand to clasp in his.

"At least we need not worry about such things. There are no oceans in space."

Areva laughed. "I'm curious, what are you planning to do once we head out? Returning to the routine Neptune patrol is going to feel uneventful."

"I bought some new books."

"Long ones?"

"Da."

"What are you going to do in the second week?"

"Defeat you at marksmanship again."

She swatted him. "What do you mean? I scored more points tonight."

"We can compare targets."

"I don't think the restaurant would appreciate us whipping out bullet-shredded papers. This is a fancy place." She leaned forward incrementally to take another look around. "In fact, it's the fanciest restaurant I've ever seen."

"Including ones you visited in special ops?"

She made a face. "I did more lowbrow infiltration. The fancy stuff went to people with seniority. Seriously, Viktor, how are you affording this?"

A commotion at Fancy Suit's table stole Viktor's attention. The real estate tycoon had stood up, teetering with a hand on the back of his chair. His face was flushed, his breathing erratic. "Dizzy ... room's spinning," he mumbled.

Viktor's hand automatically checked to make sure the projectile gun tucked in his concealed holster was still there. It was. His senses leapt to alert as he watched Fancy Suit stagger against the chair. There was no way he'd gone from lucid to this drunk in such a short amount of time.

With a shudder, he collapsed.

Viktor was halfway to the man's table before he hit the ground. He pulled his pocket computer from his slacks and flicked his UELE badge onto the screen, flashing it at the startled man still at the table. "Police. What happened?"

He knelt to check Fancy Suit's pulse as the other man sputtered. "I don't know! One second we're talking, and the next he starts sweating and his eyes go blank, and he says he doesn't feel well …" The man cast a suspicious look at his meal and dropped his fork.

Areva appeared beside Viktor. He didn't flinch; he was used to her stealthy arrivals. She'd worn slacks and a nice blouse rather than an evening dress, giving her free range of movement. She held her pocket comp in her hand, the screen set to a fingerprint identifier, and pressed the fallen man's thumb to it. Data crawled across the screen. She read it in a low tone. "Jarry Rin. Forty-two, no criminal record, no prior health problems."

Jarry Rin moaned and clenched his hands into fists. "Stable pulse," Viktor told Areva, "but unstable breathing. Keep him still and call the hospital." He stood to inspect the table as she began calling in the emergency on her comp.

A steak the size of a lunar dome sat untouched on Rin's plate next to equally unsampled greens that looked like lettuce but probably had a nicer name. The silverware hadn't even been unwrapped. The only object at Rin's setting that showed any sign of interaction was the bottle of Château de Montes 2118 with a rather overstated image of its originating vineyard on Venus, and Rin's glass of the purple liquid. Spun strands of edible gold decorated the plates, and little flecks of it floated in both glasses.

Viktor leaned over the bottle, careful not to touch

anything, and sniffed.

It smelled like wine.

Then he did the same to Rin's glass.

A faint odor of garlic surged into his sinuses. He exhaled sharply by instinct and crouched back beside Areva.

"Poison," he whispered, "or a drug."

"Medhovers are on their way," she replied. She'd mostly obscured herself beneath Rin's table. "I called for backup. UELE officers are two minutes out. They'll close off the building and question witnesses."

"Rin?"

"He's not getting worse, but he's delirious."

Rin groaned and clutched his stomach.

Again Viktor stood and faced Rin's tablemate. He flipped his pocket comp to its fingerprint scanner and held it out to the man. "Your thumb."

The man blinked confusedly before comprehension dawned and he pressed his digit against the screen.

Two beeps, and the scanner displayed the man's identification.

"Ed Alvarez," Viktor said. "Tell me everything that happened since you arrived at the restaurant."

Alvarez shuddered. "We've been in business talks for about a month now. I'm a senior vice-president at a lunar mining company, and we were thinking about investing in his project. I knew something was going to happen; property values around Median are just too high for his island to get built with no trouble."

"Stop," said Viktor. "What do you mean, you knew something would happen? Did you suspect danger?"

"I thought Jarry was being paranoid. He kept saying there were competitors who wanted to halt his construction, that they would stop at nothing to ruin his project. He even bought this device for testing his food before consuming it, some attachment for his pocket comp."

"Did he use this device tonight?"

"I think ... yes. Yes, he tested a drop of wine, but not the food. He hadn't had a chance."

"Just the wine. You are sure?"

"Yes. He said it was clean, but when he tried it he said the texture was wrong. I thought he was just showing off, flaunting his expensive tastes."

Viktor frowned and turned to search Rin. Apparently Areva had been listening. Though she'd by now obscured herself entirely beneath the white tablecloth, her hand appeared from beneath it, holding aloft Rin's pocket comp.

Viktor switched the device on and located the food analysis program—software for evaluating nutritional content, operated by depositing a miniscule sample in an attachable mini mass spectrometer, which would evaluate the chemicals present. Apparently Rin had co-opted the device as a poison tester.

A chemical breakdown was present for a sample of wine. Tartaric acid. Fructose. Multiple words Viktor couldn't define but recognized from other food labels as normal, non-harmful consumables.

Not a hint of any kind of poison.

"You are sure Rin tested this wine?" he asked Alvarez, pointing to the glass.

Alvarez nodded.

"And no one touched it after he tested it?"

"No. There was no time; he drank right afterward."

Viktor linked the nutrient analyzer to Rin's pocket comp and dipped a corner of the silk napkin into the wine, shook off the edible gold that clung to the fabric, then placed a drop on the device's clear screen and activated it. A metal cover slid over the screen, and a faint humming vibrated the table. A minute later, the comp began displaying graphs and lists breaking down the chemical contents of the wine.

This time there was an added ingredient.

Arsenic.

That explained the garlic scent.

It did not explain how the poison made it into a glass that, a few minutes earlier, had not contained a hint of lethality.

Viktor inhaled, exhaled slowly. He had a mystery on his hands.

And he'd left his Holmesian deerstalker cap in his berth on the ship.

Pity.

"Mr. Alvarez, tell me again what happened after you entered the restaurant, with every detail you can remember."

After Alvarez repeated his story twice more, neither time producing any more usable information, Viktor noticed Areva staring toward the entry hall. He held up his hand and knelt to speak with her. "What is it?"

"Backup should be here by now. What's taking them so long?"

"I do not know."

From the entryway, a waiter in full dress attire strode into the main dining room. "Attention, please," he said, and lifted the tails of his coat to produce an energy gun from the back of his cummerbund.

The patrons, most of whom had been sitting and watching the situation unfold from their tables, screamed.

Viktor's hand was on his gun at once, but the waiter was too quick. "We don't want to tangle with the police," he said. "Place your weapon on the ground and kick it over here, please, Officer."

"Lieutenant, actually," said Viktor.

"My apologies, Lieutenant. No disrespect intended. But I do need your gun."

Viktor slowly pulled his p-gun from its holster and laid it on the tile. "What do you want?"

"Funding."

"Who are you with?"

"Your weapon first, please."

With a gentle kick, Viktor's service weapon skittered across the floor. The waiter stepped forward and picked it up.

"Now then," he said, scanning the room with a pleasant smile, "I'm afraid you'll all have to stay here for a while. My colleagues and I represent the Uprising, and we have temporarily seized this building."

"Uprising!" wailed a woman wearing a national park's worth of fur.

"No need for alarm," said the waiter. "We don't want to hurt anyone."

"Then let the paramedics in," said Viktor, pointing to Rin. "This man is dying."

"Yes, he is. But once our demands are met, we'll ensure his survival."

"What demands?"

"Everyone knows the Uprising's demands," scoffed a man with an honest-to-god monocle hanging from his pocket. "If they think taking over one restaurant will lead to the breakup of planetary government and a return to nation-states, they're out of their addled minds!"

"Believe it or not, we do have other goals besides that one," said the waiter. "Tonight, we need money. Most of you may not know this, but the man currently lying on the floor is Mr. Jarry Rin, owner of Arbor Landing, the artificial island just off our lovely artificial capital's coast. He's procured investments from several dozen sources, promising a ten to one return once he turns it into a luxury community. One such source was our organization."

Indignant murmuring came from the patrons.

"We've recently discovered that Mr. Rin has been squandering his funding, and that his proposed project may never actually come to fruition. Naturally we want to discourage our other business partners from defaulting on their loans, so we're here to collect what's ours. We have sealed the entrances and one of our outside agents is currently speaking with Mr. Rin's company. Once they have returned our funding, we'll leave you all to enjoy your dinner and him to his hospital visit." A smile turned up one corner of his mouth, though it didn't meet his eyes. "And for those of you in this room who are currently using Uprising money among your various investments, take notes. We'd hate to spoil another of your evenings."

Through all of this, Viktor did not look down at the table. He knew Areva was crouched beneath the tablecloth and had no desire to attract attention to her. Surely she had her gun out and was waiting for the moment to strike. She might not be willing to fire point blank on people anymore, but she had no qualms about shooting those who couldn't see it coming. And very few ever saw her coming.

"Where's your date, Lieutenant?" the waiter asked Viktor.

"Restroom."

"I'll have someone check on that." Though Viktor didn't turn, he saw the waiter nod to someone across the room.

"How many of you are here?" Viktor asked.

"Enough."

"How did you get the arsenic into Rin's glass? You must have known he checked his food before eating, so somehow you poisoned the wine after he had scanned it."

The waiter's smile became genuine. "You're quick, Lieutenant."

"Yet you did this without so much as touching it."

"Maybe we've invented teleportation."

"Unlikely."

A woman's voice drew Viktor's attention to the back of the restaurant. "The restroom's empty," she said. She was wearing an evening gown and huge, fake pearls. They had people posing as diners, then. Probably more than Viktor had spotted.

He didn't have time to look around for suspicious faces before the waiter's smile vanished and he aimed his energy pistol at Viktor's chest. "Where's your friend?"

"Perhaps she stood me up."

"I'm not playing games with you, Officer." The waiter aimed at the nearest patron, a middle-aged man seated at the edge of a crowded booth. "Where is she?"

"Under the table!" The fur-clad patron shouted, pointing. "Don't shoot anybody, my god!"

Viktor's heart leapt into his mouth, but before he could react the waiter and Pearls converged on Rin and Alvarez's table. They unceremoniously flipped it over, flinging steak and greens to the floor. Glass shattered, and the wine spilled out of both bottle and goblets, staining the floor and fallen tablecloth blood red. A few flakes of edible gold stuck in the liquid.

The area under the table was empty.

The waiter whirled on Viktor. "Where did she go?"

"I do not know."

"I won't ask you again!" He pressed the barrel of the e-gun against Viktor's chest.

Viktor didn't blink, but slowly raised his hands. "Your shoe is untied."

Confusion crossed the waiter's face. In that instant, Viktor moved.

He pivoted to one side, simultaneously bringing his raised hands in to grasp the gun and twist the waiter's wrist. Bones snapped and the waiter screamed, and then the gun came away from his broken fingers in Viktor's hand. Before anyone else had moved, Viktor stepped back and aimed the gun at the waiter and Pearls.

"Disarm yourselves. Now. You are under arrest."

Another patron seated in a booth opposite Rin's table stood, revealing an energy gun from beneath his jacket. Another metallic device hung from his belt, though Viktor couldn't make out what it was in the mood lighting. The man had a magnificent mustache that trembled as he shouted, "You disarm yourself! Nobody's getting arrested!"

So the Uprising had Mustache and Pearls posing as patrons. Adding in the waiter and estimating two people to guard the doors, there were at least five individuals involved in this attack. Could there still be more?

Viktor did not drop his gun, as he had an clean angle of attack on both the waiter and Pearls. Alvarez had dived out of his chair for the protection of the rows of booths. Mustache kept his e-gun squarely on Viktor, his stance firm.

"We are in a standoff," said Viktor, "but I have the advantage."

"How d'ya figure that?" said Mustache.

"More officers are descending on this building every

second. Your backup cannot reach us."

Mustache didn't reply and Pearls simply curled her lip, but between hisses of pain the waiter chuckled. "Our backup has been here all along."

Behind Viktor, the kitchen door banged against the wood paneled walls. He spun to try to keep the entire restaurant in view while also watching the newcomer, but the downside of his large size was a reduction in agility. By the time he turned, a woman in kitchen garb stood in the doorway, a projectile gun in hand. They all stared at each other for a moment before she said, "Hi. How were the appetizers, asshole?"

Two weapons against his one, from opposite directions. Viktor could not win this alone.

Of course he wasn't alone, but if Areva didn't make her appearance soon, this might go very badly. Where could she be?

He began lowering his gun. "A poor choice of catchphrase," he told the Uprising cook. "You should have said, 'Hot bullets, compliments of the chef.'"

"The bullets are for dessert."

"Fair enough."

Viktor had just crouched to set down his gun when the first shot rang out.

A loud zap crackled the air, and a blue-white ball of energy the size of a marble struck Mustache in the chest. He gasped and flopped back in his booth, spasms contorting his limbs.

Viktor snapped his gun up and fired on the chef. Another zap, another blue blast, and she too went down.

That left only the waiter and Pearls, and whoever was guarding the doors. Viktor felled the waiter, and another shot from somewhere in the general direction of the kitchen took down Pearls. That left only the door guards to—

Pain exploded in Viktor's left arm as the crack of a projectile gun and the acrid stench of powder filled the air. Fire lanced through his biceps, down into his forearm and up into his shoulder. He groaned and clutched at the wound. His hand came away sticky and red.

He knew in that instant that he'd been shot, and that a second bullet would no doubt follow. This one would probably have better aim.

Before he could duck, or turn, or do anything else to try to save his life, a buzzing sound filled his ears. This wasn't the crackle of an e-gun. It was more like the hum of the Adkinsium reactors that powered UELE spaceships.

Something heavy hit the floor behind him, and someone let out a low moan.

He pivoted to see a plain-clothed man splayed on the floor, a p-gun fallen by his side. He wasn't twitching like the others who had been stunned, though. Instead he pressed his hand against a burn in his shoulder that was far too small to have been made by an e-gun.

On the other side of the restaurant, near the booths, Ed Alvarez stood wide-eyed, trembling hands clutching the device that had been attached to Mustache's belt.

Viktor surveyed the room. All opponents were down, and the remaining patrons were all cowering in their seats. Not likely that any Uprising agents remained among them. "Mr. Alvarez," said Viktor through gritted teeth, "please put the ... object on the floor."

Alvarez blinked and opened his mouth, then complied. "S-sorry," he said as he stood back up. "T-the guy was shooting, and I j-just ... am I under arrest?"

"No."

Another zap rang out from the back area of the

kitchen, and then Areva appeared at the swinging doors. "Exits are clear," she said. "Once we radio, backup can come—Viktor, you're hurt!"

She was by his side at once, inspecting the wound. "Just a graze," she said. "You'll be okay. But your suit is ruined."

"Damn." Viktor stripped off his jacket and then tore off one his shirtsleeves and tied it around the wound.

Areva activated her pocket comp and relayed to the officers outside that the situation had been contained. In seconds the entire restaurant flooded with cops. The uninvolved patrons were escorted outside, Rin was rushed to the hospital, the Uprising agents arrested and removed, and Viktor's arm treated by medics. He and Areva remained on scene, as did Ed Alvarez, for questioning.

Viktor found the shaking senior vice-president seated on a booth. "Thank you," Viktor said.

"Oh, um, you're welcome," said Alvarez.

"What was that device?"

"It's a thermal beam. Our facilities use them to separate contaminants out of the ores we mine. On low settings it's pretty harmless, but I ... I turned it up all the way, and ... well ..."

"Do not worry," said Viktor. "He will live. You only hit his shoulder."

"That's good. I guess we were lucky that guy had it on him."

It was curious. Why *did* the Uprising bring such a device into this heist? Viktor thought through the details of the operation. A chef, a waiter, two guards, and two fake patrons, one armed with a mining tool, all to pull off a simple poisoning against a hyper-paranoid diner. He surveyed the destruction around what had been Rin's table. The cloth was fully soaked with wine, and the steak had long since stopped steaming. The edible gold flakes had sunk into the wine puddle.

A hunch flitted through Viktor's mind.

He retrieved Rin's fallen pocket comp, complete with its mass spectrometer, and used a fork to fish one of the gold flakes out. He placed it on the spectrometer and waited for the analysis.

90 percent gold.

10 percent highly refined arsenic.

"I have solved it," he said.

Areva peered over his arm at the screen. "Ooh," she said.

"Yes. The Uprising used their false chef to switch the edible gold for these flakes," Viktor said, gesturing to the fallen pieces. "Then a false waiter brought the poisoned wine to Rin. Then the patrons used bursts from the thermal beam to melt the arsenic into the drink after Rin had already tested it. That is why Rin said the texture was wrong."

Alvarez gaped at them. "They used the beam? That's incredibly dangerous. If they'd hit his skin, or the tablecloth ..."

"Caution has never been one of the Uprising's priorities."

"Why go to so much trouble?"

"They enjoy spectacle. It keeps them in the public eye and ensures their cause continues to receive attention."

Areva huffed. "They got their wish tonight, then."

"At least they did not get their money."

"True."

They left Alvarez to speak with a department counselor and surveyed the ransacked room.

"Too bad," said Areva. "I was looking forward to this dinner."

"As was I."

She slipped a hand into his. "It's not too late. Once we're cleared by the department, want to get ice cream?"

"Whatever you like."

"It'll at least be cheaper than this place."

"The money was not going to be a problem."

Areva glanced up at him. "Do I need to ask for a raise, or are you running some sort of side business outside the corps?"

Viktor laughed. "Neither. Remember the island Jarry Rin was building?"

"Yes."

"I invested in his competitors. They had the foresight to buy land that was not in a flood zone. Their first dividends were paid last month. Not a lot, but enough for one night of fine dining."

Areva laughed. "Next time I'll order filet."

"Will we need to go shooting to set the mood again?"

"Of course. Or are you scared I'll beat you again?"

"After tonight, I should be." He paused, then said seriously, "Thank you for saving my life."

She shrugged. "It's what we do. In fact, tonight was one big string of what we do."

"It was. Perhaps the evening was not ruined after all."

She reached up and used his tie to pull him down into a kiss. "No," she murmured. "In fact, I think it was absolutely perfect."

Book Five

Wet Ducks

The *Endurance* was the best ship in the United Earth Law Enforcement fleet.

Matthias Habassa had never served on any other ships, but he was pretty sure it was true.

For example, what other ship was currently receiving a heavily encrypted message from the Phobos colony on a classified priority channel, with a subject line reading: "HELP"?

None of them. That was for sure.

"Progress, Habassa?"

Matthias glanced over his shoulder at his commanding officer. Captain Thomas Withers leaned forward in his chair, chin resting on steepled fingers, blue uniform creases sharp enough to cut paper. "Working on it, Cap," Matthias said with a grin. "Decryption protocols only go so fast."

"What, you haven't improved their efficiency?"

"Not since the extra fifty percent I wrangled from them last year." Matthias turned back to the console at the front of the bridge, which currently flashed a dizzying array of numbers and symbols. Through the viewport just above the station, the heavy blue depths of Neptune swirled against a backdrop of stars.

It really was a pretty planet. Boring, perhaps, but the lack of activity in this part of the system gave more time for science projects. Like boosting the efficiency of the standard decryption software. Matthias wasn't bothered by the captain's jibe about his progress. As his mom used to say, be a duck. Quack, quack.

He entered a new algorithm and watched the first letter of the message resolve on the screen:

I.

A deep voice rumbled behind him. "The Dispatch officers think they are jokers."

"Really, Ivanokoff?" asked Captain Withers. The command seat creaked as the captain leaned back. "You think the message is a prank? Even they wouldn't stoop that low. More likely it's some kid with a broadcaster just screwing around."

The tower of muscle that was the *Endurance*'s first officer growled in the back of his throat. "It is from Dispatch. They hate us, sir. This mockery is the exclamation point on the insult of our assignment to this part of space."

"Was that a poetic metaphor, Lieutenant?"

"I do not do poetry."

"You're the literature guy."

"Da. I read it. I do not write it."

"Maybe you should give writing a try. Areva might like it."

"Areva is a stoic, like myself."

"You can't write stoic poetry?"

"Captain, your jokes do not change my original point. Dispatch is again mocking our crew. The message will contain a rude word and nothing more."

Matthias extracted another few letters from the encryption: *Ivano*.

"Actually," he said, swiveling his stool to face the center of the bridge, "I think it's addressed to you, Viktor."

That got the huge man's attention. Viktor Ivanokoff crossed to the console and leaned over the data-strewn screen. Even so bent, he would dwarf Matthias at full height. "What is the rest?" Ivanokoff asked.

"Working on it." Matthias watched as the computer put together the remainder of Ivanokoff's name, and then the letters *thi*. It seemed each letter of the message had been encrypted using a different cypher, and the computer was beginning to pick up a pattern from one to the next. "The rest should go a little faster," he said.

Ivanokoff grunted. "It is still likely a prank."

Matthias shrugged. "I dunno. I think we were put out here for a reason."

The captain laughed, making his chair creak again. "Sure we were, Habassa. To keep us out of the way."

"That's not what I mean," said Matthias. "I mean a greater purpose. Look how things have turned out. *Endurance*'s routine gave me time to invent a lot of cool stuff. It's the reason we were able to leave the solar system and find all those planets. We weren't out of the way. We were in the middle of everything."

A small smile crossed the captain's face. "That we were. Short as it was, we had a good run."

Another grunt from Ivanokoff. "Until they found an

excuse to return us to our cage."

"We killed a hundred aliens, Lieutenant," said the captain.

"They were already dead."

"Still counted, to Dispatch."

Matthias swung back and forth on his stool. "At least we tried to help. That's what matters."

Neither command officer replied.

More letters.

Ivanokoff, this is O ...

Ivanokoff's hands formed fists, his knuckles white as they pressed on the metal bank of computers. "It is O'Dell, from Oversight and Investigations. He is mocking me."

But the next letter was a *K.*

A sudden weight descended on the bridge. The banter and speculation fell silent.

O.

Ivanokoff's knuckles popped. Even Matthias felt his usual chipperness fade. If the name was what they all suspected, this was a lot more trouble than a prank from Dispatch. Traitors never got in touch with those they betrayed unless something was very wrong.

R.

O.

Ivanokoff swore. "Okoro."

Captain Withers came to stand over Matthias. "No."

"Looks that way," said Matthias.

"Delete the message," said Ivanokoff. "We do not need more of his lies."

But the computer was decrypting faster now, and more words appeared amidst the shifting, streaming code:

I'm sorry for what I did.

Matthias pointed at the screen. "That's a good sign."

Captain Withers and Ivanokoff both scoffed.

The blue-black symbols continued to resolve on the screen. *P25NORKZL* ...

"The decryption isn't working," said the captain.

Matthias slid his stool to the adjacent console and activated its screen. "I think it is, Cap. That looks like an unaffiliated lightcom frequency." His hands flew over the controls. "Yup, there's a video message embedded in the signal. Playing it filtered through that frequency now."

On one of the two screens suspended from the ceiling above the line of viewports, a plainly dressed man appeared, filling the frame. Gloomy lighting behind him threw a grainy haze over the message, which appeared to have been recorded on a cheap pocket computer.

"Ivanokoff," said Okoro, "I need your help."

No scathing remarks came from Matthias's two companions. The engineer's heart began to race, and from the corner of his eye he saw the captain and Ivanokoff stiffen. Every one of them saw the same thing in that moment. Though the dim setting made it hard to distinguish details, Okoro's wide eyes were haunted by desperation.

He spoke quickly, but in an undertone, his voice trying to tiptoe its way through a sprint. "I know you don't trust me. But I swear, I thought the Uprising was only bluffing about wanting to send a message to the Haxozin. The threat wasn't supposed to be real.

"But they sent the message, Viktor. They contacted the Haxozin. They told them how to find Earth. I found out yesterday, when they received a reply."

Matthias's skin turned to ice.

Okoro's next words confirmed what they had all feared for the better part of a year: "The Haxozin are coming."

Captain Withers jabbed a finger at Matthias's console. "Forward this to Dispatch, now."

"On it, Cap."

The message kept playing as Matthias sent the decrypted data on a priority channel toward Earth. On the screen, Okoro shook his head. "I can't risk sending this intelligence to Dispatch; anything aimed at Earth would be intercepted. But you're way out there at Neptune. The Uprising signal scrubbers will let it through." He paused and checked something on the pocket computer. "It's still broadcasting, so I know you'll receive this much. Ivanokoff, you have to find a way to stop them. These Uprising loons don't understand what they've done. They think the Haxozin will ally with them. I tried to stop them, to make them turn themselves in and share the information the Haxozin sent, but they won't listen to me. You have to—"

Okoro jerked and straightened up, his head disappearing off the screen. A muffled voice shouted, "Hey, bad cop, what are you doing in there?"

Then Okoro's face filled the screen again, his eyes scanning something on the computer. "Shit! They detected the broadcast." He tapped several buttons, shaking the recording as he did so. Something heavy thumped off screen, the sound of a body ramming a door. Okoro looked directly into the camera, and his face went through a subtle hardening, a draining of emotion that left him looking nearly lifeless. "At least I reached you," he murmured. "At least you know."

He stood, his torso almost swallowed by the shadows in the room. His left hand moved to his waist, drew a standard-issue UELE projectile gun, and aimed it off screen.

A crash sounded, then a thunderous bang as Okoro

fired. A man screamed. Okoro chambered another round.

Shouts. A second bang.

Okoro jerked, his body convulsing inward, shoulders caving in and arms clutching at his chest. His gun tumbled from his hand and clattered onto a tile floor.

A third bang.

He spun as if pushed and collapsed with a thud. Then multiple bodies in dark attire crowded the frame.

One bent to where Okoro had fallen. "Dead."

"His computer's on," said another.

"The signal?"

"Already sent."

"Shit!"

"Turn it off!"

"Do we have anyone to interce—"

Playback stopped. The screen went dark, and the computer flashed the options to replay, save, or reply.

Matthias swallowed and pushed his stool back to the console. "That's it," he said. "That's all there was."

Captain Withers cleared his throat. "I'm sorry, Ivanokoff. I know he was your friend."

Ivanokoff stared at the black screen. "'He gave his honours to the world again, his blessed part to heaven, and slept in peace.'" He closed his eyes for a moment, then faced the captain. "He regained his honor. We have warning of the attack to come."

Matthias churned over the information contained in the message. Some detail was prickling his mind, but he couldn't yet articulate what it was. Some word, some phrase had given him a deep uneasiness. Memories floated across his mind, disparate pieces of information. He let them drift, watched them bump against one another until they coalesced, atoms joining to form a molecule with a name.

When the last pieces came together and he was able to articulate that name, the bottom dropped from his stomach. He sprang from his chair, hands flapping. "Captain, it's too late!"

"What?" Withers took a step back, his face contorted in the wary incredulousness Matthias had come to expect from others when he made a breakthrough.

He made an effort to calm himself and speak slowly enough for understanding. "They said the Haxozin sent the Uprising a message. A message they received yesterday."

"Right," said the captain. "So?"

"So the Haxozin don't use multidimensional travel like we do," said Matthias. "Their interstellar engines are based on gravitational manipulation, and that means they can't send messages while in transit. Their ships' own gravity would prevent it."

"What's your point, Lieutenant?"

Matthias paced the bridge, pounding a fist against the opposite palm. "If they'd sent their message to the Uprising from their homeworld, it would take years to arrive, and there's no reason they'd stop midway just to broadcast their approach." He stopped, whirled, and brought his fist against his palm one last time. "Cap, they have to have sent that message after dropping into normal space at the end of the trip."

Withers inhaled a sharp breath. "Are you saying—"

"Yup. Wish I wasn't, but I am. We're too late. The Haxozin are already here."

While Matthias found the silver on every cloud, even he couldn't muster a smile now.

* * *

Captain Thomas Withers stared at his chief engineer and wished he could disbelieve what he'd been told. "How close?" he asked.

Matthias shrugged. "Hours. Days. No more than that."

Ivanokoff folded his arms. "It takes three and a half hours for lightcoms to reach here from Phobos."

"And four to make it to Earth from us." Thomas pinched the bridge of his nose. "That's too much time."

"We have no other option," said Ivanokoff. "Even with gravitational assists, we would need four days to return to Earth. The message we sent is the fastest way."

"If the Haxozin are at our front door, it's not enough. You saw the devastation they created on Thassis. They could commit the same atrocities on Earth if they show up with no warning." Thomas's heart fluttered with concern for his girlfriend, currently employed in Lunar Dome Three. Far too close to the coming catastrophe. He whirled on Matthias, who had sunk back onto his stool, his bouncy ball personality flatlined for once. "Lieutenant, there has to be a way to contact Earth right away."

"Not through communications, Cap."

"Can't you create something that will warn them?"

"That's not really how inventing works. We're limited by the speed of light."

"But the D Drive lets us go faster than—"

"No, it doesn't. It lets us travel through a higher physical dimension and bypass parts of three-dimensional space. We travel at the same speed we always do."

Thomas gritted his teeth. "Can't you use that to somehow send a message to Earth?"

"Sorry, Cap. Dimensional travel only works for the ship."

A thought crystallized in Thomas's head. "The ship," he said. "We have to use the D Drive to jump to Earth."

A multitude of expressions rippled over Matthias's face, finally settling on bemusement. "Cap, like I told Dispatch, D Drive only works over long distances. The engine can't turn on and off fast enough to make a jump that short."

"There has to be a way," said Thomas. "You're a genius. Think of something!"

Matthias opened his mouth, and Thomas was sure he was about to hear another reason why the futility he felt was inescapable.

But then the engineer's eyes took on a faraway look, and he sat there, mouth hanging, for several seconds. His fingers tapped his thighs like a keyboard, and his gaze darted about in space as if reading invisible messages in the air.

When he refocused on Thomas, his signature grin had returned. "This is kinda dumb, Cap, but I think it'll work."

* * *

It was more than kind of dumb. Thomas sat in his chair, surrounded by Ivanokoff and two other officers manning the bridge's front consoles. A screen hanging from the ceiling over the viewports showed one of the interior security camera feeds. On it, they watched the security chief's progress. Areva Praphasat was dwarfed by her spacesuit, yet somehow she still moved with serpentine grace.

She stood in the center of the *Endurance*'s main loading ramp, anchored by tethers affixed to hooks in the bulkheads. The airlock between her and the rest of the ship was sealed, her progress only visible through the visual feeds from the ship's security system.

The bulkhead to space was open. Far beneath the edge of the ramp, Neptune's gas oceans glowed with ethereal light, the planet's reflection of the sun unblocked by the satellite rings and space lanes seen in settled regions of the solar system.

Thomas tried to ignore the enormous projectile gun in Areva's hands and instead focused on the bridge's other hanging monitor, which currently showed a feed from the reactor room. He tapped his ear-mounted intercom interface. "Habassa, time?"

The engineer spun and waved at the camera before tapping his own interface. "Thirty seconds, Cap. We've got the main reactor feeds offline. The D Drive will start up all on her own."

"You're sure this won't blow up the ship?"

"Mostly."

"Habassa ..."

"Yes, Cap. I can't scientifically guarantee everything will be fine, but the statistical chance of implosion or explosion is very small."

"Good. Praphasat, you catch that?"

The spacesuited figure in the airlock flinched at her name before answering over her own open intercom line. "Yes, sir. Am I still on the monitor?"

Thomas managed not to sigh. "Yes, Lieutenant. It's a necessary precaution."

Areva Praphasat didn't like being watched. Or seen at all, if possible.

Thirty seconds ticked by. Thomas watched the stars through the viewports and tried not to think about how distorted they were about to become.

His earpiece buzzed. "Ready, Cap," said Matthias.

Thomas leaned forward, hands folded to stop them from shaking. "All right. Fire it up."

Energy thrummed through the deck plates, vibrating up Thomas's legs. Bulkheads rattled, and unsecured equipment crashed to the floor. One unoccupied stool at the front of the bridge began stuttering its way toward the rear hatch.

This was such a bad idea.

At the same time, the stars warped and twisted, dissolving into spirals that rotated both directions at once, and simultaneously rushed forward to swallow the ship and charged away to leave it alone in darkness. Black space itself rippled, bunching up like carpet in impossible contortions, shapes that only existed in theoretical math and nightmares.

Thomas tore his eyes from the chaos happening outside the ship and swallowed the nausea that crawled up his throat.

Matthias spoke again. "We're four-dimensional, Cap."

"I see it."

"We can start moving any time."

Thomas focused on the non-distorted floorplates and said, "Praphasat, one shot. Now."

He didn't watch the monitor, but he heard Areva's grunt as she discharged the rifle.

Ivanokoff gave a grudging humph. "I should have done it."

"This is her job," said Thomas.

"It is my gun."

"And it's my ship. My orders."

Ivanokoff gave up, though he muttered, "*I* wanted to test the vacuum firing feature."

Thomas chanced a glance at the viewports. Space

was still misbehaving outside, refusing to abide by any patterns his brain could follow. Instead he looked up at the monitors.

Neptune was gone. More writhing stars filled the view outside the open airlock.

"Habassa," Thomas said, "it's working."

"I see it on scanners, Cap," said Matthias. "The shot gave us a push, but we're still drifting too slow." Someone in the background screamed, and Matthias hushed them. "Sorry, Cap. Officer Lee got scared."

"Why?"

"We just passed through some space debris. Boy, imagine if we returned to 3D space with *that* inside our hull!"

Thomas ignored his own surge of panic at the thought. "Praphasat, fire again."

The spacesuited body on the screen hefted the gun and pulled the trigger. Another small grunt from Areva's comm line.

"That's it!" shouted Matthias. "We're going a fraction of a kilometer per hour. At this rate, we'll reach Earth in ... three minutes."

"Don't bring us out inside a satellite," Thomas said.

"We'll stop outside the ring, Cap. It'll be fine."

Thomas focused on his breathing, in and out. It would be fine.

"Praphasat," he said, "close the hatch and get back inside."

The spacesuit waved an acknowledgement, and then Areva began pulling herself along one of the tethers toward the airlock controls.

At two minutes to go, she triggered the outside door closed.

At one minute, she repressurized the airlock and

clomped back through the hatch into the ship proper.

At thirty seconds, the sickening view through the bridge viewports flashed from black space to earthen brown for the blink of an eye.

That was an asteroid, Thomas thought. *We just flew through solid rock.*

This was such a bad idea.

At ten seconds, he gripped the arms of his chair and forced himself to focus out the viewports.

At five seconds, one of the other officers covered her mouth and gagged. Thomas pushed down his own wave of nausea triggered by the sound.

At one second, he crept forward to the end of his seat. The chair creaked under his weight.

Zero.

The rattling in the bulkheads ceased.

The view through the ports resolved, the stars spinning back into points of light, space flattening to its proper texture. Yet something was still off. The sky was too full.

At minus one second, Thomas stared through a haze of laser fire crowding the space between a ragged handful of UELE vessels and a hundred five-pointed star ships encroaching on his homeworld.

* * *

A jolt threw Thomas back against his chair and threatened to make his already upset stomach empty itself. A moment later his equilibrium returned.

"Sorry, sir," said the woman at the helm. "The gravity plating couldn't compensate in time. I had to swerve to avoid that ... that ..."

Thomas needed no explanation. The viewports and

overhead screens displayed swaths of destruction. A UELE ship burned atmosphere on the right screen, and on the left the mangled wreckage of something—a police satellite, a civilian transport, who knew—careened through the battle zone.

The remaining UELE vessels peppered the attackers with guided rockets, energy bursts, and EMP discharges, but they were outnumbered. Another ship lost a stabilizing engine and had to retreat toward the atmosphere. A dozen Haxozin stars swooped in, nipping the flank now left undefended.

Thomas pointed, though the gesture wouldn't help. "Over there, fill that hole!" He glanced at the data streaming across the screens on either side of his chair. "Relative coordinates 189 by 236 by 47." He slapped his intercom. "Habassa, I need regular engines operational five minutes ago!"

"Ten seconds, Cap."

Those ten seconds crawled past in fire and debris. Haxozin ships assaulted the opening in the grid, rotating around their central spires, able to travel in any direction indicated by their five points. The smaller UELE craft had an edge on maneuverability, but not by much.

Endurance finally surged forward, gaining momentum beyond the pitiful crawl that had been inching her toward the combat. They dove behind the defensive grid and surged upward into the spot vacated by the crippled ship.

"Let's get 'em!" whooped Matthias over the comm. "The reinforcements are here!"

Thomas doubted anybody was cheering on the other UELE ships. *Endurance* had been around the sun a few more times than any other cruiser. Her carpet outdated most of the vessels fighting alongside them. Her crew wouldn't inspire much confidence either.

Nevertheless, this was their job. They were protectors, and they would do their damnedest to defend Earth from this invasion.

Viktor Ivanokoff swiveled his stool to face the captain. "Ten rockets."

Thomas knew their limited stock. Self-guided missiles served little purpose around Neptune. He'd have to make them count. "Save them for now. Try to hit the biggest ships with EMPs."

When he tore his gaze from the havoc and looked toward the defensives station, Areva Praphasat had appeared there without his notice. She'd removed the spacesuit and sat in her uniform blues, rank and certification patches black on her shoulder, short dark hair curling around her ears and framing her olive-skinned face.

Thomas couldn't remember the last time his chief of security had willingly seated herself out in the open. "Praphasat?"

"The EMPs aren't working; the ships' hulls are shielded. We need to strip some of the exterior to expose the circuitry. Recommend a precision rocket strike to blast through." Areva's hands flew over the controls, preparing the commands she had just recommended.

Beside her, Ivanokoff supported her preparations with his own. "The EMP must follow exactly behind the rocket, otherwise the Haxozin ship will move."

Thomas cleared his throat. "You okay to do this, Praphasat?"

"Yes, sir. They won't see it coming."

Ivanokoff reached over to squeeze Areva's hand. She gave a return squeeze.

Thomas gripped his armrests. "Then fire."

The two officers looked at each other in a silent

countdown. Areva fired first. A gleaming cylinder of metal shot from the front of the ship and screamed across the thin barrier of space. Ivanokoff depressed his controls a second later. The EMP wasn't visible, but the pulse emitter on the front of the *Endurance* shivered and contracted as it fired.

Areva's guided rocket tore into the ventral side of a Haxozin star. The explosion stripped away bulkheads and exposed a mess of circuitry.

Ivanokoff missed. The star ship executed a minor turn, and the target area rotated out of the EMP's field of impact. He yelled an incoherent sound of rage and slammed a palm on the console edge. "That was not my fault!"

Another star closed in, and Thomas ordered, "Evade!" The helmswoman went into a dive, again too fast for gravity plating to completely counteract, and pulled up sharp beneath the damaged hull of the first ship. Each arm of the star was easily as wide as the *Endurance* was long. The Haxozin ship could swallow a few dozen UELE craft whole.

Thomas focused on that little point of exposed circuitry. Even a giant could be taken down by a slashed tendon. "Track them," he said. "Keep that spot in the EMP's range."

Whoever was piloting the star seemed to realize their goal, because the larger vessel went into a spin, rotating one way, then the other, executing jerking movements, then doubling back. Tiny *Endurance* kept pace. At such close range, they were a fly swarming the head of a bull, too tiny to swat, too rapid to evade.

Thomas watched the vulnerable point dance in and out of the EMP's line of fire. "Whenever you can, Ivanokoff."

The big man growled.

There. The melted edges of the weak point drifted across the *Endurance*'s front, right in range of the EMP cannon.

Ivanokoff fired.

This time the shot hit.

Sparks flew from the Haxozin star's open hull plating as too much energy entered the system. There wasn't enough tactical data about Haxozin ships to know if they'd struck a vital series of circuits, but Thomas just had to hope so. "Pull back," he ordered.

As they swung back toward the defense grid, he was treated to the sight of lights darkening all along the ventral side of the star's damaged prong. Its darting movements ceased, and it dragged to a halt before hauling itself back toward its brethren.

One down, Thomas thought. Ninety-nine to go.

Endurance swung around and the viewports once more showed rows of UELE defenders, Earth's cloudy surface looming behind them.

Half of them were on fire.

Plasma and atmosphere vented from Earth's fleet. Scorched hulls and cracked viewports marred the few vessels that held together. Not one was undamaged, and their collective return fire had only managed to cripple a handful of the larger Haxozin ships.

The imbalance of the fight struck Thomas like a blow to the gut: *We are not going to win this.*

As if to underline his realization, Ivanokoff looked up from the scanners station. "Incoming message."

"Play it," said Thomas.

A grating voice filtered through a Haxozin helmet boomed from the ship's speakers. "... all surrender immediately. The Haxozin Sovereignty has claimed this planet and will now exact tribute from its population. Cease firing and return to the surface at once, or we will destroy you."

At the same time, some of the Haxozin vessels began branching out, going around the minimal grid the UELE was able to form with its remaining defenders. A few of the more functional UELE ships broke formation to chase after them.

Thomas shouted a series of coordinates. "That one's ours. Same tactic. Stop his advance."

A moment later the *Endurance* shot after one of the penetrating ships. Areva watched her console, executing minute changes to the targeting system of the rockets. She fired.

"Up three degrees," Ivanokoff yelled at the helmswoman. *Endurance* tilted a fraction.

Ivanokoff fired.

Another EMP from the *Endurance* hit the hull of the Haxozin star just behind Areva's rocket.

The star faltered. Its lights dimmed.

Two down, courtesy of *Endurance*. Perhaps eight from the rest of the fleet.

Endurance's turn back toward the defense grid showed another two UELE craft adrift, lights flickering.

They'd crippled no more than ten percent of the invading fleet, destroyed none, and by Thomas's quick count, lost over seventy percent of their own. The worst of the injured ships had retreated back to the surface, but a good number had been destroyed or left limping. They were only putting off the inevitable.

One of the Haxozin stars finally took notice of the *Endurance*'s attack runs and spun after them, rotating so that one of its prongs aimed squarely at them. The star's central spire loomed behind the prong like a skyscraper.

Hundreds of weapon emplacements targeted the little vessel.

"Sharp climb!" Thomas cried, but they were too late to pull out of range. A white line of energy streamed from the prong and struck *Endurance*'s starboard dorsal wing.

Thomas was flung against the side of his chair as the entire ship jolted under the impact and went into an uncontrolled roll.

"Turn it into a dive," he ordered. "Bring us up right beneath them."

"I can't, sir," said the helmswoman. "The starboard aileron-thrusters are gone."

Thomas checked his computer readouts and saw another thermal buildup in the front of the Haxozin ship's arm. A glance at their relative position told him the shot would hit. *Endurance* would not survive a second blast. They would either overload a vital capacitor and explode, or lose more aileron-thrusters and spin off to burn up in the atmosphere.

He stared at the growing red readout of energy that would soon end his life, and could think of nothing to stop it. At this point they couldn't even heed the Haxozin warning to retreat to the surface. They were flying straight away from the planet, and their chaotic rolling wouldn't allow them to correct their trajectory.

There was only one way left to escape the impending blast. Thomas whacked his intercom. "Bridge paging engineering, activate the D Drive, now!"

He felt the familiar vibration as the ship began to project into four-dimensional space.

The ship's intercom crackled as a new voice broke on the same frequency as the Haxozin. Thomas recognized Commissioner Wen, the UELE officer in charge of the capital city of Median, and also his boss.

"Median City paging all UELE vessels," said the commissioner. "We are not going to win this fight. Therefore—"

Wen's signature snap was missing from her tone, and Thomas's heart sank. He knew what she was about to say.

The D Drive activated. Visible stars and Haxozin ships began to contort.

The commissioner's voice came through distorted, drawn out for one word and then jumping to high-pitched speed the next, but Thomas could still make out the message. "—get out of this system and go find help. Bring back hell for these bastards."

The last word lingered on the speakers, a deep rumble that faded as the *Endurance* slipped into D Drive and the twisted view through the ports became impossible to watch.

* * *

No one spoke for some time. Four-D travel had taken them out of the solar system almost instantly, and Thomas had no destination in mind. He ordered a halt after several seconds, bringing the ship into an empty region of space. He didn't know how long the *Endurance*'s Adkinsium reactor could keep the ship in four-D, and they needed to conserve power output. Damaged stabilizers continue to rotate the ship in place.

Thomas sat in silence. The commissioner had surprised him by ordering everyone away from the planet. That would leave Earth without any functional defenses, should they wish to stage a counterattack later. But then, the Haxozin ambush had left them without much recourse.

If the *Endurance* could find allies to return and fight

with them, they might stand a better chance. The Haxozin weren't invincible, after all. But Thomas's crew had only encountered one species with technology to rival the enemy's, and unfortunately they were all dead. No other crew had done much better.

He finally refocused his eyes and scanned the front of his ship. Ivanokoff sat regarding space, arms folded. The helmswoman and scanners operator were both staring at Thomas. Areva Praphasat had disappeared, though Thomas suspected she was still within earshot.

They were all waiting for him to decide their next move. To be the captain and come up with a plan.

For the first time in his career, he didn't know what to do.

He heaved a deep breath and looked each of them in the eye. "Everyone okay?"

Nods.

"We're going to get them for this." He didn't know how, but it seemed the right thing to say.

"How?" asked the helmswoman.

Leave it to his crew to ruin his rousing moment. "I'm open to ideas."

"We must destroy them," said Ivanokoff, finally swiveling to face Thomas. "This insult cannot go unanswered."

"I agree," said Thomas, "but the question is how. Unless you've got a starship-killing gun in that collection in your berth."

Ivanokoff grunted. "I do not."

"I didn't think so. Which means—"

"Yet."

"Which means we need to find some sort of weakness. Some way to drive the Haxozin away from Earth."

The rear hatch to the bridge banged open, and a blond man with a hawk-like nose stormed in. "I knew this day would come!"

Thomas squeezed his temples. "Not now, Fish."

Chris Fish, lead scanners operator and head of the various scientists performing experiments on the ship, charged forward, gesticulating wildly. "Alien invasion, Captain. I've been predicting this since—"

"Since birth," said Ivanokoff. "Add something useful or leave."

Chris folded his arms. "I'm just saying. It finally happened. People will have to pay more attention to my other theories now."

A moment later, Matthias Habassa appeared on the bridge as well. Though the bounce had left his step, an attempt at an encouraging smile played at the corners of his mouth. "We can fix the ailerons," he said, "and the starboard oxygen filters are fine. No permanent damage. So there's some good news."

"We needed some," said Thomas. "Now let's try to generate some more. Is there any way to tell how many other ships made it out of the system?"

"No," said Chris. "Not unless we go back to check."

"I don't think that's a good idea," said Matthias. "We can't handle any more Hax attacks."

Despite everything, the engineer's face brightened at the rhyme. God help him, he still could find his optimism. Thomas fixated on that fact, that point of stability, and used it to ground his thoughts. He had his ship. He had his crew, among them some brilliant, if eccentric, minds. He had a functional D Drive and an engineer who could manage the reactor's power output to give him the maximum four-D travel each day.

And he had orders. Bring back hell for these

bastards.

For publicly issuing that order, Commissioner Wen would likely be killed when the Haxozin landed. Thomas had had his differences with her, but he would not let her final command go unanswered.

"All right," he said. "We need a good strategy for taking down the Haxozin ships. We know they have limited manpower, which means there aren't too many soldiers on each one—"

"We think," said Areva's voice from somewhere in the back of the bridge. "We don't know."

"We think," said Thomas. "And that means if we can destroy their fleet, they'll be far outnumbered on the ground. Without the ability to threaten cities from orbit, they won't hold the planet for long." He pointed at Matthias. "Habassa, you understand their technology better than the rest of us. Can we overload their engines, anything like that?"

Matthias straddled a spare chair and tapped his chin. "Maybe. They use the gravity on a stick method of interstellar travel. Each star prong has a generator that produces a gravity well, pulling the space ahead of the ship toward itself. They use that to propel themselves forward. Technically they're not going faster than light, they're going around it."

"Gravity well," said Thomas. "How does that work?"

"It's not that different than D Drive," said Matthias. He produced a folded piece of paper from his uniform pocket, unfolded it, and held it out before him like a tray. "Think of this paper as three-dimensional space. Viktor, put a bullet on the center of the paper."

"*On*, not through," Thomas said with more than a little alarm as his first officer went for his gun.

Ivanokoff's eyes narrowed, but he retrieved a

projectile from one of his weapons and set it on the paper Matthias held in the air. It rolled to the center and bent the paper where it settled. Matthias nodded to it. "The bullet represents something with a lot of mass. Mass causes space to bend around things, like how the paper is bending around the bullet. This bending makes other things roll toward the massive object. If I put something tiny, like a microfilament, on the edge of this paper, it would slide down to the bullet. The more mass something has, the more it distorts space, and the more gravity it has. This part's theoretical, but I suspect mass is a four-dimensional property, and that's why it causes gravity."

"This is all fascinating," said Thomas, "but how do we use that to destroy their ships?"

"Their ships generate artificial massive objects in their prongs, and that bends space to propel them forward," said Matthias. "I can't say for certain without knowing more about their technology, but anything generating artificial mass like that must be using a lot of power. It's probably not too hard to overload it. The only problem is, doing that might do something weird."

"Weird as in ...?"

"Weird as in create a black hole next to Earth."

"Oh."

"Yeah. It's probably not the safest unless we know what we're doing. If I saw a schematic, I might be able to come up with more ideas, but for now I'm mostly guessing about the Hax facts."

"Habassa ..."

"Sorry, Cap. Just trying to lighten things up."

"This is not a time for lightness."

Matthias shrugged. "My mom always told me to be a duck. Sometimes you can't do anything about the situations that soak you, so you have to just let the water roll off your back."

"I will not let an attack on our planet roll off my back!" Thomas realized he was shouting and calmed his tone. "We all have families there. Friends. Our lives are there, or in the lunar domes, or the planetary colonies. For all we know, we're the only humans who escaped the Haxozin's control. If we don't find a way to defeat them, it may never happen. We are the only chance we've got."

Thomas made eye contact with each of his officers, ensuring they understood the gravity of their dilemma. Then he looked at the ship's name and serial number engraved over the aft hatch. "You know what this ship is named for? In 1915, a sailing ship called the *Endurance* got stuck in the ice floes of Antarctica. The captain and his crew survived and set off on foot. No one knew where they were or that they needed help, but they found their way back to civilization and not one person was lost. That's the fighting spirit that gave our ship its name. So we are going to fight."

Chris Fish stuck his hand in the air. "Didn't the ship sink, though?"

"And weren't they lost for a whole year?" asked Matthias.

"Two," said Ivanokoff.

"Seems a little ill-fated," said Chris.

Thomas held up his hands, eyes closed, willing himself to stay calm. "The point is, they didn't give up."

"No, not when giving up meant freezing to de—" Chris Fish went silent under Thomas's glare.

"The point," Thomas repeated, "is that they didn't give up. There's a way out of this, and we're going to find it. Now, Habassa, I want you to go over everything we know about Haxozin technology. Find every weakness you can. It may take a while, but we're going to—"

Beep beep beep. A light flashed on the scanners station.

Chris Fish leaned over the console. "Power's being shunted from the bridge to the lower deck."

"What?" Thomas asked. "Why?"

"I don't know. It looks like—hang on—oh, that's clever—somebody's rigged up the EMP emitter to broadcast a message without having to go through the bridge console's filters."

"Really?" said Matthias, scooting closer to look. "How did they compensate for—"

Thomas had no time to be fascinated. "Shut it down."

"Almost there," said Chris. A moment later a section of the scanners console went dark. "Outgoing messages are closed down for the whole ship. Once we undo whatever rewiring was done, we can start them back up."

Thomas felt the back of his neck prickle. This could not be a coincidence, coming so soon after the attack on Earth. "Who was it?"

"How should I know?" asked Chris.

"I've got this." Matthias began pulling up screens on the next console. "There's a security camera right near the EMP emitter. This rewiring must have been done in the past few minutes. Just one second, and ..."

Video footage appeared on the console, already in mid-playback. A figure stood over an open panel, adjusting the various light signal sensors and receivers in the EMP's electronics.

The figure looked up.

Thomas's mouth opened in shock.

That person was not on his short list of suspects.

"Where was the message sent?" His voice came out

in a harsh hiss.

Chris Fish looked up, ashen. "Phobos."

The larger moon of Mars. The moon from which Okoro had sent his warning. The moon on which the Uprising had a confirmed presence. The Uprising that had just arranged the capture of the entire solar system.

"Ladies and gentlemen," Thomas said, "we have a traitor on board."

* * *

The rec room had been turned into a makeshift interrogation space. The furniture was pushed up against the bulkheads, the two fake plants removed to another compartment. The coffee maker was stowed, the cards and games stashed in cabinets, leaving only a sparse single table in the center of the fraying carpet, one chair on either side of it.

Thomas sat on the side facing the compartment's hatch. Ivanokoff stood behind him. Areva lurked somewhere behind the extra furniture. Thomas had no doubt she'd pick up any useful detail he missed during the questioning.

He glowered at the figure sitting across the table. When he took command of the *Endurance* a year ago, this was not a situation he'd imagined in his future. "Who's on Phobos, Mr. Cleaver?"

The *Endurance*'s 104-year-old janitor, Archibald Cleaver, rubbed the back of one wrinkled hand. "Not sure I know anybody there, Captain sir," he said in his creaky twang. He glanced across the room to where his equally ancient beloved vacuum cleaner was parked.

Thomas unfolded a pocket computer on the table and pushed it so its display faced Archibald. "That's security footage of you hanging around the EMP emitter controls, just before they were used to bypass the bridge's communication filters and send a message to Phobos."

"I was just vacuuming."

"Where's the vacuum in this footage?"

Archibald stared down at his yellowing nails. "I forgot it. I'm old, you know. Been around the solar system a few times."

"Bullshit. You take that thing everywhere." Despite his anger, Thomas couldn't bring himself to actually scream at the old man. Such an act might shatter his bones. "Mr. Cleaver, this is very serious. You know what happened earlier?"

"I'm a civilian. Not s'posed to be privy to official happenings up on the bri—"

"But you know what happened earlier."

A pause. "Yup."

"The Haxozin have taken Earth. They only knew where to find it because of the Uprising."

Archibald's shoulders hunched. "I know."

"So why were you contacting them?"

The janitor took a rattling breath. "'Twas a long time ago."

"What was?"

"Way beyond the statute of limitations."

Thomas leaned forward and dropped his voice. "Were you involved with the Uprising, Archibald?"

The janitor's head snapped up, and he pierced Thomas with his milky blue eyes. "Promise I won't get prosecuted for that message."

"I can't promise that," said Thomas.

"Well, the way I see it, what I tell you could help us fulfill that last order from the commissioner, which I did not officially hear. Bring back help. That's why I sent that message, to ask questions. You want the answers, you let me off the hook."

"I'll do my best."

"Promise? I know you keep your word, Captain sir."

Thomas ground his teeth. "Fine. I promise I will do my best to keep you out of court for that message. Tell us who you contacted and what they know."

Archibald placed his palms on the table and rubbed them across the metal surface. "You know I volunteered to clean starships way back, oh, over eighty years ago, when us civvies could still do that. Lived most of my life here on the *Endurance*. Loved it, too. Kept this ship sparkling. Still do."

Thomas glanced at the fingerprints on the hatch handles and the dust bunnies in the corner, then at Archibald's aged eyes. "Sure."

"Just after I joined up, the Uprising gained lots more popularity. This was just after the new United Earth justice system got implemented. People who wanted to stick with nation-states were real mad. And so they started paying for information. Paying lots."

"You sold out." Thomas's hands formed fists.

"Kinda. Cleaning the whole ship, you hear stuff. Some of it's not s'posed to be heard. UELE plans to ambush Uprising ships, that kinda thing. I traded them recordings, and they paid me enough that I could live on my little UELE salary. When I started collecting informing for the Uprising, they gave me some contacts. Places I could message when I had data to sell."

"How long did you keep doing this?"

"Just a year or two. After the Uprising invaded that part of South America 'n United Earth had to kick them out, I thought maybe I didn't want to support the wrong side anymore. So I stopped. Gave away all the money they'd paid. Told them never to contact me again." His fingers interlaced, and his arms trembled.

"Archibald," said Thomas quietly, "have you had any contact with the Uprising in the last year?"

The janitor dropped his head and closed his eyes. "I didn't know. I promise, Captain. I didn't know what they were planning. Just after Mattie invented the D Drive and that business with the People of Tone and the Haxozin went down, one of the Uprising folks contacted me. They said they'd pay good, let me retire in luxury if I told them what the UELE was doing."

"Did you?"

"No! But they gave me a signal to use, a way to get in touch if I wanted to talk. Said to send a message to Killian Yang's people on Phobos."

Thomas and Ivanokoff both stiffened at the name. They'd run into Yang before.

Archibald didn't notice. "After ... after all those ships showed up at Earth ... I thought maybe they'd realize they messed up. Maybe they'd tell us anything they know about the Haxozin so we could find a weakness."

"You broadcast our position to a known enemy."

"I'm sorry, Captain. I didn't know what else to do."

"How about telling us your story up front?"

Archibald looked up again. "Would you have given me the chance?"

Thomas paused. "I guess not."

"Didn't think so." The janitor sat back in his chair and tapped one hand absently on the table. "You've got honor, Captain, but you're not the best listener."

Ivanokoff snickered.

Thomas ignored him. "Now that you've told us all this, how do we use it? Do you know where exactly your message to the Uprising went? Where they're hiding on

Phobos?"

"Nope. But betcha if I took a look at the area where the message reached, I could make a good guess."

"The Haxozin will be spreading out through the solar system," said Ivanokoff.

"Not yet," said Thomas. "It's only been a few hours. They need to solidify their hold on Earth, then the moon before they start going for the planetary colonies. We've got a little time." He said a quick prayer for Loretta's safety. She was smart. She would keep herself safe. Thomas appraised the ancient man across from him. "You realize even if this leads us to a solution, your time in the UELE is done."

Archibald nodded. "I figured. Just want to help now. You got any other questions, you ask."

Thomas pushed back from the table. "Just one, for the moment. You said you sold the Uprising recordings. Did you sabotage any of the ship's systems?"

"Oh, no, nothing like that. I'm not so good with technology."

"Then how'd you get the recordings?"

Archibald nodded toward his vacuum. "There's a reason I never traded her in for a newer model."

Thomas blinked. "You put surveillance equipment in the vacuum?"

A shrug.

"Is it still there?"

"Nope. But it leaves a mark. Anybody gave it a serious look, they'd know what used to be in there."

"Which is why you couldn't risk letting it out of sight." Thomas shook his head. "And I thought you were only attached to that thing through sentiment."

Archibald's smile lines appeared. "That wasn't a lie. That vacuum's my best friend."

"Let's just hope some of your other friends are still home when we come calling."

* * *

Phobos had never been a popular place to live. After Matthias calculated another micro D Drive jump back into the solar system, and everyone held their breaths and hoped they wouldn't emerge inside a rock, they arrived at Mars and its moons safely. Through the bridge's viewports, a handful of livable Martian domes contrasted with the red surface of the planet. Mars was nowhere near as built up as the lunar dome network, which had almost crowded out the natural rock of the moon. Mars's red terrain retained a rugged otherworldliness, the promise of adventure on what was still half frontier.

Phobos and Deimos were all frontier. Nothing had been built on their surfaces. Instead, a few holes showed the way into the airlock-secured tunnels where a handful of ambitious individuals struggled to create something resembling civilization. Thomas had never visited those particular moons, but from what he'd heard, the colonists weren't succeeding.

Thermal scans confirmed those rumors. "Uh, I'm not getting any warm bodies," said Chris Fish. "Looks like nobody's here."

"At all?" asked Thomas.

"At all. Heat readings are completely negative."

"It is possible," said Ivanokoff, "that the residents of the moon relocated to Mars after learning of the Haxozin attack."

"That makes sense," said Thomas. "Strength in numbers. But it does leave us with a problem. Mars has a large population. We don't have time to locate the

Uprising contacts there." He turned toward Archibald, who sat on the passenger seats along the aft bulkhead of the bridge. "Did they give you any other way to contact them? Anything that might pinpoint their location?"

The janitor tapped his fingers together. "Not for Phobos, no. I don't know any other currently operating bases. But ... there might be someone from the past who can help."

"Who?" asked Thomas. "One of your old contacts?"

"Sort of. Never spoke to him myself, but I know a handful of Uprising bigwigs from the twenties and thirties retired to the Enceladus colony."

Ivanokoff was already shaking his head when Archibald finished speaking. "We surveyed Enceladus thoroughly after the incident with Yang and Okoro. There are no Uprising operatives left there."

"Not active ones," said Archibald. "But their geezers are still around."

"Would they know anything about the Uprising's current intelligence?" asked Thomas.

Archibald smiled. "Do I know anything about the UELE's current intelligence? Retirement doesn't stick so well when you're part of a sedition, Captain. If we find one of the old-timers, they'll know something. Not everything, but something. Being old has its advantages. We can act deaf or asleep and you young folk will spill all sorts of information around us."

Thomas turned to the front of the bridge. "It's worth a shot. Head to Enceladus."

As the helmswoman routed the Adkinsium reactor's power into the *Endurance*'s propulsion system, Thomas leaned over to Ivanokoff. "Did I ever drop classified information around Cleaver?"

Ivanokoff answered in an undertone. "Not to my

knowledge."

"Has he pretended to be asleep around us?"

"I do not recall."

"Well, don't let me discuss things around old people in the future. It's hard enough keeping secrets with Areva hiding everywhere."

A squeak came through the open hatch of Thomas's office. "I don't hide everywhere."

Thomas gestured toward the hatch. "See? I don't need more people overhearing my every word."

Chris Fish shook his head as he did two different things on two different screens at once. "Too late for that. *They* hear everything. I'm working on a helmet to block their reception of our brainwaves, but in the meantime you can read my dissertation on exercises to resist telepathy."

Thomas settled back in his chair and didn't acknowledge that with a response.

* * *

Enceladus was, in some ways, a suburb of the solar system. Houses with picket fences lined underground streets. Little tunnels connected interweaving caverns. Many areas looked like any quiet neighborhood on Earth, save the rocky roof covering everything.

In other ways, Enceladus was an armpit, or maybe a spleen. Some part of the body where sweat and toxins could hide from the outside world. Particularly in the more urban areas, where the buildings almost reached the cave roofs, criminal rot had started to grow, secure in the moon's out-of-the-way location and quiet culture to help preserve anonymity.

By the time *Endurance* arrived a day and a half after

the attack on Earth, Matthias and Chris had calculated that they had at least six hours' head start on the Haxozin. The gravity on a stick technology couldn't function at full power near the natural gravity of planets. As long as Thomas's crew worked quickly, they could scour Enceladus for information and be on their way before the invaders arrived from Earth.

Endurance passed through the double airlocks in the moon's surface and landed in a parking lot. Thomas led the way down the boarding ramp. Areva Praphasat left the ship with Thomas and Archibald and promptly vanished behind the rows of parked ships. Thomas let her go; she'd be around when she was needed.

"In case you're thinking of turning on us," Thomas muttered to Archibald, who shambled along next to him, "you should know Areva's watching."

"Hah!" hacked the old man. "She's always watching. If she'd been around when I was tryin' to sell information, I'd never have managed it. Same with Mattie; that boy's a genius. You got yourself a good crew, Captain."

"I know it."

They picked their way through the narrow streets, dodging pedestrians and two layers of hovercar traffic. Thomas tried not to feel claustrophobic under the dark ceiling. He missed the stars.

The local UELE offices occupied a prominent place in the center of Portsmouth City. A freshly painted UELE logo stood out in vibrant color above the door, and the offices had expanded since the last time Thomas was here. The pervasive smell of salt water from the nearby underground ocean hadn't changed.

Thomas climbed three steps to the front entry, passed through the sliding doors, and flashed his pocket comp badge at the young man behind the front desk. "I need to see your captain."

He and Archibald were ushered to the third floor, to a moderate-sized office with refurbished furniture. Awards and family photos adorned the walls, and a well-tended vine spilled out of its pot on a bookshelf. A female officer sat behind the desk, captain's patch on one shoulder of her blue uniform shirt, certification patches on the other. Her sleeves were rolled up to the elbows, a concession to her position, but the uniform indicated that she hadn't lost touch with street work. She was engaged in spitfire dialogue with someone via her desk monitor. A flush showed beneath her dark complexion.

"I don't know!" she said. "Yes, I got the same message from Dispatch, but I have no more information than you do." She glanced up as Thomas and Archibald entered, nodded to the desk officer, and waved him out of the room. "I'll let you know if we learn anything else. Right now I have to go." She tapped her intercom earpiece to end the conversation.

She stood and extended a hand to Thomas, glancing once at his rank patch. "Captain."

"Captain," he answered, accepting the shake. "I'm Thomas Withers."

"Sekai Nandoro. You here to tell us what the hell's going on? That was one of my counterparts on Titan. We all got this message from Dispatch saying Earth had been invaded, and to launch all ships."

"Did you?"

"Yes, but I didn't know where to send ours. They're hanging out in orbit of Saturn with everyone else from the area. We haven't heard from our commissioner, so we're just waiting. It's been a bad time."

"Yes. Yes it has."

Her eyes widened. "So it's true?"

"The Haxozin fleet ambushed Earth two days ago. Once they've secured that part of the system, they'll be on their way here."

"You escaped?"

"Yes. Have you heard from any other ships?"

"No. We guessed any ships that escaped would either use their D Drives if they had them, or find somewhere in the interplanetary void to regroup. I was going to send my patrol ships to help once we found out where they went."

"There might not be a regrouping. The fighting was bad. It's possible no other Earth-based ships made it."

Captain Nandoro took a deep breath and began to roll down her shirtsleeves. "All right. Then the regrouping starts here. What do we need to know?"

Thomas shook his head. "I'm not here to bolster your defenses. My ship has D Drive. I'm leaving the solar system and looking for some way to fight back."

"Alone?"

"It's the only chance, and we're the only ones. Any D Drive ships returning from outside the system will be captured as soon as they reach Earth."

Nandoro finished buttoning her cuffs and straightened her shoulders. "Fair point. Anything you need from us before you go?"

"Actually, yes." Thomas motioned Archibald forward. "This is my ship's janitor."

"You still have one?" asked Nandoro.

Archibald smiled and shrugged. "Legacy position."

"I need you to show him your arrest profiles," said Thomas. "We think someone he used to know has information we can use to track down any Haxozin weaknesses."

Nandoro nodded and spun her monitor to face them, then began tapping commands on the screen. "Of course. Anything I can do."

"Start with criminal records from about eighty years ago," said Thomas. When Nandoro gave him a puzzled look, he jerked his head toward Archibald. "He's been around for a while."

Nandoro set Archibald to scrolling through old arrest records and mugshots, filtering the results to only include those individuals still living on Enceladus.

While the janitor tapped at the screen, Nandoro spoke quietly to Thomas. "Give me your honest opinion. Can we win?"

Thomas studied the wall. "I don't know. But this has been coming since we first left the solar system. I can't help but feel partially responsible."

Her brow furrowed. "Why?" Then her mouth opened. "Oh. *Oh*. Withers. You're the captain of the *Endurance*."

"Yeah."

"Look, just because your ship found the Haxozin ..."

"Doesn't mean it's my fault they tracked Earth down, I know, but I doubt everybody else will be that understanding. I wouldn't."

Nandoro folded her arms. "I know *Endurance* has a bad reputation in the fleet."

Thomas laughed humorlessly.

"I used to make fun of it with everybody else, but you should know, the last year changed some things. The suits at Dispatch and O&I might still see your crew as a liability, but out here, on the fringes, some of us are impressed by everything you accomplished. You don't hear much joking when you mention *Endurance* here anymore."

Thomas blinked at her. "Really?"

"Yes. In fact, that desk officer who showed you in wants to transfer aboard your ship someday."

"Wants to? My ship? Why?"

Nandoro chuckled. "Asked the man standing here on a mission to save the world."

Thomas lapsed into silence. He'd focused only on Dispatch's opinion of his crew. He'd never given thought to what his fellow officers might think of them. Of him. "Thanks."

"Sure." Captain Nandoro moved behind her desk and pressed a button to slide out a drawer. She retrieved her service belt and buckled it around her waist, then stocked its holsters with her service weapon and pocket comp. "Once we're done here, I'll begin organizing a rendezvous for survivors."

Thomas nodded. "Don't start trouble with the Haxozin. They're big, and there are a lot of them. Without some strategic advantage, we don't have a chance."

"Understood. We'll pick an empty spot in space. Probably somewhere in Mars's orbit, so we're not too far from Earth when we're needed. When you get back, look for us there."

Thomas had time to give Nandoro a brief analysis of the Haxozin star ships' capabilities and the tactic for overloading their circuitry with EMPs. "It's hard to hit them when they're moving around, but it'll buy some time. Use that if they find you."

"We will."

"Tell the civilians here not to resist. If they don't fight, the Haxozin will leave them alone."

"Got it."

Thomas glanced toward the door. "That kid really

wants to serve on my ship?"

Nandoro smiled. "After today, I'd bet more than ever."

From the desk, Archibald made a hacking sound. "That guy. I know him." He pointed at the computer screen.

Thomas and Nandoro moved in to look. "Destrier Michaels," read Thomas. "Nicknamed Disaster?"

"I know him," said Nandoro. "Lives in one of the suburban tunnels. Calls in every couple weeks to complain about his neighbors. No recent criminal record, though."

"He used to be Uprising," said Thomas.

"He served ten years," Nandoro read from the screen. "We've never had real trouble from him. You think he has the information you need?"

Thomas looked at Archibald.

Archibald nodded. "I got a feeling."

"His feelings have an eighty-six percent accuracy rate," said Thomas.

"Eighty-six point one five one," muttered Archibald. "Not just eighty-six."

Nandoro gave them a bemused smile and gestured to the door. "Good luck."

"Thanks. You too." Thomas let Archibald precede him into the hallway.

Just before he left, Nandoro's voice stopped him. "It was an honor to meet you, Captain."

He froze. The words sounded foreign, like they were directed to someone else. Yet they also felt like a welcome home. He turned and smiled. "Likewise."

They exchanged a salute.

He left her to organize the beginnings of human resistance against the Haxozin. If he did his job and brought back some way to defeat the enemy, they might eventually stand a chance.

If he didn't, every one of them would die.

* * *

"Disaster" lived in one of the sleazier areas of the colony. No picket fences here, and the cave roof had only been carved to the minimum height necessary to accommodate houses. In some areas it dipped so low, Ivanokoff would have been able to reach up and touch it. Only half the artificial sunlamps worked, and the bumpy street was marred by multiple ditches from hovers that landed too fast. Disaster's house was dropping shingles and had lost half its paneled siding, but the lush lawn was trimmed and lined with varicolored blossoms.

A block from the house, a musclebound man whipped around the street corner, riding a bicycle three sizes too small for him. "Move it, loons!" the man yelled, and Thomas had to pull Archibald into the street to keep from being run over. The man flipped them off as he passed.

Thomas thought about drawing his badge and pulling the guy over, but he had no time. He contented himself with a snide comment. "Tough guy. Bet he knocked over a whole lemonade stand to afford that bike."

They knocked on Disaster's door. The bony stack of wrinkles and liver spots that answered lived up to his name. "Birds orbit my ass, will you kids stop bothering—oh." The aged Uprising agent looked Thomas up and down. "You're at the wrong door, Officer. The punks who keep squashing my flowers live two houses down."

"It's captain," said Thomas, "and we're not here

about your flowers."

Archibald poked his head around Thomas. "They do look nice, though."

Disaster adjusted his thick glasses. "You look familiar."

"Archibald Cleaver. From the old days."

"Oh no." Disaster glared at Thomas and began to shut the door. "The Uprising can rise up somebody else's nose; I've kept mine clean. I did my time. You leave me alone."

"We need your help," said Thomas.

"That's police code for 'putting me in hot water with old buddies.' Nope."

"If you don't help, you'll have alien invaders tramping across your petunias by tomorrow morning."

The door stopped closing, screeching to a halt across misaligned floor tiles. "Hah?"

"You heard me."

Disaster scanned the street, then slid the door back open. "You better come in." As Thomas and Archibald passed him, he added, "And they're chrysanthemums, idiot."

Thomas didn't sit down. He stood between a cheap broadcast screen and a cheaper sofa and faced Disaster. "Has anyone from the Uprising contacted you in the past year?"

Disaster shuffled to the couch and seated himself with the creaking of several bones. "On the record, no."

"Off the record."

"Promise nobody's gonna knock on my door and arrest me for this?"

"I promise I won't tell anyone you talked to us."

"Off the record, then," said Disaster. He began picking dried leaves off a plant on the side table. "I hear from Killian and his crew pretty often."

"Did they say anything about their current operations?"

"Oh yeah. Couldn't stop talking about how they were gonna contact the Haxomen, use them to teach United Earth a lesson. 'Strike like a hammer,' all that stuff."

"What about in the past few days?" Thomas asked. "Did anyone tell you what was coming?"

Disaster's hand trembled, and a few dead leaves slipped and tumbled to the floor. "You need to understand, son, Killian talks a lot. Never shuts up about this plan or that plan. Most of them? They go no place. So I didn't think anything of it when he started talking about the Haxomen."

"Haxozin," said Thomas. "What did he say about them?"

"That they'd agreed to help. That in their messages they all wore these red suits and he had no idea what they actually looked like. He didn't like that they hid their faces. Made them hard to read."

None of this was helpful. "Did he say anything he *could* read?"

"Not a lot. It was odd, though. He spoke directly to their leader."

Thomas stiffened. "Are you sure?"

"Yup. Killian thought it was strange. Bigwigs don't like to mingle with the masses, yeah? Leave that to their flunkies." Disaster adjusted one of the green leaves to receive more sunlight. "Actually, that's something. Killian thought maybe they had a personnel problem. Like there weren't that many of them. He said he only ever saw two or three at a time, and their boss never mentioned troop numbers. Just ships. 'Our fleet's full strength will be at your doorstep.' That kind of thing."

"Full strength," said Thomas. "Are you positive that's what was said?"

Disaster shrugged. "I'm hearing it from Killian, so I don't know. But that's what he said the bigwig said."

"That's good. That's very good. Is there anything else?"

"Sure, but jump my flowerbeds if I can remember."

Thomas stood. "If you remember anything else, contact Captain Nandoro in Portsmouth." He programmed the appropriate information into Disaster's wallscreen controls.

Disaster crunched a fistful of leaves as he watched them head to the door. "Can I ask you something, Officer?"

"Captain. What is it?"

"Are we all gonna die?"

Thomas stopped with his hand on the knob. "Not if I can use what you just told me."

"Ah."

"If anyone asks questions, deny you talked to us."

"I ain't stupid."

"Never said you were. Thanks for your help."

"Don't step on the chrysanthemums on your way out."

"We'll be careful."

Thomas let himself and Archibald out and picked his way back toward the street, giving the flowers a wide berth.

"Did that help?" asked Archibald.

Thomas thought over what Disaster had said. "Yes. I think it did." He turned his steps back toward the city tunnels. "Come on. We need to get going before—"

A burly young man stepped out from behind one of

Disaster's well-pruned bushes. Then three more large individuals emerged and took up positions flanking him. One of them pushed the tiny bicycle that had nearly run Thomas and Archibald over earlier. Bulges beneath their jackets warned Thomas that they were armed.

Thomas halted. Archibald retreated behind him. "Hi there."

The lead figure advanced. "First cop I've seen in months. What's the UELE doing around here?"

"Business. Back off, kid."

"One officer, all by himself? Heard rumors about some shit going down on Earth. You part of that?"

"No."

"Prove it. Tell us why you're here."

"There are aliens invading Earth." Thomas saw no reason to hide it. The more warning people had, the less panic the Haxozin would cause when they eventually made it here.

The burly young man stared at Thomas. Then he flashed his teeth and looked over his shoulder at his buddies. "This loon thinks aliens are invading." To Thomas, he asked, "Been off the moon too long, loon?"

"Watch your language, kid. My girlfriend's from the moon."

"I bet you're not even a real cop. Walking around here with some old geezer and no backup." The young man shook his head. "Not buying it. What's really going on? You with the Uprising? Because we don't want any of that here."

"I'm not Uprising."

"Prove it."

"I could arrest all of you right now if I had time." Thomas reached for his pocket comp to show his badge.

The movement startled the young man, and his hand

went toward his hip. "Hey, don't you draw on me!"

Before the young man could unholster whatever weapon he had under his jacket, a flash of white energy struck the concrete at his feet. He yelped and leapt backward, then turned panicky eyes on Thomas. "What was that?"

Thomas couldn't help but smile. "My backup."

"I didn't see anybody."

"That's the point." Bolstered by the young thug's retreat, Thomas took a step forward. "Look, kids. I get that you're scared. You're hearing strange rumors about Earth, and you're trying to get a sense of control. But we're not the enemy. So let us go about our business, and we'll take care of the aliens. Go home and wait. The aliens won't hurt you if you don't give them reason."

The young man licked his lips. "I'm not good at waiting."

An idea occurred to Thomas. "If you want to help, the UELE's a little shorthanded right now."

"None of us are cop material."

"Maybe not, but you could be alien fighting material. If you want to do something, go see Captain Nandoro in Portsmouth City and say you want to join the resistance."

A blink. "Seriously?"

"Yeah. It's dangerous, but it's more productive than standing out here harassing those of us trying to get things done."

The young man exchanged dubious looks with his friends. "We'll think about it."

"You do that. Now, if you don't mind, my backup and I would like to leave."

With a few glances into the surrounding foliage, the young men vacated the sidewalk and let Thomas and Archibald pass. "Loons," he heard one of them mutter.

"Loons, all of them."

"But fighting aliens sounds awesome," said another.

Thomas didn't know if they'd actually bother to help. Confrontational bullies tended to be cowards. But even if his words only sent them off the streets, it was worth it.

He waited until he entered the pedestrian tunnel to Portsmouth to say, "Thanks, Praphasat."

"It's my job." Her voice came from right behind him. He turned to see her slinking through the shadows near the wall. Over her shoulder was slung a long-barreled weapon of unearthly design, definitely not standard issue.

Thomas eyed it before facing front again. "In the future, if you want to take one of the bazooka rifles off the ship, let me know first."

"Yes, sir."

"Carry on."

When he looked back again, she'd disappeared.

He smiled. Maybe working with his crew *did* have a certain appeal.

* * *

The *Endurance* left Enceladus's airlocks with a few hours to spare. In orbit, Captain Nandoro had already scrambled all remaining UELE ships from the moon, and a few civilian ones as well. They exchanged wishes of good luck before Thomas set heading toward the solar system's edge.

At the moment, he worried those staying behind would need more luck than he would.

Matthias Habassa tinkered with the D Drive controls on the bridge. "Where we going, Cap?"

Thomas settled in his chair. "Our source said the

Haxozin sent their entire force for this invasion."

Across the bridge, Ivanokoff's eyes lit up. "Their *entire* force?"

"Yup," said Thomas. "Emptied the barracks, as it were. And since they came to our homeworld, it's only fair that we go to theirs."

* * *

The last time Matthias had seen the Haxozin homeworld, he'd been fighting half a dozen technical obstacles at the same time. It was hard to sightsee when you were overriding the controls for alien airlocks, calculating trajectories for a crash landing inside a hanger bay, and estimating the warhead yield necessary to blast through a bulkhead without collapsing the entire ship.

He'd pulled it off, though. The rescue mission worked. He and his engineering team had downed a full bottle of champagne for that one.

Now, though, he stared out the viewports and finally understood why so many bridge officers had been unnerved by the sight of the Haxozin planet.

It was dead.

Not just kinda dried out. Not undead like the planet Thassis. Like really, seriously dead. Matthias doubted anything had lived down there for decades. Impact craters riddled the dark brown surface. The few structures visible from orbit were hard to make out, nowhere near as prominent as Median City on Earth or the lunar domes. Most troubling, thermal scans picked up not one sign of heat from the entire surface.

What in the world had the Haxozin done to this place?

Matthias wondered if it was possible to stimulate

plant growth in such a sterile environment and restore habitability. He'd have to add that to his list of future projects, right after disproving Alfson's take on unified field theory and finding an application for the antiderivative of position. It was neat that math could discover things that didn't exist, but applying that discovery was a pain.

Still. All problems could be solved. The obstacles didn't bother him. Be a duck.

He wondered, in the back of his mind, if even now the Haxozin were starting their planet-killing process on Earth. If so, his parents and friends might be—

No. Not now. He was doing the only thing he could to solve that problem.

Be a duck.

He turned his mind to analyzing the various scanner data streaming across the console. "No ships in orbit, Cap. Got a few satellites, but they're pretty busted up. Probably been there since the planet was inhabited. A few dozen years, based on what I can see of them."

Captain Withers drummed his fingers on his armrest. "Can you access the satellite computers, look for strategic information we can use?"

"Not without bringing them aboard and taking them apart. Their systems are all burnt out."

"We don't have that kind of time," said the captain. "Let's do a full orbit of the planet. There might be something more usable on the other side."

Halfway around the dead world, the captain got his wish. Matthias pointed at the overhead screen. "Look, look. That station has thermal readings!"

The station in question was small, about one and a half times the size of *Endurance*. A few mechanical messes had been pasted onto its hull, probably serving as data transceivers. A dozen or so weapons had been grafted on as well, though Matthias couldn't tell how potent they might be.

Most importantly, ambient heat radiated from the station, with a single prominent heat source visible in its center. At first Matthias thought it might be an active reactor or a miniature fission chamber—how he'd love to see one of those! But over a few seconds, the heat source moved from the center of the station toward one of the edges.

The captain folded his hands, and Matthias caught a vengeful gleam in his eye. "Looks like someone was left to mind the farm. Let's go have a chat."

"Hey," said Chris Fish, "can we keep our metaphors straight? There are no farms in this entire solar system."

Matthias grinned. "If they don't farm anything, where do they get their Hax snacks?"

The captain sighed and pinched the space between his eyes. "Just go dock us with that station."

* * *

Dozens of little projectiles impacted *Endurance*'s hull as she swooped in along the station's z-axis. Her thick hull plates absorbed the impacts, but every strike vibrated the ship and rattled Thomas's teeth. Small the damage might be, but his ship was going to look like the surface of the moon when this was over.

The station's energy weapons proved a little more modern. After the projectiles failed to halt *Endurance*'s approach, a series of amber lights streamed from the top of the station, burning holes into the wings. Number eight air cycler failed, but their approach was too fast and too zigzagging for any other precision shots.

They braked to a stomach-turning halt just above the station's surface, safely beneath the range of the guns, and rotated until their top-deck airlock aligned with the station's hatch. The ship jostled as the two ports sealed with one another.

Ivanokoff drew his guns, Dickens and Dante.

"Don't kill him," Thomas said.

Ivanokoff scowled more than usual and stomped toward the bridge hatch. "Never any fun on this ship."

Matthias spun in his chair just as Ivanokoff disappeared into the corridor. "Cap, the guy knows we're here."

Thomas didn't bother pointing out that "the guy" had just fired a couple hundred shots at them. "Oh?"

"Yup. About fifteen other thermal sources just showed up on scanners. I can't pick out his specific spot anymore."

"Clever."

"Not really," said Chris Fish. "It's the obvious strategy."

"It doesn't matter," said Thomas. "The station's not too big. Areva and Ivanokoff can search it in no time."

"Saying that guarantees something will go wrong," said Chris.

"Aw, stay positive," said Matthias, patting the scientist's back.

Thomas watched the thermal scan of the station. He saw the moment his two officers disappeared into the mish-mash of color that made up the rest of the structure. Stay positive indeed. Let that water roll off his back.

When five minutes passed without a confirmed capture, Thomas's gut began to feel queasy and the knots in his back no longer allowed things to roll off. He tapped his intercom. "Ivanokoff, what's taking so long?"

His earpiece crackled. All the active equipment must be interfering. "No ... yet. Still looking," said Ivanokoff.

Thomas shifted restlessly in his chair and tapped his earpiece again. "Bridge paging airlock, any sign of activity?"

He expected the voice of one of the officers guarding the open door to the other ship.

He received nothing.

He bolted up, jabbing a finger at the scanners station. "Airlock view, now!"

Chris Fish jumped and typed quickly. A moment later the overhead screen flashed to live footage of the top deck corridor alongside the airlock.

Two UELE bodies lay motionless on the floor.

Thomas swore. "Get Maureen down there to see to them. Scramble another team and start searching the *Endurance* for—"

A scalding blow struck him in the back like a flaming baseball. His muscles went rigid, and pain shot through every nerve. His jaw clenched and white haze flashed across his vision. Then his senses were dulling, his equilibrium failing. He had the sense of his knees hitting the floor—

* * *

Matthias stared open-mouthed at the red armored warrior standing in the hatchway, brandishing a hot bazooka rifle. A cube-shaped computer hung in a pouch by his side—a talky box for translating between languages. Matthias's gaze darted to the captain's unconscious body beside the command chair. No burns. The weapon was on stun.

Chris Fish froze with his hands still on the scanners

panel. An unbroken high-pitched squeak came from his mouth.

Matthias glanced around the bridge. Besides Sergeant Fish, there was one other sergeant and an officer. He was the only lieutenant. That put him in command.

Huh. This was new.

He put on his most disarming smile and slowly raised a hand to wave at the soldier. "Hi."

The Haxozin stepped through the hatch and came around the command chair, weapon trained on the captain's fallen form. "Who are you?" The voice used the grating, guttural sounds of the Haxozin language, but the talky box at his hip emitted an intelligible translation.

"We're from Earth," said Matthias. He heard his own words being broadcast from the box in the harsh Haxozin sounds. "You know, the planet you guys are invading right now? I guess they left you behind to watch over things. Or maybe you were sick? We have an infirmary if you need some anti—"

The Haxozin swiveled his gun to target Chris. "Back away from the technology!"

Chris jerked from the console as if it bit him. "Yes, sure thing, Mr. Killer. Won't go anywhere near it. Please don't shoot me."

"Or anyone else," said Matthias, still smiling. "We're really nice people, once you get to know us."

The bridge crew retreated to the center of the ring of consoles. The Haxozin prowled toward the scanners station and glanced down at its readings. "You move, I kill your sovereign."

"Sovereign," said Matthias. "Is that what you call your boss? We call ours 'Captain.' How about we sit down and discuss this peacefully. A Hax pax."

The Haxozin paid him no mind. The red helmet

turned as he scanned the consoles. "Where's your emergency shutdown?"

"Our what?" asked Matthias.

"To seal all doors and disable all systems. Where is it?"

Chris Fish snorted. "With one command protocol? Why would we have something like that?"

"Yeah, that violates, like, all the safety laws," said Matthias. "The UEAA would throw a fit if someone submitted a design like that."

"Shut up!" The rifle rose to target Matthias's chest. "Tell me how to shut down this vessel."

"You can't," said Matthias. "We have all kinds of backups in place to prevent that sort of thing. But the reactor room is that way." He pointed toward the hatch.

Chris Fish jabbed him in the shoulder. "What are you *doing*?"

But Matthias kept his attention on the Haxozin. When the soldier turned to look in the direction he'd pointed, Matthias stuffed his hand in one of his pockets and retrieved a handful of assorted objects—ball bearings, gaskets, washers, paperclips—all useful to have around. He slipped one between his two forefingers and flicked it toward the unconscious captain.

It hit the captain in the face. He didn't stir.

The Haxozin spun to face Matthias again. "Show me the reactor!"

"It won't help you much," said Matthias. "It's got tons of safety features in place, too. I mean, imagine what would happen if we lost containment. Fission bomb, right in the middle of the ship. Boom. I bet it would take out your entire station, too. I can run the exact figures if you want." He moved toward the nearest console as if to start tapping buttons.

"Back off!" The Haxozin crossed the bridge and shoved Matthias away, then checked to make sure he hadn't activated anything.

Matthias tossed another bit of metal at the captain.

The washer struck Captain Withers on the nose. This time he stirred, his head twitching at the impact.

Chris Fish made a little "oh" sound, and Matthias assumed the scientist had caught on. Chris folded his arms and looked down his long nose at the soldier. "You're not going to find a way to seal everybody in their berths. We use hatches. Manually controlled hatches. Go have a look. There's no digital controls anywhere on them."

The soldier strode toward Chris. The scientist meeped and backed up until he tripped over the captain's chair and fell into it. The ancient chair groaned under the sudden weight. The soldier loomed over Chris and pressed the end of his rifle against Chris's forehead. The scientist crossed his eyes to watch it, his hands trembling on the armrests. "Or don't. That's fine."

The Haxozin leaned close. "You show me." He moved to give Chris a sliver of space through which to escape the chair.

The scientist darted from the confined space and backed toward the open bridge hatch. "Oh, I d-don't think you really need someone to show you. It's not complex. Right, Matthias?" His blue eyes begged Matthias for help.

The soldier had his back to the group, his focus on Chris as he followed him toward the hall. Matthias took a step toward the captain's unconscious body, eyes on the p-gun holstered at his side. His foot made the faintest bump against the deck plating.

The soldier heard. He whirled, gun now targeting

Matthias. "Don't move!"

Matthias froze. "Sorry."

The soldier returned to investigate. When his helmet turned down toward the captain, Matthias knew it was over. There was no way the soldier would miss the gun.

He didn't.

The Haxozin bent to unbuckle the captain's holster. "You thought you could ambush me by—*gah!*"

Captain Withers's sprawled arm shot up and under the Haxozin's elbow, twisting around it and clamping onto his shoulder. Then the captain rolled, his other hand hooking the soldier's ankle. The soldier flew over the captain and crashed to the deck on the other side, shuddering the network of floor plates. The captain used the momentum to roll to his feet, drawing his p-gun from its unbuckled holster in the process. He strode to the Haxozin soldier and kicked the fallen rifle away, beneath the bridge's front consoles. His hand rose to tap his intercom. "Bridge paging Ivanokoff and Praphasat. Return to the *Endurance*. We've got him."

Matthias pumped his fist in the air. "Woo!"

The captain didn't turn. "Was that you throwing stuff at me, Habassa?"

"Yessir, Cap." To demonstrate, Matthias tossed one of the remaining washers across the deck at the captain's leg.

"Thanks. Don't do it again."

"Sure thing, Cap."

He'd known everything would work out. You just needed to keep a positive mindset.

And a pocketful of loose parts.

Good thing he hadn't needed to get to the *really* unusual stuff he carried around. The captain might not have appreciated Matthias launching protractors around the bridge with his fold-up trebuchet.

* * *

Thomas glared at the Haxozin soldier sprawled on his bridge. "What exactly was your plan? Shut down our ship and leave it locked up for your buddies?"

The soldier moaned and rolled over to face him. "I will tell you nothing."

Thomas's earpiece buzzed. "Maureen Habassa paging you," said the computerized voice.

"Answer."

A moment later the ship's de facto medic spoke in a lyrical soprano. "I've checked the two airlock officers, Captain. They might have concussions. Or not. It's hard to tell. But they're conscious now. They should be fine."

"Thank you, Maureen. Help them back to their berths and keep an eye on them."

"Yes, sir."

The comm line cut. Thomas glanced at Matthias. "Your sister's getting more confident."

The engineer grinned. "Yup."

Thomas refocused on the Haxozin. "Your entire species is attacking our home planet right now."

The helmswoman raised her hand. "I'm from Mars, sir."

"System. Our home system," said Thomas. "We take that personally. And since they left you and *your* home system defenseless, we thought we'd return the favor. You're going to provide us with a way to disable your ships."

"Never," said the soldier.

Thomas shook his head. "We can just get it from your station's computers. It'll be easier if you help, but we don't need you. You're dead weight. I'd advise you to make yourself useful."

It was an idle threat. The UELE would kick him into the sun if he fired on an unarmed arrestee.

But the Haxozin didn't need to know that.

The soldier pushed himself to a sitting position and folded his arms.

Thomas jerked his head toward the hatch. "Habassa, Fish, head over to the station and find some schematics for their star ships and weapons."

"Okey dokey, Cap," said Matthias.

"What?" said Chris. "I should be here. I know the most about prior alien invasions of Earth, and the abductions that happened throughout the twentieth century, and the cryo lobby's conspiracy to—"

"Now."

"Ugh. Fine. No appreciation, I swear." Chris followed Matthias out the hatch.

Thomas rotated so he could keep the Haxozin in sight while addressing the two remaining officers. "One of you take his rifle to the armory, and then both of you cover the airlock."

"Yes, sir," they both mumbled. They followed the others, leaving Thomas alone with the prisoner.

Thomas let the soldier sit in silence, studying him. The man made a pretense of nonchalance, but little twitches revealed that he was scanning the environment, very much alert.

Thomas tapped one finger on the barrel of his p-gun. "It's funny. The first time I met you people, you were interrogating me."

"You'll be back to that before long," said the soldier.

"Maybe. What's your name?"

No answer.

"If you don't tell me, I'm going to have to make up a nickname. As the People of Tone probably told you, my species isn't great at naming things."

Pause. "My people call me Vinlin."

"Great. Here's the situation, Vinlin. We never wanted this war. We found your empire completely by accident."

"You inspired some of our worlds to revolt."

"That wasn't our main goal. We were just exploring. If a single visit from another spacefaring species was enough to convince them you weren't all-powerful, you had revolution coming sooner or later anyway. Those worlds were reactors waiting for a leak."

"Your intentions don't matter. We must punish you to ensure the others learn their place."

"That's the problem with revolutions, Vinlin. Killing the thing that sparked them tends to make them bigger. My point is, we would have been happy to just stay off your lawn, but you made it personal. Now we have no choice but to fight back. We may not have a fleet of enormous warships, but humanity is stubborn. Sooner or later, we'll find a way to stop you."

He crouched to Vinlin's level. "I have a few less pleasant ideas, but I'd rather you helped me find something agreeable to all of us. Something we can all survive. I don't want my world to end up looking like yours."

Vinlin twitched his head toward the viewport, through which the dead hulk of the Haxozin planet loomed. "That's not ours."

Thomas raised an eyebrow. "Whose is it?"

"They're extinct."

"You people make a habit of wiping out other species, don't you?"

"They deserved it."

This topic seemed to rile Vinlin. Thomas decided to probe, to see what usable data the Haxozin might let slip. He put on a scornful sneer. "I doubt it."

Vinlin uncrossed his arms and leaned forward. "You know nothing. They were monsters."

"Said the monster right in front of me."

"We are what they made us!"

Thomas's heart began to pound. Eager warmth burned in his veins. "Who were they?"

"You'll die just like they did."

"What did you do to them? Bombard them from orbit with your fleet?"

Vinlin scoffed.

"Wipe them out with a genetic disease, like you did the Thassians?"

No scoff this time.

"That's it, isn't it? You poisoned their planet with targeted genetic warfare. That's why there's no greenery left down there."

"They outnumbered us. It was the only way."

"Why? What did they do to you?"

"What didn't they do? Enslaved our species, killed any who resisted, forced long hours of hard labor, bred us as they saw fit. It was only fair. We built their technology. We should have it!"

The excited warmth in Thomas's veins reached his chest. "You mean your ships. You stole them from the people who owned that planet."

"We made them! The ships were ours."

"Why not use them to run away, go back to your own homes?"

"After so long in servitude, the ships *were* home."

"Then why use them to oppress others? Is it just

payback? Anger against the rest of the uninvolved galaxy?"

"Uninvolved?" spat Vinlin. He pushed himself to his feet, and Thomas rose with him, gun still ready in case of trouble. But the Haxozin was trembling now, anger overriding any kind of strategy. "You call them uninvolved, when they had it easy compared to us? They paid tribute but remained on their own worlds, ran their own societies, lived their own lives. They were the favored thralls. *We* were the Haxozin's real victims!"

A sharp breath hissed through Vinlin's helmet as he realized what he'd said.

The hot energy pulsing through Thomas's body went cold. "Oh, shit. That's why you're terrified of anyone seeing you as weak. That's why you don't have enough soldiers to man your fleet or your planetary outposts. That's why your empire seems too big for you to manage. *It isn't yours.*"

"It is ours!" shouted Vinlin. "We took it."

"How many of you are there, really? You have about a hundred ships, but how many people are on them?" He threw out an impossible number to gauge Vinlin's reaction. "Fifty? Seventy?"

"Of course not."

"Then how many? A hundred? One per ship? Two? There were twenty or so on the ship that captured some of my officers a few months ago, but that was your leader's own flagship, so maybe ten? A thousand of you total?"

Vinlin shook his head. His armored fingers drummed in the air. "It doesn't matter. You can't defeat us."

His reactions told Thomas that the thousand number was around the mark. "One thousand soldiers," he said, "to run an interstellar empire. That can't be an easy life."

"We're used to hard work."

"Why do it? Why spend your time running from planet to planet, putting out fires and maintaining control when you could be settling somewhere, having lives, having leisure time?"

"The Sovereign knows what's right."

"Your boss?"

"Our leader. He has kept us safe. We will not disobey."

The Sovereign. All the Haxozin and their thrall species had referenced this figure with near reverence in the past. The nebulous plan in Thomas's mind began taking on distinct features. If they could discredit or eliminate the Sovereign, the rest of the fake-Haxozin army should crumble in the face of Earth's far superior numbers. Better technology couldn't save them when they had no leader to direct its usage. "Vinlin, I feel sorry for you."

"We want no pity."

"You have it whether or not you want it. But feeling sorry for you doesn't change what I need to do to protect *my* people. To keep my species safe." Thomas moved his finger from the barrel of the p-gun to the trigger. "Take off your helmet."

"No."

"I imagine you all kept them on so other species wouldn't recognize that you're not the real Haxozin, but that secret's out. So unless you're incapable of breathing our atmosphere, which I doubt since yours is similar enough for us to breathe, that helmet's coming off. You can do it yourself, or I'll have you restrained and remove it by force."

Vinlin's trembling hands formed fists. He growled an unintelligible word that the talky box didn't bother to translate, and then reached back to release the clamps around his neck.

Thomas didn't know what he expected to see when the alien drew the red metal helmet from his head. Vicious fangs, maybe, or multiple eyes with the dead irises of a sociopath. Instead, the head that emerged was the most similar to humans of all the aliens he'd so far encountered on his travels. Two eyes, a nose, a mouth, two ears. The skin was a rich plum color, and the jaw looked like it could be distended like a snake's, but Vinlin even had hair atop his head. Granted, it was purple and only grew in a circle that capped his skull, but compared to third arms, spider legs, and claws, Vinlin looked almost benign.

Ivanokoff chose that moment to re-enter the bridge. Thomas saw a quick figure slip behind him and assumed Areva had come too. Ivanokoff surveyed the Haxozin standing unhelmeted for the first time. "I am not impressed." He turned to Thomas. "Habassa and Fish will finish gathering data soon. Where are we going?"

Thomas continued watching his captive, who stared resolutely back at him. "Once the reactor produces enough power to charge the D Drive again, we're returning to Thassis."

He heard a quiet gasp, and then Areva appeared by his elbow. "Captain," she said, "as your chief security officer, I need to recommend against that. They almost killed us all the last ti—"

Thomas waved a hand to cut her off. "I know. But we need the Thassians' medical technology. I want to create a very specific, very targeted plan of attack."

He made eye contact with Vinlin and inhaled slowly. "Sorry about this, but I'm going to need a sample of your DNA."

* * *

Alien technology was so *cool*. Matthias scrolled through the code as he searched for an operation to initiate DNA analysis. The computer mainframe was small, just a little box with a screen on the front, sitting on a table in a chilly, sparse room at the top of one of the decrepit buildings of Thassis. The *Endurance* had blown up an identical room in a different building on their last visit.

Ivanokoff paced the wall of windows on one side of the office, hands toying with the grips of his two holstered projectile guns. "Hurry."

Matthias paused on an executable file that looked promising, but dismissed it after the talky box hookup translated the file as a power control program. "Patience is a virtue," he said with a smile.

"I do not do patience," said Ivanokoff. His pacing took him toward the office's entryway. He rapped twice on the closed door. "Areva, anything?"

"No," came the security chief's voice. "All quiet out here."

"For now," Ivanokoff muttered.

"Don't be so grumpy," said Matthias, pausing to analyze another potential file. "Just because you were almost eaten by zombies last time you were here—"

"They do not eat people."

"That's not what Chris said."

"Chris Fish is an idiot."

Matthias chuckled. "Tell that to his resume."

Ah, there it was! Matthias confirmed that he'd found the hospital's DNA analysis program, a segment of the DNA mapping technology contained in the basement.

"Got it," he said. "Initializing now. I think I've got everything working." He glanced over the array of split wires, spliced connections, and jury-rigged adapters he'd needed to make the alien technology compatible with his own.

He slipped the Haxozin blood sample from its biohazard container. The liquid in the tiny cylinder was deep red, almost purple. Matthias donned protective gloves and dabbed a bit of the blood onto the portable scanner plug-in attached to the side of his pocket computer.

The lid of the scanner pad slid closed, and the device began to hum in operation. Matthias quickly transferred the analysis protocols from his pocket computer's limited software to the more expansive programming in the Thassian hospital's computer. He would now be able to read every nuance of the blood sample's makeup, including genetic weaknesses.

While the computers worked, Matthias watched Ivanokoff continue his circuit of the room. "You okay, big guy?"

"I do not do nicknames."

"You okay, Lieutenant Ivanokoff?"

"No." Ivanokoff stared out the windows again. "The longer we stay, the more likely the aliens will come."

"I'm almost done."

"Hurry."

"Take a deep breath, buddy. There's nothing you can do to make things go faster. Remember, be a duck. Let the stress just roll off."

"I do not do metaphors."

Matthias laughed. "I guarantee some of the novels in your berth are full of metaphors. Come on, just take a deep breath."

"No."

A light flashed on Matthias's pocket computer. He leaned over the desk and pecked a few controls on the flat device. "Analysis complete. We've got a full study of this guy's DNA. It'll take time to go through, but this should show us any predisposition to certain poisons, toxins, all sorts of—hang on, what's this?"

Ivanokoff strode toward the door. "No time. We leave now."

"Wait, wait, this is important," said Matthias. He skimmed the data, eyes flicking back and forth across the screen. He scrolled to the bottom of the analysis, then back to the part that had caught his attention. A tremor ran through his hands, and he swallowed. *Be a duck*, he thought. *Focus. Any problem can be fixed.*

This one was a doozy, though.

"So," he said, trying to maintain a light tone, "remember how the other hospital's DNA scanner stored an analysis of your genes last time we were here?"

Ivanokoff froze by the door. "Da."

"It's still here."

In seconds the first officer had crossed to the table. "We destroyed the scanner and the mainframe storing the information."

"I know, but apparently all the hospitals on this planet were networked. Your DNA analysis was transferred to every other DNA scanner on this planet."

Ivanokoff swore. "Delete it."

"I can't. That requires administrator privileges. But that's not the important part."

"The Haxozin are invading Earth. If they visited this planet and looked into these computers, they have likely made a genetic virus to wipe out humanity," said Ivanokoff. "Yes, it is the important part."

"No," said Matthias. "It's really not. Part of the analysis program I ran compares the DNA sample to other stored information. When it analyzed the Haxozin DNA, a close match was found."

Ivanokoff stared down at him. "No."

"Yep."

"But they appear nothing like—"

"I know, but genetics don't lie. The Haxozin, whatever else they are, are part human."

* * *

The *Endurance* had secluded itself in a park enclosed by overgrown hedges, about two blocks from the hospital. Broken windows, tattered flags, and stained walls lined the walk back. The Thassians hadn't been dead long enough for their buildings to collapse, but darkened rooms and empty doorways loomed in every direction.

Matthias trotted behind Ivanokoff and Areva, toting a backpack full of his equipment. Ivanokoff spoke quietly into his intercom to inform Captain Withers of the situation. Matthias wondered which swear words the captain was using.

He tried to think positive. Now they had something in common with their enemy. Maybe they could use that to reach an understanding. Also, if the Haxozin deployed a bio toxin on Earth, it would wind up killing them, too. They had enough human DNA for that. Poetic.

Somehow that thought didn't comfort Matthias.

They had just rounded the corner of a run-down grocery store and glimpsed the hedges protecting the *Endurance* down the street when he felt someone's hand on his back. Areva's voice whispered in his ear, "Don't look."

Matthias kept his attention forward. "Don't worry, Areva, I know how you feel about being seen."

"No. Not at me. Don't look back."

A prickling feeling crawled up Matthias's neck. "Why not?"

"They're here."

"The Haxozin?"

"No. The Thassians."

Oh.

Oh.

Not good.

"Keep walking slowly," Areva said. "I'll tell Viktor."

Matthias forced himself to maintain a measured pace while Areva slipped in front of him and whispered to Ivanokoff. He tried not to watch her, considering it impolite given her eccentricities, but he found it comforting to remember that two deadly fighters were out here with him. It wasn't just his brain against the teeth and claws of the undead Thassians.

Ivanokoff stiffened as Areva murmured to him. He reported something into his intercom. His hand slipped over Areva's, and they shared a reassuring squeeze.

Then they let go. In slow movements, Ivanokoff drew his p-guns, Dickens and Dante, from their holsters. Areva slipped her bazooka rifle down her arm and hefted it with both hands.

Areva slowed her pace until she was even with Matthias again. "Run when I say," she whispered.

"Kay."

"Don't be scared. We'll make it."

"I'm not." Matthias made himself grin. "I'm a duck, remember?"

Areva rolled her eyes and disappeared out of sight at the back of the group.

The narrow passage through the hedges that led to *Endurance* lay at the end of a crumbling bit of sidewalk, across an abandoned thoroughfare. Matthias fought the urge to quicken his steps. Slow movements. Don't be a target—one of the first things they told mechanically-minded recruits in UELE training. Leave the shooting to the fighters.

A scrabbling noise drew his gaze to the second floor of the grocery store on his right. Sunken pink eyes stared out of a sickly orange skull from one of the windows. Two hands clutched the sill alongside the head, bearing the curving talons that let the Thassians climb walls.

Matthias gulped. Be a duck. Be a duck. Let the fear just roll off.

More scrabbling. A lot this time, most of it from the second story.

Some from up ahead.

They were about to be cut off.

Something shoved Matthias in the back, and Areva shouted, "Run!"

Matthias broke into a sprint, clutching the straps of his backpack to keep his arms from flailing. Ahead of him, Ivanokoff raised Dante to target a second-story window and fired. A crack split the air, and an inhuman shriek followed. An undead Thassian tumbled from one of the windows.

Ivanokoff continued firing, clearing the way ahead, while Areva fended off those encroaching from behind. Matthias just ran. They left the grocery store behind and darted across the road, projectile and energy shots screaming through the air.

Matthias chanced a backward glance. Thassians were swarming over walls, sidewalks, even streetlamps. Hundreds of pink eyes fixed on the three fleeing humans.

Hundreds of lethal talons stretched out to stop them. Thousands of fangs glinted in the sunlight as the aliens snapped their jaws.

The team reached the hedge. Ivanokoff turned sideways and slipped between the plants ahead of Matthias. Matthias, being smaller, ducked his head, raised his arms to deflect hanging twigs, and charged straight through.

Halfway to the other side, something scraped his shin, tearing straight through his blue uniform. Pain flashed through his leg, and he stumbled. Another impact against his ankles brought him to his hands and knees in the dirt.

He scrambled to get his footing and spied a pair of pink eyes gleaming at him beneath the hedge. An open maw gaped, full of red teeth.

"Areva!" Matthias screamed.

The security chief nearly tripped over Matthias's fallen form. She pulled back just in time, aimed her energy rifle into the hedge, and fired. White lightning blasted through the leaves, vaporizing several of them instantly and setting many more ablaze. The pink eyes disappeared. Matthias couldn't tell if the shot had hit the zombie, but he didn't care. He pushed himself up and hobbled the rest of the way to the *Endurance*'s waiting airlock ramp. Ivanokoff stood at the top of it, firing first with one gun, then the other, fending off the attacking horde from both sides.

The second Matthias and Areva cleared the ramp, Ivanokoff punched the control to seal the airlock. Hydraulics whirred to life, and the ramp raised to enclose the *Endurance* interior. Matthias collapsed, leaning on his full backpack for support. He stared down at his torn pant leg and bleeding shin. Areva slunk into a dark corner.

Ivanokoff told the captain to take off and initiated the airlock decontamination procedure. Only then did anyone pay attention to Matthias. "You are hurt," said Ivanokoff, holstering his guns.

Matthias nodded.

"He tripped on the hedge," said Areva.

Ivanokoff grunted. "Your sister can take care of it."

Matthias grimaced. "I'm not sure about that."

"Why not?"

"It wasn't the hedge." *Be a duck*, Matthias reminded himself. "One of the Thassians was hiding under it. I saw his mouth. His teeth were bloody."

Areva gasped. Ivanokoff's grip tightened once more on his gun.

This time Matthias felt the strain in his own smile. "Yeah. He bit me. I'm infected."

* * *

Thomas gaped at Ivanokoff across his desk. "He was bitten? Where?"

"The shin. He is in the infirmary now. Maureen is treating the wound."

"Is he ... you know?"

Ivanokoff shrugged. "So far he has not shown signs of dying. But the virus was created for Thassian bodies. It may take longer to affect a human, or not affect him at all."

"How will we know if he starts turning?"

"The Thassians became zombies—"

"Please don't use that word."

"—almost instantly. I imagine if his body begins to die, but his brain remains active, we will know."

Thomas sank onto his threadbare desk chair and dropped his head into his hands. "I've never lost a crew member."

"You still have not."

"Thanks, Ivanokoff." Thomas indulged in only a few seconds of rest before rising. "Have Maureen start preparing any ideas for treating the infection if it does start to affect Matthias. In the meantime, is he up to studying the data we downloaded from the Haxozin station?"

Ivanokoff's mouth twitched in a rare hint of a smile. "One cannot stop an engineer from studying things. He has already begun."

* * *

Matthias sat on his bunk in his berth. The single-person bed was built right into the wall, with storage drawers beneath it and a two-step ladder to climb up. Maureen sat at the desk built into the opposite wall. The room's hatch stood open, implying freedom of movement, but Matthias knew he wasn't at liberty to leave. Areva stood guard outside, and should he get all bitey, she'd stun him before he cleared the doorway.

It was comforting, really. Matthias didn't think he could look at himself the same way if he went around nipping his coworkers.

A series of unfolded pocket comps lay strewn across his bedspread, each displaying a different set of files downloaded from the Haxozin space station. The schematics for their star ships required multiple reference files to understand—glossaries, numerical codes, molecular structural formulas, and engineering manuals—hence he needed multiple screens to display it all. He'd also found the Haxozin linguistic database; he might as well teach himself some of their language while he studied their data. At the moment he was puzzling through what looked like a diagram of the gravity-on-a-stick drive, except all the labels were given in symbols, requiring him to cross-reference between multiple other files. He stuck his tongue out as he scrolled through the various data. He concentrated better that way.

At his desk, Maureen studied her own spread of pocket comps. The captain had asked her, along with Chris Fish in the science lab, to look through the Haxozin DNA analysis for any possible weaknesses. The report from the Thassian hospital was very thorough, so it would take hours to skim it all.

Matthias picked up one of his screens and skipped to the next file from the database. He snickered as he read the translated text. "Hey Sis, I found their tax code. You think they call it the Hax tax?"

Maureen dropped the pocket comp she'd been holding. The clatter made Matthias's desktop maglev train start zooming around its homemade track. Maureen reached up and shut it off, and Matthias saw her hand tremble.

"You okay?" he asked.

"Mattie, how can you still joke?" Despite her scandalized tone, Maureen's voice retained its soothing airiness.

"How can I not? It's just who I am."

His sister spun the desk chair to face him. "I think this could be the one time you take things seriously."

Matthias set down his own computers. "Sis, what's bothering you?"

"What's bothering me? What's *bothering* me? Our home planet's been conquered, we're millions of miles away, and now you're ..."

"I'm not dying."

"I didn't say you were."

"For all we know, this disease won't even affect me." Matthias shifted his posture to hide the growing grey patch of skin on his bitten leg.

Maureen noticed. Her lithe arms folded across her chest. "Mattie, please."

"All right, so it's affecting me. That doesn't mean I'm gonna die. If it gets bad, we can still try the Revixophin you used on the zombies last time we were on Thassis."

"Yes, that turned out so well."

"Different physiologies, different results." Matthias smiled. "Look at how much progress we've made already. And I'm *this* close to finding a way to disable the Haxozin engines. If they can't maneuver, they can't evade our EMPs anymore."

"They can still shoot at cities from orbit. Or release a toxin that wipes out humanity. If I—if we don't find a way to wipe them out first." Maureen tucked her legs up against her chest and rested her chin on her knees. Her voice dropped to a murmur. "I didn't know it would be like this."

Matthias decided his little sister needed a hug. But when he swung his legs off the bed, she jerked to an upright posture. "No, stay there. You said the leg hurts. Don't walk on it."

He obeyed, slipping back onto his bunk. "We never really talked about why you decided to become a UELE officer. You were supposed to be dancing with the Rashiq Ballet. Why'd you turn them down?"

Maureen bit her lip. "Why did *you* pick this job?"

"I love astrophysics."

"And?"

"And ... I wanted to use astrophysics to help catch bad guys?"

Maureen shook her head. "And you wanted to annoy Mom and Dad."

Matthias laughed. "Maybe a little. I was never gonna be a good sculptor. Not everyone can be famous artists like them."

"That's why I did it," said Maureen. "When you decided to go into law enforcement, it made me think. I wondered if I was doing the most useful thing I could with my life, and when I compared it to yours, I had to answer no. I had never thought of doing something outside the arts, but you made me realize it was an option, no matter what Mom and Dad said. I thought it would be a grand adventure. That I'd see different planets and help people. I didn't expect ... this."

Matthias traced the bandage on his shin. Around it, the grey translucence had spread halfway up his kneecap and across his instep. "None of us did. But that doesn't mean we can't make the most of it."

Maureen looked at him with the wide eyes that used to beg him to check for monsters under the bed. "Do you think Mom and Dad are all right?"

Matthias spoke with absolute conviction. "Yes. I do."

"How can you know?"

"I don't. But until I do, there's no reason to assume the worst." He smiled again and picked up two of his screens. "We'll be the most helpful if we don't waste time worrying about things we can't control."

Maureen managed a small smile. "Be a duck?"

"Quack, quack, quack," agreed Matthias.

* * *

Thomas faced Vinlin across the makeshift interrogation table in the rec room. The Haxozin soldier had been stripped of his armor, and instead he now wore a borrowed uniform of Ivanokoff's. With the alien's large frame, the first officer's uniforms were the only ones that fit him.

Areva was keeping an eye on Matthias, but Ivanokoff stood near the rec room hatch to stop Vinlin from posing a threat. Thomas hoped that after he told the Haxozin what they now knew, the threat might be eliminated entirely.

"We analyzed your DNA," Thomas said. "Found some interesting things, too."

Vinlin didn't reply.

"You people seem to like using targeted genetic viruses against your enemies. Turns out you'd better not do that on Earth. Whatever you do will end up killing yourselves, too."

This time the alien's purple brow twitched.

Thomas nodded. "That's right. A whole bunch of your DNA is identical to ours."

Vinlin scoffed. "Impossible."

"Oh yeah? You said your people were taken as slaves by the original Haxozin."

"Yes."

"From where?" When the alien didn't answer, Thomas pressed. "Where's your original homeworld, Vinlin? You don't know, do you?"

The alien shifted in his seat. "Those records were lost generations ago."

"Not surprising. Your owners wouldn't have wanted your people yearning for a specific place."

"This does not prove any bit of your story."

Thomas ignored the protest. "What we think

happened was after your ancestors were taken from Earth, they interbred with the original Haxozin, leading to how you look now. We can't know for sure, since there are none of them left to compare to your DNA. But at least half of your heritage is from the planet your people are currently trying to conquer. Use a genetic virus against us, and you stand a good chance of wiping yourselves out."

Vinlin worked his jaw. "Even if this is true, which I do not believe, why would you tell me?"

Thomas leaned forward. "We don't have to fight, Vinlin. Your people are human at your core. You don't have to keep struggling to preserve the illusion of a dead empire. We can call off the war, and you can all come home."

Vinlin shook his head. "The Sovereign would never agree."

"I'm not talking to the Sovereign. I'm talking to you."

"I will not betray my people."

"No matter what you choose to do, you're betraying your own. The difference is that we offer a life of peace, comfort, and the ability to define your own life. Does your Sovereign offer the same perks?"

The alien didn't answer, but he didn't have to.

"We'll give you full access to the DNA analyses," said Thomas. "You'll come to the same conclusion we did. And then you'll have a choice."

"I serve the Haxozin Sovereignty. I have no choices."

Thomas folded his hands. "Is that something the Sovereign said, or your old masters?"

Vinlin stiffened.

"Think about it. We'll be heading back to Earth's

solar system soon. I hope it'll be with you on our bridge as ambassador." Thomas stood and headed for the hatch.

Vinlin's voice stopped him. "You would truly allow us to settle among you?"

Thomas looked over his shoulder. "I can't promise everyone will welcome you as neighbors, but yes. You belong with us. I'm sure we can find space for you."

A pause. "Show me the analysis."

Thomas smiled.

* * *

After all the research and debates, the *Endurance* crew had one final meeting before enacting their plan.

Thomas stood at the head of the long tables in the rec room, their benches crowded with the twenty-some members of his crew. The ship currently held position in an empty part of space, waiting for the Adkinsium reactor to generate enough power to use the D Drive again. Thomas left two officers on the bridge in case of emergencies, but everyone else was supposed to be present.

Thomas cleared his throat. "Where's Nina?"

"Food poisoning," said three different people.

"Officer Lee?"

"Monitoring the reactor," said an engineer.

"Areva?"

"Here," said a quiet voice from beneath one of the tables.

Thomas surveyed the room. A year ago, he would not have entrusted these people with the survival of the planet. He wouldn't have even trusted them to water his houseplants. Now, he knew better.

"I'm sure most of you know what's happening," he

said. He recapped the invasion of Earth and the discovery of the human elements of the Haxozin DNA. "Once the D Drive charges, we'll head to the World of Infinite Tones to pick up some supplies, and then we'll return to Earth to try to disable or destroy the Haxozin fleet. I know none of you signed up for this. We're law enforcement, not special forces. We're also on an older ship with inferior weapons, and airlocks that take three tries to open. If any of you want to stay behind on Tones, I'll understand."

He paused, not sure what to expect. In any other crew, he'd assume every officer would feel the need to show courage. Here, he didn't know.

Chris Fish spoke up. "Joyce and I will stay behind."

His wife, scientist Joyce Fish, elbowed him. "What now?"

"Honey, I don't want to blow up on a foolhardy mission to take on a thousand enemy ships—"

"A hundred," said Ivanokoff.

"You *saw* a hundred," said Chris. "You're not counting the reinforcements I'm sure they have shrouded in dark matter or hiding in false asteroids or—"

Joyce patted his arm and talked over him. "Captain, we'll be returning to Earth with you. I'll convince him later."

Chris folded his arms and hunched in his seat, scowling.

Thomas scanned the tables. "Anyone else?"

Sergeant Ramirez raised his hand. "Uh, is this l-likely to get us killed?"

Thomas saw no reason to lie. "Yes."

"Oh. So, er, you'll need people, um, to be at their b-best. Sir. Captain, I mean."

"Relax, Sergeant. I won't bite."

"Matthias might," muttered Chris. Joyce elbowed him again.

Ramirez swallowed, avoiding eye contact with anyone who outranked him. "Uh, if it's okay to say then, sir ... can we make extra coffee rations before the trip? I, uh, do better with caffeine." A few other officers murmured in agreement.

More coffee. That was their biggest concern. "Are you all sure about this?" Thomas asked.

Ivanokoff raised his chin. "We are UELE officers. Not cowards."

"I m-might be a coward," said Ramirez.

"Me too," said Chris.

"But," said Ramirez, "that, uh, doesn't mean we don't have to do this. So, um, yeah. I'll go."

Thomas made eye contact with every officer—his officers, who had yet again surprised him. "Thank you," he said. "All of you. I ... I know you'll make me proud."

All was quiet for a moment.

Then Chris asked, "So is that a yes on the extra coffee?"

Once the coffee controversy had been resolved, Thomas let his department heads explain their research findings for the coming mission.

Chris Fish went first. "We the scientists of this ship—the most important team, by the way—have been reading the Haxozin DNA analysis."

"I helped," said Maureen.

"Fine, we the scientists and the scientist in training. We don't have the technology necessary to create a targeted genetic virus or anything that precise—"

"Which we wouldn't do anyway," said Maureen. "Because it's awful."

Chris didn't comment on that. "But the analysis

revealed a weakness to carbon monoxide. Haxozin hemoglobin will be affected by the gas far faster than human cells, meaning unconsciousness or expiration from oxygen deprivation will set in far faster. And we can collect carbon monoxide as a byproduct if we misalign the superconductors on the ship's—"

"Basically," said Thomas, who had heard this already, "we can knock the Haxozin out, disarm them, and pump fresh air in before there's any permanent damage. Low risk to them, almost no risk to any humans they're holding. We want to come to peaceful terms with them, but we can't do that if they have hostages. So one team will be infiltrating the Haxozin's main base on Earth, seeking out their Sovereign, and using this method to subdue him and then negotiate. Vinlin, our Haxozin guest, has been convinced by the DNA analysis and has agreed to help."

"Won't their helmets filter out the gas?" asked Maureen.

"Vinlin says no," said Thomas. "They're armor, not hazmat suits."

"The Sovereign may not listen," said Ivanokoff.

"I know," said Thomas. "That's why we have the second part of this plan."

Thomas pointed at Matthias Habassa, who sat alone on a chair in one corner. Thomas tried to ignore the grey, translucent quality of the engineer's infected skin, which had now encroached partway up his neck. There was a clear, jagged line on the throat where the grey infection battled Matthias's natural copper color.

Matthias spoke as if he wasn't possibly dying. "Okie dokey, guys. We've analyzed the Haxozin ship schematics and found the most vulnerable place to target. If we EMP a certain spot on the ventral side of the prongs, we can shut the ships down entirely. They'll be dead in the water and unable to shoot back. Of course, in order to hit that spot, we have to disable their gravity-on-a-stick engines first. Once they can't move, we'll have a much easier time blasting away bits of their hull and EMPing their insides. So here's how we do that:

"We have to fly, in D Drive, through the gravity wells on the prongs of their ships."

"Whoa," said Chris Fish. "Whoa, whoa, whoa. Do you have any idea how dangerous that is? What if you come out of four-D inside one of the prongs? What if the star ship moves?"

"D Drive jumps are too fast for them to evade," said Matthias. "Once we engage the jump, it'll hit its target. And we can avoid any complications with math."

"Math," said Chris dubiously.

"Sure. Based on the amount of force Areva's gun used to push us to Earth a few days ago, I've written a program to calculate the same kind of micro-jumps and perform them automatically. We'll have to make the jumps at, like, a billionth of a percent of max thrust—I wrote a program for that, too—and each jump will be so fast you can't even see it, but it'll work. It's the same thing we did to get from Neptune to Earth, but now with technology instead of guns."

Chris looked at Joyce. "Are you sure you don't want to stay behind?"

"Guns are technology," said Ivanokoff.

"What coding language did you use for the program?" asked an engineer.

Thomas took over the meeting before it could get sidetracked. "Most of you will be staying on *Endurance* and bringing Matthias's plan to the other UELE ships gathering near Mars. Ivanokoff will be in charge."

"Oh, goody," said Chris.

Ivanokoff arched an eyebrow. "I do not do backtalk."

Chris shut up.

Thomas continued, "A few of us, including myself, will take another ship and sneak through the Haxozin lines to land on Median Island. Vinlin said the Sovereign is probably going to stay at Earth's capital, so we'll go in, locate him, vent a few canisters of carbon monoxide into the room, and come in after to secure him and any guards he's posted. Then, if all goes well, we'll talk this out."

"I hate to bring up the obvious problem," said Chris.

"You *love* to bring up obvious problems," said Joyce.

Chris ignored her. "How are you going to sneak past a hundred alien spaceships?"

Thomas smiled. "By borrowing one."

* * *

"Absolutely not," said the grey-skinned alien, waving all three of her arms in negative gestures. Her two-foot ears vibrated to underscore her point, and her voice lilted in melodious fluidity. The talky box translation probably lost the nuances of her refusal.

"Echo," said Thomas, "we need your help."

Echo shook her head again. "That captured ship is ours."

"Only because we helped you liberate your planet."

"We gave you our translation technology and linguistic databases. You promised us new languages to study in return. But you have so far not kept that promise."

"We gave you over a thousand languages from Earth."

Echo folded two of her hands and made a dismissive gesture with the third. "We finished studying those ages ago. Your speech patterns are so dull, Dirt Person."

"Earthling."

"That is what I said."

Thomas sighed. Translation issues aside, he needed the People of Tone to lend him the Haxozin shuttle they'd been studying for the past year. Otherwise he had no chance. "I promise to bring the shuttle back right away. A few days at most."

"Unless you destroy it in a foolish attempt to fight *the entire Haxozin Sovereignty* at once."

"I told you, they're not the real Haxozin. There are only a few of them, and they're vulnerable. This will work."

Echo's ears drooped. "I am sorry, Captain Thomas Withers. It is too big a risk. We will not enable you in destroying yourselves."

Thomas ground his teeth. "It was a big risk when I saved your life. And when we shot the Haxozin soldiers occupying your city. Your world is free because of what we did, Echo. I'm only asking you to return the favor." He looked into her black-rimmed eyes. "Please. If we succeed, the whole galaxy would be a more peaceful place. If we fail, the Haxozin are going to finish solidifying their control of my world, and then come back to re-conquer yours. One shuttle won't do you any good against their fleet, but if you lend it to us, it might prevent that threat from ever coming to you."

Echo's ear tendrils rose and fell in the equivalent of a sigh. "I will try again to convince the First Leader. If only your species were more eloquent and gifted with verbal harmony, you could explain your position yourself. Such a shame."

* * *

After another hour, Echo returned with good news. The People of Tone would agree to lend their shuttle to the Dirt People (their term, not Thomas's) in exchange for the rest of Earth's language databases, current and past, to be delivered with the return of the shuttle. Thomas agreed at once. If he wasn't able to deliver them, it would be because he'd failed. His dead body wouldn't be too inconvenienced by having an unpaid debt.

The Haxozin shuttle was about a quarter the size of the *Endurance*. Tangled wires and messy interface screens bore testimony to the People of Tone's year-long study to learn how to fly the thing. Thomas received an explanation of the controls and a translation program to convert the interfaces to something he could read.

Only once he made sure he could pilot the shuttle did he have Vinlin brought aboard.

The Haxozin soldier was still in his borrowed UELE uniform, his purple neck straining against the shirt collar. He was unarmed, but Thomas had no illusions about how dangerous he could be. He had Vinlin secured in the shuttle's cramped berthing compartment, and the door locked. He didn't need any ambushes while he was trying to fly through a blockade.

The only other officer accompanying him was Areva Praphasat. The rest of the crew would be needed on the *Endurance*, and would be in less danger there. Areva was ex-special ops. She could handle danger, so long as it didn't see her.

Thomas seated himself in the pilot's chair, facing the pyramid of viewports on the front of the narrow bridge. "Ready?" he called over his shoulder.

Areva's voice came from somewhere amidst the displays and control panels behind him. "Ready."

Thomas located the communications system and activated it. "Withers paging *Endurance*."

His first officer answered. "This is Captain Ivanokoff."

"You're not a captain."

"I am in command of the ship. The title applies."

Thomas rolled his eyes. "Just remember that I want it back later. Are you ready to go?"

"Da. The D Drive is ready for the final jump."

"Good. Once you meet up with Captain Nandoro, proceed with the rest of the plan immediately. You'll distract the enemy and give us time to land. If things go smoothly, they should all surrender to you shortly afterward."

"And if it does not go smoothly?"

"Then start disabling their ships, and don't stop until they're all adrift. Then have somebody land at the capital and come find us. We might need help."

"Understood."

Areva appeared at Thomas's side, making him jump. "Can I say something?"

"Uh, sure."

"Viktor?"

Ivanokoff answered. "Areva?"

"I love you," she said.

"And I, you. 'Only in the agony of parting do we look into the depths of love.'"

She paused in thought for a moment. "Eliot?"

"Da."

"Apt."

A muffled groan sounded over the intercom line. "Great, Ivanokoff," said Chris Fish's voice. "Now something awful is going to happen because you had a touching departure."

Areva smiled and disappeared into the back of the shuttle once more.

Thomas hesitated before closing the channel. "Ivanokoff."

"Yes?"

"Put me on shipwide."

A few beeps carried over the line. "Ready."

Thomas took a deep breath. "I know I didn't get off to the best start with most of you. Or any of you. I'm sorry for that. I'm sorry for the misconceptions I carried onto the ship with me. When I first received this assignment, I couldn't wait to transfer to another ship. But over the last year, I've realized that beneath the nonconformist, confrontational, unconfident exterior, you all are an excellent crew."

He heard a whoop. Matthias.

One side of his mouth turned up. "We're all cracked, but sometimes those cracks are just what we need to get results. I've been proud to be your captain, and I'm proud of how we've started to reclaim the *Endurance*'s good name. Let's finish that process today."

An auditory slush of "yes, sir!" "all right!" "woo-hoo!" and "UELE!" blared through the speakers.

With the voices of his crew ringing in his ears (literally—the volume had been turned up too high), Thomas engaged the Haxozin shuttle's engine and lifted off.

* * *

Matthias sat on the bridge's aft bench and tried to ignore his icy fingers and shivering arms. His body was in trouble; he knew that. But despite the clear encroachment of the zombie virus through his veins, despite the ever-present security guard waiting to stun him should he turn, his mind felt no symptoms whatsoever.

That was good. His mind was his most important part. If it stayed intact long enough to liberate Earth, medical researchers would be able to do something about the rest of him. For now, he surveyed the ragtag fleet of UELE fighters, cruisers, and civilian craft gathered near Mars and tried to quiet his pounding heart.

At the scanners station, Chris Fish cleared his throat. "Captain Nandoro is paging us. Video call."

"Answer," said Ivanokoff.

A moment later, one of the overhead screens blinked to Nandoro's face. "We're all set, *Endurance*. Once we get there, focus on disabling the Haxozin gravity drives. I'll oversee the rest. A few Haxozin stars have broken off to visit the other planets, but we'll still have to face the majority of their fleet. Disable one star, then move to the next."

Ivanokoff nodded. "Understood."

"Good luck."

"I do not do luck."

"Good luck anyway."

The feed switched back to *Endurance*'s external thermal scanners, currently showing the bulk of the fleet. All the UELE's mustered forces totaled no more than fifty vessels, most of them the size of *Endurance* or even smaller. A swarm of mosquitos against a herd of rhinos.

"Engage engines," said Ivanokoff. He raised his chin and deepened his voice. "'Either victory, or else a grave.'"

"Um, dark," said Chris Fish.

Matthias hefted the computer panel he'd rigged to display reactor output, D Drive stability, and the positions of all targets simultaneously. He'd need to stay on his toes to make sure the jumps were long enough to pass all the way through the star prongs, but short enough not to drain the reactor too fast.

Good thing his brain still worked.

Endurance fell into place on the right side of Nandoro's ship. Together humanity's remaining law enforcement crews engaged their engines and headed off to serve and defend, possibly for the last time.

* * *

The Haxozin shuttle handled poorly at high speeds. Thomas gritted his teeth against the rattling from every bulkhead, every console, every bone in his body. The view outside, though not as nauseating as D Drive, still turned his stomach. Most stars were too far away for this speed to make them appear to move, but the bending effect of the ship's false gravity well rippled space like an optical illusion.

Thomas didn't start to slow down until the last possible second. He wanted to appear in the midst of the Haxozin fleet in the hopes that, with their less-than-skeleton crews, they'd miss his arrival and assume he'd been there the whole time.

"Here we go," he murmured, and disengaged the gravity generator at the nose of the shuttle.

The illusory bending of space boggled his eyes for a few more seconds, and then slowly the night returned to a solid pattern, no longer broken by sloping lines and curves. Earth loomed ahead, big and blue. It looked almost normal.

Except for the grid of grey hulking vessels surrounding it. Thomas's deceleration brought the shuttle right beneath one of the largest star ships, and he had to force himself not to stare upward as they drifted along the length of one of its prongs.

Scanners beeped. Thomas held his breath. Had his entrance been noticed?

But none of the giant ships turned to intercept him, nor did any of them show a buildup of stored weapon energy. He didn't get so much as a "hello" on the intercom.

He exhaled and engaged a meandering path that wouldn't look too determined, but that brought him slowly toward the surface. He passed from the shadow of the first ship and crossed a patch of empty space before passing over the arms of a second. He gave the central spire a wide berth, not wanting to get their attention, and changed course to drift a bit closer to the atmosphere.

"Come on, Ivanokoff," he muttered.

"Viktor will be here," said Areva, making him jump with yet another sudden appearance in the cockpit.

"I know. Just talking to myself."

"Did you mean what you said? That you're proud of us?"

Thomas made another turn to avoid a Haxozin shuttle heading in the opposite direction. This maneuver directed him away from Earth, but that was just as well. He didn't want to look suspicious. "Yes. I did."

"Even me?"

Thomas laughed. "Areva, you're one of the most capable members of the crew."

"Sometimes."

"When it counts."

"Not always." She lapsed into silence, and Thomas had the sense that she wanted to say something important but couldn't find the words.

"When we're on the surface," she said, "I'm not going to shoot anyone who can see me. No one should see death coming."

"I'm familiar with your habits."

"I mean it, Captain. Even if it's the last chance to save our lives, I'm not going to break my principles. If they see me coming, I won't kill them."

Thomas pursed his lips. "So don't let them see you."

"I don't intend to. But I thought you should know, since you're depending on me."

Another turn, this time back toward Earth's surface. Where was Ivanokoff? Where was Nandoro? "I appreciate the warning, Praphasat. I trust you."

"Thank you." Another pause. "If we succeed, we'll be heroes."

Thomas nodded and stifled the flutter of excitement the word put in his stomach. "Probably."

"I'm not good at that. If we succeed, I'm quitting law enforcement. I thought things would be fine if we stayed in our quiet orbit of Neptune, but we're back in the middle of things. I'm not suited for it. One way or another, this is my last mission."

Thomas couldn't claim to be surprised. "Does Ivanokoff know?"

"He knows."

"What does he think?"

"He hasn't decided yet."

Thomas ducked the shuttle beneath the spire of a star ship rotating on its axis. "I'll be sorry to lose you. But I understand."

"Thanks." Like a whisper, Areva disappeared into the background again.

And like chain lightning, a series of blips appeared on Thomas's scanners, rapidly growing larger. Ships.

The UELE was on the scene. Ten seconds out, at their current speed.

Thomas pointed the shuttle's nose at the center of the Mediterranean Sea and prepared to dive.

* * *

"Now!" shouted Matthias.

Ivanokoff gave the order. *Endurance*'s D Drive engaged. One second the viewports showed the rapidly oncoming bulkhead of a Haxozin star ship's prong. The next they showed empty space. The jump was too minute for even a blinking eye to catch.

"Bring us around," ordered Ivanokoff. Every bridge officer held their breath as the ship pivoted to face their struck target.

The star was pitching, one of its arms darkened, its ability to maneuver gone. A trio of UELE ships followed the *Endurance*'s path, opening fire on the unpowered prong and stripping away sections of the bulkheads. Then a fourth vessel swooped in and fired an EMP into the crippled target.

The rest of the star dimmed and went out. The red thermal readings from its charged weapons began to dissipate to blue.

Cheers erupted. It had worked. Matthias breathed a sigh of relief.

Or tried to. His lungs wouldn't quite obey. He gasped a few times and got them working, but each inhale was laborious.

"Next target," said Ivanokoff. Matthias shook himself and began checking the computer's plan for the next jump. Some portion of his brain concentrated on filling his lungs, but he had no time to worry.

His mind was still working. As long as it was, he could let the rest roll off.

* * *

The Haxozin shuttle plummeted through the atmosphere. Waves of heat rolled off its bow, creating a haze over the viewports. Thomas piloted by instinct and scanners. The rickety barge shuddered with every bump, and his knuckles went white as he fought to keep an even angle of descent. He had no idea what he would do if he lost control and went into a spin. Die, probably.

A glance at one of the side scanner panels showed the havoc breaking loose in orbit. The UELE had fallen upon the sitting Haxozin ships much the same way the Haxozin had done to them a few days ago. The tiny UELE craft darted in and out of attack runs, never maintaining one course for more than a few seconds.

One of those blips represented his ship, his crew. Somewhere up there, they were fighting for their lives.

He refocused on the approaching ground, now dimly visible through a final layer of clouds and his re-entry shockwave. He slowed his descent and changed direction a few times to shake off any weapons tracking him. His heart hammered in his ears. As the re-entry haze began to clear from the viewports and he broke through the last wispy clouds, he searched for any sign of surface-to-air assault. If the Haxozin had landed ground troops, they might have taken over Earth's defunct, pre-unification military installations and found some way to re-initialize them.

He flew in a high circle before descending toward Median Island, an artificial landmass in the sparkling blue Mediterranean, equidistant from European, Asian, and

African soil. Skyscrapers covered the island from shore to shore, leaving only minimal swaths of white beach. On a normal day the skies would be filled with multiple layers of hovercars, the streets crowded with pedestrians. But the city lay quiet, its air and ground still. If it weren't for thermal scanners showing heat signatures in the buildings, Thomas would have thought Median was deserted.

"Areva," he said, "expect trouble. They've got the city locked down."

He heard the whirr of a bazooka rifle coming to life and the click of a round being chambered in a projectile gun. "Ready," said Areva.

"Got the carbon monoxide canisters?"

A backpack zipped. "Got them."

Thomas passed the tops of the tallest buildings. He couldn't see through any windows; the blinds were drawn, the lights dark.

"Better get our friend ready." He rounded an office building, and the grey ten-story cube that housed Dispatch headquarters came into view a few blocks ahead. "I'm going to land right at the back entrance. With luck they're too short-staffed to notice our approach."

"If they do," said Areva, "they'll think we're more Haxozin."

"I hope so."

He glided in over the walled-off parking lot that normally sheltered off-duty patrol hovers.

It was empty.

An eerie feeling crawled up Thomas's spine. Commissioner Wen must have dispatched all hovers right after ordering spacefaring ships to retreat. It magnified the deadness Thomas sensed over the whole metropolis.

He landed a few feet from the rear entrance into Dispatch headquarters, straddling one of the lines delineating parking spaces. He powered down the Haxozin shuttle and held his breath.

Nothing happened.

Where *was* everybody?

He motioned Areva to follow and headed for the berth where they'd stowed Vinlin.

The Haxozin was standing by the door when Thomas triggered it open. Thomas barely avoided jumping back in surprise. Without a word, Vinlin stepped into the hall and walked toward the airlock. "The Sovereign will be with your military leaders," he said.

"We know," said Thomas. "The people here are the closest we've got to that."

"He will be armed," said Vinlin.

"We know that, too. We're prepared." Thomas glanced over his shoulder. Areva had made herself scarce. No doubt she was still nearby.

The thought that he had an assassin watching his back gave Thomas comfort. He let Vinlin trigger the airlock open and walked with him down the ramp toward the UELE's back door.

Still no challenge to their approach, no sign of recognition.

A suspicion began to twist in Thomas's mind, whispering fears. *It's as dead as Thassis.*

No. *If* the Sovereign really did have a genetic plague to use against humanity, and *if* he'd had time to deploy it, there wouldn't be so many warm bodies in the buildings.

Right?

... right?

Thomas pressed his palm against the door scanner, and a moment later the entrance unlocked.

He grabbed the handle and yanked it open.

One way or another, he'd know soon what had happened.

* * *

The Haxozin ships were beginning to regroup. Once the initial surprise wore off, the star ships spread out around Earth, forcing the smaller UELE ships to leave the protection of their group in order to pursue them. *Endurance* had taken multiple hits, though none had yet caused serious damage.

"Next target!" Ivanokoff shouted, and Matthias continued his feverish calculations. They had only disabled a dozen or so ships, but already it felt like a never-ending ritual—sitting on this bench, feeling the ship jolt and bounce with every sharp maneuver, forcing his mind through complex calculations and double-checking algorithms, because a single mistake by the computer would doom not only the ship but the planet. Feeling ice encrust his finger bones and dig through his arm muscles. Realizing his legs had gone numb some time ago, and he hadn't noticed. He had to focus on the work. Everything else could roll off.

Maureen had arrived at some point and sat beside him. She had a hand on his shoulder, her dancer's muscles stabilizing both of them through the shaking of the ship. She said nothing, but he felt her concern radiating, as if its warmth could thaw the illness putting his body to sleep.

"Good to go!" he shouted, and Ivanokoff ordered the thirteenth D Drive jump. Another Haxozin star lost power to a prong and began to spin. Another quartet of UELE vessels dove in to finish it off.

The next target was a good distance away. Matthias

okayed the computer's jump calculator and the reactor's output levels with almost a minute to spare. This gave him a chance to finally look at his sister. He forced his lungs to breathe in.

"Hey. I'm okay."

"Are you sure?" she asked.

"Yeah. Why?"

"Part of your face is turning grey."

Matthias pressed a chilled palm to his cheek, felt no responding warmth. "Huh."

"Mattie, you need to go lie down. Somebody else can do this."

"Not as well as I can."

"Please."

"Sis, either the disease will get me, or it won't. Quitting won't help. Besides, if I keep thinking, keep calculating, it might let my brain stay fully alive. That was the point of the zombie drug, wasn't it? Keep the Thassians' minds active even while their bodies died?"

"They were shells of people, not really there."

"But I'm human. Maybe it'll be different. My brain feels fine."

"How can you be so optimistic?"

"How can you not be?" Matthias smiled. "We're saving the world, sis. That's kind of awesome."

She shook her head. "I don't understand you."

"Few people do. But I'm happier than they are."

"I just worry—"

"Worry won't help me any more than quitting would. Let it roll off, Maureen. Besides, once the captain makes peace with these guys, I can go to the best hospital on the planet and receive a hero's treatment. Right?"

Finally Maureen managed a small smile. "I suppose."

The next star ship loomed large ahead. Soon

Matthias would need to dive into his computer panel once more. Before turning back to his calculations, he said, "Hey, sis."

"What?"

"What will they call the documents everybody signs to officially end this war?"

She gave him a blank look.

"Hax pacts."

Maureen let out a genuine giggle.

* * *

The lobby of the headquarters building was empty. Thomas and Vinlin rode the lift up to the fourth floor. Areva took the stairs. Or maybe she teleported herself there. Thomas wouldn't be surprised.

The hallways were dark, and their steps echoed off the tiled floors as they crept through shadows. Again Thomas was reminded of Thassis. Again he pushed the thought aside. Thermal scans had showed warm bodies. That meant they were alive.

He stopped outside the offices belonging to Commissioner Wen's division. Though Thomas suspected she hadn't survived the attack, and that the Haxozin would have clustered on the higher floors with the other highest-ranked officers, he felt he owed it to his CO to check. To his surprise, raised voices came from inside the long room that housed the rows of desks and a few corner offices.

A harsh, guttural voice spoke in the raspy tones of the Haxozin, the sound filtered through the metal of a crimson helmet. The computerized talky box translation followed. "I will use it!"

Vinlin froze beside Thomas. The alien's purple skin

drained to lilac, and his eyes went wide. He pointed at the door. "The Sovereign," he whispered. Thomas had his own talky box turned down, so the translation was barely audible.

Well then.

Never mind the higher floors. They'd found the party.

Here we go, Thomas thought. He made a series of motions, hand signals used to communicate silently during stealth operations. He couldn't see Areva, but he had no doubt she could see him.

Target inside. Proceed with plan.

Before he could communicate anything else, a female voice answered the Sovereign. "Then what? What does that gain you?"

Thomas sucked in a startled breath. Commissioner Wen was alive. Not only alive, but fighting back, from the sharp knives lining her tone. He'd been on the receiving end of that tone once. It was an experience he never wanted to repeat.

The Sovereign barked something that Thomas couldn't make out. A moment later, Wen made a pained hissing sound.

Shit.

Whatever they did, it didn't subdue her, because her next words contained just as much steel as before. "We know you only have a handful of soldiers. You can't hope to conquer us."

Thomas withdrew his pocket computer and unfolded it, then engaged the thermal sensors. Half a dozen patches of warm light glowed on the screen. The smallest one, the commissioner, was seated. The largest one, likely the Sovereign, stood before her. The others were scattered around the room, and Thomas couldn't tell whether they were enemies or other captives.

The shape that was the Sovereign drew an arm back and struck Wen. Her head jerked to one side, but snapped back to face him just as quickly. Thomas could imagine the venom in her stare.

"Perhaps I should demonstrate what I'm capable of," said the Sovereign. "We have dozens of your subordinates and colleagues held in this building. They can serve as a test case for what will happen to the rest of your species if you continue this refusal."

Shit. *Come on, Areva*, Thomas thought.

"The emergency orders I broadcast sent everyone on the planet to hide in the most secure locations they can reach," said Wen. "Even if you manage an orbital bombardment of the entire planet, which I doubt you can with your forces under attack—"

Good, thought Thomas, *they know about that.*

"—it'll take hours to infect everyone, and that's assuming this disease you claim to have actually works."

Oh. Shit. Shit. Shit.

They had a biological weapon. One of them had discovered the human DNA analysis in the Thassian computers, and they'd used their other stolen technology to make a virus that could wipe out humanity.

Thomas had to admire Commissioner Wen's stoicism in the face of the end of the world.

"Even if you eliminate Earth," said Wen, "you'll have to contend with our other colonies spread throughout the system, and most of them don't even have exposed atmospheres. If you keep going with this invasion, we can hold out for a very long time. And as you can see from what's going on in orbit, we like to fight back."

The Sovereign growled. Actually growled. "Tell me

how to access the surface-based military installations."

"Those are off limits."

"Answer!"

"You must be losing pretty badly to be this desperate."

The Haxozin struck her again and stormed across the room. Thomas heard the wall rattle as he smashed a fist against it.

The next time the Sovereign spoke, it was in a calmer tone. "Get three of the prisoners. Preferably the younger ones."

A clamp closed on Thomas's chest.

One of the other warm bodies performed a bow, then marched straight toward the door behind which Thomas and Vinlin lurked. Thomas heard the pound of the soldier's boots on the other side.

Time was up. If Areva hadn't gotten the room's ventilation system to start pumping the carbon monoxide yet, it was too late.

Thomas stood, tossed his pocket comp aside, and brought his p-gun to bear. He shifted his weight, bracing for the proper angle of attack. Then, with all the force mustered from his strength and pounding fear, he kicked down the door and charged in.

* * *

Halfway done. They'd been at this for almost an hour. Fifty Haxozin warships hung useless in space, their windows dark, their engines idle. Fifty more still rotated out of reach, using their five propulsion points to jerk one way, then another, keeping out of *Endurance*'s path and firing on the other UELE vessels all the while. The *Endurance* had attempted the last dimensional jump three times before succeeding, and the one before that twice.

The Haxozin were growing wise to the plan.

Worse, the misses had used up crucial power reserves from the reactor. Already they were approaching maximum daily output. Matthias wracked his brain for another strategy, another method to use to pin down the star ships. But the enemies were just too big, the UELE forces too minimal.

"Now!" Ivanokoff shouted.

Another jump. Another miss.

"Come about and repeat," said Ivanokoff. "Dive toward the planet and come up beneath them."

A quick turn, a lurching movement, and the *Endurance* once more faced the star prong.

"Now," said Ivanokoff, without even waiting for Matthias's confirmation. This time the jump worked. They passed through the gravity well, and the star's limb went dark.

Fifty-one.

"We have three ... no, four ... no, *eight* of the remaining stars converging on us," said the scanners operator.

"Perhaps they finally noticed we are the head of the spear," said Ivanokoff. Matthias could swear the man was enjoying himself. "Target the first and ..."

Ivanokoff's sentence disappeared in rumbling chaos as something enormous impacted the starboard wing. The ship pitched, and the deck tilted a full thirty degrees. Matthias's back pressed against the aft bulkhead. Officers clung to their consoles to stay in place. Then artificial gravity compensated, and up and down returned to their proper positions.

"What was that?" Ivanokoff barked.

"They *hit* us," said the helmswoman. "They rammed

us with one of the prongs. The starboard wing is crunched, but still there."

All eyes looked toward the smoking end of the star ship that had effectively hobbled them.

It appeared to be moving away.

"Are they retreating?" asked Matthias.

No one answered as everyone checked their consoles.

"No," said the pilot. "We're falling. That attack shoved us out of orbit. *Way* out of orbit. We're in an uncontrolled re-entry."

Ivanokoff stiffened in the captain's chair. "Full engines."

"They struck one of our aft thrusters, sir, and all stabilizers are gone except one. If I engage engines, we'll go into a spin. We can't get out of this. We're going down."

The star ship shrank rapidly in the viewport as *Endurance* fell. Bits of heat distortion began to creep over the glass.

"We must aim the nose down and ride it out," said Ivanokoff.

Matthias cleared his throat. "If we engage the last stabilizing engine just a little, it could give enough rotation to turn us around. Air resistance should stop it from becoming a full spin."

"Do it," Ivanokoff ordered.

"Engaging engine," said the helmswoman.

A moment later the ship began to shudder under the forces of re-entry. The viewports still faced the stars.

"More!" said Ivanokoff.

The helmswoman wiped her brow, her other hand flying over the controls.

Bulkheads screamed as *Endurance* swung about, the

view panning from space to the green and blue of Earth's surface.

Which was growing bigger.

A lot bigger.

Matthias pushed himself to his feet. He couldn't feel his legs, but he held the wall to keep his balance. "We're going too fast. We'll break apart."

"I've got all the flaps open, brake thrusters firing, and I'm holding the pitch as even as I can!" said the helmswoman. "It's not enough."

"We need more drag." Matthias's thoughts raced, his gaze darting here and there, seeking inspiration. He stopped with his eyes on the starboard bulkhead, behind which he knew the mangled starboard wing protruded from the ship. "I've got an idea! Vent the air!"

"What?"

"The air cyclers in the wings always have a supply of air in them. We need to poke holes in the front of those systems so the air can vent through the front of the ship. It's high pressure air; it might slow us down just enough!"

"Poke holes with what?" demanded Ivanokoff.

But Matthias's brain was miles ahead. "If I deliberately overload the forward—"

"No talk!" said Ivanokoff. "Just go!"

"Sis, help me." Matthias leaned on Maureen, and she shuffled him to an empty spot on the consoles lining the front of the bridge.

Matthias settled in the chair and flexed his fingers to get them moving. Then he was off, hands flying, brain soaring, mouth muttering calculations. He disabled capacitors, short-circuited surge protectors, deleted security coding. "Everybody back away from your consoles," he said. "This might blow a few things."

The planet filled the entire viewport now. Clouds

rushed past. Matthias could make out rivers and mountain ranges in detail.

"Here we go!"

With one final button press, he attempted to turn the wing thrusters up to 2,000 percent capacity.

An indecent amount of power surged through the circuitry lining the wings' leading edges. As Matthias expected, the resistors spaced evenly along the wiring blew up. And with safety features disabled, those miniature explosions blasted holes through the forward plating and the air cyclers within the wings, creating an escape route for the compressed air.

The ship bucked again at the sudden resistance. The pilot scrambled back to her console and fought to maintain a steady trajectory. "It's working!" she called. "We're slowing."

Matthias grinned.

Then his console exploded, and all he could think about was pain.

* * *

The door struck the Haxozin officer in the face, knocking him back before Thomas's charge. Thomas ignored him, instead targeting the large armored body he now knew to be the Sovereign. The gold and silver stripes on his crimson helmet gave it away.

Commissioner Wen sat in a metal UELE desk chair, looking a bit worse for wear. Her wrists were handcuffed to the chair arms, and her face showed several bruises from the Sovereign's blows. Her dark hair was free of its bun and hanging around her shoulders, and one sleeve of her uniform was torn. But there was nothing beaten about the vindictive smile she flashed at the Sovereign when Thomas came bursting in.

"I told you," she said. "We fight back."

"Keep your distance," Thomas told the handful of Haxozin soldiers lingering around the room, "or I'll blow a hole in your leader's face. Vinlin, free the commissioner."

The purple alien moved to the chair and snapped the chains on the handcuffs with his bare hands.

"Vinlin, what did they do to you?" the Sovereign demanded. His deep voice threw each word like an attack.

Vinlin didn't look up. He helped Commissioner Wen out of the chair, and she gave him a nod before crossing to the closest desk and retrieving a key to remove the dangling ends of the broken cuffs.

"I asked you a question, soldier!" The Sovereign started to step toward Vinlin, but backed off when Thomas gestured with the gun.

With a heavy sigh, Vinlin finally looked up. "I'm sorry, Sovereign. But you must hear what they have to say."

"They can say nothing of use. They are conquered, just like we have conquered so many other—"

"They know about the real Haxozin, Sovereign."

That shut the big guy up.

"You told them?" cried another armored body across the room.

"No. They figured it out. And there is more." Vinlin waved a hand at Thomas. "Tell them."

Thomas didn't take his eyes off the Sovereign. "Yeah, here's the thing. If you shower our planet with that genetic disease you made for us, you're all dead, too."

There was silence. Wen was the first to understand. "Oh," she murmured. "Oh, you've got to be joking."

"Sorry, ma'am. I'm not. These guys, purple as they

are beneath that armor, are partially human."

"Impossible!" shouted the Sovereign. "We are from a lost world. Our ancestors were taken from it many—"

"Not so lost, it turns out. It's this one. You thought you were invading, but you were actually coming home. Think about it." Thomas slid his feet forward, closing the distance on the Sovereign in case he needed to make a point blank shot. "We share a lot of instincts. You go around collecting technology from other species. We do, too. We don't steal it, but the idea is similar. We feel the need to explore the galaxy and spread out through our solar system. You spread out to rule the Haxozin empire. We both fight for freedom and survival. Your expansionist tendencies are just like ours, only they've been twisted by what your people have been through."

"You know nothing about us," the Sovereign growled. He did not retreat from Thomas's advance. "We are superior in every way."

"Your stuff is better, sure. But there are only what, a few hundred of you? So let's say you kill all of humanity off. You don't have a viable population. Sooner or later, some other species is going to figure out that you can't handle the empire you've inherited, and they'll wipe you out. Then all of humanity disappears."

"We are not dirt people."

"There's enough dirt in you to make you one of us. So here's what I propose. You call off your invasion. We call off our attack. We all sit down and figure out a way for you to settle somewhere peacefully, where you can live real lives instead of frantically trying to run something that's too big for you." For the first time, Thomas glanced around the room, making eye contact with each of the other Haxozin's helmets. "Vinlin's decided he's sick of nothing but work and fear. What about the rest of you?"

"Hold your positions!" ordered the Sovereign. "This is a lie. A trick."

"We've got all the DNA models saved. You can compare them for yourselves. If you really need proof, we'll all go back to Thassis and do a fresh analysis of your DNA against ours. But the answer is the same. This is where you came from. This is where the real Haxozin abducted your ancestors, and this, I think, is the real thing you've been seeking all this time. Security."

"It's true," said Vinlin. "We can finally stop."

The other Haxozin began to murmur.

The Sovereign surveyed the room, then glared at Thomas. Thomas couldn't see his eyes, but he felt the glare all the same. "Even if all you say is true, even if we came from here, why did your ancestors not see fit to protect ours?"

Thomas frowned. "What?"

"You allowed enemies to take us away."

"They were *aliens*. Do you know how many people go missing in any given year? There was no way to know aliens were involved."

"No," said the Sovereign, "not if you were all living peaceful, content lives here, forgetting us."

Slow horror crept through Thomas's mind. "You're not going to see reason, are you? You're so bitter that you'll lash out at anything in front of you. Even if it's trying to help."

"Our anger is justified."

"Your anger," said Vinlin quietly. "Not ours. Not anymore."

A hissing sound came from the ceiling. Thomas's head snapped up, eyes riveted on the air vents. The carbon monoxide.

The distraction came at just the wrong time.

A trainload of metal and muscle crashed into Thomas, throwing him up against the far wall. His gun fell and slid beneath a row of desks. Then the Sovereign's hands closed around his throat, and a white halo flashed around his vision as the metal-clad fingers pressed against his windpipe. He struggled to throw off the attack, but his feet dangled off the floor, and his sight rapidly darkened. Panic set in.

"Liars," hissed the Sovereign, the crimson metal helmet inches from Thomas's face. "I will take at least one of you with me."

Hands that could snap metal chains like twigs tightened around Thomas's neck.

* * *

Burning, aching, pain everywhere. Matthias groaned and tried to focus his eyes, but his vision swam. People shouted, the ground shook—*no, not the ground. You're on a spaceship, silly*—and his body throbbed. One voice, deep and gruff, rose over the others, and the sounds came to Matthias through a long tube: "Enjay linding jots."

Matthias giggled. Those weren't real words. The vocalization hurt his throat, and he swallowed a fit of coughing. His ears popped.

"Engage landing jets!" Ivanokoff repeated.

Oh. That made much more sense. And now Matthias remembered—the *Endurance* was crashing. Except not anymore, because he'd fixed it. He was a genius. He'd never say the word out loud, but he knew it. That was enough. He smiled, but didn't risk another laugh.

Apparently he wasn't *so* smart, though. His chest and face felt like they were on fire. The hot pain was distant, felt through a translucent wall, but still there. He recognized that as a bad sign, but couldn't find enough room in his mind to care. It was too full of things like breathing. Yes, his brain had finally quit on him. Lazy slacker.

Except the grey on his face hadn't reached his skull yet. The infection wasn't fast enough for that. So why was his brain starting to shut down?

Through the bonfire of pain, he registered a hand on his arm. A woman's voice. "Mattie? Stay awake, brother. Stay awake."

Hi, Maureen, he tried to say, but his throat still ached, and all he managed was another cough.

A sharp jolt shook the entire ship, and Matthias's body left the floor before crashing down again. The pains on his skin flared, as if doused in oil. He swallowed a scream. Let it roll off. Let it roll off.

The shaking continued. Voices shouted from all directions. Then, mercifully, the rattling stopped, and the pain faded to a regular throb.

"We're down!" cried someone, somewhere. "Computer's offline, but we're on the east shore. Sand's half buried us."

"I smell smoke," called someone else. "We might have a fire."

"Evacuate!" Ivanokoff ordered. His voice was too loud, and it thrummed in Matthias's ears, which were trying to muffle themselves again.

"These burns are really bad. He needs a hospital, now!" That one was Maureen. Matthias wondered who she was talking about.

"No time." Ivanokoff. Now closer. Through the fog in his eyes, Matthias could just make out two human-ish shapes in the air above him.

"I don't know what to do. I'm not trained for this kind of injury. We're losing him!" Maureen sounded hysterical. Matthias tried to reach out to comfort his baby sister, but his arms wouldn't move.

Another head-and-torso blob moved into the mist above Matthias. This one had a long, pointy nose. "We need to stabilize him long enough to reach a hospital. Do we have any more of the zombie drug?"

Maureen said, "Yes, from the research we did, but why would—"

"Get it," said Ivanokoff. "Now."

The Maureen shape disappeared. Matthias tried to wish her good luck, wherever she was going, but his throat ached and let out only a croak.

His eyelids felt heavy. He let them close, blocking out the foggy shapes. There hadn't been much to see, anyway. His brain was working harder now to keep his chest moving. It was such hard work. Maybe he didn't need to do it anymore. The pain was fading, too. This wasn't so bad. All he'd had to do was let it all roll off. Let everything roll off ...

Something jabbed into his skull, a slender puncture just behind his ear, but he barely felt it.

Everything—pain, fear, worry—all of it was rolling off his—

* * *

In the seconds after Thomas's neck bones groaned, but before they could actually splinter, the office exploded.

No, that wasn't quite right. For one thing, no shockwaves threw Thomas across the room, and for another, nothing was on fire. Maybe it was just his ears that had exploded, a loud sound deafening them under the pressure of the choke.

The Sovereign's grip lessened, and Thomas gasped in air. Then the enormous man crumpled forward, pinning Thomas against the wall with his weight. For a moment Thomas thought he'd be smashed, but then the Sovereign rolled off him. Thomas, no longer pinned, fell and landed with just a slight jolt through his ankles. He staggered against the wall, his throat on fire, his pulse pounding in his temples.

The Sovereign landed on his knees, then keeled the rest of the way over and lay sprawled.

Thomas's hands found his throat and he focused on choking down mouthfuls of air. Next time he looked in a mirror, he was sure he'd see a ring of red marring the dark brown of his skin.

The pain in his chest eased as his lungs filled again and again. The white fog slid back from his vision. Thomas realized he didn't feel lightheaded; the air he sucked in was pure. The carbon monoxide should have filled the room by now. He glanced around and saw the source of continued ventilation—he'd left the door open when he charged in. It wasn't much, but it was enough for the building's circulatory system to compensate for the gas.

So why had the Sovereign dropped him? With another choking inhale, he looked around for an explanation.

Commissioner Wen stood in a shooter's fighting stance, hands clasped around the grip of a pistol. It wasn't Thomas's—she'd probably retrieved it from one of the desks. Her hair had fallen over one eye, but ferocity burned in the eye he could see. Her lips were set in a thin, determined line.

Thomas peered down at the fallen Sovereign. The back of the man's helmet showed an entry hole.

Thomas looked back at Wen.

A year ago, she'd chewed him out and thrown him onto the worst posting possible, because he'd shot a valuable enemy and killed him.

Her visible eye flicked its gaze from the Sovereign's body to Thomas's face. They stared at each other in silence.

Slowly, Thomas gave her a small nod.

A long pause.

Then she returned it.

Thomas only broke eye contact when one of the Haxozin near the rear wall cried, "You killed him!"

Wen spun, weapon aimed at the ground, but ready. "He was strangling one of my people. What matters is he's not here to refuse reason anymore. Our offer stands. Surrender, and you can all come home. Keep fighting, and we'll keep at it too until one or both of our kinds is dead."

The Haxozin who'd spoken took a step forward.

An energy blast ignited the carpet right in front of him. The flame burned itself out immediately, leaving a hole chewed through the rug and exposing the metal underneath.

Then a voice boomed out of the vents around the ceiling, coming from every direction at once. "If you don't take her offer, your kind in this room dies first."

Thomas scanned the vents. "Areva?"

"Hi." Again the booming echos from every wall.

"No one can see you?"

"No."

Thomas nodded to the approaching soldier. "That means she can shoot you. I wouldn't push her."

The soldier backed away from the smoldering carpet.

Wen looked at Vinlin. "Who's the second in command?"

Vinlin pointed to a soldier wearing armor with one silver line on his chest. "Atrik."

"What's your choice, Atrik?" said Wen. "Leave the room alive, or not?"

Atrik looked around for help but found no support from his fellows. His armor rustled as he folded his arms. "We ... we surrender. And ... I want to come home."

Wen rewarded him with a small smile. "You can. Get over here and contact your ships."

As Atrik crossed the room to call off the war, Thomas clapped a hand on Vinlin's shoulder. With the thrill of near-death wearing off, he felt giddy. "Earth's a nice place, but it's a bit crowded for some. If you want another option, you could always join the team preparing to start a colony on Triton. Neptune's not so bad, once you get used to it."

* * *

They liberated the captive officers locked on the other floors and funneled orders throughout the solar system, beginning the logistical nightmare of clean-up. When Thomas, Commissioner Wen, and the others stepped out of the building, a bright sun was beaming down. Thomas couldn't see the hundred-some ships in orbit, but he knew the Haxozin stars were powering down and allowing UELE vessels to dock with them. Their skeleton crews were surrendering, to be brought back to UELE bases for questioning and then, with luck, integration into society. Thomas breathed deep, letting the sea salt air fill his chest and cool his skin. For the first time in over a year, he felt light.

It took only a few minutes before a dark speck in the sky grew larger and resolved into the descending form of a UELE spacecraft. Thomas didn't recognize it, but when it landed and opened its airlock, he did recognize the woman who stepped out.

"Commissioner." Captain Nandoro flashed a salute to Wen. "Everything's under control up there."

"Good work," said Wen. She paused when the rest of the crew began to stream out of the ship. In addition to uniformed UELE there were muscled thugs, plain-clothed civilians, and even a few faces Thomas recognized from the list of ex-Uprising operatives. Disaster debarked among them and scowled at the bare parking lot. Maybe he thought it needed some begonias. The thugs who had nearly assaulted Thomas ran past, and Disaster stumbled and waved a fist at them.

Captain Nandoro swept her hand across the group. "Meet the Enceladus reserve, Commissioner. When we didn't have enough backup from Earth, they volunteered to run unstaffed consoles, calibrate torpedoes, and keep us flying."

Wen opened her mouth, then closed it.

Thomas grinned. "Irregular, but effective."

Nandoro's face fell. "Captain Withers, I don't know if you heard yet, but your ship—"

Thomas's heart stopped. He knew the face she was wearing, the tone she'd adopted. "No," he said.

"I'm sorry. They were falling upside-down. None of us saw whether—"

"Captain!"

That booming voice could only come from one person. Thomas spun toward the gate and nearly buckled in relief at the sight of his first officer striding across the parking lot. "Ivanokoff! What happened?"

More of his crew trickled in through the gate—Archibald Cleaver, vacuum in tow. Chris and Joyce Fish, in the midst of a squabble. Ramirez, coffee pot in hand. With each face, Thomas breathed a bit easier.

Ivanokoff stopped right in front of Thomas. "We crashed. Matthias saved the ship. We walked from the shore."

"You crashed on the beach?"

"Da. It was the only open space."

"Not in the water?"

"I do not do swimming."

Before Thomas could ask his next question, Areva appeared from the crowd (how long had she been there?) and leapt onto Ivanokoff. Thomas expected a flurry of passionate kissing, but the two shared only a chaste peck before holding hands and staring into one another's eyes.

The flow of people through the gate ended. Thomas scanned the faces of his crew and his stomach sank. "Ivanokoff, where's Matthias? Where's Maureen?"

Ivanokoff's face fell.

* * *

The hospital wasn't as large as the one on Thassis. The room Thomas entered had only enough space for a bed and a chair. Maureen sat curled in the latter, asleep.

Matthias lay in the former.

Bandages covered much of his face and chest, protecting the burns he'd sustained in the explosion. But when Thomas saw the engineer, he still broke into a smile.

The skin that he could see was a healthy copper. No trace of grey in sight.

Matthias stirred and opened his eyes. His signature grin brightened his face. "Hiya, Cap. What happened to your neck? You look terrible."

"Hey, Lieutenant. Just a fight with the Haxozin Sovereign. What happened to you?"

Matthias shrugged. "I died. You know how it is."

"Did it hurt?"

"The burns hurt, but after they gave me more of the zombie drug—oops, I forgot you don't like that word."

"It's fine."

"Anyway, they injected me with enough to override my human physiology and fully turn me. Heart stopped, organs shut down, all of it. After that, my brain kinda stopped processing things like pain."

"Do you remember anything?"

"It's hazy. I know they called a medical hover from the beach. I remember wanting to infect other people, just a little."

"I imagine you weren't mobile enough to do it."

"Yeah, blowing up will do that to you," said Matthias. "I don't remember much before they gave me the Revixophin and revived me."

"Did *that* hurt?" asked Thomas.

"Coming back to life? Nah. Well, maybe a little. They'd treated the burns by then, but they're still healing. The worst part was feeling my brain slipping away. But it's a good thing it did, or the Revixophin wouldn't have worked."

Thomas leaned against a table in the corner. "Any side effects?"

Matthias cocked his head. "Maybe a few. No urges to bite people or anything icky like that. Why?"

"It's been a few days since the invasion ended. I don't know how much news you've gotten, but the

Haxozin Sovereignty has officially dissolved. The other planets out there need to be told they're free. The UELE's putting together crews—a real exploration force, not seat-of-the-pants like we've been. I'll need an engineer."

Matthias brightened. "Does that mean they salvaged *Endurance*?"

"No. There was too much damage. They saved the reactor, but the rest of the ship is scrap. I'm sorry."

It was hard to watch the grief pass the engineer's face, but it only took a few moments. "I'll miss that engine room. I built the D Drive there."

"I know."

"But I'll get used to a new space. I'm with you, Cap." The last remnants of sorrow slipped from Matthias's face. "Hey, it's kind of appropriate, isn't it?"

"What is?" asked Thomas.

"*Endurance*. Crashing. But we all survived. Just like in that story you told about the ship's namesake."

Thomas hadn't thought of that. But it fit. He nodded.

"And you get a new ship. That's what you wanted when you first got assigned to ours, right?"

"It was. Now I think I'll miss the old barge. The new barge won't be the same."

Matthias adopted a scandalized expression. "Captain, don't say that word. You'll hurt the ship's feelings."

Thomas laughed. "I won't say it while aboard."

He started to leave the room, but paused and looked at Maureen asleep in her chair.

He wanted the same engineer, but his new ship would be staffed with a proper doctor. He had no need for untrained, inexperienced, and often incapable youngsters barely out of high school. Yet he couldn't in good conscience turn any of his old crew away. "Your sister's welcome too, if she wants."

Matthias shook his head. "Sorry, Cap. That won't work out."

"Why not?"

"Didn't anybody tell you? She just made up her mind the other day. She's going to medical school next year."

* * *

Matthias stayed in the hospital for a week, then was discharged to recover at home. His parents fussed over him and Maureen the whole time. Saving the world had a way of making your folks approve of your career choices.

A month later he received his new assignment. The UELE *Alegría*. He laughed when he translated the name.

Joy.

This was definitely his ship.

A few people would not be joining him on it. Maureen, for one. Archibald Cleaver for another. At 104, with a new criminal record, the ancient man finally decided to retire. Matthias didn't know what he'd do, but suspected it would involve cleaning. Some habits couldn't be broken. Matthias would, in a twisted way, miss repairing the decrepit vacuum.

The biggest surprise to him had been when Viktor Ivanokoff and Areva Praphasat announced their resignation. Areva was quitting entirely; Viktor was returning to Median City criminal investigations. Matthias wondered if Areva was going to become a PI or a consultant or maybe a hitman. Or perhaps the two of them would become philosophers. He didn't know.

By the time Matthias was ready for space again, the *Alegría* had been outfitted with a D Drive, a talky box, and even experimental weapons developed from the Haxozin bazooka rifle technology over the past months. He couldn't wait to take one apart.

He stood on the bridge and looked around at the improved technology, new carpet, and non-shaky command chair. Captain Withers swiveled to greet him. "Lieutenant, welcome aboard."

"Thanks, Cap. How was your vacation?"

"More a working vacation than a restful one, but Loretta and I still had a few nice dinners out." The captain smiled. "Ready to go?"

"Yup yup!" said Matthias.

"Then helm, take us up."

The ship barely rattled as it revved to life. The liftoff was smooth, the glide up into the atmosphere smoother. The only turbulence came as they punched through the clouds and rocketed into the welcoming volume of space. Then all went still again.

Matthias studied the stars and found himself grinning. "Where we going first, Cap?"

"Well, Captain Nandoro's taking her ship along one edge of the galactic arm. We're covering the opposite side. Shouldn't be too eventful."

"Perfect." Matthias's smile grew. "It'll be a great time to work out my new project."

The captain swiveled the chair to face him again. "What project?"

"Nothing too big, sir. Just an idea I've been bouncing around for a while. I have a research proposal here for you to approve." Matthias held out his pocket comp. "It's for a way to use D Drive to visit alternate universes. Wouldn't that be cool?"

Captain Withers groaned and pushed the pocket comp away. "Not right now, Habassa. We just solved this universe's problems. We don't need more."

Matthias folded his pocket comp and tucked it away, but didn't lose his smile.

He'd try again later.

After all, they had plenty of time.

Until then, refusals were just so much water off his back.

Ivanokoff's Quotes

From *Enduring Endurance*

> "What a terrible thing, war is."
> - Leo Tolstoy, *War and Peace*

From *Mightier than the Sword*

> "Yon Cassius has a lean and hungry look. Such men are dangerous."
> - William Shakespeare, *Julius Caesar* (1.2.204-205)

From *Preferred Dead*

> "I have never died in all my life."
> - Cervantes, *Don Quixote*

> "Before the government threw me over, I preferred to throw the government over."
> - Cervantes, *Don Quixote*

> "Once more unto the breach ..."
> - William Shakespeare, *King Henry V* (3.1.1)

> "Ten soldiers wisely led will beat a hundred without a head."
> - Euripides

From *Wet Ducks*

"He gave his honours to the world again,
His blessed part to heaven, and slept in peace."
- William Shakespeare, *Henry VIII* (4.2.29)

"Only in the agony of parting do we look into the depths of love."
- George Eliot

"Either victory, or else a grave."
- William Shakespeare, *Henry VI Part III* (2.2.173)

Author's Note

I hope you enjoyed the *Endurance* series. If so, please drop a review on Amazon or Goodreads. Every review means the world to me, even if it's just a few words long.

Throughout this series I have tried to be as scientifically realistic as possible while dealing with decidedly unrealistic storylines. A few people are to thank for that: Jeff Adkins, for correcting my astrophysics, Chris Adkins (no relation) for critiquing my medical science, and Justin Spahn, for fixing my aerospace engineering and flight mechanics. Any remaining scientific errors are entirely my own fault.

Thank you to Robert for providing insight into the workings of the police force, to Jenny Zemanek for the beautiful cover design, and to Shauna, Mitch, Hercules, the members of the East County Writers Group, and my parents, Marjorie and Walt, for beta reading, editing, and providing feedback. I couldn't do this without all of you.

Thanks be to God, for creating this awesome universe in which we live. May we one day explore beyond the boundaries of our little corner of it.

Finally, thanks to you, Reader, for deciding to pick up this book by an unknown indie author. I hope the story took you for a great ride.

Blessings to you!

About the Author

A. C. Spahn is the author of the *Endurance* series and the *Arcane Artisans* series. Her shorter works have been published by *Daily Science Fiction*, *Star*Line*, *Outposts of Beyond*, *Disturbed Digest*, and others.

She wanted to be an interstellar starship captain when she grew up. Since nobody was hiring, she became a writer instead. She enjoys training in martial arts, organizing messy rooms, and cooking, sometimes all at once. When not commanding imaginary starships, she lives in Pennsylvania with her husband, son, and feline overlord.

To get in touch and check out her other books, visit www.acspahn.com.

Also by A. C. Spahn

Made in the USA
Las Vegas, NV
18 February 2021